THE FALL

DESKTOP REVELATIONS VOL 2

THE FALL

L.A. CARNEVALE

an elci**Production**
www.elciProductions.com
www.desktopRevelations.com

elci Productions
PUBLISHING

First, IngramSpark Unedited | Unabridged | Limited | Rookie Edition Paperback Pre-Release [Fall 2020] • Second, IngramSpark Edited | Soft-Release [Fall 2023] • Third, Unabridged | Official Release [Fall 2024]

Cover design, by elci Productions: www.elciProductions.com

elci Productions Publishing
elci Productions
NRH, Texas 76180

Contact elci Productions Publishing:
elciPro.Books@gmail.com
elciPro.Music@gmail.com

This book and other elci Production titles may be found at:
www.elciProductions.com
www.desktopRevelations.com

Available from Amazon.com, IngramSpark.com, BarnesAndNoble.com, DesktopRevelations.com, and other retail outlets.

ISBN: 978-0-578-71903-0 (sc)
ISBN: #### coming soon (hc)
ISBN: 978-0-578-71904-7 coming soon (e)
ISBN: #### coming soon (sc|eco version)

Revision date(s): 09/22/2020, 09/22/2023, 10/19/2024 | [GEN5]

DEDICATION

To every overcomer, and future overcomer, ever.

ACKNOWLEDGMENTS

Where to begin? This book has cost me everything. Friends, family, dreams, reputation, health—it has tested me at every level. The twelve blistering years spent honing this manuscript were filled with the polar extremes of life. From raising the dead, to burying first-borns. Establishing families, to progressive family fall-outs. Impossible genetic healings, to decade-long, ongoing battles with Vaccine Injury/Autism. From dismantling Fear & destroying porn addictions, to discovering War Boards, War Walks, War Calls, War-Ship … and did I mention the Shame Dumps? Oh, the Shame Dumps. All I can really say is, *Thank you!* Thank you for crushing me. Thank you for putting up with me! No really. No matter what part you played: Protagonist. Antagonist. Avoid-ist. Critic. Enemy. Friend … you played a crucial part in shaping me, and thus, in shaping this book. *Thank you.* I take very little credit for any of this: I didn't choose to write this book. This book, chose me. (I was just crazy enough to never give up, and to let it do its complete work … *I think* :)).

AUTHOR'S INTENT

Desktop Revelations, Vol 2, The Fall, was written as an Action/ Adventure, Quasi Historical **Fiction** Novel and therefore, intended to be taken as such. While all accounts, dates and truths were done as accurately as possible, this book was never intended to follow or adhere to any sort of 'strict theological guidelines.' It was never intended to tell you "how to think," or even "how it is." But rather, to paint a picture of Biblical History, and thus, Ancient World History, in a way you may never have seen it before. Like *The Chronicles of Narnia, The Lord of The Rings*, and *The Matrix–Desktop Revelations, Vol 2, The Fall* was written as entertainment first, allowing any intended/ unintended allegory to land where it may. While this book *was* divinely ordained—written strictly out of obedience to the one, true, living, Papa God—my personal heart-felt desire was that it would spark your imagination, get you thinking outside of the box, open up brand new conversations, release brand new eyes of understanding, turn the heart of the Father to the children and the hearts of the children to the Father, and if applicable—to occasionally blow your mind. With that in mind, *enjoy!*

INTRO: AWAKENINGS

"Welcome!" the voice rippled like thunder. Though scarcely a whisper, it permeated the atmosphere. Living and breathing, it expanded—saturating everything.

Haylel *('Hah-lel')* didn't budge. Eyes closed, he basked in the energy of the inexhaustible greeting. The barbershop-style chair—in which he comfortably sat—shook violently beneath him. Every fiber of his being trembled. He inhaled deeply. He could feel the greeting coursing through his body in wave after liquid wave—pushing, pulling, stretching—evolving his very DNA. He grinned. There was a growing sensation that at any moment he might burst into a million tiny, irreparable pieces ... *and he loved it! The rush was exhilarating.* He settled back, fully relaxed, eagerly soaking it all in. *One thing was certain,* in the presence of this kind of power, *he wasn't about to miss a drop.*

Pitter, patter, pit.. the sound of padded footsteps arose. Haylel's ears perked up. *What was this?* He raised a half-interested eyebrow as the footsteps approached, paused, and then moved on. His eyelids fluttered, opening just in time to see a handsome young man in a white-linen robe disappearing through a nearby doorway. For a moment he stared, watching as the man stopped and turned around, each catching the other's eye as two perfectly polished doors glided seamlessly shut between them.

Then the man—and the doors—were gone.

Haylel blinked. The incident, in itself, was completely forgettable ... except for the belt which had girded the young man's waist. Its golden appearance had blazed with an energy that was, *almost irresistible.*

"Welcome!" the voice boomed again, this time extending its greeting in a bit more than a whisper. Immediately Haylel was back in the moment, riding the brand new wave. His breathing deepened. His grin widened. His heart quickened. *What an invitation!* He could feel abundant-life dancing in its overtones, unending-possibility coursing through its timbre, and a wild, relentless love churning savagely underneath. *Who was this, who held such power within the sound of his voice?*

Instinctively, he turned to the source.

His jaw dropped..

There, looming before him—towering galaxies tall—stood a being like a man. Two arms. Two legs. A torso and head. A smile that lit up his face. Lightning flashed, electric in his eyes. And truth blasted from his nostrils like a wild stallion's breath on a cold winter day. A cloud of blazing stars bathed the crown of his head. And a ring of spinning planets orbited his thick, powerful fingers. Water, clear as crystal, rushed like a mighty river from where he stood. And when he moved, his robes pealed with the sound of distant thunder.

Clearly, he was matchless in power—the thought of which was terrifying—yet there was an air of gentleness about his demeanor. His face, both young and kind, was crowned only by an unassuming shock of woolly-white hair. His stubble beard, neat and trimmed, held a sort of fatherly appeal. Living lights danced around him—no, through him—pulsing and breathing, changing color in playful adoration. Laughter was heavy upon his lips, a twinkle always about his eye, and he shown with the light of ten thousand suns.

Breathtaking was too inadequate a word.

What is … all this? Haylel marveled, lost in a whole new world of wonderment.

"I have given you all knowledge. You have only to receive.." the response came clear as crystal, quiet as a dove.

Immediately, Haylel understood. He relaxed, allowing the wisdom to flow through him.

'Elohim.. Creator.. Throne room.. Home..' The answers resonated deep inside.

"WELCOME!" came the third and final roar. This time, a burst of delight-filled laughter followed close behind. It was a burst, that with every heartfelt utterance, set off waves of plasmic solar energy, like little strings of atom-bombs detonating back to back to back. Haylel's body trembled. He smiled, fully embracing the new surge of life. He could feel metamorphosis erupting in his soul. Breathing deep, he closed his eyes, sinking further into the confines of his cozy comfy chair. *Ahhhhh—, if this was where eternal life lived.. than he never wanted to leave!*

A great cheer exploded in the heavens.

What—? Haylel bolted upright. Somehow the thought had never occurred, *he might not be alone.* Turning fully in his seat, he saw that the seemingly intimate room—ending shortly in front of him— actually stretched on endlessly behind, disappearing into a vast expanse of newly awakened, highly energized beings. He surveyed the crowd: Trillions upon trillions. Creatures of every size, shape, and creativity. They were an endless family. A countless army. A virtual 'sea' of heavenly hosts. All cheering for their Creator—*cheering for Elohim ('Eh-low-heem').*

Haylel stood and joined the celebration, raising both hands in wholehearted agreement. A euphoric grin shot passionately across his face. *What a rush!* His heart pounded. His spirit soared. *This was sensory overload to the max. Everything he could have ever possibly wanted, and more.*

He glanced up. Fearless. Focused. Slowly, his surroundings began to fade, until only Heaven's spoken energy remained. It shot across the sky in iridescent trails of lingering luminescence—arrayed like multicolored musical strings of interdimensional light. He couldn't look away. They were fascinating. Mesmerizing. Calling to him..

Calling to him?

Haylel closed his eyes. He couldn't resist. Reaching out, he stretched all twelve fingers into the freshly strung sky. And then, with every bit of his prowess and might, he played them like a prodigy.

CH1: CREATION BEGINS

A second cheer arose. Then a third.

Haylel listened closely, attempting to make out the words. "Whole-E? ... Oh, Lee? ... HOLY!" came the unified cry. It was massive. Intense. Authentic and raw. But mostly—*OMG, it was beautiful.*

Haylel snapped to attention, instinctively channeling the energy, focusing it back on Elohim. He trembled under the weight of its purity. This was supercharged, unbridled love, multiplied beyond belief. It was—*how to describe?*—as if every fiber of his being was fully aware of every fiber of every other being—all at once, from every possible angle, in every possible dimension, down to the smallest detail. *Wow,* he gasped, desperately attempting to reframe his instantly pulverized worldview, *nothing was withheld.* All power, all knowledge, all understanding—*it flowed freely through his grasp, his to control!*

Then, it happened: At the very climax of connection, revelation dawned.

Haylel never would be able to fully articulate the sense of infinite pride he felt the moment he realized: *It was his OWN voice he'd heard leading the charge. His OWN energy, outshining the rest.* And they were—*by far*—the *MOST BEAUTIFUL OF ALL!*

Then, there was silence.

As if scripted, everyone—and everything—paused. Listening. Haylel alone understood. Each creature was receiving their very own, 'personal revelation.' A tailor-made set of instructions, hand-delivered by Elohim—detailing the very reason for their existence. He smiled fondly. He wasn't sure about anyone else, but his had been comprised of three empty boxes scribbled on a cocktail napkin, reading, 'Care to join me in ruling the universe? Check, Yes. No. or Maybe.'

Haylel grinned, that was a definite check—*Yes.*

For a moment, the silence continued.

Then—download complete—all of Heaven inhaled, accepting its collective assignments in one single, unified breath.

Everything sprang to life!

Haylel could scarcely take it all in. Like New York City on a paid government holiday—laughter, excitement, and activity were *everywhere.* Angels scrambled a million different directions. Creatures parted ways. Hosts shot to and fro. And the noise … *oh, the noise!* It was order. It was chaos. It was everyone doing everything they had been created to do—*building a universe.*

Haylel glanced around.

In one corner, a group of fairy-like creatures giggled as they fluttered about, oversized brushes and paint-laden palettes in hand. Like budding artists fretting over their latest design, they raised their brushes high, darting around the vast canvas of space, expertly splattering stars into existence.

In another corner, seven mountainous creations dug—rather feverishly—through seven personal organizers. Talking soberly, in hushed tones, they disputed the best possible ways to "shape developing culture," while they earnestly scoured their Caboodles for the perfect-sized asteroids to weave into their ever-growing asteroid belts.

In the distance, heavyset beings—decked to the hilt in full welding gear—produced anvils, hammers, and tongs. Plucking choice 'red giant' stars from the ever expanding space around them, they forged ahead, hammering in perfect unison, until each had piles of fiery white dwarfs stacked neatly alongside.

Nearby, a bucket-brigade emerged, singing raucously as it passed colorful buckets of plasmic solar energy down its ever-lengthening line, to where a rather large, rather muscle-bound creature awaited. Haylel chuckled. Clearly, this creature had not given his legs the same meticulous, 'power-lifting' attention it had so obviously granted its torso. Still, the bullish being masterfully handled each bucket, effortlessly tossing their shimmering contents into the various corners of the visible universe—solar clouds beginning to form.

Laughter erupted.

Haylel spun around.

Angels on bleachers sat giggling behind him, empty cans and plastic lids strewn liberally about. Joking jovially, they molded new planets out of what appeared to be some sort of, 'cosmic-looking play-dough.' Haylel gasped, gawking as each masterpiece was then lobbed towards a large field of bat-swinging, backwards-cap wearing, All-Stars, who smashed them—albeit a bit over-theatrically— 'hopelessly out of the park.' Haylel stared in wide-eyed wonder as each heaven-sent body landed precisely in its place, even to the most distant of galaxies.

Beyond them, lining the edges of the universe, a row of masculine beings stood—well-built, clean-cut—clad with 'Q' letter-jackets and oars. At their leader's command, they submerged their oars, stirring the space around them—slowly at first, then faster and faster, until their arms were just a blur. Haylel watched as bits and pieces of the surrounding cosmos moved steadily toward the center of each letter-men's vortex until it was swirling around like a sort of cosmic alphabet soup. *Boom. Boom. Boom.* Massive amounts of energy erupted from each swirling quasar, lighting up the universe in succinct succession.

What was this—? Haylel frowned. In the sudden clarity of the brand new light, it was almost impossible not to notice the growing disarray: Prepubescent angels, armed with large safety-pins were haphazardly poking black-holes in the interstellar fabric of space. Motherly seamstress-types, raced along behind, laboring to stitch them back up. Self-absorbed adolescents, darted and dashed, playing tag throughout their midst. Planets were streaking. Stars were splattering. Galaxies and solar clouds, swirling. Haylel swallowed hard. Dare he say it? *Things were out of control!*

Instinctively, he began to direct.

The universe began to respond.

Like a conductor commanding his orchestra, Haylel directed the world around him. Harmony sparked. Momentum grew. Order took hold: Evolving. Expanding. Consuming. Until every swell of disarray had been transformed into a virtual symphonic masterpiece.

Haylel became completely engrossed in his work, new life overwhelming his being. He laughed. He cried. Directed. Deferred. He sang. He played. He joked. His skin began to shine, radiating light in every direction. Energy poured out of him in liquid flame, spilling to the floor around him. His robes shimmered. His arms blurred. His jewelry flickered and sparked. A peculiar ring of keys—tethered to his left shoulder—blazed bright in the fiery light. Tongues of fire danced above his head. And flames lapped about his feet.

Engulfed, he paced—to and fro—until it became impossible to tell where fiery robes began and blazing glory ended. To all who watched, it was a thing of extravagant beauty.

Suddenly, far away, somewhere in the distance, a new event began: a spectacular display of music and lights—tucked within the recesses of a remote galaxy on the back side, of the wrong side, of the far side, of the multiverse.

Haylel spun to face it. *What's this?* He scowled. *Bursts of light—flickering like camera flashes in a darkened stadium?* He had authorized no such thing.

All of Heaven stopped too. Curious. Confused. *Wasn't that the Milky Way Galaxy?* they nudged one another. *A galaxy of trivial rocks and stars? Had it not been left on the dark side of the multiverse for a reason?* They scratched their heads in wonder. *Could it really be that Elohim had chosen this lackluster space as his personal canvas to create?*

Everything came to a halt, everyone waiting for someone to make a move.

Haylel alone knew what to do.

Reaching up, he pinpointed the target, zooming in for all to see. The sky became his touch-screen as he refocused the image, adjusted the volume, and triggered the subs. What currently sounded like muffled, "outside-tha-club" music, suddenly hit in full 12-D, 15.3, quantum surround-sound.

Boom—astral doors flew open, bursting out of thin space, torrents of heavenly hostesses pouring through. Beverage trays high, they served up a brilliant sparkling water that went down like a fine red wine. Everyone began to move.

Dance music started.

Flashes from the interstellar display spilled over into the festivities, swirling freely among the celestial bodies, pulsing in perfect time to the kick-snare beat.

"Let there be light! Le-Let there be light!" The *hook* rang out, over and over again.

Slowly, the flickering lights grew: Bigger. Brighter. Closer together. Until they were completely divided from the dark. At last, it was possible to see what was going on. Excitement gripped the crowd. *A brand new planet?! Made entirely of—water?!* They could hardly believe their eyes. The seas raged: Churning. Crashing. Chaotic. *Yet… there…* hovering above the chaos, rested the Spirit of Elohim. *Waiting patiently for..?*

"Day. —Night," Elohim's voice boomed with explanation.

Of course! A boisterous cheer arose—glasses clinking, toasts raised high. *Clearly this was, 'Day' and 'Night!' And it was good!*

For twenty-four hours, the celebration continued: Full force. Non-stop.

Then, as day two began, a gentle breeze began to blow. All night long it grew—slow and steady, gathering momentum. Finally, as daybreak approached, a new sound emerged. It was air. It was strings. It was wind. It was pipes. It was melody *and* ambiance: Haunting. Organic. Enchanting. Hopeful.

"SKY—," Elohim's voice called out again.

Immediately, the waters began to separate—evaporating, rising, condensing. Clouds formed above. Oceans flowed beneath. The atmosphere took on a rich pink and blue hue.

Once again, Haylel knew what to do.

Reaching up, he zoomed in. Way in. Now they were flying at a fantastic pace, hundreds of feet above the cresting waves. He cranked up the music, grabbing each new sound as it arose—visible stems of frequency and light—weaving melody and ambiance together like a seasoned DJ.

The air grew rich and thick, energized with life.

Haylel mixed and mixed.

By the time his hypnotic trance-beat hit full force, the new planet's atmosphere had become just like that of, *Heaven itself!*

Waves of electricity raced through the crowd, they could sense the potential energy surrounding them. *Anything was possible!*

Day two was done, and—*Wow. It was good!*

Night fell for the second time.

"Sea. —LAND," Elohim's voice released another command.

This time everyone understood. They paused, waiting for the separation, listening for the sounds of emergent earth.

There was a groan. A creak. A sound like gears and chains … *and there it was!* They peered into the thick, atmospheric fog. Even through the swirling mist, the crowd could see a great continent rising. Emerging from the ocean floor.

A new song began: Heavy on bass. Plenty of swing. Just a touch of R&B soul.

Haylel reached out, working his mixing magic, spinning the fading trance-beat into the budding trip-hop jam.

"Weeping Willow, Coriander, Myrtle, Thyme—,
Periwinkle, Poppy seed, Apple 'n Lime—.."

Elohim spoke, playing to the cadence of the new trip-hop flow. All through the night and long into the next day, his voice called every manner of grass, plant, and fruit-bearing flora into existence. Trees erupted from the earth. Flowers burst into bloom. Vegetation developed in seconds. Everything expanding from the sound of his voice like extravagant carpets unrolling. Nothing aged. Nothing died. Everything remained perfect, in its prime. Even the fruit didn't ripen until it was plucked from the vine.

It was flawless. It was brilliant. *It was good!*

Day three was done.

Once again, night fell. And as it did, everything in the budding, tropical paradise began to slow and settle: Vegetation. Music. Energy.

Even Haylel felt the need to bring their racing flyby down to a casual troll.

Then, everything stopped.

What's this? murmurs rippled through the questioning crowd. *Had the show already come to an end?*

'Twinkle, Twinkle Little Star,' the crisp melody rang out in response, played on nothing more than a child's opened music box.

'Little—star?' The crowd's attention instinctively turned to the skies.

Ba-Boom, a bass drum thumped.

Brrrrrrr, kettle drums rolled.

The ground began to tremble. Temperatures began to spike. The orchestra began to build on its own.

A gut-wrenching roar—like that of a thousand fighter jets— screamed overhead. The crowd shrieked, delighted, as out past Earth, the sun was *FLUNG* into the heavens. 'Day' went careening with it, shrinking over the horizon in one big orange glow. In the distance, the setting rays caught the earth's unblemished atmosphere for the first time: *Oh, the colors. Oh, the lights*. Dancing. Glowing. Morphing. Glittering. Fading back into night.

The orchestra sprang to life.

Pop, pop, pop. Zoom, zoom, zoom. Stars, 360 degrees around, shot like fireworks, up from the horizon and into their permanent places in the sky. Up, up, up—millions at a time—streaking into the heavens overhead.

A particularly bright star rocketed skyward. *Going, going, going—BOOM*. It exploded into ... the Little Dipper. *Ohhh!* the crowd gasped.

Another one launched. *Whoosh, zip—BANG*—the Big Dipper. *Ahhh!*

Orion. Virgo. Scorpius. Cancer.

Constellation after constellation took its place.

The crowd applauded.

The orchestra escalated.

The Milky Way was coming to life.

Vroom—a planet flew by.

Vroom, vroom—another, and another.

Mercury. Venus. Pluto. Mars. Each pausing just a moment before racing to its home in the heavens. Uranus. Neptune. Saturn. Jupiter. Each a separate timepiece in the sky, each more wondrous than the last.

Finally, the moon was hung—carefully strung between Heaven and Earth. Like the others, it too passed by, but where it paused, it remained.

CREAAK—the galaxy began to shake.

Now what?! The crowd fought to keep its balance.

Whirrrr—like a tightly wound watch the Milky Way began to move and unwind. Constellations: chronicling seasons and times. The sun: dividing the day from the night. The moon: tracking holidays and months. Even the earth counted hours, minutes, seconds, and years.

The crowd was speechless. *What could they say? What a display! It was so good!*

Day four's work was done.

Haylel zoomed out, casually trolling the newly formed coast. Light from the brand new, rising sun sparkled through the air, bathing Earth's atmosphere in a shimmering array of pinks, purples, and blues. Mountainous waves crashed wildly below, casting themselves relentlessly onto glittering, white-sand beaches. Trees and plants swayed warmly in the breeze, the occasional star still streaking skyward. The winds ebbed and flowed. The land and oceans settled.

The crowd relaxed—laughing, mingling, enjoying each other's company until, at long last, the sun sank slowly behind the horizon.

"Come forth. ABOUND!" Elohim's voice thundered above the pounding surf.

There was a trembling and a quaking—the ocean vibrating and shaking. Suddenly—to the crowd's utter delight—sea creatures of every phylum and species began to germinate directly from the water itself. Embryo to adult, they evolved, birthed within the swirling molecules of the foaming, frothy waves. It was astounding. Across the entire shoreline a wave would grow, metamorphosize, crest and break into a billion brand new, wriggling, squiggling, splashing, flopping, squealing, thumping sea creatures. For a moment they would lie, thrashing about in the brilliant moonlight, literal fish out of water—until the following wave would break, dragging them all gleefully back out to sea. Over and over, it repeated:

Starfish. Crab. Barnacle. Jellyfish.

Wave. Wave. Wave. Wave.

Dolphin. Shark. Tuna. Octopus.

Wave. Wave. Wave. Wave.

Even the inland waters joined in on the fray, producing freshwater creatures anywhere a wave crested, broke into waterfall, and/or bubbled around impediments.

Once again, Haylel found himself back in the musical driver's seat. This time mixing the mashup to start all mashups. All night long he mixed: Rock, Country, Pop. Blues, Reggae, Jazz. Emo, Screamo, Dreamo, Latino—nothing was off limits.

The crowd perked up, they'd never heard anything like it. *What an absolute smorgasbord of sensation!* Between the Two-Step and Dubstep, the Break-beat and Neo-Soul—they were certain they detected a little Tex-Mex ... some J-Rock, Redemption Pop ... and— *was that actually some, Quiet Storm?*

"Arise. Fly. *MULTIPLY!*" At the first sign of light, Elohim's voice ordered the skies.

Immediately, the water molecules along the edges of the newly formed clouds began miraculous transformations of their own. Like the oceans below, birds and winged creatures of every kind began to metamorphosize directly from the droplets themselves, peeling off from the clouds in mid flight.

Eagles. Kites. Storks.

Robins. Swallows. Jays.

Haylel mixed relentlessly, matching wits—and tracks—with each of Elohim's marvelous displays.

The day budded, bloomed, and withered away. Yet even as day five was ending, day six was already beginning.

"Creatures, BE!" Elohim's voice boomed again. This time calling to the land. "Rise up. Each according to your kind."

The earth began to shake, continents began to quake, patches of hardened ground vibrating like loose sand.

Up from the dust, forms begin to rise. Monkeys from the jungles. Lions from the plains. Crocodiles from the wetlands. Lizards from the desert. From mammoth to mouse, aardvark to alpaca, zebu to the Cape Mountain Zebra; each creature came to life, evolving in the time it took to simply rise up and walk.

Then, in the midst of the fray, the Spirit of Elohim paused. Between two towering trees, at the heart of the continent, in the midst of a garden, it gathered. Glowing. Blazing. Growing. Un-ignoreably bright.

Immediately the crowd was hooked. They couldn't look away.

What was going on?

Haylel dropped everything and zoomed in close.

The crowd squinted and strained. *There!* Through the fog. *See it? There it was again!* A figure, like an angel—*No, like the very son of God*—moving freely in the mist, clothed in white, dazzling bright, so brilliant he could barely be seen.

A reverential hush fell.

Haylel's *mashup* faded away.

The figure—*was he ... kneeling?* He seemed to be sculpting. Molding. Shaping. Scooping up the dew drenched dirt.

Between glimpses, the crowd did their best to fill in the pieces.

Slowly a form began to take shape. Miraculous. Complex. Compelling in concept. The very essence of Elohim, himself.

It was a new creation, a being—*a Man.*

There it lay: bare, lifeless, alone.

The crowd held their breath as the glowing figure knelt, cupping Man's head in his hands.

Then Elohim bent down, his Spirit gathering around—and leaning over the glowing figure's shoulder—gave his new creation a holy, awakening kiss.

CH2: LET US MAKE MAN

They sat alone. Three figures, deep within the recesses of space—walled in by nothing more than the absolute darkness around them. The only light present was the soft ethereal glow that emanated from within the figures themselves. They spoke earnestly, in hushed tones, occasionally pausing to crack a smile or share a joke, but never lingering for longer then the briefest of moments before they were wholeheartedly back on track. The circular table, around which they gathered, overflowed with books, blueprints, songs, and scrolls—orders and edicts too. Each bursting with blank pages just waiting to be authored, down to the smallest details.

The first book was opened.

"Let us make Man," spoke what appeared to be the youngest of the three. He was clothed completely in linen, purest of white, a single golden belt encompassing his waist. He leaned forward, resting his elbows casually on the table hovering between them. "Someone we can shower lavishly with our love!" He flashed a winsome smile, belt beaming with the reflection of his heartfelt emotion.

Elohim turned to address his son, affectionately titled, 'The Angel of the Lord.' "Someone who can *choose* to love us in return." He grinned, lifting his pen. "Someone who looks like us. Talks like us. And *loves* like us." The eternal father leaned forward, putting earnest pen to paper, meticulously composing the text.

"A child—," the third figure spoke. "One to call *our very own!*"

Two heads slowly turned.

Spirit beamed a brilliant, adventurous smile, acknowledging both father and son. With a shrug and a giggle she dropped back in her chair, closing twinkling eyes. Long, shimmering locks of multi-colored hair fell adoringly around her glowing, joy-filled face. *Ahhh—* she loosed a deep, contented sigh. It had only been a moment, yet she was already in love.

Elohim smiled at his darling companion. *What a delight!* Even in this light, Spirit's petite stature and unassuming demeanor did little to hide her dauntless personality. He looked at her fondly. Soft, inviting features complimenting a well-defined frame—what at first glance seemed so simple and plain, upon a closer look revealed stunning, relentless perfection. Elohim's heart swelled. *Was his counterpart not drop-dead gorgeous?!* He leaned forward, longing to call her by any one of her many given names, but he wisely held his tongue. This was her time to speak. He was more than happy to wait.

Spirit opened one purple, rainbow-rimmed eye, smiling at her eternally powerful partner. Strong but gentle, passionate but capable, infinite yet clearly defined—one moment Elohim could be towering galaxies tall above his creation, the next he could be sitting down intimately alongside. "Someone," she continued, relaxing in the unconditional acceptance of her matchless king, "who actually *wants* to love. Not because they *have* to—but because it's truly their deepest, strongest, most heartfelt desire."

Elohim nodded, his pen already back on the move. "Someone who can truly connect with the heart of God." He grinned, making careful note. "Someone like us. *Exactly*—like us."

—| |—

Ahhh—back in the garden, Elohim exhaled—deeply, deliberately, lovingly.

Even in the midst of the blinding haze, all of Heaven could see Elohim's essence—a glimmering piece of his very own Spirit—flowing out from his lips. It rode gently on his breath, tumbling and twirling, entering the man made of clay.

Immediately, life began. Lungs rose and fell. Blood pumped and flowed. Nerves twitched. Skin ambered. Auras glowed.

Man's eyelids fluttered.

Elohim leaned back.

Man inhaled his first breath. "Ahh–ba … *Daddy,*" he smiled.

At this, Elohim threw back his head and laughed—a long, hearty laugh. He reached down, extending a welcoming hand. The earthen man took it. As he rose, he became fully clothed in the light of eternal life. His hair glimmered and glowed. His skin beamed and shone. Light coursed throughout his veins. *Woah*—the crowd 'oohed' and 'aahed.' *How was it that this man made of dust, was suddenly clothed like the sun? Was he not the very son of God?*

Introductions commenced. A garden tour was taken. Two trees displayed. One rule given: "Eat freely of any tree in all of Eden," Elohim urged, "save the one tree at the center of the garden. That tree—*The Tree of the Knowledge of Good and Evil*—is reserved for me, and me alone. For in the day that you eat of it," he warned, "you will surely die."

Man turned aside and grabbed an orange.

Elohim, a fig from his tree.

Cheers, they saluted, "It was agreed!"

The remainder of the day was a blur, full of discovery and disclosure. Still, he—Man—felt curiously incomplete. It wasn't so much that he could put it in words, as the fact that innately, he just knew. Elohim had friends—at least two others who were just like him. But as far as anything that was 'bone of his bone,' Man seemed strikingly alone.

Heaven chuckled as Elohim brought beast after beast before Man in the hopes of finding a suitable mate. *Bluebird?* Nope. *Polar Bear?* Nope. *Panda? Monkey? Dog?* Nope. Nope. Uh—nope.

The day lingered on, Father and son searching out the matter together. *Where would a suitable match be found?* They were on a mission. There was no giving up. Man had determined, they would—*yawn*—find his match—*Yawwn*—right after he … *took … a..*

..Nap?

He plopped down on a super-fluffy patch of uber-green grass and passed out.

Murmurs reverberated through the quizzical crowd. *What was this thing, '—sleep?'*

Before their confusion could fully conceive, out of Elohim's midst, the blazing figure once again reappeared—this time looking a bit more like a surgeon. With masterful expertise, he opened Man up, removing the rib closest to his still beating heart—and upon extraction of its DNA—began to delicately form a Woman.

The crowd leaned in, this unusual break in the "name-game" was strangely riveting. *What a dazzling new creation!* Compelling and beautiful. Shapely and soft. Even the angels found it hard to look away. Woman was Man's glory. His comforter, teammate, helper, friend. She was everything he was, and more. If he was streamlined, she was elegant. If he was glowing, she was radiant. If he got it done, she looked good doing it. She was bold and powerful. More than a conqueror. Better than beautiful.

She was, Woman.

When Man awoke, you can imagine the scene: Large, sparkling meadow. Appropriately placed, waist-high grass. A warm inviting breeze.

Elohim beckons to Man. "Come, there's one more thing I have to show you."

Man slowly turns, peering intently across the plush, luxurious expanse.

Elohim's presence thins—parting like two drawn curtains—revealing, in all her blazing glory, *Woman.*

Man jumps for joy. "This is it!" he shouts, spiking the recently named, 'Chipmunk,' he's been holding. "This is, bone of my bone, flesh of my flesh!" He finishes doing a quick floss-dab dance, throws two hands in the air, and takes off running across the lengthy field.

"Goooaaaaaaaaaaaaaaaal!" the cry just naturally erupts.

Woman follows his cue, sprinting to embrace her clearly athletic lover. Time slows. The camera cuts back and forth: Man/Woman. Woman/Man. Man/Woman..

"Goooaaaaaaaa—"

How … wide … is … this … field?

Man stops to catch his breath, chug some water, and of course—spike another chipmunk. Woman stops to freshen up, double-check her hair, and make a few dozen "essential" phone calls.

Man/Woman, Woman/Man..

"—ooaaaaaaaaal!"

Finally, history's first ever streakers fall gleefully into one another's arms. Both are laughing. Elohim is chuckling. Birds are chirping. Chipmunks are running for their lives.

It's glorious!

And then it's done. Elohim names them, *Adam*. Man names woman, *Eve*. Elohim blesses their union, commanding them to, "Be fruitful and multiply. Fill the earth and subdue it. Rule over every living thing in it!" The bride is kissed. The lovely couple turn and— Mr. and Mrs., Man & Eve Adam—are finally introduced. (To clear up any confusion: Adam—as would any true sports enthusiast—goes by his last name.) And everyone reconvenes to the Crystal Lakeside Reception to cut the fresh fruit cake.

> *..For this reason man will leave his*
> *Father & Mother, unite with his wife,*
> *and the two will become one..*

The post-party starts. The lovers retire. Tonight, there will be little sleep for anyone. Tomorrow will surely be a day of rest!

Whew. Day Six is done.

CH3: COSMIC MISUNDERSTANDINGS

Heaven's collective head was spinning. *What just happened?* Never, in all the time it took to create the universe had Elohim ever talked or walked with anyone one-on-one in the cool of the day. Certainly, he was good, powerful, epic, amazing—and a myriad of other things—but personal? Informal? Intimate? Tender?

What new side of God was this?

It didn't take long to find out. Word quickly spread. "Effective immediately, there was to be an 'all Heaven meeting.'" A new era was beginning. A new normal rolled out. Upgrades would be given. Promotions bestowed. Jobs and positions reassigned.

Heaven could barely contain its excitement. For the first time since its inception, things were about to radically change. *Yes*—this would be a time of advancement for all!

—| |—

"Haylel adores you," The Angel of the Lord spoke first.

The round table—hovering just inches above its inverted pyramidal base—gave way, ever so slightly, as Elohim's beaming son plopped both elbows down and leaned in. "He wants nothing more than to be like his Father."

"I know. It's certainly endearing." Elohim casually looked up, lifting his busy pen. "After all, it *is* his destiny to be like me. And his deepest, most passionate desire."

"So, we'll grant it to him?"

"Of course," Elohim fired a wide, genuine grin. "We'll make him Earth's covering cherub—enforcing the edicts of Heaven, empowering the Laws of Love. It will be his test, his eternal right of passage. If he handles it correctly, the new world and all its inhabitants, will become his forever!"

"..And if he handles it incorrectly?"

Elohim loosed a long slow sigh, a wave of sorrow washing over his face. "Then, it will be his undoing."

"But what of the innocent lives?" The Angel of the Lord's voice sparked with concern. "Can something as precious as 'innocent life' be entrusted to someone who has never had to work *ever*, for anything?"

Elohim shook his head. "We will not place Earth—nor its inhabitants—directly in his hands. Rather, we will make him like us—a servant to all—subject to the will of the people."

"But there is darkness in his heart!" Spirit erupted, the truth bursting from pursed lips. Heaven's darling powerhouse looked at her fearless teammates and slowly cleared her throat. Up to now, she had kept mostly quiet, content to simply enjoy the two-way conversation. But in the light of this new line of questioning she could no longer contain herself, she *had* to interject. Especially, when she knew the truth.

"He will eat from The Tree," she cut to the chase. "I've searched his heart and examined his ways," twinkling tears began to well. "He will eat from *The Tree of Knowledge*, and when he does, a seed will become lodged within his bosom. Rooted in pride, hidden in darkness, it *will* germinate within the depths of his soul." She cleared the growing lump from her throat. "If left unchecked, it *will* expand, clouding his judgment; rendering him blind, irrational, unstable— and worse.." her voice trailed off.

"That seed," Elohim stepped in, "is exactly why he *must* be given the opportunity." He smiled reassuringly. "If his deepest desire is to be like us—and that desire is truly to be fulfilled—than Haylel *must* be afforded the same opportunity as us. The opportunity to lay down his own life, and to serve others above serving himself— whether they deserve it *or not*."

Elohim turned back to his son, the mighty, matchless Angel of the Lord. "Of course, we will *not* place the earth—nor Man—

directly in his hands," he continued. "*Rather*, Man will have full authority *over him*." He paused a moment, letting the distinction sink in. "Even so—Man has been granted free will. He has the right to choose. At any time, Man may eat from the *Tree of Life* and remain under our tutelage forever. OR he may eat from the *Tree of Knowledge* and transfer all authority over to Haylel."

At this, Elohim stopped and shifted his gaze, staring lovingly into Spirit's wide compassionate eyes. "Do not fret, dear one. Even when Man does fall, all will not be lost. Heaven will *most certainly* provide a way of escape."

—| |—

If nervous chatter in Heaven were possible, the throne room was full of it. Angels arriving from every side of the multiverse were eagerly discussing the past week's miraculous events and speculating as to what the coming, 'New Era,' would be.

The throne room itself was no less interactive—self-renovating and expanding to accommodate each new attendee. Haylel was last to arrive. The wall-to-wall crowd curiously parted as he made his way casually to the center of the now endless room. At just the right spot he stopped, waiting, a stage slowly rising beneath his feet.

The expectant crowd moved back, adjusting accordingly.

With a wink and a nod, the room lights fell, a single beat thumping in the darkness. Haylel's hand shot up, flipping "on" his personal light-switch. Lit from within, he began to stomp—pop. Stomp, stomp. Pop.

STOP—the drop occurred.

Up from the floor sprung an entire troupe of dancers—stomping, popping, moving, and glowing in mesmerizing unison.

A cheer erupted from the crowd.

The meeting had finally begun.

Everyone joined in, moving in corporate unity, brilliantly portraying a stunning recreation of the era they had just completed. As they moved, a song rose steadily from their midst, its tangible substance spilling from their lips.

Rising, it gathered. Stacking. Building. Beckoning. Thickening. Resting just above their heads.

Suddenly Elohim appeared. Tapping. Snapping. Moving and grooving. Filling the entire space. With a silly little grin, the King of Kings sat down. Enraptured. Enthroned. Fully engaged. Seated on the praise of his people.

For eons they danced, Elohim's presence energizing the crowd, the crowd's worship empowering Elohim. The room blazed brighter and brighter, building until the energy was almost unbearable.

Then, it was over.

As suddenly as it began: The music ended. The dancers stopped. The lights reset. And the ceremony commenced.

The crowd waited on pins and needles as awards were given, accolades bestowed, and promotions accepted. Each reward was bigger and better than the reward before, each recipient more appreciative. Applause was abundant. Encouragement prolific. It was a whirlwind of smiles and laughter, fun and appreciation—of life, and life more abundantly.

At long last, it was Haylel's turn.

"Come," Elohim beckoned.

Haylel proudly approached the throne, the crowd releasing a deafening roar. *Surely the best had been saved for last,* Haylel bowed low. After all, he *had* orchestrated the birth of the universe to perfection, *and that was no small feat by any stretch of the imagination.*

Patiently he waited, the crowd's energy surging through him on its way back to Elohim. He breathed deep, thoroughly enjoying the rush. It was exhilarating. Invigorating. Completely addicting.

The crowd grew louder.

For the most fleeting of moments Haylel almost considered holding back the tiniest portion for himself, just as a personal memento. But the thought quickly passed. And soon Haylel's full attention returned to the one who favored him most.

"For services rendered," Elohim presented a jewel-studded crown.

"For initiative taken—above and beyond."

A second crown was given.

"For unmatched wisdom, whits, and beauty."

A third, a fourth, a fifth..

Haylel glanced at the crowd. The awards, the applause, the energy—they were quickly piling up. He stared at the crowns by his feet, and then at the newly twinkling accolades up-linked to his lapel. *What a marvelous leader he was! Certainly, an example to all!* He lifted his chin. His chest swelled. He could only imagine what must be in store for the most brilliant, beautiful, highest ranking angel in all of Heaven.

"For you, my anointed cherub," Elohim leaned in. "I present the possession, dearest to my *heart*." Five little letters, 'h-e-a-r-t,' floated visibly up from his lips; circling in the air until they slowly settled on, 'e-a-r-t-h.'

"My—*Earth!*"

An awestruck hush fell.

Haylel's ego soared.

"Should you accept my offer, you will be set in place as Earth's primary covering," Elohim explained for all to hear. "Your responsibilities will be as watchman, guardian, protector—and most importantly—governing body."

Haylel grinned from ear to ear. He could no longer hide it. Elohim was giving him everything he ever wanted. *Everything he deserved!* He would be like God! *No, wait*—to Earth—*he would BE God!* He couldn't believe it. It was like a dream come true. *Earth*—the pinnacle of all pinnacle creations, handmade by Elohim—*it would be his!*

"I will gladly rule over Man and its kind!" Haylel gushed, albeit a bit rashly. "All of humanity *will forever be mine!*"

"Not quite so fast!" Elohim chuckled, lifting a cautioning hand. "You will be God of the Air, God of All Things," he quickly corrected. "Anything spoken by Man—*YOU will bring to pass*. I will place Powers, Authorities, and up to one-third of my Heavenly Hosts under your charge. With them, you may guide the hearts of mankind—leading them to walk in my ways. You will be his protector, defender, his shelter and shield; assisting, furnishing and facilitating his every word."

Haylel felt his cheeks flush, then redden, as it slowly dawned exactly what he was being asked to do. He wasn't being given a world to rule and reign. He was being given a world to ... *baby-sit?*

A thunderclap of anger disrupted his soul. He shuddered violently, instinctively stuffing the offense back down.

"So—I will be Earth's—Ambassador?" he quickly redefined for everyone to hear.

"Yes—Earth's gatekeeper," Elohim nodded. "Governing what goes in and out. Guarding all of mankind. Watching over their every word, and bringing those words to pass."

Haylel bowed deeply. "Then I—humbly accept your ... *promotion,*" he winced, his reply suddenly tasting quite bitter against his ego-bruised tongue. "May it be as you say."

"You're certain?" Elohim gently confirmed, a flicker of concern sweeping across wide, fatherly eyes. He paused for the affirming nod, responding with a nod of his own. Then, springing from his seat, he gave a mighty handclap. "*You will love it!*" he grinned, motioning Haylel forward. "Come, let's debrief you, anoint you, and set you into office!"

CH4: DOWNHILL FROM HERE

A small, elite company of angels fell into lockstep behind Haylel and Elohim. Two by two, they moved through the halls of Heaven, retiring from the dazzling throws of the soaring throne room and into a small, privately-sequestered—yet equally dazzling—office.

With a bow and a blessing, the group began the process of setting Haylel in as Earth's Covering Cherub, or as Haylel later put it, "Chief Errand Boy." Documents were drafted. Oaths were taken. Authorities assigned. Powers given. One-third of all Heaven's Hosts activated and commissioned.

In all honesty, it *was* quite a responsibility. Looking after Earth—Heaven's most prized possession—was no small undertaking. There were many details to discuss.

Haylel went down his list of concerns.

Elohim highlighted a few of his own.

Undeniably, it *was* the perfect fit, almost to Haylel's chagrin. He would be Earth's gatekeeper, the filter between God and man. His jurisdiction would be neither spirit nor flesh. Rather it would be the intermediate realm, *Soul*. Just as Elohim reigned over Heaven (and Mankind over Earth) so too, would he reign over *Soul*—the vast, *Second Heaven, solar system expanse* connecting the two.

And so it was set, Haylel's duties would include: Governing what was allowed in and out of Earth's atmosphere. Appropriate direction/redirection of mankind's worship. Appropriate direction/redirection of mankind's heart. Diligent observation and documentation of everything mankind did. And of course, attending to the physical fruition of mankind's every word.

This was no small undertaking. To start, Haylel would have

to oversee all of Heaven's *Watchers:* a unique authority of angels created with embedded audio, video and transmission capabilities—designed specifically for documenting, recording and relaying information between Heaven and Earth.

In short, they were Heaven's daily news crew.

Likewise, he would also spearhead an elite division of *Powers:* beings gifted with the singular ability to motivate the fickle hearts of Man; compelling mankind to instinctively (and spontaneously) follow in the "way they should go."

Lastly, Haylel would command a large, angelic body of *Heavenly Hosts*—messengers, healers, warriors, builders and the like—commissioned to facilitate creativity, growth, and when absolutely necessary, direct connection between the resources of Heaven and Earth, facilitating the spoken words of Man.

Of course, such a vast group of specialized forces would need a home base; a place from which to run daily operations.

The nearest planet, Mars, was Haylel's first choice. A mirror image of Earth, it too boasted rivers, forests, mountains and moons. Set in precise orbital resonance, its shared spin and relative orbital space kept it in perfect synchronization with Elohim's young Earth, crisscrossing the brilliant red planet spectacularly through Earth's sky once every fifty-four years; making it perfect for "rubber-necking media crews" attempting to transmit regularly scheduled broadcasts whilst keeping close, attentive ears to the ground.

Earth's own, Moon, was Haylel's next selection. As openly noted, it was, "Big, and bright, and close!" For Haylel and his Power Team Elites, this was prime-time real estate. Its perpetual 'dark side' made it ideal for any angelic influencer wishing to maintain maximum anonymity, while enjoying minimal distance & proximity. Moreover, the Moon's unique ability to rebroadcast any internalized frequency made it the perfect instrument for daily repairing, reprogramming, and reshaping mankind's DNA—even while Earth's inhabitants slept.

Of course, every planet in Earth's immediate solar system eventually became some sort of "home base" for Second Heaven's ever-expanding, over-reaching political operations. "This was always to be expected," Haylel often bragged to anyone who listened. "After all, can perfection ever truly be contained?"

As for the mysterious set of keys which hung plainly from his lapel? Those were to be kept under the strictest of guard. With the power to unlock the nuclear capabilities of *Death*, *Hell*, and *The Grave*—no other being, in all of Heaven or Earth, was *ever* to be granted access. Even he, Haylel, was to use them *only* under the strictest of supervision—*the direct expressed consent of Elohim.*

And that was that.

The groundwork was set.

For quite some time, the dialog continued. Until Haylel was fully satisfied that every request had been met. And Elohim, that every instruction had been received. Only then, was it reiterated: "Second Heaven was to faithfully uphold Third Heaven's highest ethical standards and to adhere to every word that emanated from the mouth of God and mankind."

"Absolutely," it was agreed. "It would certainly be so."

And so with that, the meeting adjourned, both groups going their separate ways. Elohim, to flawless relationship. Haylel to flawless implementation.

—| |—

Back on Earth, Team Adam was living it up. There were dinosaurs to wrangle. Bullfrogs to race. Hopscotch Hoopla's and Treetop Toga Parties to attend. There were clouds to surf. Mountains to climb. Oceans and jungles to explore. Not to mention, chatting with the chimpanzees, lounging with the lions, or the ever enchanting 'playtime with the penguins.'

And that was all before breakfast.

Adam's personal favorite, was cliff diving. He would search out the tallest bluff, scale it to the top, and proceed to jump—head first—over its looming edge. It was exhilarating! The rush of air on his face, the feeling of free-flight. *It couldn't be beat!* He would tumble, twist, and turn to his heart's content before—*WHAAM*—slamming, face-first onto the soft earth below.

Admittedly, it did sting quite a bit, but the fleeting pain was nothing compared to the total awesomeness of the free-fall. Thus, he was always in search of bigger, taller, steeper cliffs from which to dive.

The whole process made Eve giggle. One second they would be picking wild-berries, and the next, Adam would be gone—only his wild shouts of ecstasy and the eventual resounding THUD demarcating his new location. No worries though, after a moment, Eve would come floating down, reclined atop a low flying cloud, or riding the back of some sort of watchful winged creature. What she would find was always the same. Adam would be busily brushing himself off—bones popping back into place, bruises quickly disappearing—grinning from ear to ear as he eagerly looked for another cliff to conquer. Eve kept it to herself, but it was kinda cute to see her man so fearless and free. Especially the times he would show off, just a little, just for her, on his way down.

Eve's favorite thing—aside from intimate walks on the beach, long honest conversations, hot-spring bubble baths, red-clay mud facials, counting shooting stars, collecting hidden gems, braiding daisy chains, singing in the meadow, dancing in the forest, and cuddling with her man—was the food. *Oh, the food! There were so many options: Fruits. Berries. Veggies. Nuts.* Every meal was its own excursion—its own fully immersive, culinary experience.

"First, one has to spot just the right fruit," Eve would often explain, "any old piece won't do!" Of course, with a properly trained eye this was quite easy to accomplish, since each piece of fruit had its own aura—a sort of plasmic, colorful energy—surrounding it. The more saturated the color, the stronger the energy. The stronger the energy, the more ripe the fruit. All one needed to do, was to pluck an appropriately glowing target from its protective branches, wait a few moments until it fully ripened, and then, as Eve liked to say, "Chow out!" *Oh, the tastes. Oh, the smells. The colors and textures. It was beyond compare!* Each new bite was always better than the last!

And that was just the start. As each piece of fruit was consumed, its energy, its aura, and oh, yes—*its wisdom*, became a permanent part of its consumer. For example: An orange would be eaten, and suddenly the understanding of, "the orange peel's diverse health benefits to the physical body" might be revealed. A second orange enjoyed might leave its partaker full of wisdom for, "cultivating orange groves in cooler, more arid climates." A third fruit might introduce expanded knowledge of, "drying and planting orange seeds." A fourth, sparking the idea for making, "orange zest in the kitchen."

The possibilities were literally endless!

But best of all, as each fruit was plucked, a new, better tasting, more revelatory fruit would appear—growing almost instantly in its place. *It was captivating.* Eve would often get lost for hours, feasting at a single branch: *Need a deeper understanding of animal-husbandry and the interbreeding of preferential genetic markers?*

There was a fruit for that.

How about the migration habits of the Madagascar Sunset Moth?

There was a fruit for that.

Calligraphy? Jujitsu? Quantum Physics? Hooked on Phonics?

There was a fruit for that.

Of course, all personal interests aside, Team Adam's favorite thing to do was to walk with Elohim in the cool of the day. More and more, they found themselves looking forward to their casual evening strolls with Abba—*Daddy God*. There was rarely an agenda. Never an ulterior motive. It was simply time set aside to enjoy one another's company, and to just 'be.'

Often their evenings were spent discussing the day's prior pleasantries, exploring new intellectual concepts, and/or revisiting new-found discoveries. Team Adam might bring Abba to taste their favorite berry bush, or go for a dip in their latest swimming hole. Abba might lead Team Adam to a hidden fruit grove, reveal an undiscovered mountain range, or point out some new extreme cliff.

Often the trio never made it out of the garden at all. On those evenings, they were typically found lounging at its center, hammocks stretched between its two towering, most notorious trees—laughing, joking, and sharing holy ghost stories.

Of course, spoken conversation was a rarity. Certainly their communication was nonstop—clearly heard, plainly felt—but it was thoughts and emotions which did the brunt of the work, not words. Like birds flocking south or schools of darting fish, they instinctively acted and reacted, flowing with Elohim's *Special Spirit* seamlessly, as one. There was little need to waste the time or the physical effort that audible speech required. *And honestly, why would they?* Words in Earth's fertile atmosphere were exceedingly powerful. If Abba spoke, *it became.* If Team Adam spoke, *it would soon become.* No, it was understood—spoken words were reserved for times of creation, creativity, and cataclysmic change.

And so the years passed, angels under Haylel's command nurturing the happy couple into their eternally brightening future. There were no worries. No doubts. No fears. No frustrations. No unmet needs or desires. Unity and inhibition were simply *the* way of life. Intimacy and joy, their natural by-product. Selfishness didn't exist. Lack was unheard of. Rejection wasn't a thing. Self-awareness, completely unnecessary. Iniquity had yet to be birthed.

It was: Two lovers.

Three friends.

One amazing experience.

Truly, it was *Heaven on Earth*.

CH5: LIKE TAKING CANDY FROM A BABY

This table wasn't round. No, this one was square. And it certainly wasn't hovering in space. This table sat grounded on four legs of stone—fused together like fire-tempered iron. There was no light coming from this permanent fixture. No glow within the two figures seated around it. The only light, came from the bubbling cauldrons of boiling lava scattered liberally about the surrounding cavern. Stalactites hung low across the ceiling. Stalagmites rose eerily from the floor. The air was thick, hot and heavy. And everything about this god-forsaken hollow reeked of death and sulfur.

"Remind me again why we're here?" growled the first figure, clearly on edge. A cauldron flared behind him, highlighting his looming frame.

He leaned in close.

Way too close.

The second figure scrunched his nose and smirked at the malodorous piece of work. His cohort had the body of a strong man: muscles on muscles with muscles. Yet, he was covered with a wiry coat of thick, dark hair—fur, would be more accurate. It was short and shaggy, course as wool, and somewhat unkempt. On his fingers were claws, like that of a bear. And his feet were cloven like hooves. His head resembled that of an ox, an iron ring hanging loosely from his nose. The long horns on either side of his head had been cut to stubs and filed into jagged points—visually intimidating, but practically useless. His ears were full of studs, and rods, and tags. His eyes were bold and dark. And when he spoke, his voice rumbled like a lion. Rumor had it that his name was actually an acronym for something much darker than himself, and was thus spelled in all caps. But most thought it was simply because his name was usually being shouted when spoken—most often by himself.

"BEAST, you know full well why we're here," came the irritated reply. "The heart of the earth is the only place we may freely speak without threat of compromise."

BEAST grunted. "—because nobody in their right mind.." he trailed off, looking around, grumbling mostly to himself.

"Hey—you don't have to be here ... *OX.*"

BEAST flinched. That barb stung ... mostly because barbs in the spirit-world were actually—*barbs*. He reached back, over his right shoulder, and popped the tiny dagger from his thick, rolling flesh. "You're lucky you outrank me," he trailed off, sending the sharp tack sailing briskly off the end of the table. "Or, I'd.." For a moment he paused, sizing up his offender. The figure was easily as slender as he was tall—not physically tough by any stretch of the imagination. In his hands he held a primitive staff, almost like a shepherd's rod. Dark and gnarled, it appeared sensational, but in reality it wasn't good for much of anything except beating sheep. He wore the cliché 'hooded robe,' pulled low around his face. Piercing yellow eyes blazed underneath. His cheeks were high and gaunt. His lips stretched thin and pursed. And when he moved, it was with slow, deliberate motions—an obvious overcompensation for his quick, sharp tongue.

No one actually knew his real name, he was simply called, *Prophet.*

"I'm lucky I outrank you, *or you'd what?*" Prophet thumped the end of his cane hard against BEAST's thick skull. "You'd pull your thumb outta your mouth just long enough to *call your mama?*"

BEAST didn't hesitate, both hands were instantly around Prophet's neck—*squeezing hard.*

The dark Shaman lurched and reeled, caught completely off guard. Jaw wide, he struggled for air. Typically he would've muttered an incantation, waved the tip of his staff, and—*voilá*—confrontation over. But he couldn't breath, not even to force a whisper. And his staff had been unwittingly knocked against the edge of the empty chair beside him—*just out of arms reach.*

"Never—EVER ... talk about *my mother,*" BEAST snarled

through clenched teeth.

Actually, BEAST didn't have a mother. However, Jezebel—the spirit to whom he was referring—*had* raised him since Creation. To him, she was everything. In fact, he was here solely on her behalf. It was actually Jezebel who had received the secret underworld invitation—her presence, the actual presence requested. But there was, quote, "No way she would be caught dead sneaking around Middle Earth." Not until she was absolutely certain they were on to something. So naturally, BEAST had been sent in her stead.

Prophet clawed and choked and sputtered.

BEAST squeezed harder.

For a long, semi-comical moment, they remained. Poised like a still photo, diabolically unmoving, stuck in a sort of "frozen limbo." Prophet contending for any sort of air whatsoever, and BEAST utterly unyielding. Of course, this was the spirit-world, BEAST couldn't actually *kill* Prophet—just make him incredibly uncomfortable. At some point he would *have* to let go ... *maybe.*

"Gentlemen!" A new voice erupted from the darkness. "Let's not overextend our prepubescent frustrations prematurely," it chided. "We all know *a house divided will not stand.*"

Two heads slowly turned.

The arrival was tall, dark, and debonair—and in an unusually good mood. He would have been handsome as well, had he not been hidden behind an overly-polished, highly-tinted, jet-black, motorcycle-like helmet; and sporting a shock of thick, dark dreads, cascading boldly down the length of his back. He wore a form-fitting, heat-resistant suit, which seamlessly concealed his stunningly chiseled body. And there was a curious set of three rubber-wrapped keys tethered to his left shoulder. He was the perfect cross between The Predator and Batman, Dark Knight—an irresistible blend of charisma and charm that, if given the chance, would absolutely eat you alive.

"Ha-satan!" BEAST bowed low, dropping Prophet hard against the back of his chair.

Prophet popped up, coughing and sputtering, doing his best to regroup and follow suit. Cane back in hand, he cleared his throat loudly, observing their mentor with the sliest of smirks. *He already knew Ha-satan's dirty little secret:* In the Heavens above, this was Haylel—*the bright and shining one.* But down here, in the dim and the dark, he was simply called, Ha-satan *('HAH-say-tahn'), The-deceiver.*

Ha-satan brushed past the duo, nodding "hello" and securing his seat at the head of the table.

"What, no cape?" BEAST quipped, doing his best to lighten the mood. "Not even a forked tail?"

"I thought about hooves," came the dry reply. "But you beat me to it." Ha-satan dropped three fresh figs dead-center on the table. "Besides, you should already know, every tale I tell is forked."

"Touché." BEAST flashed a crooked grin, bowing just a smidgen lower.

Ha-satan moved to tip an invisible hat and froze. "Are you here alone?" He glanced around for Jezebel. It *had* been her name on the invitation, *no?*

BEAST snorted. "Belle wouldn't be caught dead in this hell-hole," he motioned to their picturesque surroundings. "Suffocating isn't exactly her cup of tea. But no worries," he produced a wad of pale-yellow sticky notes, and a well-chewed pen. "I'm here to represent." His chest slowly swelled with pride, "—and BEAST takes *GOOD NOTES!*"

Ha-satan rolled his eyes and dropped to his seat. *What was there to say?* That was Belle—always throwing a wrench in things. It was for that exact reason, he both loved and hated her. Still, he wasn't going to let her obstinance ruin his day. *Not today anyways.* He waved a dismissing hand and motioned for them to be seated.

"There *is* a way," he began, "that puts us back at the top of the food chain." He glanced around the table. "A way that no matter how it's played, will be a win for us." He paused, waiting until he was sure he had their full attention. "Gentlemen, how does no more babysitting sound?" He glanced first to BEAST, and then to Prophet. "No more, 'Errand Boy..' No more, 'Mr. Fix It,'" his eyebrows instinctively raised.

"Sounds ... magical," Prophet dryly responded. "But what's the catch?" He wasn't keen on the pitch, but he was more than tired of healing the same bruised bones from the same tired cliff dives.

BEAST was already nodding.

"No catch." Ha-satan motioned to the fruit. "The key is in *The Tree.* If we can get Adam to willingly eat from it," he grinned, "he will have—in essence—bowed his knee to *us*, and the revelation housed within the fruit will immediately become a permanent part of his DNA." A chuckle escaped. "Not only will it breach the impenetrable firewall which protects his relationship with Elohim, but it will provide a port—a permanent opening—through which we can connect with him, any time we want."

"A LoJack—," nodded Prophet. He'd heard of such things.

BEAST was thrilled. "You mean to say—we'll be able to talk to Adam through his thoughts, *LIKE ELOHIM DOES?!*" He looked up from his ball of notes like he was ready to bust a move. He wasn't the sharpest tool in the shed, but what he lacked in mental fortitude, he more than made up for in enthusiasm.

"That's just the start," Ha-satan waved a dismissive hand. "Have you noticed the extent to which Man's fool-hardy agreement moves the heart of Elohim?" He scooted to the edge of his seat.

"More than any other substance in the universe," Prophet tipped his cane.

BEAST was already nodding.

"Well gentlemen, that's because: *Man's agreement is free.* And free agreement, when *freely* expressed, unleashes a kind of radical energy which is second to none. In fact," Ha-satan paused for emphasis, "that energy is the very energy *of Elohim, himself!*" He stared at two blank, emotionless faces. "Did you hear me boys—*the very energy of Elohim, himself!*"

More blank stares.

Ha-satan threw up both hands and sat back. This was pointless. *How could he make them understand?* "Gentlemen," he shifted gears. "I've found a loophole. A loophole which, if utilized, would give us unlimited access to Adam's *free radical energy.*" He was literally shaking with excitement, his inner lawyer taking over. "Gentlemen—if we can simply persuade Mankind to turn his agreement away from Elohim and direct it towards us instead, than we can freely—*and legally*—receive it!"

At this, Prophet began to chuckle. Not because he liked the plan, but because there was *no way* Man would *ever* turn on Elohim.

BEAST, however, was completely sold. "So—uhm." He fumbled with a sticky note. "If we can get mankind to do things *our way.*" He flipped one note around, swapped it for another, scribbling something on a third. "Than this 'magical, super-power, energy' of Elohim's is ours ... *for the taking?*" He glanced up, beginning to grasp the full picture.

"And it's all, one-hundred percent, *totally legit!*" Ha-satan leaned forward, slapping the table for emphasis.

"Ha, eh—heh, he-hehhhhh!" Something resembling—and sort of smelling like undigested laughter, gurgled up from BEAST's fourth belly. His eyes lit up. He had a thought. He cracked a toothy grin. "Wanna know the *BEST PART?*" he bellowed, leaping up from his chair. "The best part is—*we can blame it ALL ON MAN!*" His gravelly voice was rolling like thunder. "Your EXCELLENCE," he bowed, doing his best mock throne room impression, "I'm SOOO hating all this extra power and control. But how long will mankind continue to insist on agreeing with ... *ME?!*" BEAST howled with laughter, stumbling about like a peg-legged sailor, the back of his hand flopped disdainfully across his broad, perspiring forehead. "Gov'na. Oh, Gov'na," he kept repeating. "What's a deity to do? What's a deity to do?"

Prophet shot BEAST a wicked look. As much as he wanted to kill him, he was unfortunately inclined to agree. Playing middle-man and quietly blame-shifting *WOULD* drive a wedge between God and Man. Especially when Elohim saw that Man only loved him because Man had never really been given any viable alternatives.

He opened his mouth to say just that, but BEAST was already rambling on. "*AND—.*" The blathering Ox pontificated. "When Elohim sees that Man's agreement is only making *US* stronger," he came to a teetering halt against the back of his chair. "Elohim will have no other choice *BUT TO PERMANENTLY DELETE HIS BROKEN RELATIONSHIP WITH MANKIND.*" The words exploded from deep inside. "That, or to let us grow so powerful that we can *OVER-*

THROW HIS VERY THRONE OURSELVES!" BEAST cleared his throat, pawing at the drool suddenly racing down the cleft of his chin. His bellies rumbled—loud and long. He did his best to stifle a belch. *"EITHER WAY,"* he roared, stepping back to bust his move. *"IT'S A WIN-WIN-WIN!"*

Ha-satan did his best to ignore the dancing ox beside him, shooting Prophet a sideways, knowing glance. "Wanna know the kicker?" He held out an empty hand.

Prophet grudgingly scooped up some dirt. Waved his staff. And—*poof*—handed Ha-satan a fist-full of hay.

"The kicker, Gentlemen, is that we also have the *Powers of Heaven* at our disposal." He handed the hay to BEAST. "Not only will we be able to speak to Man in thought, *but in emotion as well.*"

They watched as the great bovine slowed his roll and began munching blissfully away.

"Which means," the dark lord added, "that once we've gained legal access, Adam will not only *think* like we want him to think, but he'll *DESIRE what we want him to DESIRE! He will practically BEG to follow us!"*

This was almost too much for BEAST. His blood-sugar began to spike. His vision tunneled. His body shook. Snack or no snack, he was quickly sliding into a power-hungry coma.

Prophet nervously cleared his throat. "But how will we ever get Man to fall for it?" He shifted uneasily in his seat. "He will never disobey a direct command from Elohim. He physically cannot. There's no rebellion in him, he doesn't even know how.."

Uh-oh, BEAST froze mid-coma.

Total buzz-kill.

"The woman." Ha-satan smirked. *"She's* our ticket. She was never given the same face-to-face instruction as Man. Technically, she can freely eat." He leaned in. "We simply get the woman to eat, and when nothing happens, Man will surely follow." His tone shifted to one of total disdain. "Besides, they are clueless, trusting, bumbling idiots. Like their father, they'll believe anything you tell them ... *anything."*

BEAST relaxed, *game back on!* He inhaled deeply, letting the last bit of good news push him right back over the edge. His eyes rolled back in his head. All feeling was leaving his legs.

He began to sway violently.

"Brilliant—*except* for one monolithic detail," Prophet scowled. "Team Adam will *know EXACTLY* who tricked them."

Instantly BEAST was sober. He fell, crashing to his seat—one huge, hairy head falling into one huge, hairy hand. "He's right," he mumbled through the last of his hay. "If we mislead Adam—what's to stop Team Adam from simply telling Elohim everything?" He sighed pitifully. "The jig is up, even before it starts.." BEAST's eyes began to well with tears. His lower lip began to quiver.

At this, Ha-satan leaned back and smiled his most winsome smile. Of course, no one noticed because he was wearing a big, black, tinted helmet. "Gentlemen," he exclaimed, "that is *exactly* why I called this meeting."

Both heads turned in slow unison.

"I've found a way." Ha-satan reached forward, casually lifting the fruit. "A back-door—if you will." He tossed one fruit to Prophet, another to BEAST. "A way to enter the soul of every earth-bound creature." He paused, motioning for them to eat. "*Take a look!*"

They each took a bite.

Ha-satan waited for the byte to take root, then boot.

The understanding uploaded.

"Using this technique," he continued, "we can enter any creature's soul, putting them on like a glove, compelling them to do our bidding." He chuckled a sort of creepy Puppet Master chuckle. "I've been perfecting the art for quite some time now, practicing on reptiles and fowl, observing our marks for years.."

He pushed back from the table and stood.

"Gentlemen, I am willing to put my own neck on the line. To take *all* the risk. To do *all* the tempting. But only if you're *both* all in." He looked each cohort dead in the eye. "Because once we do this, there will be no going back. Things will never be the same."

For a moment, the question hung clumsily in the stagnant, boiling air.

"..What say you both?"

BEAST was first to stir.

Power? Control? Deception? AND delicious snacks? He glanced around. *What wasn't there to love?!* He popped the last of his fruit into his wide-opened mouth. *Of course, he was all in!* He chewed and swallowed. *After all—he'd been snacking on these fruits for years. Ever since he'd happened upon his mom sneaking a bite one mid-summer's morning from one of The Tree's many low-hanging branches.*

Eagerly, he rose from his chair.

Prophet, on the other hand, was slower to rise. A no-risk, high-reward deal to ruling the universe seemed almost too good to be true. He needed to know: *What were the responsibilities? The drawbacks? The unforeseen repercussions? Was there some sort of hidden catch?*

For quite some time he rode the fence. Analyzing. Thinking. Rethinking. Analyzing again..

But in the end, the fruit was sweet. The forbidden knowledge sweeter. And permanently quitting his job as, 'Mr. Fix It,' sweetest of all. So eventually—and against his better judgment—Prophet slowly stood.

"Welcome aboard!" Ha-satan gleefully slapped each crony on the shoulder. He brazenly raised a gleaming fruit of his own, pocketing it as he moved to make his exit. "Have no fear," he reassured. "This will be like taking candy from a baby!"

"Ehh—?" BEAST grunted, watching his unlikely associate disappear into the surrounding darkness. "Whaa—What's a baby?"

—| |—

The day had been especially brisk.

Eve leaned back, nestling further into the comforting arms of her best friend and teammate lover. She breathed in the thick, honey-sweet air, loosing a long sigh of content. From where they reclined at the center of the garden, Eve could see her favorite grove of willow trees waving gently in the breeze. She waved back. Halos of shimmering gold-dust flowed tranquilly around their majestic, swaying branches, swirling like a million free-floating fireflies. A smile alighted on her lips. For a moment she studied her surroundings—the butterflies fluttering playfully about, the bees buzzing from flower to technicolored flower, each carefree blade of grass singing quietly in the setting sunlight—they all seemed entirely unaware, carrying on, business as usual.

Nearby, the two trees stood, towering overhead, a thick carpeted path running right between them. Birds sang sweetly in their branches. Furry woodland creatures scurried among their roots. Daisies and dragonflies were everywhere. Eve's brow slowly furrowed. On the surface, the garden was its usual picture of perfection— innocent, inviting, serene. Yet somehow, underneath, something seemed amiss.

Today, Eve thought, *just feels like change.*

With a gentle squeeze Adam shifted, standing to his feet. By the look of his aura, Eve could tell, *he felt it too*. She studied her man, positively stunning in the glow of the surrounding gold-dust. Like a work of art, he posed—strong, striking, confident—the atmosphere especially responsive to his present, questioning hue; bathing him in a sort of snow-globe of ever twinkling lights.

"Evening arrives soon," he spoke playfully, his voice sing-song in nature. "Time for the clouds to break so we can count the stars!" He looked eagerly to the already thinning heavens.

"YES—*and Abba arrives!*" squealed Eve, grabbing her lover's hand and pulling herself up. She could barely wait. "What do you think Abba will bring us tonight?" She was already imagining a million things: A brand new story. An exciting, epic adventure. A shiny new piece of jewelry.

"How about a talking serpent?" The voice came suddenly, calculatedly, mischievously.

Eve squealed again.

Adam turned excitedly.

Whoa! There it was, the biggest talking serpent they'd ever seen, stretched out—six, twelve, eighteen feet long—resting comfortably beside them in the *Tree of Knowledge*. Its body lay coiled, wrapped tight around a thick, low-lying branch. Its arms crossed and tucked beneath its chin.

"What are you doing?" Eve squinted at the silly new creature—*so long and smooth and red. Its teeth looked big and razor sharp.* "Isn't this tree forbidden?" She took a step closer and cocked her head.

The snake smiled and stretched, twisting slowly along the thick, sweeping branch. "So what if it is?" he grinned, reaching out with a slender, salamander-like arm and plucking a low-hanging fruit.

Eve gasped.

Adam blanched.

"What?" The serpent chuckled, casually popping the snack into its mouth. "Tastes absolutely amazing!" The creature smacked and chewed, licking each finger one by one. "Want some?"

The question made Adam flinch, although it blew right past Eve. "No thanks," she responded. "We don't eat from that tree."

"Why not?!" the serpent hissed, feigning surprise. "Has the Creator not said, you may eat of *any* tree in the garden?"

"Of course—of *all* the trees in the garden we may freely eat," Eve clarified. "But of the fruit of this tree, here in the center of the garden—Abba said: 'You shall not eat of it. Neither shall you touch it. Lest you surely die.'"

"*You* will not surely die," scoffed the snake. He plucked a second fruit, tossing it to Eve. "See for yourself."

The fruit landed neatly in Eve's outstretched hands.

This time Adam gasped.

They both froze, waiting for certain, imminent death— *whatever that was.*

Nothing.

Eve slowly exhaled the breath she didn't know she was holding, turning the pretty little fruit over in her hands. She glanced to Adam, then back to her fruit. It looked spectacular, shimmering, a deep ruby red with a fiery yellow center. The outer edges of its aura looked almost to be made of pure gold, and it felt firm yet delicate to the touch.

Eve's mouth began to water.

"Well, Abba didn't actually tell me directly," she slowly backpedaled.

"Because—Abba knows," the serpent slyly baited the hook, "that in the day you eat of it your eyes will be opened and you will be like God, knowing good and evil."

What great news! Eve could barely contain herself. *She had always wanted to be just like Abba!* She studied the fruit. *It was so pretty... so pleasant... so innocent... so—CHOMP.* Even before she realized what she was doing, she was already chewing on a delicious mouthful—sweet, sugary juices running slowly down her chin.

Mmmm, it truly was amazing! Refreshingly good. In fact, it was so yummy, she couldn't help herself—*she simply had to swallow.*

Adam stood stunned. *What just happened?* No really. *What?* One second ago, they were planning a magical evening with Abba— *and now... THIS?* It didn't compute. *What was he supposed to do?* He could never disobey Abba, he loved him too much. But then again, Eve—she was flesh of his flesh, bone of his bone. *How could he ever turn his back on her?* He felt sick, conflicted, caught unexpectedly off-guard. For the first time ever he was stuck—trapped between opposing worlds—pressing him from either side.

Eve turned and handed him the fruit.

Adam blinked, wide-eyed—*waiting..*

Waiting.

He turned to the snake. Then back to Eve. She still seemed very much alive. *Had he gotten it wrong?* He opened his mouth to rebuke the lie, but then again—Eve had never looked so radiant. *Was the snake actually telling the truth?* Numb and reeling he lifted the fruit, trying to find the words.

Crunch—he too, took a bite.

Wow. It WAS fantastically good.

Slowly he chewed, analyzing his conundrum, fully expecting to spit. But it was just—*gulp*—easier to swallow.

GONG... GONG... GONG.

What was this?! Adam dropped the fruit with a start; bells— like those from a clock tower suddenly piercing the air.

The dumbstruck couple turned to one another, their world already beginning to unravel. Fibers shook. Molecules shifted.

Perceptions flipped. DNA twisted. For a moment, even the serpent seemed rattled.

Then, silence..

confusion..

darkness..

W-Where did everything go?

Adam's eyes fluttered open. Eve's eyes followed suit. The plasmic life-force covering everything around them had completely … *vanished.* Their eyes went wide. *Everything was dim and dark—as if it had been unplugged.* They stared at one another, suddenly as dull as a couple of bare light-bulbs. *What had they done?! Had they broken the machine?* Why did they suddenly seem so simple … so unimpressive … so—*naked!* Guilt washed over them. Then shame. Then fear. *Abba would know that they ate!* There was no way he wouldn't. One look at their stark, lightless bodies … *and he would know!*

Then, the unthinkable happened.

"ADAM!" Abba's voice rang out. "ADAM! Where are you?"

They were busted.

They turned to the snake, but the snake was already gone.

They turned to each other, but—*awkward.*

They turned to the sound of Elohim, but how could they face him now?

What to do? Elohim would arrive in: *Five … Four … Three … Two …*

Adam reached for Eve's hand.

RUN!

CH6: THE COUNTDOWN BEGINS
4035:00:00:21:02:00

Since the beginning, the clock tower stood—silent as the grave. Dormant, it loomed, crafted from a single white stone, towering atop a floating hill. Its frosted frame and glowing infrastructure, pulsed and gleamed, beaming for all to see. Sure, its prominence was puzzling, especially considering the fact that its face had never moved, *and* that it was visible from nearly every location throughout Heaven. Still, no one was the wiser. Time in Heaven was little more than a fabled whisper, mere water-cooler conjecture. Certainly, there was no need for any sort of device to actually keep track of it.

That was, until..

GONG ... GONG ... GONG.

In a single moment, the lofty tower sprang to life—publicly proclaiming the tragic fall of Man. Like a cosmic combination lock, its countdown began: years, months, days, hours, minutes and seconds, ticking away to ... *what?* The question bothered Haylel to no end. At first, he tried to ignore it, to remain focused on the lucrative rewards of his recent global acquisition. But the clock's steady tick grated his soul, and the moment he realized he would *never* find relief, it was fully resolved—that by any and all means—*the countdown must be stopped.*

—| |—

"So—how do you catch a liar?" The question hung burdensome in the crisp, clean air. Elohim let it hang a moment longer. "Tell me," he repeated. "How do you catch a liar?"

The King of the Universe glanced around. The resounding

silence said it all. Everyone at the round table was fully aware, '*Love ALWAYS trusts,*' and in a culture of perfect love, honor, and *trust*—how *could* you catch a liar?

—*You can't.*

He probed a bit further. "So then, when the deceiver fails—when he gives himself fully to selfishness and self-promotion—how will we deal with the lies? The trickery? The gossip and deceit?"

"With love," came the reply. "We will love."

Elohim nodded his approval. "And what does love do?"

"Love always trusts." Spirit looked up from her clipboard of doodles and notes. "Always trusts, *and always* believes the best." She licked the tip of her pencil and went right back to work.

"Then that's what we'll do," Elohim replied, matter-of-fact. "We will trust. And we will believe the best—*about him.*"

"*But love also protects!*" Elohim's son, The Angel of the Lord, erupted. "*It defends! Takes no pleasure in deception! Does not excuse injustice! Nor does it sweep rebellion under the rug!*" His blue eyes were flashing, belt glowing fiercely. "Love is unstoppable. Incorruptible. Undefeatable. Unpredictable. Utterly fearless. *Love never fails!*"

"Well said," Elohim turned, giving his son his full attention. "And so I ask, once more: How do you *catch* a liar?"

There was a brief pause.

"You set a trap? Catch him in the act?"

"Yes—and how do we do that?"

"..Give him a test. An opportunity *to do* the right thing!"

Elohim chuckled. "Precisely!"

"Then—I will go." The Angel declared. "I will be that test." A determined smile flickered across his resolute face. "I will insert myself into the system, and place myself within his hands," he leaned in, passions beginning to rise. "Just as the deceiver disguised himself—*I too, shall hide in flesh.* Just as he enticed creation—*I too, shall become his temptation.* Should he uphold me, the earth will remain his forever. Destroy me, and he will have been caught red-handed!"

He pushed back, rising from his seat. "Let the books reflect, we will not muddy our relationship with futile attempts to confront or accuse. Neither will we force him to do anything he does not *want* to do." Flames leapt from his lips, fire churning in his belly. "NO—the deceiver is free to do what he wills, and we will let him *do just that!* In time, *HE will reveal HIMSELF.*" He leaned across the table. "Then the world will know the truth, and The Truth will set her free.."

"No, no, no—I will go." Elohim cut him off. "This is far too much to require of another!" His voice brimmed with emotion. "I will simply insert myself into man's midst, and we will.."

"Impossible," came the indignant reply. "Would you truly vacate your throne to another? *Most certainly not*—we will have lost, even before we begin!" The Angel flashed his most winsome grin, dropping back to his seat. "Father, this is my fight to fight. My position to claim. My inheritance. Besides, have you already forgotten? *It's impossible to lose!*" He shrugged and leaned back. "If he passes the test—I will become Heaven's permanent advocate on Earth. And if he fails—I will become Earth's permanent advocate in Heaven." His smile grew bigger and brighter. "It's not only the *surest* way," he beamed, "—it's the *only* way."

"You know this won't be easy." Elohim's voice grew somber.

"Excruciatingly painful."

"I'll be forced to turn my back on you."

"You'll leave me in the depths of Hell for three days."

"—even forsake you," tears were flowing.

"I know—," The Angel of the Lord exhaled. "But in the end, *it will be worth it!*"

Silence.

"Well then—," Spirit briskly cut in, bringing the Hallmark moment to a screeching halt. "If you are to go, there are a few things we will need to address." She donned a pair of smart-looking glasses, scanning the pages on her clipboard. "First and foremost, you must remain a mystery. Top secret. Highly classified." She tapped her clipboard authoritatively. "The serpent is beyond wise. If we truly expect to sneak attack, than you—," her pencil spun in the air around The Angel's stunning profile, "—must remain a mystery."

Spirit tipped her head, glancing over the top of her glasses. "You'll need a name," she declared. "A code name. Something ambiguous, but not too ambiguous. Catchy, but not too catchy."

A mischievous twinkle sparked in The Angel's bright eyes. He immediately launched into his best Medieval accent. "Then from this moment onward, I shall hence-forth be called: *The Word of Which We Dare Not Speak!*"

Spirit's face lit up, a silly little grin on her lips. "Your subtlety, my Lord, *is atrocious.*" A giggle erupted. "I think I speak on behalf of everyone, *ever,* when I suggest we call you simply—*The Word.*"

"*The Word,*" Elohim smiled, mulling it over. "*It does have a ring about it!*" He looked up thoughtfully, turning to address his angel. "My son, from this moment forward—and until further notice, it's agreed—you will be called simply, *The Word.*"

—| 4035:00:00:21:00:00 |—

"ADAM," Elohim's voice rang out again. "*ADAAAM!*"

The cries grew ever distant as Team Adam fled, scrambling towards the outskirts of the garden. The pair was frantic, guilt-ridden, driven by shame. Escape, the only thing on their minds. *How could they face their Abba? ..see his disappointment? ..admit to what they'd done?*

"Adaaam—!" the final cry faded in the distance, leaving silence—sweet, safe, silence.

The pair slowed to a halt, ducking beneath the cover of a sprawling fig tree. Falling back against its gnarled trunk, they paused, gasping for air. Strange how they used to run for hours on end without ever feeling so much as winded. *What was this new thing— fear?!*

They glanced around.

How in the—? Jaws dropped simultaneously. *Somehow they were back... exactly where they'd started?!* Hearts began to pound. Thoughts began to race. They peered out between the twisted branches of that troublesome, *Tree of Knowledge.*

Had they really run, full circle?

They turned to each other, but no answers came—only an

overwhelming desire to cover their shame.

What about the big, broad leaves above them?!

Eve brushed aside a fruit—the same fruit that had seemed so irresistible before, now looked dull, and brown, and ... lifeless. *Ugh*— she pushed away the feeling of growing disgrace, tearing off fistfuls of precious, protective leaves. The daisy-chain around her neck was the final piece of the puzzle. Stripping off its pedals, she began to stitch the leaves together, using it like thread, crafting a primitive sort of covering. Adam quickly followed suit. And in a matter of minutes, two makeshift aprons were donned.

Just in time..

"ADAM!" Elohim's cry rang out again, this time only a few yards away. "Where are you?" The branches of *The Tree* began to rustle. Then part.

The jig was up.

Deep breath, Adam stepped out.

"I-I heard your voice in the garden," he sheepishly admitted. "And I was afraid because I was naked, so I hid myself."

Elohim looked in the direction of the voice. He could no longer spot Adam's unique glow among the multitude of auras and energies present. He sighed, a sad little sigh, he knew what that meant, *it had happened—Adam had gone dark.*

"Who told you, you were naked?" he squinted, eyes readjusting. "Have you eaten from the tree of which I commanded you not to eat?"

Everything in Adam screamed—*Yes, yes, Abba yes!* Yet instead, he found himself pointing and saying, "It was this woman you gave me. *She* gave me fruit from *The Tree*, and I ate."

Elohim's face dropped. "What is this that you've done?" He turned, peering back into the thick foliage of the forbidden tree.

Eve too, stepped out. Like her man, she also longed to spill her heart—to bawl and beg forgiveness. But something rose within her. Indignant, she pointed to the snake, now cowering among the roots. "The serpent deceived me," she blamed. "And I ate."

The snake was speechless, not to mention a bit dazed and confused. No longer possessed, it wasn't exactly sure *what* was going on. It stared blankly, forked tongue flickering, trying desperately to get a handle on what was going down around him.

"Because you've done this," Elohim rebuked the snake, "you are cursed; more than all cattle, and every beast of the field. On your belly you shall go, eating dust all the days of your life. Enmity, will be between you and the woman, and between your seed and hers. For he shall bruise your head, while you shall bruise his heel."

There was a loud pop, followed by a long piercing whine, almost like a balloon deflating. Immediately the snake's legs began to whither and shrink, wasting away to almost nothing.

The serpent writhed in protest, making its objection vehemently known. Confusion or no, *this injustice, it did understand.* It hissed and snapped violently, slowly sinking to the confines of its belly.

For a moment, no one moved.

Then the snake dropped its head and slid hurriedly away.

Elohim watched it go. He felt for the snake—left to bear the brunt of the punishment, while the one who'd hidden behind its smooth exterior stood cowardly by, eavesdropping beneath the shadowy foliage of a neighboring weeping willow.

With a sigh, Abba knelt. Gathering his team to himself, he quietly unpacked what life would be like now that they had chosen 'knowledge' to be their guide.

First and foremost, access to the garden would be completely removed—lest they attempt to eat of the *Tree of Life* and remain in their fallen state forever. Furthermore, they were now on their own. Cut off from the abundance of the garden and forced to inhabit its surrounding wilderness—growing, maintaining, and recreating their personal gardens alone.

It wouldn't be easy, Elohim gently explained, *now that the serpent was god of their souls.* Pain and frustration would be their companions. Death and discord, their reward. Every day would be a fight just to keep their hearts in touch with the love and life they had once, so effortlessly enjoyed in the midst of the garden.

Still, Heaven would not leave them high and dry. Elohim lifted their chins, promising to look after them, and to teach them anything and everything they asked. He urged them to wait patiently on him for answers and to look forward to the day of their coming salvation.

Until then—he stood to his feet, lifting each one in turn—*their new relationship would a bit more … formal.* He took a bull, and sacrificing it, covered their souls with its blood, their flesh with its skin. Then—filling their pockets with everything they would need to start a new life on their own—he dried their tears, pointed them in the right direction, and sent them on their way.

Slowly, they went from his presence.

For a long while he watched, standing until well after the couple had fully disappeared from view. Then he turned and sat down, waiting silently in the shade of a nearby weeping willow.

In time, there came a rustling, accompanied by a particularly brisk breeze. The branches parted.

Out stepped—*Haylel*.

"Anointed Cherub!" Elohim called, not bothering to turn around. "Just the one, I wanted to see!"

Haylel would have jumped from his skin, had he any more skin to jump from. For a split second he froze, shell-shocked, the look in his eyes said it all. Still, he managed to keep his cool—turning casually towards his Creator.

"At your service." He bowed low.

Elohim slowly turned and upon flashing a dazzling smile, immediately cut to the chase. "My perfection. My son. My right-hand-man. The one who presides over *everything* in my garden. What do you know about talking snakes, forbidden fruits, and both my children suddenly compelled to eat from your tree?"

"I know … exactly what you have just said," Haylel replied, so smoothly that it was hard to tell he was calculating each word in real-time. "Unfortunately, I, who preside over everything in the garden, was myself en route to said garden whilst the aforementioned transaction did fully transpire." He waved a mildly apologetic hand. "Regrettably, I can speak no more of it."

"That's it?" Elohim pressed, overlooking the faint smell of skunk wafting through the air. "There's nothing more to tell?"

"Not a thing."

"Nothing?"

"*Did Man not say it was the serpent?*" Haylel replied rather abruptly, an edge of irritation coloring his voice. He raised both eyebrows and folded his arms. Clearly, he was done with the conversation.

"Very well," Elohim eased up. "Keep an eye on that snake, will you? And congratulations on Man placing his authority in your hands! You're a very capable leader." He stood to his feet, offering Haylel a welcoming hand and the scroll containing Earth's new deed. "Son, I look forward to working with you directly," he smiled, embracing his fiery cherub. "Only one small caveat," he motioned to Haylel's lapel. "Your keys—all application and use *must* be fully co-signed by me." A single eyebrow raised before he flashed a quick grin. "And of course—you may drive my rebellious couple completely out of the garden at your earliest convenience."

Then, with a wave and a nod, he was gone. Disappeared. Stepping out of the garden and back into the throne room of Heaven.

Haylel's grin stretched ear to ear. He reached for his keys. "It will be my pleasure," he called out after him. "My pleasure, indeed."

CH7: GAME ON
4035:00:00:00:00:01

And so the game began: Haylel to divide mankind from Elohim, Elohim to bring mankind back to himself.

Haylel had already made the first move. Rather than encouraging Man to eat from *The Tree of Life*—and thus, solidifying a perfect Heaven, Earth, and his own position forever—Haylel had chosen to use his influence self-servingly—tricking Man into eating from *his* tree instead. And while the move *had* established him as permanent 'Middle-Man,' handing him Earth's deed lock, stock, and barrel—it had also left him on surprisingly shakier ground. Had he known about the everlasting side-effects hanging between the branches of the 'other tree' in the center of the garden, he most certainly would have offered Eve a second fruit—solidifying the fall permanently, ending the game immediately. Yet, having failed to tie up that single loose end, he suddenly found himself engrossed in an on going, ever developing, epic battle.

To cover his mistake, Haylel wasted no time in making his second move—recruiting key angels from under his own charge. One by one, he singled them out—Watchers, Powers, Authorities, Principalities—demonstrating the ways in which they could simply speak into the atmosphere, energize fringe emotions, and 'magically' sway the decisions of men.

The untapped potential of the new soul connection left his team in awe, and with a bit of a personal dilemma. *Would they remain content to simply sit back—acting only in response to the promptings of man? ..Or would they begin to speak up? ..Proactively move? ..Take control, manipulate, and rule?*

Of course, *technically,* Haylel assured them, *they were*

doing nothing wrong … definitely nothing illegal. They were simply, *"providing an alternate path on which mankind could freely trod."* Sure, mankind would most likely mistake Second Heaven's emotions as their own, confusing Second Heaven's voices with the thoughts in their own heads. *But that fact was inconsequential.* After all, *it was man who was breaking-up with Elohim. Mankind, whose affections were changing …* was it not?

Second Heaven seemed inclined to agree. So when they saw how easily man was moved, the power they personally gained by it, and how Elohim seemed none-the-wiser—they quickly began to fall; one by one, pledging their unwavering allegiance to the secret societies of Hell.

Haylel was elated.

Surely now, Elohim would recognize his error in making Man and wipe the "tarnished slate clean," he reasoned. *That, or turn a love-blind eye until Second Heaven had absorbed enough power to overthrow Heaven directly.* Either way, it would only be a matter of time until his minor oversight had been corrected.

Still, he was troubled.

Elohim's initial response had been something of a curve ball—promising a "seed," a "savior," and a personal "resolution?" *The whole premise raised more questions than answers. What exactly was this, 'seed?' How exactly would they identify this, 'savior?' And when, exactly, would this 'resolution' occur?* Of course, all these unchecked boxes left Haylel feeling a bit, *outta control.* Odd, since Haylel had never actually been more *in* control.

Still—, the Cherubim puzzled, stroking the keys on his lapel, *the ultimate solution remained essentially the same: Whatever it took. No matter the price. No matter who he needed to remove. This 'seed,' this 'savior,' MUST BE STOPPED.*

—| 3985:06:12:18:00:00 |—

Back on Earth, the mystery of 'seed' didn't remain a mystery for long. Without an aura to hide their differences—and now that their evening chaperon had gone quote-unquote, *permanently missing*—Adam and Eve quickly found themselves pregnant. Another complication, Haylel wasn't entirely ready for.

First came a baby boy, *Cain.*

Shortly thereafter, *Abel*, arrived.

Abel was a special boy. Thoughtful. Attentive. Loving from birth. Like his father his heart naturally leaned toward the things of Elohim. He had a mouth slow to speak. An ear quick to listen. And a soul that was practically airtight. Aside from his parent's sin, there was not so much as a thimble-full of additional space into which Second Heaven could squeeze a manipulative finger.

Haylel was not at all impressed.

Was this the dreaded, "Promised Seed?" The boy who remained so obedient—year upon sinless year? If Abel was not so easily swayed— what might the implications be? What might Elohim suddenly compel him to do? The thought made Haylel exceedingly uneasy. It was entirely unacceptable. *This new wildcard simply had to go.*

Luckily, Abel's older brother had an access-point the size of a barn door. And Haylel had an idea even bigger! He stroked his keys. Certainly, Elohim required a co-signature for *him* to use them. *But what if he managed to convince someone else to?*

The plot was set.

Even after Elohim spoke directly to Cain, warning him of the temptation to come—Haylel was still able to persuade Cain's fatally offended heart that, '*Abel must go.*'

So one day, when the two brothers were alone in a field—in a fit of fury, and with the iron from his plow—*Cain consumed Abel's life.*

The murderous act rocked Heaven and Earth. *Was such a thing even possible?* The cry from Abel's blood went straight to the top, compelling Elohim to step in and do Haylel's job of policing the situation.

Once again, Elohim confronted.

Once again, man pointed and blamed.

Once again, Haylel denied.

The deception worked like a charm. Even after Elohim side-stepped middle-management and dealt with Cain directly, no mention of foul play was ever brought up again.

Second Heaven was completely dumbstruck. *Had their manufactured charade truly become Earth's reality?! Could it really be this easy—to simply persuade man, provide him access to Death's key, and then to deny all involvement?* They couldn't believe their eyes. *With power like this, who could stop them?*

Suddenly everyone wanted in on the action. Overnight, Haylel's mutiny became a movement, defectors flocking daily to his cause.

Haylel was beyond thrilled. Yet something had shifted. He couldn't quite shake it. He'd tasted first blood: *The death. The power. The instant level-up.* It was utterly intoxicating. Irresistible actually. He couldn't get enough. From that moment onward, he was consumed by it—every moment of every day spent hatching his "next big, 'eugenic' scheme." He could think of little else. All he needed was another "trial," another "tribulation," just one more "affliction" that ended in death. *Sweet, sudden, delicious, power-up—death.*

Days turned into months, months turned into years, years turned into centuries.

The plot thickened.

And thickened.

And thickened.

Then—as if it weren't already—things sorta got weird.

CH8: THE WAR BEGINS

Now a population explosion took place upon the earth. And it was at this time that beings from the spirit world looked upon the beautiful women of Earth and took any they desired to be their wives.

In those days—and even afterwards—when the evil beings from the spirit world were intimately involved with human women, their children became giants, of whom so many legends are told. And when the Lord God saw the extent of human wickedness, and that the trend and direction of men's lives were only towards evil, all the time, he was sorry he had made them. It broke his heart.

"*PFFZZIZZZFF—,*" a dull, static-blue light filled the smoldering grotto. Once. Twice. Then once more, it flashed. Flickering, as three shadowy figures entered, single-file.

It was no accident that BEAST, Prophet, and Ha-satan had arrived together—the transient portal they'd secretly commandeered was weak at best. Already it was beginning to jitter and wane, signs that it desperately wanted to close. Sixty minutes tops, and they would be leaving this place of their own accord—*on foot.* Nobody wanted that, especially not Prophet. As such, the general consensus was that this meeting would be a short one.

"Man's increasing numbers are becoming a burden," Ha-satan began, even before the trio had dropped to their seats. He glanced around securing his place at the head of the square table. "Man is becoming harder to anticipate. Harder to control."

BEAST stifled a yawn.

Prophet held his tongue.

"Which is why," Ha-satan continued, "a resolution was drafted, and its appeal sent before the Courts of Heaven."

"..*And?*" Prophet egged the conversation along.

"And it pleased the Supreme Judge to send a delegation down."

Prophet raised a skeptical eyebrow.

"Two-hundred ambassadors, under my charge," Ha-satan quickly reassured. "Sent to instruct Mankind in the ways of righteousness."

"*Righteousness?*" Prophet was incredulous.

"More or less." Ha-satan raised a shushing finger. "Either way, a ground presence *is* the most efficient way to both police and school mankind in the secret arts of Second Heaven."

There was a long pause.

Prophet looked relieved.

BEAST not so much. Perhaps it was his thick coat. Perhaps his thick skull. But whatever the case, the heat always seemed to get to him the quickest.

"That's it?" the mighty ox growled. "You called us to this blistering hellhole—for that?" An angry fist was already pumping the air. "That's public news—," he bristled. "Common knowledge. You could have told us this over tea and crumpets in the Throne Room, itself."

"Gentlemen—," Ha-satan raised a silencing hand before BEAST could spout any more stupidity. "*There's so much more.*"

He flashed a quick smile and leaned forward, motioning for them to do the same. Then, in an excited whisper, the destroyer of the universe, divulged his entire plan.

—| 3364:06:06:12:06:06 |—

The air was thick and balmy. The wind blew soft and warm. A lone shepherd sat, nestled peacefully among his weary flock of sheep. The drone of crickets filled the evening air, their pensive song broken only by the occasional splash of a pebble bombarding the nearby brook. *Plunk*—the sleepy shepherd loosed another stone and settled back. It had been a long day of grazing, and the calm of the night was a welcome change. One by one, flickering stars began to ignite, piercing the blackened skies above. The shepherd closed his eyes. *No need to keep watch*, his shoulders drooped. *This was Hermon's Peak— nothing exciting ever happened here.*

Slowly, his mind began to drift.

His head began to nod.

WAAARRRRRRRRR—the shepherd was up with a start, groping wildly for his staff, dust pelting his body like sandpaper. A whipping wind tore at his clothes. He sputtered and gasped, burying his face in his sleeve. The earth seemed to tremble beneath his quaking hands and knees. Slowly, he slid to the ground, flattened like the tall meadow grass around him. Pressed and shaking he waited, trembling beneath the wild, turbulent wind.

CLICK—blinding lights suddenly flooded the meadow.

The shepherd squinted, raising a hand to shield his eyes. Up, up, up he peered, trying to make some sense of the roaring darkness above. His free hand continued to move, locating his staff, tightening instinctively around it. Nearby, his panicked sheep stumbled and staggered, blowing about like cotton balls in a blender. *What was happening?* The shepherd exploded with fear.

Then, as suddenly as it started—it stopped.

Only the lights remained.

The shepherd froze, straining to see, grass slowly standing back up around him. *Something was moving. Something was coming. Something was..*

Out of the light stepped a being. First, one. Then another and another. They were tall. Fierce. Well-built. Iron-clad. Walking around, like gods among men.

Like gods among men!

The thought hit the awestruck shepherd harder than a Hickory-switch with a vendetta. Dumbstruck, he stifled a gasp, jaw dropping squarely to his chest.

OMG—the gods have come.

OMG—THE GODS HAVE COME!

With a gasp and a shriek he was gone, his flocks scattering before him. Through the meadow. Over the brook. Down the rocky mountainside. His feet were a blur, barely touching the ground. His arms flung wide, desperate to keep him upright.

Only two things to do, he heaved, barreling towards the suddenly antiquated securities of home. *Change my shorts. And warn EVERYONE—THE GODS HAVE COME!*

CH9: TO THE BRINK

Haylel's ambassadors never gave a first thought to true righteousness. Upon landing, they immediately taught mankind to manipulate the system for themselves. Honesty, prayers, and peace soon gave way to sorcery, weapons, and war. Under their dark tutelage, the amicable culture of Earth flipped; violence, deception, and death rising to supremacy as mankind twisted each new "enlightenment" to his own advantage.

Of course, the devolution of mankind was exactly what Haylel intended. His plan was simple enough: *Pollute the gene pool by any means necessary*. Devolution was step one. Pollution, step two. Implementation however, proved to be a bit more challenging. So when it was discovered that mixing heaven-sent ambassadors with earth-bound women was not only feasible, but genetically preferable—the green light was immediately given.

The ambassadors didn't know what hit them. It was almost as if they had become victims of their own virtual reality. Women— who previously would have left only the most bitter of tastes in their mouths—suddenly appeared irresistibly ravishing.

Not surprisingly, Haylel was behind the sudden confusion. In fact, it had been his plan all along: to build a kingdom of dark, eternal children, all his own. The perversion was brilliant; providing Hell with the ever-growing, inexhaustible army it needed, while doubling to insure that Elohim's own seed could never be born.

Almost immediately, the plan took hold. Haylel's ambassadors succumbed. And with binding oaths—sworn in secret atop Mount Hermon—they took for themselves, wives among the most beautiful of earthen women. Their inevitable conceptions released powerful, irreversible pollutants deep within the human gene pool—resulting in an illegitimate race of half-human, half-angelic hybrids. Fatherless creatures, created apart from the life-giving power of Elohim, and far from any nurturing acknowledgment of Haylel. They were illegal, eternal, decaying anomalies. Disconnected from Heaven. Abandoned by Hell. Spiritual nomads with nowhere to go, and no hope for future redemption.

Needless to say, these creatures had no incentive to care about anything or anyone, save themselves. They were self-absorbed, self-obsessed monsters. Hellbent on destruction. Earth was their playground, and they weren't leaving until they had stripped it of its beauty, ravaged its pleasures and burned it to the ground.

Naturally, Haylel's grinning lips were sealed. So when the news *was* finally relayed to Elohim, Elohim was deeply disturbed.

Heaven's first order of business was to round up the trouble-making ambassadors; binding them in chains, and locking them deep within the earth until the day when the consequences of their actions could fully be weighed.

Only then, did Elohim speak the sixteen little words Hell had been dying to hear.

"Man's days are numbered," Heaven's decree went forth. "He will have one hundred and twenty years to mend his ways."

—| |—

"*We must agree to send an assembly of angelic ambassadors?*" Spirit could hardly believe her ears. "Are you serious? Even when we understand the consequences?" Delicate fists rained down hard upon the manuscript-laden table.

The Word (formerly known as The Angel of the Lord) couldn't help but crack a smile. This was one of those rare moments when the round table discussion was actually getting ... heated.

"We *must*," came Elohim's calm reply. He pushed aside his latest book and looked up. "We must, because *we*, in turn, will do the same."

"We most certainly *will NOT* take earthen women to be our

wives!" Spirit fired back, a visible blast of heat exploding from her body like an unspoken exclamation point.

Elohim chuckled. "No, we most certainly will not," he assured. "But we *will* infiltrate Earth in a similar manner.."

Spirit held her tongue.

"And," Elohim continued, "if we want to be completely justified in using a willing feminine participant for our little, 'undercover operation,' than we *must* allow the enemy to do the same."

"It's only fair?"

"Only fair."

"By the books?"

"By the books."

The answer seemed to appease Spirit. She relaxed a bit, sinking back into her chair, twirling a stray lock of color-changing hair. "Acceptable—," she slowly conceded, "as long as we orchestrate a way for mankind to escape the growing perversion." She spun her hair thoughtfully. "A way to escape—*once and for all.*"

—| 2499:00:03:07:07:07 |—

Noah's breath blew white against the early morning air. He stifled a yawn, rubbing puffy, sleep-laden eyes. For a long time he stretched, savoring the moment, surveying his recently completed vineyard. *What a sight!* One hundred acres of pure, unadulterated wine country. He grinned. Harvest was only days ago, yet the vines were already beginning to bud again, their dew-drenched flowers shimmering spectacularly in the ever brightening light.

With a grunt, the seasoned agrarian hoisted his pack, moving briskly towards the northernmost fence-line. His wind-chapped lips whistled the broken melody of an ancient tune, his heart skipping merrily along to its beat. This day was starting out like most of his 175,319 previous days on the planet: Lots of work to be done. Lots of upgrades to be made. Lots of overgrown fence to mend. Still, this day was different, Noah adjusted his pack, *today he turned the big—four, eight, zero!*

Ahhh—an enormous smile warmed his lips. He imagined how he and the Mrs. would celebrate. *Friends and family? Balloons and streamers? An extra-large bottle of home-brewed, Noir?* He paused, robustly sniffing the air. *Whew—maybe just an extra-long, bubble bath!*

A chuckle erupted. He waved a not-so-agreeable hand. *The overlooked grapes weren't the only thing currently "fermenting on the vine."* Broad shoulders shook with laughter as his merriment grew. *Maybe that's why he'd been sent out to "mend fences" today.* He laughed out loud. *Duly noted! He would stop by the hot-springs on the way back.* No need to perpetuate the scenario, especially now that the only thing left on his bucket-list was to actually start a family.

Family.

His knees buckled a bit. *No doubt, starting a family would be awesome. But the challenges. The responsibility. The pitfalls of a world full of perversion.* He breathed a quick, heartfelt prayer. *At a mere four-hundred and eighty, was he really ready?*

*Wreeeeeeaaa*α*K*—Noah's ears perked up, locking in on the all-to-familiar sound: *Broken fence, twisting in the wind, about a quarter of a mile away.* He glanced ahead, adjusting his trajectory, trudging silently up the final hill.

There it was, he peered past the remaining rows of vines. *Just inside that random patch of fog.*

Random patch of fog?

He looked again. *What were the odds?* A particularly dense patch of fog was resting over the *exact* portion of fence he was hoping to mend.

Well—no sense in going back, he reasoned. *Might as well see what I can see.* With a deep breath, he lowered his head, stepping squarely into the billowing mist.

The broken fence was only a few yards further.

..Wasn't it?

He groped his way forward. Then forward some more. *Just a couple more feet,* he yawned. *Had to be within inches.* His eyelids were sinking. His pack was slipping. *What was going on?* He yawned a second time.

Everything was slowing down.

Everything was getting heavy.

Everything was going ... *black.*

"NOAH—." Elohim's voice rattled Noah back to consciousness.

"NOAH!" it roared again.

Noah strained to lift his head. He couldn't move. From where he lay, he could already tell, he was face down in the dirt. The air was strange—sweet and thick, like a honey-drenched blanket pressing him down. The atmosphere was electric. Riddled with joy. Coursing like fire down his spine.

He relaxed, letting his face fall back into the soft, wet soil. There was really no point in fighting it, he had felt this presence before. This was the amazing, incredible, unmistakable presence of..

"I have decided to destroy the earth," that familiar voice began. "Perversion and violence have grown to pandemic proportions. No one has gone untouched." The voice softened, "You alone have found favor in my eyes, because you alone have kept your bloodline pure, always trying to conduct your affairs according to my will."

..Elohim!

Noah's stomach was instantly in knots, his mind flashing back to previous days: Elohim had spoken with him before— his great-grandfather on many occasions—but the tone of this conversation was different. *Way different.* In fact, it was terrifying. He wasn't entirely sure how to respond.

So he listened.

"Make a boat," Elohim instructed. "Seal it with tar. Make it 450 feet long, 75 feet wide, and 45 feet high. Construct three decks inside the boat, adding stalls throughout. Leave a skylight all the way around the top, and put a door in its side."

Instantly, Noah felt a rushing wind, air beneath his belly. He glanced down. He was certain his eyes were closed, yet he found himself a mile high, staring down at Earth.

"Look!" Elohim pointed below. "I am going to cover the earth with a flood. Nothing infected will remain."

Noah scanned the horizon.

All he could see was water.

He regrouped and searched again.

Only wind and waves.

"I promise to keep you safe," Elohim continued, noting a tiny boat rising in the distance. "You, your wife, your three sons, and their wives."

The boat grew larger and larger—massive, by the time it drew near.

"Bring a pair of every animal, male and female, into the boat with you. Keep them alive throughout the flood. Store away all the food that they, and you, will need—every kind of food that can be eaten.."

Noah listened carefully as Elohim continued with what seemed like a dozen more details. If he was really going to pull this off—*one boat, every kind of animal, three kids AND their wives*—he couldn't afford to miss a thing.

When Elohim finished, he paused.

There was a long, thoughtful silence.

"Yes—my Lord." Noah finally came to himself. "I will do everything as you have commanded."

Immediately, the wind and waves were gone.

Noah glanced up. He was back in the dirt, Elohim's spirit beginning to lift.

One last detail came to mind.

"Of what, shall I make the boat?" he quickly called out.

"Of wood," came the waning reply. "Resinous, Opher Wood."

"G-Gopher-wood?" Noah clarified, somewhat surprised. The back forty acres of his vineyard were virtually littered with those towering, useless trees.

"Yes, my son—," a distant chuckle responded. "Gopher—barkey, barkey."

CH10: SALVATION BY WATER

The dark lord raised his glass—silver-lined, diamond-studded, and overflowing with a stout, Second Heaven brew. "To a perfect plan—perfectly executed!" he sloshed, saluting each member at the square table in turn. "To our seed—or Elohim, himself—completely destroying man within the next dozen decades!"

BEAST and Prophet each met Ha-satan's glass with a glass of their own, resulting in a resounding *CLA—CLANG* that echoed sharply off the shadowy cavern walls.

The two cohorts promptly guzzled their drinks, immediately pouring another. Ha-satan placed his brimming beverage neatly back on the table, pondering how he had not quite thought through all the implications of choosing a fully helmeted disguise.

Still, that thought—nor the occasional groan of a recently apprehended ambassador locked away deep within the smoldering darkness around them—could spoil his mood.

No—today was a day of victory! He lifted his mug to 'cheers' another round. *Today was a day of celebration!*

—| 2499:00:02:03:00:00 |—

To say that Hell went immediately to work overtime, was a bit of an understatement. With only twelve decades left, Ha-satan threw everything he had at mankind—doubling, tripling, even ten x-ing his infectious efforts. He mixed and mingled, twisted and tangled, perverted and procreated every chance he got. Sure, his ambassadors were bound in chains, leaving him scrambling to redirect the blame. But Heaven's word had gone forth, and Earth's judgment would surely arrive. There was no way he was going to give mankind so much as an inkling of opportunity to change Elohim's heart or mind.

Noah, on the other hand, paid little attention to the swirling storms around him. He continued to work diligently—day after day, year after year—quietly erecting his aquatic, Resinous Wood monstrosity.

It wasn't long before Shem, Ham, and Japheth—the three hard-working, fun-loving sons Elohim had promised—appeared on the scene. To Noah, their arrival was everything. It served as confirmation of Elohim's word. Incentive to intensify efforts. Relief that help had arrived. And most of all, proof to his wife, that he hadn't gone entirely crazy.

Together, the family was relentless. For more than a century, they persevered. Nothing could stop them. Sure, there were setbacks: The Great Beaver Infestation of 2447. The tiki torch fire of 2411. And of course, who could forget, the infamous, "tar and turkey" incident of 2398—don't ask—but through it all, they plodded on.

Certainly, there were days, months, even years where the monotony was so strong, it was almost unbearable. And of course, there were entire decades where the family was forced to face the blatant opposition that comes from building a towering monument to the 'death of humanity' in one's own backyard.

Yet, the day finally came when the last beam was hoisted. The last peg was fastened. And the last log, secured and tarred. Noah slowly put down his hammer, and breathed the longest, most grateful sigh ever heard by all of mankind. He was six hundred years old.

There were definitely balloons and streamers that evening, and baths all around.

That night Elohim spoke again. And seven days later, with Noah, the animals, and his entire crew safely on board *The Ark*—Elohim shut the big boat's front door with a bang.

The rains came.

The earth was washed clean.

The battle was over.

Mankind was freed.

—| |—

Ha-satan was furious.

"*ONE MAN*," he screamed, slamming a supercharged fist down on the thick square table. "One stupid, delusional, stubborn, arrogant, narcissistic, bumbling, grape-growing, stink of a MAN has ruined *everything ... EVERYTHING!*"

BEAST and Prophet sat silent, waiting for the hammer to drop.

"You mean to say," Ha-satan continued, "that life goes on? Earth remains? The game continues? All because of ... *ONE STINKING MAN?!*"

BEAST winced, he identified a little with the stinking remark. Still, he held his tongue, waiting until..

"*WE HAD THE BETTER PART OF ONE HUNDRED YEARS TO DEMORALIZE, INTIMIDATE, ACCUSE AND ATTACK. ONE HUNDRED YEARS TO HUMILIATE, EMBARRASS, BLAME AND DISTRACT. YET HERE WE ARE, BACK AT SQUARE ONE—ALL BECAUSE OF ONE STINKING MAN!*"

..the hammer had dropped.

Ha-satan's facemask fogged. His body trembled. He was literally frothing at the mouth. He slammed his fist down a second time, the square table tilting and cracking under the force of his blow. The atmosphere was thick, unstable, crackling with a dark, savage energy.

Prophet shot BEAST a sideways glance. Somebody needed to say something, or this wasn't going to end well.

"*Uhh—uhmm—eh.*" BEAST bumbled. "Perhaps—*uhm*—if he had not stunk so much, my Lord, he—*err*—would not have needed such a—*ahem*—large bath?" he nervously reasoned.

Ha-satan didn't even respond. He just dropped with a crash to his seat. Slumping over, he plopped his big, helmeted head down in one big, spoiled hand. The fingers of his other hand methodically stroking the keys hanging from his shoulder. "Unless—," his voice trailed off, a thoughtful pout constricting his lips. He turned away, purposely ignoring the room. This was no time for heart change, self-improvement, or introspection. This was *his* world. *He* made the rules here. If careless oversights had gotten them into this mess, careful foresight would get them out.

The deceiver took a deep breath, closing dark and slanderous eyes, lost in a world of his own vain imaginations.

Already, he was scheming again.

CH11: REGROUPING
2123:00:03:00:00:00

It was one of those moments: You know, the kind where you pull up to work having no recollection of the drive, but suddenly realize that you've been singing at the top of your lungs, windows wide open, the entire way.

Or better yet: One of those moments when your 'significant other' elbows you in the middle of the super-lame chick-flick you were practically dragged to see, asking you—albeit, rather obnoxiously—to stop crying into your popcorn.

You know, one of those ultra rare moments where you actually catch yourself being all caught up, "in that moment?"

Yea, Abram was having one of those moments.

Plop—a bead of sweat dropped from the tip of Abram's nose to the crystal clear puddle below. He didn't move. He was lost in thought, staring blankly into the little pool as ring after concentric ring slipped quietly to its grassy edges. His breathing slowed. Then shallowed. His face and shoulders relaxed. In silent tandem, his ruggedly handsome, full-bearded, seventy-five year old reflection did the same.

It had been an exciting day of tracking. He, Lot, and the boys were, as they say, "hot on the trail." Their first target—a rather large buck—had given them a run for their money, challenging all seventy-five years of Abram's personal tracking experience. Finally downwind, and downstream, Abram was doing his best army-crawl towards his unsuspecting mark, bow and arrows in hand.

He wasn't exactly sure why he'd looked down—perhaps he was a little overconfident, perhaps he felt prompted—yet, somehow the striking clarity of his own reflection in the tiny pool below had launched him into a perpetual sea of thought.

Purpose. Destiny. Meaning. Did his life truly have any of these? He wracked his heart, searching for an answer. Certainly, he was wealthy. Prominent. Respected. Married to a strikingly beautiful Kushite. *But purpose? Or meaning?* He refrained from wiping his nose. *Could he honestly say his life had either of these?* Another bead of sweat impaled the still waters below.

He swallowed hard.

There had to be more ... didn't there?

FFFFFFFFFFft—an arrow zipped low over his head. *THUD*—the stag bellowed and reared, instantly back on the run.

Immediately, Lot and the boys were up and running along behind.

Abram didn't even notice. In that moment everything inside was screaming for something *BIGGER. Bigger than this! BIGGER than himself!* His mind was racing overtime. He was at a fork. A crossroads. Perhaps, it was a midlife crisis. But whatever the case, Abram suddenly found himself questioning everything.

Crack—a twig snapped.

Cr-Crunch—the sound of footsteps on dry leaves.

Abram lifted his shoulder to wheel around, but a powerful hand pushed him back down.

"Leave your country," a voice commanded. "Your relatives, and nation behind. And go to the land that I will guide you to."

Abram almost laughed out loud. *Leave your country? Good one, boys!* He glanced around for the fellas. *Fellas?*

"If you go," the voice continued, hand still pressing, "I will cause you to become the father of a great nation. I will bless those who bless you, and curse those who curse you. I will prosper you and make your name famous. You will be a blessing to many others. And the entire world will be blessed because of you!"

"W-Who are you?" Abram stammered, his heart skipping a beat. He seemed completely alone. Yet, the voice and the hand remained.

"I am the one for whom your soul yearns. That thing— BIGGER than yourself."

Abram could no longer be still. He *had* to look. He *had* to know. *Who was this, who could make such bold promises AND read his thoughts?!* He pushed up hard, flipping to his back, grabbing for the hand on his shoulder.

Nothing but thin air.

"My Lord?" He popped up, scanning the woods around him. The owner of that voice *had* to be nearby.

He turned and looked.

Spun, and looked again.

But the voice—and the hand—were gone.

—| |—

"We must find a man," Elohim declared, reaching across the round table and selecting an empty book. He flipped it open, putting pen to paper. "A man we can deal with face-to-face, whose generations we can trust."

"No go-betweens. No middlemen. No hearsay or hidden agendas." Spirit lifted a fuzzy, fluffy, winter-wonderland of a thinking cap and pulled it down snug.

"A man whose generations *want* to do our will!" The Word chimed in. "Who can follow our lead and keep things in check until I arrive."

"Yes," Spirit giggled, toying with her cap's dangling drawstrings. "No more worldwide floods please!"

Everyone mulled over that statement a moment.

"Certainly Earth's stripped atmosphere will slow him down," The Word acknowledged their predicament. "But it will not be enough to stop him." He was up and pacing. "The Deceiver *will* return to his old tricks: Hybrids. Giants. Lies. Disease. Mixing DNA. We will need a bloodline of our own—pure and enlightened—to guard and police the land."

"..to covenant with," Elohim nodded.

There was a brief pause.

"Idea!" Spirit's finger shot up, thinking cap suddenly ablaze. "I will search the hearts of mankind, until I find you such a man!"

Her grin was big and wide.

"And I," The Word snapped to an agreeable halt, "will go and personally recruit him!"

—| 2122:11:05:03:00:00 |—

Abram wasted no time in taking Elohim up on his word—packing up and moving his entire estate within the following year. It was only a matter of time before Sarai, his wife, and Lot, his favorite nephew, had joined the lengthy ranks of sheep and cattle, flocks and herds, tents and servants slowly filing south towards Canaan.

The sudden move caused quite a stir, especially among the relatives. Emotions ran high. Nerves increasingly on edge. Not that they could help it, Hell simply wanted to know: *Where was he going? How long would he be there? What were his goals? His intentions? His aspirations? ..Was this really what was best for his family?*

Abram fielded each question patiently and authentically. He wasn't entirely sure why, but his destiny seemed unavoidably wrapped up in the unfulfilled footsteps of his father, and in his own obedience to Elohim.

Gradually, his honest, heartfelt answers tempered the raging flames, retracting the claws of curiosity and holding devilish suspicions at bay. However, after Elohim appeared to Abram a second time—promising Canaan to him and his descendants—Hell finally did catch wind.

Haylel immediately levied the land with a curse, insisting before the Courts of Heaven that the "unrighteous acts of the inhabiting Canaanites" suddenly be rectified. In his mind, there was no way someone communicating privately with Elohim was ever going to settle in such a fertile territory, especially when that territory lay outside the scope of Hell's full and total control. Not—at least—until he could figure out *exactly* what was going on.

A favorable ruling and perpetual drought did the trick, forcing Abram further and further south until he had reached the well-watered—and well-governed—grounds of Egypt.

No sooner had the caravan stepped foot across the border,

than Haylel began to do what he did best: *A murder-filled suggestion, here. A selfish, fearful heart-tug, there*. And *violá*—before anyone could say any different—Sarai found herself alone and abandoned, given as a "peace offering" into the Egyptian Pharaoh's personal harem.

Of course, Abram was treated royally in her honor. Haylel made certain of that—lavishing favor, protection, and a jaw-droppingly large dowry upon the babe-toting, out-of-towner. Hell was taking no chances. It was pulling out all the stops. Eagerly awaiting the day when the unlikely union between king and concubine would be consummated, Abram's wife defiled, and Heaven's troublesome promise permanently derailed.

There was, however, one slight complication. Elohim's promise had been personal, and thus it kept him personally involved. So in a seemingly "ironic" turn of events, Heaven's courts ordered Haylel to rectify the situation himself. The smug watchman wasted no time in unleashing a devastating plague upon the Pharaoh's household, to be administered until the day of Sarai's full freedom.

The king didn't know what hit him. Immediately, he was at a loss. Death and sorrow were everywhere. The household body-count was quickly piling up. With his attention turned, and the royal house in chaos, all plans of consummation were quickly forgotten.

Curiously, the strange epidemic only remained until the day an inquisitive handmaiden uncovered Sarai's shocking truth: *She was already another man's wife!*

The scandal rocked the inner courts. Then the outer courts. Then the inner courts again. Eventually making its way directly to the king, himself.

"What is this that you've done?!" the short-tempered, highly embarrassed Pharaoh railed against Abram. "You have plundered my house. Capsized my life. And for what?" he scolded. "For actually trying to do the right thing?" He lifted his scepter. Honestly, he had half a mind to take this guy personally to the woodshed ... except for the fact that he wanted absolutely nothing to do with this man's strange curse.

So with a bite of his tongue and a fear-filled nod, he sent them all packing—dowry in tow—*back to the planes of Canaan.*

CH12: THE COVENANT DROPS
2115:00:03:21:03:03

Thunk—the blood-stained blade fell to the hardened dirt below. Tired fingers unclenched as Abram sank slowly to the ground beside it. He was spent. The previous forty-eight hours had been an absolute blur of events, beginning when four kings from the East had suddenly arrived to quote, "put down a growing insurrection."

And 'put it down' they did. Leaving with cartloads of the finest spoils from the nearby cities of, Sodom and Gomorrah.

Abram closed his eyes, giving his head a sharp, little shake. The blunder probably would have been forgivable had they not made off with his favorite nephew too.

That, was entirely unacceptable.

Rallying his troops, and under the cover of darkness, he'd recovered everything. Returning it all to its rightful owners—save the food his men had already eaten and the ten percent he'd already offered to Elohim.

Abram glanced around. Now—less than twenty-four hours later—he found himself sitting between the severed carcasses of one heifer, one female goat, a ram, a turtledove, and a pigeon.

Hmmm, he grinned, *maybe the last 24 hours haven't been any less strange.* He shooed away a hungry vulture.

Expectant, his mind once again returned to the previous day—midnight, to be exact. Elohim had visited him yet again; pointing up to the star-packed sky and promising, "Abram—your descendants will be just as numerous.."

In the excitement of the moment, Abram had asked for a sign.

"Prepare for us, a covenant offering," was Elohim's only

response. Not quite what Abram had had in mind. But Heaven had just awarded him the greatest victory of his life, so there was no way he was going to disobey.

Now—with the sun finally setting—all he had to do was wait.

And wait..

And..

"Abraaam … Abraaaaaaaam—," the distant call boomed in the darkness.

Abram glanced up, *had he fallen asleep?*

FLASH—a picture pierced his soul.

He froze. Petrified. *The weight. The pain. The absolute depravity.*

WHOOSH—another picture appeared. Then another. And another. *Scene after disturbing scene. Homicide. Genocide. Ritual abuse. And worse. Firing in rapid succession.*

Abram coughed, choking on air, trying to turn away. But there were more and more scenes, wrapping themselves all the way around him. *What was this?* He ducked his head. He couldn't shut them out. They were pressing in. Forcing him to watch. It was every dark deed. Every dreadful act. Every perpetration of sin along his entire family line—past, present, and future.

It was too much to handle.

Suddenly, in front of it all, a man appeared.

Oh, thank God!

Honest. Honorable. Fearless. Humble.

Yes—and … wait, what?!

Abram watched as the man was bound, bruised and beaten—sentenced to a brutal, barbaric death. Emotions shifted, peeling him off one wall and slamming him hard against another. Grief assaulted his soul. There was no getting around it. Every image seemed to depict the exact same horror—innocent life, coming to its tragically *unjust* end—and no one was doing anything to stop it.

Did anyone even want to?

Abram broke. Weeping like a father weeps for his child.

Slowly, Elohim bent the Heavens down and entered the scene.

Joy erupted.

Abram looked up, eyes suddenly dry. *Oh—but how good was this, when the light finally came bursting in!*

"Abram!" Elohim smiled his hello.

"My Lord!" Abram breathed a warranted sigh of relief.

"I have given this land to your descendants," the King of the Universe began. "And if they are enslaved, I will punish the nation who enslaves them." Abram listened intently as Elohim described his family's future—one of triumph and pain, victories and shame, of struggles and miracles beyond belief.

As Elohim spoke, Abram gradually began to see: Past the good. Past the bad. Past the faith and the fear. Past every twisted temptation that Hell could send near. *Yes, there it was! Growing strikingly clear:* Life wasn't about AVOIDING the pain. It was about OVERCOMING it. Because in the end, eternal life was WORTH it. *So worth it!*

There was a flicker.

A flash.

Wait a minute—Abram squinted. He peered deep into Elohim's midst. There stood two figures, vaguely resembling ... *a torch and a pot? They seemed to be moving together between the sacrifices he had so painstakingly prepared.* His squint got squintier, his cheeks went flush. *Son of a—those figures were making a covenant! A covenant FOR him—WITHOUT him!*

No, no, no—that wasn't how this was supposed to go!

Abram leapt to his feet, eager to remedy the situation.

His eyes flew open.

He awoke with a start.

Huh—? he glanced around, blinking two surprisingly well-rested eyes. The goat, the heifer ... that grifting vulture—*they were all still here. But the torch and the pot? Elohim? They were nowhere to be found.* Abram's brow slowly furrowed, squinting into the newly rising sun. *How—?* he gave a small shrug. *Somehow—with or without him—the deed had been done.*

—| |—

"It's not enough to simply refill the land with giants," Ha-satan sulked, fidgeting with his keys. "Not now, that God has made a covenant with Man."

There was a long, awkward silence—Ha-satan staring blankly at Prophet, Prophet staring blankly at those fidgeting keys.

"Then—why not make their covenant *WORK FOR US?*" The entire cave rumbled as BEAST stepped out from the shadows, dropping his suggestion and a massive block of ice—*hard*—beside the square table's recently fractured surface. He glanced from brooding cohort to brooding cohort, gleefully taking his makeshift seat. He wasn't exactly sure what he meant, but he was exactly sure about his new seat. It meant the immediate end of these increasingly uncomfortable, painstakingly long, highly "thermal" discussions.

"He's right," Prophet grouched. "The—*um*, God-Father, has too much personally invested. If Heaven won't let us defile or destroy Man directly, than our only hope is to convince Man to break his own covenant *willingly..*"

"..And to willingly procreate *outside* its legal bounds.." Ha-satan suddenly perked up.

"..Producing an illegal seed that will be legally covered under the legal-cover of Man's—*LEGAL COVERING!*" BEAST roared, dropping the unspoken cherry on top. He sat back, quite proud of himself for that one.

Glares.

"BUT, of course," he backpedaled, running giant paws along the sizzling edges of his quickly vaporizing seat. "That goes without saying."

"We'll approach the woman first." Ha-satan leaned in. "Doting her with promises of forbidden fruits." He glanced at BEAST, gleefully wiping melted seat against furry steaming forearms. "*TRUST ME,*" Ha-satan disapprovingly cleared his throat. "Once the woman bites, Abram *will* go for our plan. But it will *only* be at her repeated bidding.."

"Mmm—*NAGGING,*" BEAST snuckled (*snorted and chuckled*),

"you mean—*NAGGING!*" He ignored the cutting glares he was already receiving. "Oh—and, Ha-," he glanced over at his devilish overlord. "TRUST ME—*NOBODY TRUSTS YOU!*" He locked eyes with his glowering associates, threw back his head and howled with laughter, his sides quaking with glee.

Both counterparts froze, blasting frigid looks of disapproval his way. But even their icy glares weren't enough to keep BEAST's seat from melting the remaining sixteen inches. They watched as the mighty ox slowly disappeared, sinking steadily behind the formidable table until only two quaking horns remained.

"BUT of course," the bovine's muffled howl rumbled out from beneath the thick, tilted slab. "That goes without saying."

—| 2113:10:06:22:06:06 |—

"Abram—, *Abraam!*"

Abram swung to the ground, passing his reins off to an already waiting attendant. He strode to the door of his tent where Sarai was busily working inside. Pausing, he listened for her call one more time. *How was it that she already knew he'd arrived, even before he'd corralled his stallion?*

"My love ... *My love!*" he answered, ducking through the tent flap nearby.

Sarai greeted her king with a kiss and a scheme. "I've got our solution!" she beamed, toying with one of Abrams cascading locks. "Remember Hagar?" She gestured to a quiet figure entering near the back of the tent.

"The handmaiden acquired from Pharaoh's dowry?" Abram nodded slowly, it had been ten years now, *but how could he not?* There was barely a day gone by that Hagar wasn't at, or by, Sarai's side.

"Well—what do you think?" Sarai flung her arms out wide, nodding in Hagar's general direction. "Cute, smart, newly of age.." She leaned in. "Why not borrow her womb—as a surrogate of sorts?"

Abram burst out laughing. He couldn't help it. That Q-bomb was completely off his radar! He looked up, pulling himself together, hugging his delusional queen. "Thanks for that," he whispered. "I needed a good laugh! But it's late, and you're silly." He pulled her tight. "Why don't you and I just give it another try?"

But Sarai was serious.

And day after day, she persisted. It was the perfect plan, and *she* knew it. She couldn't let it go.

So, with temptations mounting–and Heaven strangely silent on the matter—Abram eventually succumbed. He took Hagar as his second wife, and nine months later a surrogate was born.

Ishmael was a rebel from birth, as wild as the plan by which he'd been hatched. And although he wasn't the promised child, both Abram and Sarai loved him like he was. In fact, to them, he *was* the son of inheritance—a heaven-sent promise, fulfilled. And because the covenant couple had *both* agreed, it was thirteen years, before anyone said anything different.

—| 2098:07:15:12:00:00 |—

"Abram!" that familiar voice called one mid-summer's night.

Elohim? Abram rolled from his bed, glancing toward Ishmael, sound asleep in the corner. *It was time!* He ducked through the open tent flap, excited to relay the long overdue news. Elohim would most certainly be pleased. He moved quickly, rounding the back of his fifty-foot tent and—*found himself standing among the very same offerings he'd prepared, some seventeen years before?*

"I *am* El-Shaddi—God Almighty," Elohim boomed. "Serve me faithfully. Walk in *my* ways. And I will make a covenant with *you*, by which I *guarantee* to give you countless descendants."

Abram dropped to the ground, knees and face in the dirt. *Elohim hadn't forgotten!* His heart leapt for joy. *He had come back to complete the covenant—the covenant with HIM!*

The King of the Universe knelt beside his budding patriarch, placing a fatherly hand on the crown of Abram's bowed head.

"No longer, will you be called, Abram" he decreed, "but, Abra*ham*—Father of Nations! For I will make you extremely fruitful. And your descendants will become many nations, and kings will be among them!"

SLOSH–Elohim's voice overflowed. Spilling down upon Abraham like a fine, new wine—over his head, down his back, dripping through fingers and toes.

Abraham had never felt so alive!

Never so drunk!

"As for your part of the covenant," Elohim was all business. "Every male among you shall be circumcised."

"Circluh–wha?" Abraham slurred.

"Separated, by knife, from foreskin," Elohim explained. "Your flesh, cut off, will be a sign between us. Proof that you—and your descendants—accept my covenant." His tone grew more serious. "Anyone who refuses these conditions shall be in turn, cut off from his people, for he has violated the terms of my covenant."

Sobriety hit Abraham like a concrete drainpipe. He squirmed uncomfortably, *what could he say?*

"As for Sarai, your wife," Elohim was moving briskly along. "She will no longer be called Sarai, but Sara*h*—Princess. For I will bless her and give you a son from *her*. Yes, *she* will be a mother of nations! And many kings shall be among *her* posterity."

SLOOSH—Abraham was sloshed again. *Really? A son from the woman he loved?!* He grinned, all doubts suddenly dispelled. *What's a little excruciating pain between friends,* he reasoned, *especially when in exchange for a SON from the woman he LOVED!*

Immediately, Abraham was back on board, his thoughts flashing back to his very first meeting with Elohim. That unlikely hunting party, when he first lay prostrate in the mud. *What if Heaven hadn't invaded that day? What if he hadn't followed through? Everything would be so diff—*

He froze. He didn't want to think about it.

But now? A chuckle began to rise. *Parents? At 100 years old?* An image emerged: Him, hobbling about, attempting to corral a toddler. He laughed out loud. *No way! At their age? That was absurd, right? Surely he had misunderstood.*

"Yes, do bless Ishmael." Abraham offered up the benefit of the doubt. "He shall be my promised heir. The son of my right hand.."

"No." Elohim sternly corrected. "*Sarah* shall bear you a son, and you shall name him Isaac—meaning Laughter. And I will sign my covenant with him forever, and with his descendants."

"Then, what of Ishmael?" Abraham persisted. It was hard to believe that the last thirteen years had all been for nothing.

"I will bless him also, just as you have asked me to," Elohim turned to go. "But my covenant is with Isaac, the son who will be born to you and Sarah about this time next year."

He flashed a wide grin, lifted a hand, and was gone.

Abraham couldn't move. For a long time he remained perfectly still, gathering his thoughts and his whits about him. Then, on the heels of the rising sun; he rose, set a date with his wife, and sharpened his knife.

CH13: PUT TO THE TEST

"ARRRraaaaaaghHH—," the gut-wrenching moan rattled the depths of the sinister cavern. All scheming paused, as the square table trio glanced down, hesitating just long enough to acknowledge the tortured lament wafting up through the smoldering stones.

Ambassadors. All two hundred of them. Locked deep within the catacombs below. Their increasing restlessness—and piercing complaints—had been relentless today. Honestly, it was starting to become a bit of a nuisance.

"Kudos!" Ha-satan began his third attempt at congratulating his cohorts on their recent Ishmael success. "Our boy still needs some work," he flashed a dark grin. "But at least we've gotten ourselves in on the covenant."

"*INDEED!*" BEAST roared, raising both paws for 'high-fives all around!'

No response.

He shrugged and high-fived himself.

"However." Ha-satan rolled his eyes. "Word has come that Elohim met secretly with Abram, changed his name to Abra*ham*, and then promised him a son through Sarai, now Sara*h*, next year." Even the dark lord couldn't mask his disgust. "Does Elohim really think that a simple name change gives him the legal right to overlook Abram's disobedience and to shift the blessing from Abram's first born son, over to Abraham's?!"

"Mmm—gotta admit, that was a brilliant legal move, Boss," BEAST snorted.

"AAAhhhuuurrghhh—!" another Ambassador shrieked its

tortured vexation.

Ha-satan took a deep breath—in through his nose, out through his mouth—regrouping from the sudden emotional outburst. Slowly, his vision cleared. "Name change or no," he snapped. "We will *not* allow Heaven's word to come to pass." With a loud harrumph, he slammed himself back in his chair, folding both arms sourly across his chest. For some annoying reason no one else seemed to mind the anomaly nearly as much as he did.

"Did I hear you say something about the covenant birth happening next year?" Prophet clarified, crunching the numbers on all twelve fingers. "Guess—that's both good *and* bad news.."

All eyebrows slowly raised. Prophet had the room's attention.

"The bad news—we only have *one year* to derail the train." Prophet paused, waiting for the lingering echo of another wailing Ambassador to fade. "The … good … news," he grimaced, doing his best to dodge three encore performances. "We only have *one year* to derail the train!"

It was silent a moment.

One long, beautifully silent moment.

"..which means we know *exactly* what resources we need to allocate, and for *exactly* how long!" Ha-satan flashed a big, discerning smile. "Atta-boy," he slapped Prophet's bony, pointed shoulder.

"Then, let's throw *EVERYTHING* we've got at them!" BEAST jumped in. He was getting excited too. And when he got excited, his mouth often took on a mind of its own. "We can release a raiding party! Conjure a prairie fire! Call down brimstone from the sky! Or maybe just unleash a pack of rabid puppies.." He raised both paws, mentioning several other, much more imaginative scenarios. All of which would have been somewhat well received, except for the fact that a particularly long, exceptionally loud moan was currently drowning them out. All anyone could see was BEAST's jaw flapping, his burly arms flailing, and rivers of spit flying.

Then stunned silence.

BEAST stood up and high-fived himself.

"Gentlemen, —gentlemen." Ha-satan reeled the conversation back in. "No need for the big guns … *yet*." He motioned for BEAST to sit down, commanding the room once again. "First, we'll re-play the 'sister' card. I have a few minor readjustments. Should that fail, and a son *is* born, we still have one very illegitimate, and very impressionable Ishmael at our disposal," he grinned, pushing up from his own seat. "And if we must go further, I have a bit of a— *uh, twist*—that they'll *never* see coming." He moved back from his chair, stepping into the darkness as another god-forsaken scream terrorized the blistering cavern.

Stick a pitchfork in him, he was done.

Ha-satan rolled his eyes, turning and making a beeline for the nearest exit. *He so couldn't wait to get out of this sweltering, hellhole of a..*

"AAAuuraarrrgggh!!" a choir of piercing cries erupted from the chasms below.

Exactly—, the dark lord stepped through his patiently waiting portal. *He couldn't have said it any better himself.* For a moment he paused, cocking his head. He could hear BEAST shouting a string of wild obscenities, and Prophet banging on the floor with his staff. "Grumpy old men," he muttered, reaching back and permanently closing the portal behind him. "Let them find their own way home."

—| 2098:07:11:06:00:07 |—

Abraham scowled, someone had set him up.

Out of his element and totally alone, Abraham had been caught completely off guard. He was out, running his usual errands— touching base with multiple flock and herd leaders. En route, he'd been flagged and detained by a peculiar band of palace scouts. The whole charade had seemed a little 'off,' so when the interrogation deviated from business, refocusing solely on Sarah, his wife, Abraham had panicked. Fearing for his life, he'd reverted to his old, "she's my sister" narrative to get him off the hook.

Once again, it had worked.

Sorta..

Hours later those same palace guards showed up again. This time at Abraham's doorstep. Flashing an edict from Abimelech, King of Gerar, they cordially summoned Sarah to the palace—*to be his wife.*

Abraham would have stepped in with the truth, right then and there, ending the whole debacle. But he hadn't even yet returned from the fields.

Instead, Sarah had corroborated the lie, admitting, "She was, in fact, his sister." And thus, had been whisked away to become King Abi's new bride.

In King Abi's defense, he *had* been looking for a way to ensure that peaceful relations remained between him and Abraham (the largest growing, independent family in the region). So when he'd discovered that Abraham had a particularly attractive (albeit elderly) unmarried sister still living at home—he was more than willing to step up and "make the sacrifice."

Ha-satan, however, was in no mood to repeat past mistakes. As soon as Sarah arrived, he lit a blazing fire in King Abi's belly. Even at 90, Sarah was exceptionally easy on the eyes—and with the king's passions supernaturally stirred, wedding preparations began immediately.

Abraham was at a loss. For the first time—in potentially *EVER*—he was entirely unsure of what to do. Should he storm the castle, or apologize? Bring the king a peace offering, or demand recompense? No scenario seemed to play out quite right in his mind. Still, his heart remained unswayed. He had a promise from Elohim. Sarah would birth *his* child. And one way or another, that promise *had* to come to pass. *Didn't it?* He fell to the ground, head between his knees, he would not stop praying until his plight had been appeased.

That night Elohim himself appeared to Abi. "You're a dead man," he thundered. "You and your nation is no more! Because the woman you have taken to be yours is already married." Pictures of Abraham and Sarah flashed before the king's wide-eyes. "Already I have sealed the wombs of the women in your household," Elohim rebuked. "Your fruitfulness *and your future* has been cut off."

King Abi was indignant. *He hadn't even visited this woman yet!* "Lord—," he challenged. "Will you destroy a nation without blame? Did Abraham not say 'She is my sister?' And she, herself said, 'He is my brother.'" A fire erupted in his belly. "*I have done this deed with innocent hands!*"

Elohim knew the king had spoken honestly. "You speak the truth," he relented. "And because you've done this with a heart of honor, I kept you from sinning against me—*I* did not let you touch her." The energy in the room softened. "So now return Abraham's wife to him. Then, he will pray for you, and you will live.."

At the first sign of light King Abi obeyed, calling for Abraham and Sarah.

"What have you done?" he demanded. "What's wrong with you, to allow such a great sin to come upon me and my nation? What have I ever done to you?" He looked at the couple with complete bewilderment. "I was trying to bridge our nations. Ensure peace and harmony between our clans. But somehow, this has become the complete opposite! *Why would you do such a thing?*"

When Abraham finally understood the lengths Elohim had gone to protect his household, he finally understood just how powerful his covenant with Elohim really was. In that moment, his trust in Elohim became unshakable.

"I panicked," he admitted. "I thought there was no fear of God in this place. I thought I would be killed for my wife, and I feared for my life. I was wrong." His eyes and voice dropped. "Although, it *is* true that she is my sister," he felt the urge to explain. "Because we share the same father."

As soon as King Abi understood the whole truth, and heard the heartfelt apology, he realized what he too had done. Returning Sarah to her husband, he offered his deepest apologies, presenting the wrongfully harassed couple with sheep, cattle, servants, and a thousand pieces of silver. "You may live anywhere in my land that you desire," he amended. "For I have made right the wrong I caused you both."

So Abraham prayed to God, and Elohim healed *everyone* in King Abi's household—including Sarah.

Heaven's rouse had worked!

In the months to come, Sarah conceived and gave birth to a healthy baby boy. They named him Isaac—meaning Laughter. For he was their delight. Their joy. *Their son of inheritance.*

—| 2083:08:07:01:05:15 |—

Ha-satan was cross when he learned of Sarah's conception, and crosser when he discovered exactly how her womb had been restored. Still, his resistance had only just begun. With great pleasure, he sowed discord among the house of Abraham. Pitting Hagar against Sarah. Ishmael against Isaac. And Abraham against—*everybody.*

Strife festered. Anger mounted. Tensions grew and grew. Building until that predetermined day when the infection abrupted, toxins erupted, and its pustulating poisons overflowed.

Today was that day.

"You know, Father loves *me* best!" Ishmael taunted, hoisting his final pot of water from the mouth of the community well and into the back of his donkey's cart. "I was thirteen years old, when the Lord spoke to *my* father, commanding him to circumcise us," he turned, casually nudging Isaac's remaining two pots back over the edge, and down—down, down—*SPLASH*, into the well. "Yet, I did not back down." He continued to work as if nothing had happened. "I did everything according to the word of Elohim which he spoke to *my* father. And from that day to this, I have given my soul unto the Lord, never transgressing *any* word of which my father was commanded!"

Isaac flinched, watching the remains of his morning's toil disappear back inside the deep, dark opening. "Is that truly something?" he shrugged. "To be so zealous over such a *little* piece of flesh? Cut—in but a moment—from the smallest appendage on your body?" A smirk settled upon his lips. He stepped back, casually slipping the bit and bridal from Ishmael's donkey's mouth. "As sure as Elohim—the God of *my* Father—lives," he reached down and flipped open the clasp to the colt's belly band. "If he were to say to *my* father, 'Take now, your son Isaac, and bring him up as an offering to me..' I tell you the truth—I would not refrain, but would joyfully agree!"

SMACK—Isaac's hand landed hard against the donkey's rear flank. With a scream the beast was off, spooked and racing for home.

Isaac smugly lifted the loosened tackle for Ishmael to see.

"*Why, you little—,*" Ishmael lashed out.

Isaac ducked and spun, but it was too late. Nearly fourteen years his senior, Ishmael was already upon him.

The rivals tumbled to the ground.

Ha-satan was right behind, pouncing on Ishmael like white on rice.

Isaac could feel the sudden squeeze. He flailed his arms and squealed, catching Ishmael's mouth with a sharp, pointy elbow.

"*You obnoxious, asinine punk!*" Ishmael trembled. "*Always looking for ways to make my life a pain—!*" Blood dripped liberally from his lip. Rage flooded his soul. He reached for a nearby rock, eager to return the favor.

Suddenly, a vision of Isaac's limp body being dumped into the well flashed before Ishmeal's racing mind. Five furious fingers tightened around the warm, rugged rock. His eyes narrowed. *He couldn't agree more. This would be fun.* He stretched his hand back..

back..

back..

"ISHMAEL BAR ABRAHAM!" a shriek pierced the air. "YOU PUT THAT ROCK DOWN THIS INSTANT!" Sarah's head popped into view above a patch of swaying reeds, her laundry-drenched physique exploding from the banks of the nearby river.

Before the pair could even flinch, she was upon them. Dragging Ishmael off by the ear. Lifting Isaac up from the ground. Wet laundry and frothy soap suds flying everywhere.

"We—were j-just," Ishmael stammered.

"GO!" Sarah bellowed, pointing to the desert.

Ishmael looked confused. "G-Go?"

"GO—," she screamed again. "ANYWHERE BUT HERE!"

Ishmael slunk slowly away, leaving his teetering water-cart and hard day's work behind.

Immediately, Sarah was on her knees, hugging her baby tight, pulling him to her chest. *Events like this were becoming all too frequent, and exactly the reason she could never leave Isaac out of her sight!* For a moment, her eyes locked on the discarded sandstone. She whispered a tearful motherly prayer. *Two heirs, battling to the death for inheritance—this simply couldn't continue.* She rocked steadily back-and-forth, calling desperately to her God. *Something. Somehow. Someway. Had to give.*

CH14: TRIM THE FAT

"Care to join the conversation?" The Word leaned in, grinning broadly at his upside-down, quietly hovering counterpart. Neither he, nor Elohim had the foggiest idea what Spirit was up to. *But whatever it was,* they shared a fond glance, *it was certainly entertaining.*

"Oh, I'm joined," Spirit playfully replied. "I'm just looking at things *from a different angle.*" She paused to reach down—which was up to her—hoisting a steaming cup of joe from her spot at the round table. The cup was full to the brim, nearly spilling over, 'St. Arbucks,' printed boldly down its green and white stripped sides. She turned it over casually in her hands, savoring its flavorful contents through a colorful bendy straw.

"So why allow this whole ... mmm, Ishmael blunder?" She sipped, eyes closed, thoughtfully watching alternative scenarios play out across the theater of her mind.

"Sometimes you can actually get further, *faster,* by allowing your enemy to take his man to the top, before you change the heart of that man," Elohim grinned.

Silence.

"Take—Abraham, for instance," Elohim reframed his answer. "See how we must watch his back at every turn? Everything ends up a struggle? The serpent throwing roadblock after roadblock in our path?"

"But that's just good 'ol fashioned ... *fun!*" Spirit peeked open one eye and giggled.

"*Certainly*—but it's not always *fast.*" Elohim flashed a smile in return. "Typically, I've found it to be much easier to fill your donkey's cart when nobody is actively kicking your water pots *back* into the well."

"Got it." Spirit smiled. "For now, we leave Ishmael alone. But speaking of kicking water pots," a slender finger wagged. "Isn't the serpent planning to force our hand *against* Isaac and Abraham?"

"Yes—well—he will not *force* it," Elohim's eyes began to twinkle. "More like, *coax it out.*" A light-hearted chuckle dismantled any undue tensions. "No worries, my dear. The serpent will only play right into our predetermined plans." The Creator sat back and smiled. "*So, yes.* This *will* be a test. And from a certain perspective, an attempted assassination. But *guaranteed*—every party involved will be a *willing and well-protected* participant."

—| |—

Elohim stepped forward, resting both hands on the thick wooden banister running full-length around the open-air porch. He gazed up into space. Outer space. Earth hanging like a big blue marble in the immediate distance.

The planet's creator exhaled slowly, watching his breath descend peacefully upon his most beloved creation. Since the fall of Adam he regularly visited this place. Usually in the cool of the day. Usually alone. In fact, he'd found himself at *Heaven's Edge* so often, he eventually had the porch installed, just so he could stand and watch.

He exhaled again. Smiling. Imagining. Watching. Waiting.

Two six-fingered hands settled quietly next to his. Their owner staring at the same swirling blue ball—*albeit, a bit less fondly.* For a long moment there was silence.

Eventually Elohim spoke.

"Haylel—my son. Where have you been?"

"On Earth, my Lord. Walking to and fro."

"What's the word—concerning my children?" A hint of longing surfaced.

"All your children on Earth who serve you, are great at remembering you whenever they require something they need!" The deceiver breathed deep. "But," he trailed off, "—whenever you give them the thing of which they inquire, they suddenly get 'Amnesia,' and remember you no more."

Elohim was slow to speak.

"Have you considered my servant Abraham? There is no one else upon the earth like him."

"Really—my Lord?! Abram?" Haylel nearly lost his lunch. "Do you not recall, all the years you promised him a child? When he made you altar upon altar, sacrifice upon sacrifice?" He paused, feigning remorse. "Yet since the birth of his son, Isaac. *Crickets*. Not so much as a sandstone of remembrance."

"Odd," Elohim frowned. "Abraham has always been exceedingly honest and upright before me. Honoring all that I say and avoiding evil at every turn." He turned to the voice of Abraham's accuser. "As certainly as I live, if I were to say to him, 'Bring Isaac—your one and only son—and sacrifice him as a burnt offering to me,' it would be no different to him than if I'd asked for a bull or a goat."

Bingo! Haylel's grin was suddenly genuine. "Speak to Abram then," he slyly challenged. "See whether or not what you have said is true. Then we will know for sure if he will honor your word, or if he will, this very day, cast it aside."

Elohim gazed a moment longer at his shamelessly calculating CEO. *If only to use his skills for life—not death.* He gave his head a curt little nod, turning back to the spinning globe.

"As certain as we stand here conversing," a mischievous grin was already tugging at the corners of his mouth. "The thing you have requested, *I have already done.*"

—| 2066:00:06:11:06:06 |—

The conversation with Abraham had been a bit more one-sided.

"Abraham!" that familiar voice had boomed.

"Yes, Lord?"

"Take your son, your only son—Isaac, the one you love—and go to the land of Moriah."

"Yes, Lord.."

"There, sacrifice him as a burnt offering atop one of the

mountains I will show you."

Silence.

"Abraham?"

"... Y-Yes, Lord?"

"Do you understand?"

"Yes Lord.."

Then it was done.

Over and out, Elohim was gone.

Abraham had tried to level his spinning head. Blink his frozen eyes. Shut his gaping mouth. But it was no use. He was beside himself. Dazed. Alone. Confused.

What to do?

He fell back against his still warm pillow, staring into the pitch black night, scouring his soul. After his scrape with King Abi, he'd come to fully trust Elohim. *No doubt, his God was good.* Even if Isaac *was* somehow destroyed, Elohim would simply raise him back up. *It wasn't so much the thought of that,* Abraham fought against the rising lump in his throat, *it was more the thought of telling Isaac's mom.* A cold sweat erupted. He rolled out of bed. *There was no way..*

No way.

Somewhere in the distance, a rooster crowed. *The day was already beginning.* Abraham stood and quickly exited his tent, gathering the essentials needed. Quietly, he roused two servants. A third he awakened with a message for Sarah. Last in line, he woke Isaac, now some thirty years old.

KAAH-KA-DOODLE-DOO, the rooster was crowing again. This time, much closer. Abraham finalized his preparations. The household would be bustling soon. In a few hours their presence would be expected. Then sought. Then missed. He stood, tossing his provisions over the waiting donkey's back. *But by that time,* he smiled, securing the last bag. *They would be long, long, long gone.*

—| 2066:00:03:06:09:12 |—

The three days it took to reach the land of Moriah were largely spent on raillery and banter. Abraham told the tales of Uncle Lot and the four Eastern Kings, the times he had spoken with angels and/or Elohim; and of course, how it had come to pass that in one single day he, himself, had circumcised over three hundred men.

Isaac joined the fray with war stories of his own. How growing up he'd been so overprotected, he'd been forced to wear a riding helmet until he was practically twenty-five years old. The top twelve reasons he could make cinnamon Challah Bread blindfolded in his sleep. And the countless times his brother had nearly taken his inheritance—and his life.

To Abraham, the journey seemed to fly by. And all too soon, he found himself staring at their intended destination—one large, rolling mountain—looming ominously in the distance.

"The boy and I will go and worship alone." Abraham slowed their tiny caravan to a halt near the base of the ever looming rise, motioning for both servants to stay. "After some time, we will return to you."

Each servant nodded their agreement, eager to spend the day trapping or fishing—anything to get them off their feet for a while.

Abraham hoisted a chord of wood from their donkey, handing it to Isaac to shoulder. Then—flint knife and tinder box in hand—the pair turned and headed up the steep incline.

Issac was first to break the silence.

"Father?"

"Yes, my son."

"Where's the lamb for the burnt offering?"

Abraham took a deep breath, he'd known all along this question was coming. *But he still had no good answer.* He whispered an earnest prayer.

FLASH—instantly the mountain transformed. Wind howling. Rain pelting. Abraham tightened his cloak. Terror seemed to be falling from the sky. He glanced up. Black as ink, it seemed to be collapsing like water. Crashing like a wave. Spilling. Cascading. Down—down—down.

SWOOSH.

Then he was back.

What—he gasped, looking around, fighting to retain

his composure. He glanced to his oblivious son. Clearly, he had experienced that translation alone. He slowed, opening his mouth to reply.

Still, no words.

Isaac pressed further, "Father, I see the wood *and* the fire, but where is the *lamb* for the offering?"

WHOOSH—again, Abraham was gone, wind and rain pelting his awestruck face. He lifted his head, raising both hands, squinting into the sky as he watched the towering wave. Thick as sludge, black as death, it barreled down to Earth—bearing down upon a single, lowly man ... *hanging from a tree?*

Abraham swallowed hard.

The man looked beaten and broken, bloodied and bruised ... yet he was shining *like the very son of God!*

*KA-BOOM—*a thunderclap jolted Abraham back. He fell against his walking staff, stumbling ahead, attempting to keep up with his son still trudging obliviously up the unassuming mountainside. Bewildered, Abraham opened his mouth. "God sees ... *himself ...* the lamb," was all that spilled out.

Isaac nodded his response.

Again, they fell silent. Steadily moving on.

...

Now, unbeknownst to them—on the opposite side of the mountain—trudged a tall and strikingly peculiar man: Gold belt. Olive toned. Dressed completely in white. He too, was shouldering a burden ... what looked to be a young, spotless ram. He smiled as he spoke to it softly, occasionally offering it handfuls of tender, leafy greens.

Within minutes, the man had reached his final destination, plopping the little ram down in a thicket and taking a seat beneath a particular tree nearby. Relaxing, he began to fade. Blending first, into the surrounding vegetation, and then back into the spirit realm from which he came.

...

Moments later, two sweaty heads popped into view. Isaac first. Then Abraham. Climbing up the steep embankment to the crest of the hill. Nearing the thicket, Abraham felt prompted to pause beside that very same, "particular" tree. *This was the place*, he motioned for Isaac to drop the wood. *He was sure of it.*

Preparations began: Isaac gathering the largest stones he could find. Abraham constructing the altar. It didn't take long. Twelve stones. Neatly stacked. A trench dug around. Then, with wood and tinder arranged on top, the tinderbox was gently revived.

Abraham glanced around. *No lamb yet?* He fought to dispel the growing knot assailing his gut. Dragging his feet, he poked and putzed—readjusting his kindling, rekindling his tinder box— graciously giving Elohim a few more minutes to provide.

Then a few more.

And a few more.

Finally, he was out of excuses.

"Isaac," he called, turning to his son. "It's time we address the inevitable.."

Dropping to his knees, he told Isaac everything. ALL of the promises of God: How Elohim had found him, rescued him, prospered and protected him. Expanded all he had in the midst of wars, conflict, and famine. He told of God's goodness. His power to resurrect Sarah's dead womb. And to bring new life from the loins of a weary old man. He boasted in Elohim's ability to defeat Kings, restore Queens, return lost loved ones, and avert countless personal mistakes. Even—and especially—in the times when he hadn't lived up to his end of the bargain.

Like a father who had suddenly lost it all, Abraham poured out the depths of his heart to his one-and-only son—*the son whom he loved.*

Finally, when there was nothing left to say. Abraham lifted tear-filled eyes, and trembling to his core, repeated the very words of Elohim. "Take now, your son—Isaac, the one whom you love—and bring him up as an offering to me."

Isaac's jaw dropped. He had a hunch, but to hear those exact words out loud.. His heart began to pound. His head began to spin. *Should he run? Should he fight? Should he resist and rebel?* There was no doubt, at the rugged age of thirty, he could easily overpower his 'delusional old dad' to save his own skin.

But, *wait*—in the very midst of his knee-jerk reaction—something jolted him to a stop. A memory. A statement. A few long-forgotten, wildly boastful words, spoken in youthful frustration to his older brother one day at the well.

"Even if Elohim were to say to *my* father," it all came rushing back, "'Take now, your son Isaac, and bring him up as an offering to me.' I tell you the truth—I would not refrain, but would joyfully agree!"

Isaac vigorously shook his head, those strangely prophetic words echoing through his mind as if they had just been spoken. *Had he truly meant them?* Not in his wildest dreams did he think they would ever actually come to fruition. Yet here he was, *would he truly sacrifice ALL of himself?*

He thought for a moment ... a long, hard moment.

Then, settling in the dirt beside his father, he raised a single hand. "Is our God, not a worthy God?" He motioned to the mountainside around them. "And his request, not a worthy request?" He studied the endless stream of silent tears dripping from his dad's thick beard and onto the rocky ground below. "Is our God not the God who makes all things new? Who brings the dead to life? Who always keeps his word?" From somewhere deep inside a new boldness arose, an unspeakable joy, rising like freshly stoked fire. He threw back his head and belly-laughed. "Is he not *well able* to restore *all things*, so that no promise is left unfulfilled?" He lifted his eyes to match his father's gaze. *His father could recount story upon story of Elohim's goodness. Was it not time for him to make at least one story of his own?*

"Not my will, Father ... but *yours* be done," Isaac completely surrendered. "I will hold nothing back, but *joyfully* agree!"

Abraham didn't know what to say.

His son? This reaction?

Only Elohim.

Willingly, Isaac laid down upon the altar. Willingly he offered up both hands and feet. No one would force him. No one would coerce him. This was his life. His flesh. He *willingly* laid it all down.

Up went the knife.

Deep breath—one last glance—*no lamb in sight.*
Down, the blade rushed with all of Abraham's might.

...

Now, unbeknownst to them—as soon as father and son had
begun to talk, the figure by the "particular" tree had begun to listen.
Their conversation was so genuine, so transparent, so authentic and
raw, that the figure had been compelled to get up and move closer.

Then closer still.

Soon he was kneeling right alongside the duo, his right elbow
resting casually across Isaac's shoulder, his left hand on Abraham's
knee; laughing and crying right along with his newly adopted,
mountain-top family. It was almost too much. He could barely
believe his ears. With supernatural, unconditional conversation like
this happening, there was no way he could ever leave his new brother
alone. So when Isaac stretched out across the altar, he too crawled
up, right along side. And when Abraham bound Isaac's hands and
feet, he too scooted over, dead center. And as Abraham repeatedly
rearranged the tinder and firewood, there he sat, Indian style, elbows
on his knees, fists tucked under his chin, barely able to contain one
huge, sloppy, ever-growing grin.

...

THUWNK—then the deed was done. Abraham froze, slowly
opening one eye. Then the other.

"—*Abraham!*" The voice of Elohim boomed like thunder.

"L-L-Lord?" he gasped, glancing fully around. Somehow his
arm seemed stuck, suspended, caught midair as if by an invisible
hand. He tried to shake himself loose, mumbling a jumbled apology.
Had he really just failed to keep up his end of the bargain?

"Do not lay a hand on the boy! Nor hurt him in any way! For
now I know that you truly fear God, because you have not withheld
your son—your only son—from me!"

"*BAAAAAA-AAA,*" at that precise moment, the little ram
bleated from the thicket. Its horns were tangled and its greens had
run out.

"Yahweh-Yireh! My provider!" Abraham exclaimed, rushing

to cut his son free. *Indeed—upon this mountain, God himself, had provided!*

When Isaac heard the words of Elohim, and saw the lamb supplied, he knew all his dad had spoken was truth. And in that moment his heart turned, wholly submitted to the God of his father from that day forward.

And as the aroma of the evening sacrifice arose, Heaven breathed a collective sigh of relief. They had found a man who would truly put God first, and whose generations would *willingly* crucify their own flesh—so that when the time was right, a mighty nation might arise and be filled with the fullness of Elohim!

CH15: PLAYER, PLAYER, MEDIATOR

The throne room was churning with life—every stone, every tile, every pillar and brick; overflowing with magnanimous personality. Its ambiance was living too. The usually soaring ceilings had completely dissolved; bright and sunny skies shining through. Its majestic walls had faded into mountains. Its pillars into trees. Billowing, golden clouds surfed peacefully overhead. Butterflies rode warm southern breezes. Birds darted merrily about. In fact, the entire room—save portions of the immediate floor—had completely disappeared, giving way to the wondrous outdoors.

Elohim sat beaming from his throne, enjoying the beautiful ruckus around him. A river—clear as crystal—flowed out from under his seat, quietly spilling down the throne room steps and dropping to its bed beneath the translucent floor below. Down the center of the great room it flowed—growing, expanding, gaining momentum—until, with a steady roar, it made its gushing exit beneath two golden-arching front doors.

In the distance, the infamous clock tower loomed. Shimmering. Stately. Foreshadowing. To most, it was a joyous reminder of the promise to come. For others, it was more of an ominous premonition. Especially now that a digital version of its vintage face was boldly projected beneath the Crystal River, dead-center of the throne room floor.

Atop the floor itself, angels scurried everywhere—interacting, networking—doing last minute preparations. Today was *The Annual Assembly*, the day when the sons of God gathered—traveling from distant corners of the cosmos to deliver their yearly reports. It was a sort of "informal, intergalactic, House of

Representatives," a time of discussion, collaboration, and multi-lateral self-governance. On the docket today was a particularly exciting presentation. Haylel—Heaven's C.E.O.—was expected to deliver a personal report concerning Earth; an account that was both highly anticipated and long overdue.

Arrruuuuugh—the opening trumpet sounded.

Bang—Elohim's gavel came crashing down. The presiding Judge lowered his sizable itinerary, scanning the bustling room.

There were smiles.

Pleasantries.

Introductions.

Then the meeting began.

Haylel was up first.

"Permission to approach the bench?" He strode forward, offering the stately, well-dressed, Chief Administrator his parchment.

The Chief Administrator turned, requesting permission.

Permission granted, the parchment was unsealed, and its contents released publicly for all to hear:

Honorable Elohim & Noble Members of The Annual Assembly. You will be pleased to know: Earth is well! Its inhabitants in great hands! Rest assured, that since the Great Flood, practically all inter-dimensional breeding has been completely and totally eradicated. Its pre-flood, prolific & undesirable effects much easier to police now that Earth's depleted atmosphere can no longer sustain such long-term, hybrid-angelic life. However, regrettably, man still seems oddly impartial and largely uninterested in anything other than himself. In fact, it seems highly unlikely that mankind will ever..

"Have you noticed my servant Job?" Elohim could no longer keep quiet, he simply had to interject. "He's a truth-loving man, full of integrity and compassion for others."

Haylel scowled. "And why wouldn't he be?" he stepped forward, a bit miffed that Elohim had the audacity to cut his flawless presentation short. "You have always kept a wall of protection around him, causing him to prosper in everything he does."

"I know!" chuckled Elohim. "Nothing can touch him!" He

clapped his hands with delight. "I have made him rich beyond belief. His servants have servants with servants. His flocks, their own flocks. Not one of his kids has ever had to do a hard days work—not a single day of their lives!" Heartfelt laughter erupted.

"But release your *Hand*," Haylel challenged. "Let *me* take everything he has away. Then we will see if he will not, most certainly, curse you to your face."

A hush fell over the crowd. These kinds of blatant accusations were rare in the Courts of Heaven. Nonexistent in The Annual Assembly. How would their infallible Judge respond?

Elohim paused, a giddy little grin plastered to his semi-contemplative face. *What a novel opportunity! ..To see how Haylel would treat a righteous man, placed completely in his hands? ..AND to extract what was truly in Job's heart?* It was two birds, one stone—the perfect scenario. He drew a long, slow breath. "Do whatever you want with everything he possesses," Elohim offered a hand to his challenger. "Just do *not* harm Job physically."

Without hesitation, Haylel stepped forward, and with a hearty handshake, eagerly accepted the deal.

The crowd erupted. *What was this? A cosmic wager?! A bet between two Gods over a single man?! ..Had this ever been done before?* Everyone looked perplexed.

Elohim and Haylel, however, were all grins. *The stakes had never been higher, and they were loving it!* Both were getting *exactly* what they wanted, and yet—as many in the crowd would later note— their smiles seemed two very different smiles.

—| 2124:06:06:20:20:20 |—

Job's blood-drenched clothes had long since dried a deep dark brown. The self-made entrepreneur tugged gently at the end of his reins, his horse eager to obey. At long last, the pair was heading home, exhausted from another long day of rigorous, religious sacrifice.

Elohim will be pleased, Job smiled. *Once again, I've followed in ALL of his ways; covering my family's sins and selfishness to a "T."* He tipped an imaginary hat, pointing a thankful finger to the sky.

Well done, he congratulated the heavens. *Here's to another season of unbridled success!*

The low-setting sun seemed to approve as it flung Job's shadow far across the prairie-land of Uz. Job looked around, deeply satisfied. *What a sight!* From the fertile, rolling hills, to the distant snow-capped mountains; every flock and herd, crop and plant that filled these planes ... *all of them were his!*

Wow, he marveled. *How good was his God!*

In the distance, a faint trail of dust began to rise. Slowly at first, then with increasing veracity it poured into the sky. *No doubt there was a rider at its front,* Job grinned, watching it billow and stretch majestically into the calm evening air. *Nothing unusual. Riders often hurried down that trail for one reason or another.* A chuckle rose from his belly. *Maybe the hasty sojourner was hungry. Or hangry. Or simply in a hurry to get home before dark.* Job shifted his reins, his heart and his horse suddenly kicking into high-gear as one last thought occurred.

Maybe that rider had a message ... for him!

The two met at Job's front gate, screeching to concurring halts. The rider—whom Job immediately recognized as one of his own—jumped frantically from his frothing beast.

"Master," he announced, visibly shaken. "The oxen were plowing the fields, the donkeys feeding beside them, when suddenly raiders fell upon us and took them all away!" He paused, heaving a convulsive breath. "Indeed, they killed *all* of your servants with the edge of the sword! *I alone escaped..*"

Before the rider had ended his report, a second rider came barreling up. This man was covered in soot, and the bottom half of his staff seemed to be smoldering. With no regard for the present conversation, he toppled from his colt. "Master, while we were out tending your flocks," he rolled to one knee, tamping out his staff in the dirt. "The lightning of God fell, catching the prairie on fire. All of your sheep and everyone tending them were consumed. *Only I have escaped!*"

While he was still tamping, a third courier arrived. This man's tattered robe was dripping with blood and he was missing both an ear and a sandal. Gasping, he raised an index finger high..

They waited.

He gasped.

They waited.

He gasped.

"Master." He finally wheezed. "The Chaldeans formed three bands! They raided your camels and took them away, killing every last one of your servants. *I alone escaped to tell you!*"

No sooner had the words left his lips, then out of the dust, a final rider emerged. Decked to the hilt in formal attire he was barely recognizable, masked beneath a viscous layer of dirt, grime, and ash. The shredded cloth he used to cover his mouth did little to stop his sputtering cough. And for some odd reason, he clung desperately to a mangled party-tray.

"Master! Your sons and daughters were celebrating at your oldest son's house," his wild eyes stretched wide as saucers. "Suddenly a great whirlwind crossed the prairie and struck their home. The building collapsed, killing everyone at the party." For a moment he slowed, noticing the three broken men before him. "I-I—alone," he swallowed hard, "..have escaped to tell you."

Time stood still.

Job dropped to his knees, sobbing uncontrollably. *How? It couldn't be. It wasn't possible.* All of this had taken place while he was out—*worshiping his God?*

Slowly the color drained from his face, running down his core and pooling in a lifeless puddle around his feet. His head dropped, heavy with shame. He couldn't breathe. With a mighty groan, he tore at his clothes. "I throw no stones, I cast no blame," he forced a broken whisper. "The Lord gives and the Lord takes away. Blessed be the name of the Lord."

CH16: THE FINAL BLOW

Arrruuugh—the opening trumpet sounded.

It was time again, *The Annual Assembly* was assembling. Haylel glanced silently around. The throne room was as beautifully hectic as ever. Elohim sat grinning on his throne, watching the sons of God—his angels—actively taking their seats. Banter was abundant. Laughter was everywhere. Life was coursing through the crowd.

"Haylel!" Elohim flashed a huge winsome grin, welcoming his second-in-command from well across the room. "From where in the universe have you come?"

"From Earth." Haylel stepped out of the crowd, bowing low. "From patrolling and governing, and watching over everything that goes on."

"Have you noticed my servant, Job?" Elohim grinned, excited to pick up right where they had left off. "After all, you know there is no one on Earth quite like him!"

Haylel cringed. Perhaps he was jealous. Perhaps, deep down, he knew it was true. After all, he *was* the Master Architect who had perfectly constructed Job's material demise ... *and still*, Job had cast no blame.

Elohim raised two triumphant eyebrows. "Certainly, you incited him against me—to destroy him without cause. Yet he held fast to integrity, and to this day remains blameless!" He shifted in his seat, barely containing his excitement.

Really—?, Haylel choked out a smile, *was Elohim really gonna throw THAT in his face! Everyone knew, it was SOLELY Elohim's fault that Job had not fallen. HE had set the limits, protecting Job physically. Of course a low-life, narcissistic, punk like Job wouldn't care what happened to anyone else around him, so long as he himself remained untouchable.*

"Skin for skin," Haylel shrewdly replied. "Will a man, not certainly, give up everything to spare his own life?" He flashed his most winsome smile, going in for the kill. "But stretch out your Hand. Let me take away his *health,*" the words practically tumbled out. "Surely, he will curse you to your face."

Total silence—you could almost hear the chins drop.

Elohim leaned back and scratched his head, putting on his best poker bluff. He already knew his next move. Heck, he already knew his next seven moves. Job had handled round one masterfully, but the exact scenario—honed to perfection ages ago—still called for Job to accomplish one last task. Elohim sighed deep. Unfortunately, coaxing that accomplishment out would take a bit more, uhm—*pressure.*

"Double, or nothing!" the master gambler grinned, offering up an outstretched hand. "You may do with him as you wish!" He waited as Haylel stepped forward. "Only one thing," the two locked eyes and palms. "You *must* agree—to *completely* spare Job's life."

—| 2123:06:06:06:00:03 |—

"Ahh-choo!" It all started with a sneeze.

Great, Job frowned, *another cold. Just what I need.* He lowered his ax, surveying his significantly downsized estate. It had been exactly one year ago, to the date, since the absolute worst day of his life. He heaved a short sigh, clearing his scratchy throat. Ever since that moment, he'd been working overtime just to keep things afloat. He bent down, hoisting another chunk of Cedar onto the well-worn splitting stump.

"Ahhh-choo!" a wave of nausea hit.

Now this..

THWACK—the ax came down again, sending splinters of firewood flying. Job's hand brushed past his nose. *What?* He glanced down. *That was strange*—an odd red lesion was somehow ruptured across the back of his thumb. He pulled up his sleeve for a better look.

There sat another, on his forearm..

And another..

And another..

Suddenly, he was searching all over: Legs. Arms. Back. Stomach. *These things were everywhere!*

Then it began.

The incredible itch.

Intense. Uncomfortable. Unrelenting.

More nausea hit.

Then more itch.

Frantic, Job searched for some relief. *A stick? A rock? A particularly stout blade of grass?* He spun around. *Nothing. Only a cumbersome clay pot of..*

CRUNCH—he smashed it, week-old goat's milk spilling everywhere.

Grabbing a sizable shard, he dropped to the dirt. Milk and all, he started attacking those little demon bumps with everything in him.

Minutes turned to hours.

Hours turned to days. While Job and his precious goat's milk shard sat huddled in the dirt—scratching and scratching and scratching.

In time, maggots arose from the dust, feasting upon the delicacies of Job's decomposing flesh. His sores began to rot. Then stink even worse than the milk. He countenance grew dim, his body overwhelmed. He felt weak. Sick. Defeated.

He was done.

Still, through all of this, he would not curse God.

As time dragged on, even his wife began to grow weary. "Why are you still so arrogantly holding on to your integrity?" she lashed out, swayed by the torment within her own soul. "Be done with it— curse God and die!"

The temptation was certainly compelling, Job couldn't deny that. It did seem that in his particular case, Heaven had seriously dropped the ball. Still, he *had* to trust that his God was good. And because of that, he could cast no blame.

Hell, of course, was furious. *How was the heart of this cretin not moved? Not by death or decay? Betrayal or disease? ..Not even by the calloused words of an overly embittered wife?*

In a fit of a rage, Haylel scoured the land, gathering his best and brightest. Three men: Eliphaz, Bildad, and Zophar—a veritable dream-team of good-looking, smooth-talking, well-meaning, yet woefully-misguided best-friends. *If Job couldn't be persuaded by his circumstances,* Haylel bristled, *surely the smooth-talking lips of a self-righteous "sympathizer" would do the trick.*

Ironically, Eli, Bill, and Zee were not at all prepared for the sight which greeted them upon arrival. Job was skin and bones, boils and bruises; a mere shell of a man lying in the dirt. Not to mention the stench, *oh the stench!* They wept loudly, covering themselves in ash, collapsing hopelessly beside their death-riddled friend.

For seven days and nights, no one said a word.

Finally, Job could take no more. "Oh curse the day that I was born," he erupted. "May it never be remembered! May it be lost forever to both God and man! Never to be accurately placed in all of history!" He shifted and groaned. "Why does God bother keeping me alive? Oh, that I had been stillborn—that I had died at birth. Then I would be at peace."

His friends began to stir, each with a reply of their own.

Eli spoke first.

"You may want to think *before* you speak," he brazenly scolded. "Has a truly innocent person ever ended up on the scrap heap of life?" He paused, listening, as if someone were whispering the words in his ear. "Certainly, it's true: God wounds. But he *also* dresses the wound. And the same hand that hurts you, will also heal you." He turned toward his dying friend, a foolhardy boldness flooding his sanctimonious soul. "Job, do *not* despise God's correction, for there must be some reason why God is correcting you."

Somewhere in the distance, a lone wolf howled.

"My so-called friend," Job fired back, waiting for the distant cry to fade. "God is not bipolar, nor is he codependent. *What*—have

I grown so rich that he suddenly feels threatened by me? Does the 'owner of the cattle on a thousand hills' need to crush me so that I might run back to his outstretched arms?" His heart sparked with righteous indignation. "*NO—I am already IN his arms*. Does a perfect test need more correction? Or a college graduate need to graduate college all over again?" Job's eyes rose until they locked with Eli's. "Tell me, sir. What's the point of all your religious babble? Why do you act like I'm the one who's full of hot air? True, I may be complaining bitterly, but I'm the one who's being completely honest. *Since when did honesty become such a crime?* Confront me with some *actual* truth, and I'll gladly shut up."

CRAACK—the campfire flared, a shower of sparks spiraling into the colorful evening sky. For a moment they hung midair, taking on the shape of a serpent, ominous in the fading light of the low-hanging sun.

"What are mortals, anyway?" Job snapped, almost as if challenging the sinister image. "And why do you feel the need to obsessively watch over them? Is it for the good of mankind? Your own personal insight? Or is it just to bother them?!" He reached down, grabbing a fistful of ash and tossing it into the crackling pit. "You beast," he snarled. "*Leave me alone!*"

POOF—the serpent was done.

But Job wasn't.

"Let's pretend I did sin—," he pressed. "How would that even affect you? Weren't you created to watch over *all* of mankind? Do you not have anything better to do than to pick on *me*?" He was so through with this. "Why don't you just forgive my sins and start me off with a clean slate? Why—? What's that to you?" His words, like the tossed ash, settled slowly in the brisk autumn air.

Eli made no attempt to respond, mostly because he wasn't exactly sure how to respond to—*whatever that was*—he'd just witnessed. *Was Job refuting him? ..or the camp fire?* He stifled a cringe. Misguided hallucinations aside, all that seemed certain was how close Job's childish rant was to being flat out *blasphemy*.

For quite some time, no one spoke, the pressure slowly mounting.

Finally, Bill caved.

"My dear friend," he lurched ahead. "Does God mess up? Does he ever get things backwards? Or out of order? It's plain your children sinned against him—otherwise, why would God have punished them?"

Job flinched.

"Do you really believe the world revolves around you?" Bill doubled-down. "I'll tell you the rule: 'The light of the *wicked* is put out.' *It's that simple.* Get down on your knees before God Almighty. If you're really as innocent and upright as you say, it's not too late—he will come running to you, and.."

"God is *NOT* my errand boy!" Job snapped, shutting down the ill-conceived prattle. "He does *not* have to move based on what *I do. He is God! I move for him!* How is it that you've so completely missed the point?" He turned to face his accuser. "The real question is: How can mere mortals ever get right with God? Even if we wanted to plead our case before him, what chance would we have? *I tell you, it's not one in a trillion!* How could I ever construct, much less argue, a defense that would actually influence *God*? Even though *I am* innocent, I could never prove it. Look at me, I shout 'Murder!' and I'm ignored. I call for help and no one bothers to stop. No, my only hope is to throw myself upon the mercy of the court."

Job stared at all the doubtful, unresponsive faces. *This was like debating a brick wall*, he sighed. *Except brick walls typically had more empathy!*

He shifted his weight, gathering the words—and the energy—to drive his final point home. "If you're thinking, 'How can we get through to him? Get him to see that his trouble is all his own fault?' *Forget it!* Instead, worry about yourselves. Worry about your own sins, and God's coming judgment for *them!*"

BOOM. The silence was deafening.

Slowly, all eyes turned to Zee, the oldest and "wisest" of the bunch. Would he have the intestinal fortitude—and providential insight—to further the case against Job?

The white-haired sage sat thoughtfully, arms crossed, frown growing as he eyed Job disapprovingly. "Who do you think you are to explain the mysteries of God?" his argument 'pulled slowly' out of the proverbial station. "Do you think you can sum him up? ..nail him down? ..box him in?" Two condemning eyes reduced to a squint. *"How can you? God is UNKNOWABLE!"* Zee's train was already off the tracks. "If he throws you in jail or takes you to court, can you do the first-thing about it? *Stop acting like you can! It's embarrassing."* He shook a cold, religious finger at Job. "Oh, how I wish God would give you a piece of his mind! He sees through your pretense and arrogance. *You fool, you haven't gotten HALF of what you deserve!* Wash your hands of your impurities and stop entertaining evil in your home. Then you will be able to face the world unashamed, living your life free of guilt and fear!"

Job's heart sunk. His shoulders slumped. *What could he do? They were hopelessly unable to see!* Only he could ever know, what he so deeply knew—*he had done no wrong!* A groan escaped his dry, cracked lips. From the most desperate depths of his ail-afflicted soul, a prayer began to rise:

> *"My friends have condemned me! My eyes have poured out tears! Oh, that I had someone to mediate between God and me. Someone GOOD! To bring us together and not to drive us apart. To mediate as a brother would mediate, between friends.."*

Even as Job cried out—an Ox of a man, far to the West, was facedown in the throws of a stagnant rain puddle, contending with the disappointments of his own reflection. No sooner had Job spilled his guts, than a portal burst open behind that man and The Word of the Lord stepped through, calling the future 'Father of Israel' into the fullness of his destiny.

Oh—if only Job had been able to see the immediacy at which his prayer had been answered! Surely, the hope that would have erupted would have instantly restored his soul.

Instead, he turned back to Zee.

"I'm sure you were speaking for *ALL* the experts," he caustically mocked. "Oh, please tell us what will happen when you die and there's no one left to tell us how to live?"

Muffled laughter rose from the group.

Job took no solace in the reaction. "I wish you'd *all* shut your mouths," he barked. "Silence is your only claim to wisdom. You have littered my life with pompous lies. Are you going to keep on lying 'to do God a service?' Making up stories to get him 'off the hook?' Do you not think he can handle me himself?" A maggot-laden hand waved them all away. "I've had it with you—*each of you! I'm going directly to God. Laying my life on the line ... do with it what He will!"*

Suddenly, a new voice pierced the darkness.

All eyes turned.

"Exceedingly, I have been patient—watching and listening from the shadows—letting age and wisdom speak its full piece. But now I realize that age is not comprised of wisdom any more than the moon is comprised of cheese," the newcomer's disdain was almost palpable. "Therefore, let me speak. For I have no ulterior motive aside from speaking the truth which God has plainly taught me."

Job lifted his head, intrigued.

Out from the shadows stepped Elihu the Buzite. Young. Dark. Handsome. Robust. Unlike the group, Elihu wore no proper headdress, no formal attire. His beard, although carefully trimmed, was thin and patchy. His soft round face emanating with the naivety of youth.

Who was this boy who spoke like a king?

Job nodded his permission.

"You have complained that God won't answer your charge," Elihu sank slowly to the dirt beside Job. "But you're wrong! *You're dead wrong!* God always answers in one way or another. Even when we don't recognize it's him talking! In a dream, for instance, or a vision at night. God might reveal his wisdom or seal-up instruction. He might allow pain and discomfort to attract our attention, making us aware of the wrong road we're traveling down." An unbiased arm plunged deep into his saddlebag, resurfacing with an unmarked flask of balm. "Job, you *know* it's impossible for God to do evil," he tossed the balm to his stricken friend. "There's no way for him to even *want* to do wrong. Can someone who hates order, keep order?" Elihu motioned for Job to apply the serum. "Are you honestly implying that someone *other* than God is in control? And that your own, limited righteousness is more righteous than God's?"

For the first time Job quieted. Partly because the serum was working wonders, and partly because *that was EXACTLY what he'd been implying.* Elihu had simply managed to put it into words! *Yes—,* he stared back at his new best friend, *it truly felt as if someone—or something—other than God was in control.* Light bulbs were flipping on, inner-eyes flying open. *It was almost as if someone was running interference—COSMIC INTERFERENCE!*

On this point alone, Job could have camped all day. Drilling down into the conspiratorial depths of who that 'mythical troll' might be. *But—,* Elihu was already moving on.

"Look at those stars," the Buzite pointed up. "See how much higher the heavens are than us? If we sin, what difference does it make to God? And if we're good, what does God get out of it? Do you think he depends upon our accomplishments—good or bad?!" Elihu shook his head. "No, God is not dependent on our behavior. The only people who truly care about whether we are good or bad are our family, friends, and neighbors."

Job was listening.

"Good Sir, God *is* all-powerful," Elihu's voice softened. "But he doesn't bully innocent people. He watches over the righteous and tells them where they've gone wrong. He helps the ones he loves to heed his warnings." Elihu reached down, hoisting the now discarded ointment from the ground beside him. "Do you not see how God is already wooing you back from the jaws of danger? Drawing you into a life of *complete freedom*—inviting you to feast at His table of blessing?" Carefully, he capped the vile, placing his mixture of aloe and colloidal silver back within the depths of his bag. "Yet here you lie," he grimaced. "Burdened with the guilt of the religious—*obsessed with putting the blame on God.*"

WOOOSH—a northern wind began to blow, rumbling across the plains. Like a mighty freight train it boomed and banged, dust and ash billowing in its ever growing wake.

Job shifted his attention, watching as the air steadily darkened around him, encasing him in a shroud, isolating him from his friends.

Closer.

Closer, the mighty storm came.

Suddenly, God was in their midst.

"*WHO IS THIS WHO QUESTIONS MY WISDOM WITH IGNORANT WORDS?*" Earth's matchless Creator thundered. "*BRACE YOURSELF LIKE A MAN, BECAUSE I HAVE SOME QUESTIONS FOR YOU.*"

Terror struck Job to the core. A moment ago he had been so ready to take on the Courts of Heaven, *but now—he wasn't so sure.* He swallowed hard, forcing his legs to move. Lightning cracked. Thunder roared. The heavens opened up. A downpour began. Against the wind and the rain (and the better part of his judgment), Job rose slowly to his feet.

"Answer me *THIS*." The God of Heaven and Earth boomed. "Where were you when I created the earth? Were you the one who decided its size? Drafted its blueprints? Formed its foundations? *Tell me, since you know so much!* Have you ever ordered the morning to, 'Get up!' Or told the dawn to, 'Go to work!' Have you ever gotten to the 'true bottom of things?' Or lay the books bare regarding death's dark mysteries? Have you ever snatched the covers of darkness away from the wicked, so that they are caught red-handed, in the very act of iniquity?! Please, by all means," the Creator nodded in turn, "speak up if you have even the beginnings of an answer.."

Job was speechless.

"Can you find your way back to the pad where lightning is launched? Or locate the place from which the eastern winds blow? Can you take charge of lightning bolts, and have them report to you for orders? Or lead them home when they get lost? *Certainly you can do that!*" Elohim grinned. "You guys grew up in the same neighborhood, didn't you? ..Hung out on the same streets?!"

The God of the Universe bent low.

"Who do you suppose carves the canyons from the rain? Or maps the route of a thunderstorm? Who do you suppose fathers the dew, or mothers the ice and the frost? You don't suppose for a minute, that these marvels of weather just happen, *do you?*" Elohim held his breath politely, his massive head lingering mere inches from Job's frail frame. "Tell me," he challenged. "Are you still planning to haul me, the Mighty One, into court to press charges?"

Job was dumbfounded. His mouth was dry. His lips trembling. *There were no words.* He closed both eyes, trying to form a single coherent thought. *How was it possible, that his mind could be frantically racing and tumbleweed blank at EXACTLY the same time!* "I—I'm speechless," he stammered. "I—In awe. I should have n-never opened my mouth!" He sank to his knees. "I've … spoken way too much." His head hit the dirt. "I'm ready to shut-up and listen."

Instantly, the world went silent.

"Then, my son," Job's Creator replied in a whisper. "I want some straight answers. Do you presume to tell me that what I'm doing is wrong? Are you calling me a sinner, so you can be a saint?" Elohim shook his head and loosened a shoulder. "Do you have an arm like my arm? Can you shout in thunder the way I can?" He flashed a curt smile. "Go ahead, show off your stuff. *Let's see what you can do!*" A hearty chuckle engulfed the heavens. "Come on, unleash your outrage! Target the arrogant and lay them flat! Stop the wicked in their tracks! Better yet," he backtracked. "Just bring them to their knees. I'll gladly step aside and hand things over to you. *Surely, you can save yourself with no help from me!*"

Job wasn't even about to respond.

"My son, can you catch the serpent, Leviathan—hidden deep beneath the depths of the sea—using only a fishhook and a bobber? Can you silence his tongue? Or pierce his jaw with a spike? Can you shoot him so full of arrows that he begs you for mercy, or flatters you until you stop? Can you play with him like you would a pet goldfish? Or make him the mascot of your toddler's daycare? Would he apply for a job with you, if only to run your errands and get you coffee for the rest of his life?" Elohim threw his head back and full-on belly-laughed. "Job, if you so much as laid a hand on him, you wouldn't live to tell the story. Why, one wrong look at him would do you in!"

Elohim reached down and gently tugged on Job's chin, lifting until all eyes were locked. "My precious son, if you can't even hold your own against Leviathan," he smiled, "how can you ever expect to stand up against me? Do you really think you could confront me and get by with it?" He tilted his head, whispering in Job's attentive ear. "I'm in charge of *everything*, son. *I RUN this universe!*"

Job's heart melted. Even Elohim's rebuke felt like a loving Father's embrace! His world refocused. *Suddenly, it all made sense*: It didn't matter that he'd done things perfectly by the book. Nor, who was "technically" to blame. The only thing that had *ever* ensured his protection, or his success, was *the unwavering GOODNESS of Elohim, himself!*

Job was undone, all pride and pretense suddenly vaporized within. "I-I had heard of you before." He fumbled for the words. "B-But now I have met you face-to-face! I take back *everything* I said. I was wrong." His heart erupted in repentance. "You can do *anything* and *everything! Nothing and no one can upset your plans.*"

And with that, Job let go of everything. His body went limp, sagging in the grip of his loving Heavenly Father. He lost all track of time. Space. And his immediate surroundings. Suddenly, *anything was possible*. No longer were there limits, walls or boundaries, enemies, disease, or terrors by night. From the bottom of his heart he knew, that he knew, that he knew: *Elohim could be trusted!*

In the midst of the darkness, Daddy Elohim placed a second hand upon his son's spent torso. Lightning arched as healing fires flowed. Job contorted beneath the power of the life-giving current, his recharging body flickering like a neon light bulb.

Then it was done.

Elohim smiled, holding his child steady. "All the days of your life, I will fully restore. And your house will be great in the land. Your grandchildren's grandchildren shall you live to see. And never again, will I remove from you my righteous right hand."

Elohim took a deep breath, while Job passed out.

A sigh. A kiss. A simple grin. And the Creator of the Universe lowered his earth bound son's wilted body to the ground. *Mission accomplished!* His grin widened. *One prayer had been prayed. One portal opened. One invitation accepted!* The plan was moving along, 'full steam' ahead! *Job*—pun intended—*well done!*

Elohim stifled a jubilant chuckle. Miraculously, Heaven and

Earth had aligned—the devil had been bested. A great victory won. And while the feat was certainly worthy of much celebration, it was already time to move on.

So lifting his head, he holstered the win—donning his best fatherly frown. And rolling up both sleeves, he flashed a terse grin, turning his rebuke toward the crowd.

CH17: OUT OF EGYPT
1559:04:00:06:06:06

It was heartless. Unimaginable. It was just plain wrong. The brand new decree demanding the post-birth abortion of all male Hebrew babies was downright, *cold-blooded.*

Sure, it was just *one* decree in a long line of similar decrees hellbent on oppressing the flourishing Israeli nation. But this decree was different. This decree had brazenly crossed the line.

To be fair, it hadn't always been like this. In fact, the past few decades had been great! Ever since Israel (Abraham's grandson) had relocated to Goshen (a lovely little suburb in the meadowlands of Egypt)—business had been booming! Yet suddenly, with the rise of a new king, life had taken on a bit more of a sinister twist.

Thutmoses *('Tuht-moe-sus'),* a self-obsessed little twitch of a Pharaoh, had—in short—no respect for his father's former friends. And Israel's nefarious oppression had begun the very moment King Thut had looked around and noticed the Hebrews were, to coin his phrase exactly, "breeding like <bleeping> rabbits."

"Well—why not try and keep up?" the court's advisers advised, touting the fact that the descendants of Israel commonly used a sort of "heightened male experience" to ensure such stunning maternal success.

"And what would you have me do?" The Pharaoh huffed. *"Mandate the circumcision of every man in Egypt?!"* Thutmoses shook his head. Everyone knew, that sort of blatant belly-flop into the untempered waters of Egyptian pop-culture was at best, "a hack," and at worst, "political suicide." *No*—it was much more PC to murder millions of faceless babies than it was to murder millions of sensitive foreskins. Besides, truth be told, the Pharaoh was kind of—*uhm*—

personally attached to his.

So, with no interest in facing the political backlash—nor any desire to depress the Egyptian economy should Israel decide to "up-and-leave"—the only practical, and indeed advantageous solution was to: "Enslave the Hebrew masses."

And enslave them, he did.

There was just one problem. When all one has time to do is work, eat, and sleep—and then repeat, repeat, repeat—one tends to look for expedient and affordable ways to, "blow off some extra steam." And thus, one tends to breed *even more,* "like <bleeping> rabbits."

Israel's population exploded.

And so did the vein in Pharaoh's neck.

"Effective immediately," the purple-faced dictator shrieked, "all Hebrew baby boys shall be thrown into the river!"

Of course, that was exactly what Elohim had been waiting for—and so, he sent Moses.

—| 1556:03:27:18:08:13 |—

"AaggghhhH!" Jochebed *('Joe-keh-bed')* gritted her teeth, grinding hard against the age-riddled riding strap jutting from the corners of her mouth.

Her contractions intensified.

"Push, Jochey, *push!* Breathe, Jochey, *breathe!*" A duo of round-faced, heavy-set, grandmotherly-type, Egyptian midwives cheered in grinning unison.

"gAAaggghhHH!" Jochey shrieked again, making absolutely no attempt to comply.

The midwives gave each other a "knowing look."

One shrugged.

Oh well—Jochey could do what she wanted. The whole "breathe, push, breathe" thing was mostly for distraction.

Slowly, the contractions subsided.

Jochey glanced wildly around for Amram, her strikingly

handsome, six-foot-four husband. In the pastel glow of the flickering candlelight she could make out his towering silhoutte, hunkered diligently over their baked-clay fire-pit, feverishly stoking a large pot of water to boil.

"Remind me again. *Why is he doing that?*" She raised a threatening eyebrow.

The midwives gave each other a "knowing look."

One shrugged. "Mostly for distraction."

"AgghhhHHH—," the final contraction hit—*HARD!*

Jochey bore down.

"Aghhh—Waaaaahhh," a new cry joined the mix. It was the piercing angelic wail of one flailing baby ... *boy?*

Jochey swallowed hard.

The midwives doted and purred, doing their best to push past the massive elephant that had just entered the room. A quick snip here, a secure tuck there, and within a matter of minutes they were handing the handsome little trespasser back to his exhausted yet overjoyed mother.

Another shriek.

This time, of pure delight.

"He glows!" Jochey beamed.

"Yes dear," came the midwives' canned reply. "They all do."

"No—really," she gasped, pulling back the swaddle to expose one perfectly bronzed baby-face.

The midwives did a sharp double-take, two voluptuous chins simultaneously hitting the floor. *The boy WAS indeed ... glowing.*

"What shall we call him?" Amram's baritone voice crashed the paranormal peering party. "Simon, Albert—Noah?" He tossed another log onto his faltering fire. "Daniel, Ichabod—Am Jr?"

Jochey absentmindedly nodded, her gaze never shifting, both eyes glued to her little golden masterpiece.

Amram stood and scratched his head, waiting for what he hoped would be some sort of further clarification. A grunt? A shrug? ..A reassuring wink?

Nothing.

He threw up both hands and sank slowly back to his

sputtering flames.

No one really seemed to notice.

"Let's see," the midwives chatted cordially amongst themselves, thumbing through a bulky checklist, busily preparing to leave. "Bed-sheets to the launders. Afterbirth to the dressers. A copy of *Concealing Newborns for Dummies* to the parents. And, of course—a smattering of pink blanketry to detour any nosy onlookers!" They unloaded a pile of fresh linen into Amram's long arms.

"But what will you tell the Pharaoh?" Jochey wanted to know.

"Oh dear child, we'll tell him what we always tell him," they giggled. "Your Excellence, the Hebrew women have their babies so quickly that we cannot possibly get there in time!"

"Yes—," the other chimed in. "They are not slow to birth like the Egyptians!"

They gave each other a "knowing look," and burst out laughing.

Jochey smiled, watching as they headed for the door—waving, hugging, and giggling their way out into the brisk, dark night. *One thing was certain,* Jochey snuggled her little man with all her might, *no matter what happened, God would take care of them. Besides,* she lifted her head, flashing one final goodbye grin, *those two were great at distractions.*

—| 1556:00:03:09:11:12 |—

Appearances were fading. The news was spreading. Three months had quickly come and gone; and already, the neighbors were beginning to notice—the whole "pink blanket thing" wasn't entirely adding up.

Jochey frowned, glancing out the window towards the group of nosy Egyptian Medjay (the king's personal gestapo) relentlessly patrolling her neighborhood. *How much longer until the cat was finally out of the bag?* she couldn't help but wonder. *And what then?* A shudder erupted down her spine. *She couldn't just let her baby boy die!*

"Heaven—*help!*" The heartfelt prayer erupted unexpectedly from deeply troubled lips.

"What did Noah do when HIS world was about to end?" a quiet thought surfaced.

Noah? Jochey squinted, her thoughts returning to long-forgotten, fireside stories at the feet of her great grandfather. *Yea—uhm, uh—that's right,* she perked up. *He made a safe-space. He made a boat!*

An image flashed before her eyes.

Small. Cute. Covered. A basket, woven from tar and reeds, sailing quietly down the Nile. She practically squealed with delight—*she would make a boat!*

Immediately she went to work constructing the tiny craft. All night long she labored; weaving, wrapping, waterproofing, waxing. Lining her creation with pillows and blankets. Arranging her precious cargo comfortably inside.

"Miriam!" she called, in the wee hours of the morning. "We must go. *Quickly!*"

Together, mother and daughter gathered their belongings. And with the dawning Goshen sun stretching pink across the plains, headed promptly for the banks of the Nile.

"May the God of our Fathers be your constant guide." Jochey choked back tears, setting her precious bundle gently aglide the river's slow lapping waters. "And may his steadfast hand prosper you all the days of your life." She planted a lingering kiss squarely in the center of her little man's forehead, stealing one last glance around.

The coast was clear.

Quietly, she pushed the boat among the reeds.

Tears erupted. She choked them back, bending and dipping her empty jug into the chilly waters below. Hurriedly she gathered the hydration needed for the day. The only thought holding her together, was the fact that she knew—*without a shadow of doubt*—this plan had come straight from Heaven.

"Please keep watch from a distance," she directed Miriam, her little sentinel helper. "Wait until you see exactly what happens to your little.."

Jochey's voice broke, she could say no more.

"Sure thing, Mom!" Miriam grinned, flopping down among a

patch of cattails about a dozen feet away. "I won't leave his side."

The words brought surprising comfort. Jochebed turned to go, blowing her babies a thousand heartfelt kisses as she slowly departed.

Miriam watched and waited, settling into her post as her mother faded silently..

into..

the..

"*MAKE WAY … MAKE WAY!*" the cry exploded all around.

Miriam bolted upright, rubbing sleep laden eyes. *How long was she out?* She spun around, quietly parting the reeds in front of her. A large band of royals noisily stepped into focus. *Was that the palace entourage?!* She squinted at the colorful banners and flags flying high. *No doubt about it. Hatshepsut ('Hat-shep-suit'), the Pharaoh's daughter, was headed her way!*

Miriam did her best to stay low. She could hear the princess' infectious laughter as she chatted amiably among her personal attendees. The group seemed to be moving steadily down the rolling riverbanks towards a divinely prescribed bathing location.

As if on cue, one tiny wicker basket began to cry.

Hatshepsut wheeled to a halt, peering down between the reeds. "Fetch me that basket!" she beckoned the nearest attendant.

Miriam watched as the makeshift watercraft was carefully plucked from the Nile.

Hatshepsut peeked inside. "What a gift the gods have brought me!" The princess giggled, reaching down and drawing her discovery up from the raft.

Her entourage went wild.

"It's one of the Hebrew babies! Yes—a Hebrew baby," the attendees proclaimed.

Hatshepsut's heart melted. The baby was so adorably cute— so helpless and literally glowing. She was instantly smitten. Her maid-servants "oohed" and "ahhed," as she snuggled her unexpected find.

There was a giggle and a burp.

Deep down inside, Hatshepsut just knew—she *had* to keep

him.

"What shall we call you?" the princess smiled. "Thutmoses, like my father and brother?" She paused a thoughtful moment, sorting through the potential confusion. Her eyes lit up. "How about ... *Moses!* For I have *drawn you up* from the Nile!"

She laughed, delighted by her own clever thought.

The baby began to cry.

"There, there." Hatshepsut rocked him gently. "I'm sure you'll grow to love it!"

The baby cried louder.

Hatshepsut furrowed her brow. The infant seemed hungry and searching for food. She patted his back, and cradled his head. But he only cried harder. *What else—could she do?*

"Excuse me!" a sweet little voice rang out. "Your majesty?"

Hatshepsut looked up, somewhat surprised to see Miriam, the spunky little sun-baked brunette, standing so boldly before her.

"Shall I go and get one of the Hebrew women to nurse this baby for you?" the little girl offered. She stepped forward, motioning to the now inconsolable infant.

The question was like music to Hatshepsut's ears.

"Please ... do!" she laughed, her burdens instantly lifting. "And—when this baby is fully weened," she caught the young girl by the arm, "return him to me. For I will certainly pay you well!"

Now it was Miriam who couldn't stop laughing. *Paid to save and raise her own brother? —The plan. The princess. The raft. The request. It was all too good to be true!*

With a wide-eyed nod, she gathered her baby brother in her arms, cradling him tight. Then, with her best royal-entourage, "thank you so much" curtsy, she turned and fled for home.

CH18: DAMAGE CONTROL

It was a bit of a toss-up, which smelled worse: *the stench of burning sulfur … or wet fur coat.*

According to Prophet, "BOTH were *equally* appalling." The unholy shaman dropped, rather uncomfortably, into his chair across from BEAST.

BEAST, already seated, was anxiously drumming his fingers, eagerly awaiting the evening's Square Table festivities.

Prophet sniffed and glared.

BEAST glared back.

"So … what do you have to say for yourself?" Prophet snidely remarked.

"Just following orders," the brooding ox snarled, a fresh batch of putrid steam rising from his bristling shoulders. His scowl darkened. He was fully convinced that *burning sulfur was, BY FAR, the worst scent. After all, he should know,* he breathed in deep to reconfirm, *seeing as he was the one WEARING the wet fur coat.*

Prophet glared harder.

BEAST pulled out a crumpled up sticky-note, squinting at its illegible chicken-scratch orders. "One." He read. "Hang out in the Nile. Two. Swallow up hallowed baby. Three," he donned a pair of extra-thick, over-sized reading glasses. "Spit out wicker basket.."

"..And?" interrupted Prophet, immediately miffed that BEAST had done no more than *ONE* of the aforementioned tasks. "What happened?"

BEAST shrugged. "I wasn't exactly counting on the Pharaoh's daughter actually *having* a heart."

Prophet glared hardest. "You mean to say, we have to smell—

THIS," he gestured over-theatrically, which for him amounted to nothing more than the slightest of head nods,"—*for nothing?*"

"Actually *THIS*—," BEAST mocked the gesture, "came from swimming across the river Styx, on my way to the meeting."

Prophet's jaw almost dropped. He regained control, slowly raising a condescending eyebrow.

"Yup," BEAST expounded. "I had long since dried off from my prearranged dip in the Nile, when I sorta … *uh … missed the portal to get here.*" He paused a moment to shake off the under-whelmingly pathetic feeling of embarrassment he suspected was being projected by Prophet towards himself. "Instead—," he shrugged, "I came on foot."

"On foot?" Prophet raised the other eyebrow.

"Yup," nodded BEAST, pulling out a second sticky-note. "One. Locate Dante's Inferno. Two. Descend, due south. Three. Forge the river, Styx. Four. Follow the smell."

He slammed the note down hard on the table. "*SEE?*" He glowered at his stoic, stick-in-the-mud friend. "The fact that I sit here before you *PROVES* the smell of burning sulfur is *MUCH* more potent." He leaned back and smirked, placing two giant smoldering hands behind one giant smoldering head. "At first," he smugly confessed, "I was a bit irritated to have missed the portal. But I must say, I'm rather enjoying it now!"

The mighty ox closed his eyes and exhaled slowly.

Prophet tried not to gag.

"Gentlemen—," Ha-satan finally spoke up. "Enough, is *enough!*" He took a deep breath, clearly enjoying the fact that he was breathing through a fully-enclosed, fully-ventilated, air-filtering, air-cooling, air-conditioned helmet. "Riddle me this," the brooding overlord released the set of keys he was toying with and leaned forward. "Superstars come and superstars go—but gatekeepers rule the world."

He paused—mostly for dramatic effect—waiting for their stellar replies.

Instead he got—blank stares.

"..*CONTROL* gentlemen." He rolled his eyes. "Have you never heard, it's all about *CONTROL?*" He growled his dissatisfaction and tried again. "Why should we continue to seek the destruction of the earthlings that El-ohhh-you-know-who favors," he gestured skyward. "When we can simply *CONTROL* them?"

More blank stares.

Ha-satan shook his head, *was he really going to have to spell this out?* "Moses, gentlemen. I'm talking about Moses." He frowned. "That basket-case has got more potential in his left pinky, than the two of you have, *combined.*" He straightened up, fidgeting hands returning to the set of keys dangling from his shoulder. "Boys—you tell me. Why should we kill all that potential, when we can simply *absorb* it into *our* system?" His countenance immediately began to lighten. "As long as *we* retain control, we can use this kid's gifts like a tool, to meet *our* needs." The dark lord stared at his clueless cohorts, an element of disgust beginning to rise. "Bottom line. It's not about talent, Gentlemen. Not money, comfort, or fame. It's not about power, or even how the world will perceive your "good" name. When you're truly at the top, boys, it's all about one thing. It's ALL about *CONTROL.*"

One by one, the light bulbs flickered on.

Prophet spoke first. "So … if we embrace the potential—human and all—we can use the earthling, even *with* his impenetrable firewall of Elohim's protection for our *own* personal benefits?"

Ha-satan waited and watched.

"..because he who *controls* it all—*OWNS IT ALL!*" BEAST slowly finished, gears finally clicking.

"Ta-Daa!" welcoming arms shot out wide. *Maybe there was hope for these two, after all.* "Our primary objective," Ha-satan grinned, "is no longer about killing the potential. Instead, we'll simply *control* it." He leaned back in his chair, kicking his feet across the corner of the table. *He was proud of himself. Why hadn't he thought of this sooner?* "Tell me." He smirked. "By promoting those who listen to us *above* those who listen to Elohim—do we not ultimately *control them both?!*" The dark overlord put both hands behind his huge, helmeted head and sighed a deep, air-conditioned sigh. "Yes gentlemen, *WE* run this show—." His voice was back to a purr. "Let good ol' El-o Cap-i-tan favor whom-so-ever he chooses—it makes no difference to us—*WE* will keep *ALL the control!*"

—| 1552:03:01:18:08:13 |—

The day of adoption had arrived! Once again, Miriam found herself standing before the beautiful daughter of Pharaoh in nervous anticipation. This time, however, she had her entire family and a four-year-old Moses in tow.

"Welcome to the palace," Hatshepsut knelt, grabbing her new son's adorable adopted cheeks. "You will make a fine, young prince!"

Moses sneezed and grinned.

Then he picked his nose.

The princess threw her head back and laughed, hugging him close. "I see we have some serious work to do!" she giggled, tousling his mop of curly-cue hair. With a wink and a grin she turned back to his family. "And now, the formalities!" she waved them forward.

Papers were signed.

Compensations given.

One Hebrew head was shaved.

The princess called for a robe and a ring—and just a hint of eyeliner. Then, taking the hand of the cutest wide-eyed Egyptian prince that you ever did see, she walked her god-given, river-son boldly into his grand new adventure!

...

The transition was seamless. Moses took to the palace like a fish to the sea. In no time at all, he was racing through its halls. Splashing in its fountains. Carousing in its stables. And excelling in its schools. He was an excellent marksmen, a skilled warrior, and aside from a bit of a stutter, a gifted statesmen. At fourteen, he was put in charge of the local Medjay; at eighteen, the Imperial Palace Guards. There was never a day when he did not perform his civic duties without excellence, character, and quality. Even his princess mother fell prey to the obscene amounts of providential favor continually funneled his way. She too, rose like magic through the ranks, taking the throne amidst a turn of jaw-dropping, gossip-worthy, heaven-directed events. And although she was eventually pressured into marrying her younger half-brother, Thutmoses II (a move demoting Moses to third in line); tensions had eased, and burdens had lifted. And for the Children of Israel, the future was looking increasingly bright.

WOOSH—then, it happened. A brick flew by, inches from Moses' head. The rockstar prince spun around, squinting into the brilliant desert sun.

WHIZ—a second brick followed close behind.

Moses set his jaw, shielding his eyes. A Hebrew slave, it seemed, was in the process of completely ignoring his supervising guard's repeated orders. Their ensuing scuffle appeared to be very real, very explosive, and very well underway.

"Fall back in line!" the fuming guard roared.

The slave bobbed and weaved as ... *crack—CRACK, crack—CRACK* the guard's whip came raining down, again and again across his hands and back.

SWOOSH—another brick was thrown.

Moses flinched, his thoughts suddenly back with his own Hebrew family. He saw their names and faces, their laughter and pain. He felt their frustrations. Considered their shame. Empathy flared. Compassion hit his heart. Like it or not, these "slaves" were people ... *his* people.

CRACK—the guard's whip finally made connection.

"Gerrrrrrr—ahhhh!" the faltering slave, at last, began to comply, struggling to retrieve his fallen pack. But somewhere between the beating, the shifting sand, and his work-weary legs, he just couldn't get the job done.

A final brick rained down. This time, it was the guard, callously bouncing the sun-dried bludgeon off the back of the stooped slave's head. Blood gushed freely. The man sputtered and stumbled, clutching his gaping wound.

That was the final straw.

Something in Moses snapped. A bellow erupted. He drew his sword and began the long, determined walk toward the clamoring duo. His perception narrowed, tunneling until all he could see was the injustice, all he could feel was the pain. He never broke stride. Two feet from the offending officer, the furious prince flipped his blade high in the air.

The guard glanced at Moses.

Moses glanced at the guard.

The guard flashed a wicked grin and stepped aside, assuming his commanding officer had come to get in on a piece of the action.

For the briefest of moments, everything paused: The slave. The guard. The prince. The blade.

BOOM—Moses lunged forward, head up, fist down. His well-practiced arm dropping the airborne blade in a fraction of an instant, butt first.

Game over.

The guard crumpled to the ground like a broken rag doll.

Moses dropped to one knee, skillfully hiding the lifeless body in the burning desert sand. Slowly he rose, dusting off sandy hands and looking around, half expecting to fend off the victory celebration that was certain to follow.

Crickets.

The young prince turned, a slow 360, scratching his wondering head. *Nothing? No one?*

His eyes darted about. Left. Then right. The street seemed strangely deserted. *Was his sentiment not shared?*

Confusion flooded his soul. Freedom had arrived, yet not so much as the slave he had just "saved," was anywhere to be found.

—| 1517:08:19:02:22:20 |—

It was the same camp. Same street. Same exact location. Twenty-four hours had come and gone. And once again, a fight was going down.

This time, it was two Hebrews.

Moses shook his head, for a second time stepping up to the plate. "Why are you hitting your fellow Hebrew?" he challenged the first, forcing his way through the growing ring of onlookers. "Don't you know that you two are brothers?"

"And who are you?" the aggressor retorted. "That you

should preside as judge and jury?" He turned to Moses, eyeing his unsheathed sword. "Are you planning on killing me like you killed that Egyptian?"

Moses froze. His world went cold. *If even THESE men knew,* he shuddered, *than who DOESN'T know?* Panic hit. His legs went numb. *How could he have been so foolish? ..so misguided? To brazenly draw a line and then to step so carelessly across it—alone.*

He stumbled back, fighting to keep his whits and balance, stuttering something about, "..n-n-not being his brother's bee keeper.." Then he blushed and turned, and promptly exited the scene.

Rushing home, he grabbed one fresh horse, his money purse, and a proper disguise. *It would only be a matter of time,* he swallowed hard, *until his man-slaughtering mugshot was plastered high across the walls of every post office throughout Egypt. Then HE would be the next Egyptian buried under six feet of burning desert sand.*

He urged his horse to a blistering gallop. Dread seemed hot on his heels. There was only one place to go. One place he could ever hope to hide and blend in. One place, where they would *never* find him.

His horse flew fast along the promenade, down through the city gates. Cobblestone turned to grass. Grass into thistles. And thistles into rocks and sand. But Moses never slowed. Not until the sun had long ago gone down, and he was securely lost—deep, deep, deep in the heart of the Midian wilderness.

CH19: TALKING TO SHRUBS
1479:00:03:03:00:03

The day was hot.

Too hot..

Moses walked the length of the sandstone ledge he'd been using as a makeshift bench, searching for a bit of reprieve. Mount Horeb loomed red-hot before him. The Midian desert stretched blazing, alongside. All around, his Father-in-law's flock of long-haired Arabian sheep lazed lethargically about, baking in the blistering heat.

Moses paused to wipe his brow. *My, my—things were different now.* A wife, two sons—a large flock of his own. Forty-nine years had passed since his sudden exodus from Egypt and that pretentious world of cut-throat aristocracy had all but been forgotten; buried beneath layers of dusty Midianite robes, a thick desert-dweller's accent, and one 'way more salt than pepper' beard.

At last—a suitable shadow found!

Quick grin, and Moses dropped to the ground, ducking below the ledge and tucking himself neatly into his new best friend's ever waning depths.

Uhm—what was that?

The seasoned shepherd squinted, staring up near the peak of Mount Horeb.

There it was again.

He raised a hand to shield his eyes, the afternoon heat rising from the rocky terrain like a flickering wall of water—dark against the towering backdrop of sandy tans and whites.

Was that … a single burning shrub?

Intrigued, Moses cocked his head. "Now that's a sight for

sore eyes!" he chuckled to no one in particular, settling back to enjoy the show.

Half-an-hour passed.

Then another.

Then two more.

The little shrub was still going strong.

Impossible, Moses frowned, *—wasn't it?* His mind began to wonder: *Maybe it was actually a really large shrub really far off? ..Or perhaps there was a pile of something much more robust burning directly behind said shrubbery? ..Or maybe, like the flickering heat, this was some sort of plasmatic optical illusion?*

Finally, curiosity killed the cat.

Moses pushed himself to his feet. *A bush that didn't burn,* he grinned. *This he had to see.*

Experienced eyes scanned the horizon. *Nothing out of the ordinary, his sheep would be alright for now.* The curious sheep-herder reached over, lifting his goat-skin canteen and sturdy shepherd's rod.

It was time to investigate.

Fifteen minutes was all it took. Moses could have laughed out loud. The burning bush was much closer—and much tinier—than anticipated. He peered intently at the strange and puzzling sight. The shrub couldn't have been more than eighteen inches tops, yet colorful flames danced nearly seven feet high from its strikingly un-singed branches.

For a long while Moses stood—transfixed and amused—gazing into the multi-colored flames.

Then he saw it.

He took a step forward. *There! In the flames.* It was almost as if he could see the outline of a..

"MOSES!" Elohim interrupted from the midst of the bush.

Moses jumped with a start. The voice rattled his bones, booming from every direction. For a moment he faltered. "H-Here I a-am?" he managed a flustered reply.

"Come no closer," the God of the Universe warned. "Take off your sandals, for the place where you are standing is holy ground."

Moses swallowed hard, bending to remove his shoes. *Clearly

he was in the presence of..

"I am the God of your fathers," Elohim introduced himself. "Of Abraham, Isaac, and Jacob."

Moses fumbled with his straps. His hands trembled. He blanched. *Who but the patriarchs ever looked upon God and lived? Certainly his timid, blood-tainted soul was not to be included in such an elite group?* Fear hit him like a rabid grizzly. He groped for the hem of his robe, pulling it up to cover his face. *He was unworthy.*

So unworthy.

..Wasn't he?

A frenzied kick loosed his remaining shoe.

He bowed low to the ground.

"I have seen the oppression of my people," Elohim lamented. "Their cry has reached my ears." Energy like an ocean's tide surged from the midst of his presence. " Now—*GO!* I am sending you to Pharaoh. *You* must lead my people out of Egypt."

What in the—what?! The weight of Elohim's words came crashing down upon Moses' broad shoulders. Immediately, he was backpedaling, trying to do the math:

One burning bush + One old shepherd's curiosity = LET MY PEOPLE GO?!

He shook his head. *Oh no, no, no—Heaven had stumbled upon the WRONG ex-con for this job. Clearly, this was a case of mistaken identity. Some sort of intergalactic clerical error.* Two bushy eyebrows furrowed knowingly—*probably due to his mountain-man beard.*

"Wh-Who am I, that I-I should go to Pharaoh and bring the Israelites out of E-E-Egypt?" Moses stammered.

Whenever he got flustered, Moses stammered. He couldn't help it, it was the residual side-effect of a particular "open fire incident" that had transpired within the first few years of his forty-year tenure in Pharaoh's court. A side-effect, he had been mercilessly teased about growing up. Over time, he'd been able to mitigate its effects with silence, prudent speech, and the occasional beat down. Yet here it was again, roaring back as awkward and debilitating as ever!

Elohim full on belly-laughed, he could scarcely believe his

ears. *Who was Moses?!* he braced his heaving sides. *Only the kid he'd hand-plucked from the Nile, placed in the house of Pharaoh, trained in the courts of Egypt, saved from certain imprisonment, and now personally commissioned to free his people.*

The Author of Life smiled fondly at his floundering creation. "I will certainly be with you," he assured. "In fact, this will be the sign to you that it is I who have sent you: When you have brought my people out of Egypt, you will worship God on this very same mountain."

The eternal ramifications of that divinely inspired statement flew right over Moses' spinning head. *Right now, he wouldn't be detoured.* "Who s-shall I say sent me?" he charged.

"I Am, that *I AM.*"

"Who shall I t-talk to?"

"The elders of Israel, and the king of Egypt."

"W-What shall I say?"

"I will give you the words."

"And if n-no one believes me?"

Here Elohim paused. "What's that in your hand?"

Moses looked down, lifting both his canteen and his staff simultaneously—almost as if it were a trick question.

"What's that in your *hand*?" Elohim reemphasized.

Moses let the canteen fall back to his waist. "A staff..?" he carefully replied.

"Throw it down."

Moses did as he was told.

Instantly, the staff was writhing and hissing, winding and coiling—a snake, ready to strike.

gAhhhHH—Moses nearly toppled himself to get away. He glared at the monstrous red serpent, dark venom dripping from its wide, gaping jaws.

"Pick it up," Elohim boomed. "Lift it by the tail!"

Moses cringed, *everyone knew that lifting a venomous snake by the tail meant certain death.* He glanced from the unconsumable talking bush back to the hissing, snapping stick-snake. *Then again— so did confronting a Pharaoh, and/or chatting face-to-face with the God of the Universe.*

Without another thought, Moses did as he was told.

Immediately, the snake became a rod.

Mhmm—Moses couldn't hide his disdain, his eyes nervously darting up and down the smooth staff in his hand. Understandably, he no longer wanted to hold it, but there was *no way* he was setting it down again.

Slowly, he started to back away.

"Place your hand inside your cloak," a seemingly oblivious Elohim redirected.

Reluctant, Moses complied, bracing himself for the sign that was certain to follow: *A mighty whirlwind? A blinding flash of light? A distant explosion?*

Nothing.

He opened one eye. Then the other. Gradually, he pulled out his hand. *Touché,* his stomach lurched. *The skin on his hand was dead and decayed—leprous as pure driven snow.*

"Now put your hand *back,* inside your cloak."

Moses plunged his hand deep within the recesses of his billowing robe. Out it came—tan and healthy. *Perfectly restored.*

He breathed a sigh of relief.

"..And if they won't believe the first two signs, they will *certainly* believe the third," Elohim grinned. "Take some water out of the Nile and pour it on the ground. Before their eyes, it will become blood."

Moses was reeling. *Sticks to snakes, water to blood, unsightly rotting flesh—wasn't this all just a little bit much?!* Insecure eyes dropped to the security of wilderness-worn feet. *He was so much better at tending to sheep—quiet, calm, UNEVENTFUL ... sheep.*

There was a long moment of courage-building silence.

"P-pardon your servant, Lord," the overwhelmed shepherd finally blurted out. "At the r-risk of offending you: Y-You don't want me—I am slow of t-tongue and s-speech." Moses bowed low, letting his clear-cut resignation slowly sink in. *Strike him dead, he didn't care;* the thought of returning to face Pharaoh seemed a far worse fate.

Elohim crossed his arms and grinned, his champion wasn't getting off that easy! "Who gave mankind their mouths?" he chided. "Who makes them deaf or mute? —*Is it not I, the Lord?*" His voice grew resolute. "Now—*GO!* I will be with your mouth and teach you *exactly* what to say!"

"But I-I—," Moses' heart sank. *What could he do?* He had just been sentenced to a fate worse than death.

"I *know* the king of Egypt will not let you go," Elohim relented, sensing Moses' cry. "Therefore, I will stretch out my hand and strike Egypt with all kinds of wonders." A reassuring laugh rose amiably from his belly. "*Do not fear*, when I am finished with him, he will be *compelled* to let you go!"

A showdown?! ..with Pharaoh?! Now Moses was no longer afraid—*he was terrified!* His stomach knotted and pitched. His knees went weaker than weak. "Lord p-please!" He begged. "Send someone else!"

Then Elohim's anger burned—Haylel leapt up from the seat where he sat watching in the Heavenlies. Keys in hand, he strode towards the viewing portal. *Enough was enough*, the fiery cherub blazed. *It was time to put this waffling buffoon out of his misery, once and for all.*

WAIT—! Elohim raised a staying hand. Clearly Moses did not comprehend the immediate consequences of rejecting a face-to-face commission with the spoken Word of God. *Or better yet*, Elohim smiled, *he didn't care*. Either way, his budding patriarch would simply have to comply.

"And what of your brother Aaron?" the master chess player pivoted. "I *know* he can speak well! You shall speak to him the words I give you. And he, in turn, shall speak them to others." Elohim dusted off his hands, delighted with the re-adjustment. "Yes—you will be as God to him, just as I am God to you."

"B-Buu—," Moses opened his mouth, the words literally vaporizing in his throat. Every fiber of his being was vehemently opposed—*yet why could he feel himself nodding?* His eyes grew wide as saucers. His mouth, dry as the desert sand. He could feel his lips beginning to move. "I will go," he relented, the words somehow spilling out on their own. "Yes—my Lord … I will go."

Outraged, Haylel dropped back to his seat.

Moses fell, stunned, to the ground.

Only Elohim was left smiling. *Like it or not,* he chuckled, *Heaven's plan was coming together!*

…

The Word lifted his head and smiled, already Moses was back on the move. He watched his newest general picking his way back down the mountain, moving towards his ever restless sheep, fading slowly into the distance.

Heaven's best-kept secret raised his hand, he was fading slowly too. His fiery silhouette disappearing from the midst of the shrub, returning to the spirit-realm from which he'd come.

Soon, all flames were gone. All smoke and sparks had ceased. In fact, the only persisting evidence that the infinite, omnipotent God of the Universe had ever intervened in the earthbound affairs of any mortal man, was a tiny blooming shrub blowing gently in the breeze.

It was at precisely that moment that Elohim turned toward Heaven and called out his greeting. "Anointed Cherub," he boomed. "ARISE!"

Immediately Haylel stood to his feet. Stepping up to the viewing portal, he snapped to attention.

"Well—whadda ya think?" Elohim put him at ease.

"Shoulda let me take him out while we had the chance," the disgruntled angel grouched. "Now we've gotta rely on the unlimited prowess of a … stuttering fool."

"A fool who will most certainly need *your* unconditional backing!" Elohim chuckled. "And your covering!"

The restless Cherub scowled.

"Ahw—he's not so bad. I'll be with him," Elohim grinned mischievously. "Stutters aside, what do you think of the signs I gave him?"

Haylel's scowl deepened. *He had certainly seen the human's pitiful reactions. Why—,* he squinted, squelching any rising understanding, *was he supposed to think something else?*

Elohim quietly examined his Chief Executive Officer's lackluster reaction. *So smart. So shrewd. So sure of himself. Yet, so unwilling to look deeper … Why—?* his heart saddened. *Was Moses' staff transforming into a sly, slithering snake, not a clear enough sign? What about Moses' right hand emerging as Death—and then again as Life? —too convoluted? Certainly the public display of 'life-giving water' becoming 'spilled-innocent blood' was nothing short of a dead giveaway … right?*

The Father of Lights slowly shook his head. *How was his right-hand man—his own, personal staff—so unwilling to consider even the most obvious of parallels?*

It was egregious.

"There will be certain signs you'll need to perform." Elohim turned back to the matter at hand. "Certain duties you'll need to fulfill." He motioned towards the Cherub's coveted set of keys. "Effective immediately, you're on standby … understand?"

Haylel nodded apprehensively, a little miffed that Elohim would force him to agree like a child. Still, the brooding angel was more interested in derailing the developing plot than in pointing out perceived belittlings. Besides, being the micromanaging legalist he had been created to be, he couldn't help but notice one glaring inconsistency.

"There is one slight—*ahem*—challenge." Haylel cleared what already seemed to be a very clear throat. "A certain *hypocrisy,* that if left unchecked, I'm afraid will, unfortunately, lead to our hero's ultimate demise."

"Yes?" probed Elohim, already knowing exactly where this was going.

"It's widely known," Haylel feigned concern, "that Moses' youngest son does not bear—*ahem*—the mark." The trickster batted puppy-dog eyes, careful to observe his Master's most subtle reactions. "How can I, in good conscious—and to the letter of the law—uphold the words of a man who does not himself uphold the words of God Almighty?" *Check*—Haylel squinted haughty eyes, sliding his proverbial Rook across the board to face his rival's king.

Elohim nodded his understanding. "Certainly, without

Heaven's covenant mark," he affirmed the bold move, "Moses is no more under our graces than the Pharaoh he goes to confront." One perfectly manicured hand stroked one perfectly manicured chin. "Therefore, it stands to reason, that any justice demanded of the Pharaoh *must* be demanded of our Champion as well." Heaven's Infallible Defender leaned in, hoping his opponent was picking up what he was laying down. "Even so—do *not* lay a finger on our Champion until *after* he has arrived in Egypt," he reached out and Castled his king, lifting it effortlessly out of harm's way. "Remember, Predictive Policing is *never* an excuse for a preemptive strike. You know as well as anyone, that with men and angels—there are NEVER any guarantees … understand?"

Haylel swallowed the snarl that leapt from his belly. "Got it," he huffed. "I am, *and will always be*—at your service."

He bowed low.

Very low.

Ah—who was he kidding, he held his disingenuous pose, *serving this progressively puritanical dictatorship was quickly becoming ALL about appearances.* For a long moment he paused, calculating his next move. Then—with a grunt, a growl, and a bit of a scowl—he vanished into thin air.

Elohim didn't waste another second. "*Go!*" he turned, nudging The Word, still hidden safely within the depths of his thick, immersive presence. "Be sure our hypocrite is no longer a hypocrite by the time he reaches the borders of Egypt!"

—| 1479:00:02:23:00:11 |—

The trip back to his father-in-law's house was anything but typical.

Snake sticks?

Divine appointments?

Talking shrubs?

Moses' head was spinning. *Was he really going to confront Egypt's Pharaoh with a burning message from God?* He swallowed hard, railing against the watermelon-sized lump in his throat—*the thought alone, made him want to lose his lunch!* Powerful shoulders slumped.

Somehow, he'd been outplayed. Outmatched. Outmaneuvered. How was it, that in only a moment, his world had gone from '*Little House on the Prairie*' to full on '*Lord of the Rings?*'

He wheeled to a stop, squinting his confusement. *Still—he HAD teamed up with the great, 'I Am, that I Am.'* He slowly lifted an eyebrow, followed by an arm. *And that meant everything was going to be OK ... didn't it?*

For the hundredth time Moses opened his hand and threw down his staff; watching it shift and twist, snap and hiss before his wide, unbelieving eyes.

He thought for a moment. Then, lay hold of its tail.

Surely this sign—, he slowly lifted the supernaturally straightening rod, *was given to convince ... ME.*

—| 1479:00:02:22:07:17 |—

When Moses finally arrived home, you can imagine the evening's dinner conversation:

Father-in-Law, Jethro: "So, how was your day?"

Moses: "Pretty amazing actually ... I saw a bush."

Jethro: "A bush?" <chuckles> "That sounds ... pretty amazing."

Moses: "Well—it was burning."

Jethro: "Oh—spontaneous combustion." <light bulb flickers on> "Must have been a scorcher." <He settles back> "I've only seen that happen two or three ... *hundred* times over the years—usually to a bush." <flashes a mischievous grin> "Now sheep, on the other hand, that's an entirely different story.."

Moses: "It didn't burn."

Jethro: "Yes.. *uh*, what? It—didn't burn?"

Moses: "It burned, but it didn't burn."

Jethro: <two eyebrows slowly raise>

Moses: "Yea. Watched it for hours—for two hours." <shifting uncomfortably> "A tiny, little, bitty bush. It never burned. Not so much as.."

Jethro: "Ohhh—." <slow head scratch> "Strange. Can't say I've ever seen that. All the shrubs, or sheep, I've ever watched were pretty well ... combusted." <raises his fork> "Tasty tho."

Moses: "I went to go see it.."

Jethro: <chewing his food> "Up close?"

Moses: "Mmm" <casually nods>

Jethro: "Anything unusual?"

Moses: "Well—," <long pause> "it kinda spoke to me."

Jethro: <swigging his drink> "Metaphorically?"

Moses: "No—it had an accent."

<beverage spews>

Jethro: "Ha!" <wiping his mouth> "Good one! That's funny. Are my cheeks red?!" <offers Moses a napkin> "For a second there, you had me going—all wrapped up in your big, tall tale." <his grin widens>

Moses: <dabbing his face> "It told me to take off my shoes.."

Jethro: <jaw drops>

Moses: <still dabbing> "And to go to Egypt."

Jethro: "This ... isn't a joke?"

Moses: <shakes his head>

Jethro: "*Ohhh*—." <deeply concerned> "So, you actually *had* a conversation with a shrub?" <he squints> "Were you in the sun all day? Short on water? Out of sunscreen?" <he raises a finger> "Wait, I know. It's getting lonely out there. I saw something like this once in a film." <fires a curt nod> "Man gets shipwrecked on a beach. Has nothing but a volleyball and a Sharpie.." <quick reassuring look> "We can send some extra help with you next time."

Moses: "It was the voice of the Lord—the Lord spoke to me from the bush."

Jethro: <benefit of the doubt> "Oh? What did he say?"

Moses: "He told me to go down to Egypt and bring two million people back with me."

Jethro: "W-What—*all by yourself?!*"

Moses: "Well, he—the Lord—he'll be there too."

Jethro: <skeptical eyebrows raise> "And what's he gonna do?"

Moses: "He—*uh*—is gonna—*uhm*—convince the Pharaoh ...

not to listen to me."

Jethro: "Doesn't sound very helpful."

Moses: "Yea, was kinda thinking the same thing."

Jethro: "Sounds like he *wants* to pick a fight."

Moses: "Mmm, not exactly thrilled about that part."

<long pause>

Jethro: "Well—saving Egypt—I suppose you'll need to take some time off, then?"

Moses: "If it isn't too much trouble."

Jethro: "And you're absolutely sure—this whole, 'fiery shrub thing,' was the Lord?"

Moses: <reaching for his staff, and grinning from ear to ear> "Well—he sorta gave me a sign.."

CH20: THE SHOWDOWN BEGINS
1478:12:05:20:20:02

The sun danced bright across the hot desert dunes, lighting them up like a sea of masquerading diamonds. Moses paused to shield his eyes, squinting through the endless swells of twinkling counterfeit lights. In the distance, he could make out the frame of a quaint little town meandering its way across the horizon. He relinquished a sigh, glancing towards the skyline and then towards his older brother, Aaron. *The sun was low, their caravan slow..*

Goshen would just have to wait another day.

With a grunt and a wave, he signaled the others, adjusting his camel's trajectory. *They would hunker down, head for the town, and find a place to stay.*

From the opposite side of the caravan, Aaron signaled his approval, affording his animal the reins to instinctively follow suit. The confident, well-spoken Levite watched his rugged, six-foot-five, "little" brother turn and plow on, full steam ahead. It had been nearly half a century since the two had laid eyes on one another, and the self-studied holy-man was completely taken by the raw, supernatural energy which seemed to radiate endlessly from his baby brother's innermost-being. *Wasn't this the same hard-headed warrior, brought up in the hedonistic house of Pharaoh? The same hot-blooded Hebrew, best known for topping Egypt's 'Ten Most Wanted' list?* His thoughts returned to their unlikely reunion in the midst of the Midian wasteland—*instigated by a burning bush and a dream.* He shook his head in wonder. Checkered pasts or not, *clearly both men could hear from God!*

Aaron leaned forward, anticipating their fast approach to the sleepy little suburb ahead. Ultimately, they were headed for home:

back to Goshen ... back through Egypt. But for now—he tugged hard on his reins—they would rendezvous right here, just inside Egypt's border, at the local inn.

Instinctively, his gaze returned to Moses. The natural born leader was already off his mount, busily 'circling the wagons.' Aaron handed off his reins and dropped to the ground beside him. Family, food, and phenomenal amounts of luggage—*it would be quite a while before anyone was fully settled in for the night.* Tomorrow would be a new day, complete with new worries of its own; but tonight—he lifted his camel's pack and bent to grab another—they would break some bread, catch-up on life, and have some cordial family fun!

...

Getting too old for these twenty-four hour days, Moses quietly chuckled, sliding into bed beside an already snoring, Zipporah. He gazed at his olive-skinned, ebony-accented, Midianite bride. *Two sons and three decades later—how was she more beautiful than ever?!* He leaned over, planting a kiss on her soft, warm cheek. *What an absolute gift from God,* Moses tugged hard at his share of the covers. *Even if she was a bit of a raging bed-hog!* He grinned, his head falling heavy against his cool, crisp pillow. *No doubt about it, he was blessed!* He yawned, eyes already closed. *Not to mention that his beauty-queen..*

was..

a..

"Hypocrite!"

Moses awoke with a start. His face was flushed, his clothes were drenched ... he was burning with fever. For a moment he squinted, trying to focus. *What in the—huh?* His blood ran cold. *There! At the end of his bed. A man!* Moses let out an involuntary gasp. The man was translucent. Dressed completely in white. And his belt—like his face—seemed to be urgently glowing.

"Hypocrite—!" the intruder spoke again, his right hand tightening around Moses' right ankle.

Hypo—what? Moses internally echoed the troubling accusation. *Where did—? How was that even—? He was a—what?* His self-talk flopped and floundered. *Deep breath,* he fought to settle his mind, willing his thoughts to fall back into line.

It was no use.

"T-To what d-d-do you refer—?" Moses struggled with the words.

The visitor lifted a grim, silencing finger, giving his head a curt nod right.

Moses' eyes followed the tightlipped gesture, squinting into the surrounding darkness. *There, beside the man—stood another figure!* Tall. Gaunt. Barely visible. Draped in hood and cloak. Sickle in hand. Its bony fingers and long thin arm clung defiantly to his *left* ankle.

Moses' head whipped back to the man in white, his eyes wide, searching for some sort of logical explanation. *What was going on?* He lurched beneath a second involuntary gasp: *Were two opposing entities truly converging in his room? ..each with a hand on his ankle?*

The man in white offered only a nod. "Any male who fails to administer the mark," he quietly acknowledged, "will *himself,* be cut off and removed." His grip tightened around Moses' right leg. "Man of God," he implored. "Your house is not in order. You have failed to comply. Should you not immediately remedy the situation, you will not survive the night."

The realization hit Moses like a punch to the gut: *His wife. His covenant. His uncircumcised son.. This was all his fault!*

He glanced at Zipporah, still obliviously pulverizing an entire lumberyard of timber beside him. Their decade-old-quarrel suddenly as fresh as the passing day—flashing defiantly across the big-screen of Moses' imagination.

"*NO WAY* is our second son going to partake in the same '*sadistic mutilation*' you inflicted upon our first!" Zipporah raged, several dishes flying across the tent for added emphasis. "Covenant or no—in *my* house, there will be *NO SUCH SAVAGERY!*"

Moses shook himself back to reality. He could still see the look in her eyes. "Zee!" He trembled, rousing his sleeping bride. "*BOTH* our boys *MUST* bear the mark, *or I will not survive the night!*"

Instantly, Zipporah was up and about, caring for her hurting husband. She was sympathetic. Kindhearted. Even mildly moved. But she was not so easily persuaded. "You are *DELIRIOUS!*" she scolded, rebuking the malignant request. "*Never again will ANY son of mine be subjected to such—,*" she searched for the words. "*BARBARIC BUTCHERY!*"

Emotions ran high as the standoff continued, but Moses would not relent. *It MUST be done*, he insisted. *It was the ONLY thing that would spare his life.*

For six long hours the battle raged, Zipporah carefully weighing the options: *Would she obediently perpetrate death unto life*—allowing her baby boy the temporal trauma needed to step into the eternal protection of supernatural covenant? *Or would she rebelliously preserve life unto death*—standing with her mama-bear gut to defend her son's 'right to choose,' and allow the man she loved—along with her family's entire livelihood—to permanently expire?

Tick-tock … she warred against the clock.

It was clear. Her husband was slipping away.

Finally, as day began to break, so did she. Brandishing a scowl and a knife—Zipporah woke their youngest son and begrudgingly fulfilled the brutal covenantal requirements. Hurling the hellish extraction at the feet of her infernal frustration, she railed against the injustice. "*SURELY YOU ARE A BRIDEGROOM OF BLOOD TO ME!*" She stormed out of the room.

Immediately, the tides began to turn. Moses writhed and reeled as new-covenant-life scoured his shipwrecked body. His seas grew calm. His vitals grew strong.

Death had gone.

Life had gained control.

When Moses could once again muster the strength to lift exhausted eyes, his room was fully aglow with the amber light of his mysterious Healer.

"Had I not remained with you this night," The Angel of the Lord smiled, "your life would certainly have been taken."

Moses moved to rise a hand and thank his unsolicited savior—but it was too late. A thick, unshakable peace had already settled heavy upon his war-worn soul. His chin stayed tucked. His hands stayed stuck. His eyes fell back to closed. Slowly his breathing deepened, then evened, as the trauma and the drama of the event-filled night slowly faded into deep, restful sleep.

—| 1478:10:16:08:00:00 |—

"The Pharaoh will see you shortly!" the matter-of-fact proclamation echoed warmly off the cold Egyptian walls.

Moses smiled, glancing down at the familiar face of the throne room attendant quietly staring back at him. The old man stretched a wrinkled hand up, up, up to Moses' broad shoulder. "*Welcome* back!" He whispered into the prodigal's bent ear. "You have been missed!"

Moses' smiled widened. He was touched. Very few from the old Kingdom still remained. Even fewer who remembered him fondly. *What were the odds that the first one to cross his path would be the Pharaoh's very own, personal assistant?*

CREEEAK—the towering throne room doors swung open. A second attendant poked his head out. "This way," he motioned Moses and Aaron through.

This was it! Moses gave Aaron a quick nod, falling into step behind his well-spoken protégé. *They had done their part—meeting with the elders, speaking to the people.* He glanced down the long, narrow isle. *Now was the moment of truth—their moment before the king.*

"When I first learned that my long-lost, Hebrew, half-brother had finally returned," the Pharaoh greeted them before they had even fully arrived, "my curiosity was peaked to say the least."

He studied them closely.

"But when I received a petition requesting an audience from his grossly under-educated, plebeian, slave brother—I simply couldn't resist." The king sat up and grinned, waiting for his insult to land. Truth be told, he was testing them; searching for an excuse—any excuse—to kick this "bumbling sideshow" out of his courts before the three-ringed circus could even begin.

Moses and Aaron bowed low.

"*Ahhhh*—to … what do I hold the distinct honor of your unexpected appearance?" the Pharaoh slowly expounded, a little disappointed they must continue. "Surely, you have not come harboring the hopes of reclaiming my throne?" A halfhearted chuckle made the room painfully aware his question was mostly serious.

"We have come *only* at the request of Israel's true and living God," Aaron calmly assured him.

At this, Thutmoses the Third seemed to fully relax. "Very well," he obliged, lifting his scepter. "You may rise and inform the court: *For what then, was your throne room petition submitted?*"

"This—is what the Lord, the Living God of Israel says," Aaron stepped forward and cleared his throat. "*LET MY PEOPLE GO*—so that they may hold a festival in my honor, in the wilderness."

Immediately, Pharaoh's walls were back up.

"Is that so?" he sneered. "And exactly *who* is this '*living Lord*' *of Israel?*" The king gestured toward the abundance of hand-carved statues lining the upper palace walls. "Tell me: Does his likeness line these hallowed halls? ..Or his image, anywhere exist? Please, if you are even the least bit able, point out the god to which you refer." He leaned in, scowling intently. "If he is so, '*living,*' how is it that he would rather send to me a deserter and a slave, than to speak with me directly?" He paused and puzzled. "I have never heard *anything* about your, '*living Lord*'..So—*no,*" he sat back. "*I will not let MY people go!*"

Aaron's stomach dropped.

"The God of the Hebrews has *indeed* met with us," the flustered priest reacted. "His word is sure! His ways are true! Kindly— oh, king—reconsider. You *MUST* allow us take a three day journey into the wilderness to worship the Lord our God. For if we don't, he will most certainly kill us with a plague or a sword.."

Shhhsht—, Thutmoses III waved a silencing hand. "I too have had a dream from god, warning me of the lies that were certain to spew from the treacherous mouths of the likes of you." A long, accusing finger lowered directly toward his harassers. "*You* are strange and vexing fools, willing to say *anything* … aren't you? Why are you giving *MY* subjects false hope and distracting them from their tasks? *Get back to work!*" he snapped, a terrible thought alighting: *Were these men not, in fact, attempting to steal his economy … right out from under him?* His eyes went dark. "*OUT!*" he roared. "You—contriving, villainous buzzards. All you spout are *FABRICATIONS AND LIES! ..GET OUT, GET OUT … GET OUT!*"

"This way!" The palace guards jumped at the words of the king, escorting the troublemakers quickly back down the long narrow entryway.

"Tell me—," the king called after them. "How is it that you have even had time to discuss such … flippantry?" He turned to his governing counsel. "*REMOVE EVERY BLADE OF STRAW WE SUPPLY TO THESE LAZY REBELS.*" The snarl burst from his belly. "Make them gather it *THEMSELVES! And DOUBLE their quotas.*" He was coming unglued. "You thought it was difficult before? *Now I'm gonna MAKE YOU SWEAT!*" He waved his scepter wildly at the two departing silhouettes. "*You hear that? Whips and chains for anyone who can't keep up!* That will teach you to guard your treasonous words—*you loose-lipped LIARS!*"

CH21: DOUBLE DOWN

"Our golden-boy has somehow returned?" Ha-satan was visibly shaken. "Tell me gentlemen—how is it that he even *STILL REMAINS?!*" He shot his henchmen a savage look, dropping heavily to his seat at the head of the square table. "You had your orders years ago." A furious fist came crashing down. "*WHY WEREN'T THEY PROPERLY CARRIED OUT?!*"

"It wasn't for lack of effort—," growled BEAST, dropping to a seat of his own. "Hell knows, I tried." He extended three claws. "Once, at birth. Once, in the Nile. And countless times in Pharaoh's court." He paused, shifting the focus to Prophet. "Tell me, old man—you just had him dead to rights … how did you manage to muddle things up?"

"Last minute change," the hooded assassin hissed. "Heaven pulled a tasteless stunt." His countenance darkened. "Some no-name, off-the-grid angel showed up and all but *forced* that Hebrew hippie to comply.."

Ha-satan had heard enough, he reached over and caught Prophet by the throat. "This is *MY* world," he snarled. "Those were *MY* orders." He shook the sputtering shaman violently. "That means, you finish the job … *Understand?*" He threw Prophet hard against the back of his chair and shot BEAST a cryogenic look. There was a long moment of blink-less tension before he heaved a loud sigh, and let his head fall back into his cradling hands.

He was moping.

"—that's what we get for once again stacking ALL our chips on the behavior of *ONE single,* swayable, free-willed human," Prophet gingerly grouched.

"NO—that's the limitations of playing both sides *IN*

SECRET," interrupted BEAST. "At some point," he brazenly flexed both biceps, "we need to take those shackles off *PERMANENTLY.*"

"..Or manufacture a way that *actually* puts ourselves back in *FULL* control."

"*ENOUGH—!*" Ha-satan lifted a silencing hand. "Your stunning incompetencies have left me no choice. *I* will handle ALL future moves—*personally.*" His voice dropped to a whimper-laced whisper. "Besides, I've already been charged with the honorary embarrassment of orchestrating every blathering directive spewed from the mouth of our resurrected golden-boy."

Two jaws dropped. *Was their "fearless" leader really beginning to whine?*

"No worries," the trickster recovered. "In the light—I will be a "good 'ol boy" and do as I'm told. But at *night.*" His tone went cold. "I will become more real to Pharaoh than the stale, desert air he incessantly breaths." A defiant fist rose sharp in the air. "I will *drive* him to do our bidding until Heaven is *FORCED* to require a national blood-sacrifice for his unyielding rebellion!"

BEAST began to tremble with glee.

*An actual, bonafide genocide? ..*Not since the days of the great flood! He closed his eyes and licked eager lips. *Was it possible? That they could actually manufacture Hades' next super-charged, tidal-wave, turbo-boost blood-harvest?* He pushed up from the table, already imagining what his new upgrades might be. *Power? Influence? Muscles? Control..?* A shiver ran down his jubilant spine. *Who knew— with all that energy flowing unrestrained from the souls of millions of unsuspecting victims—the sky was really the limit!*

"POWER-UP BOYS!" The giddy ox thunder-clapped both paws together, eyes rolling blissfully back into his thick, monstrous skull.

"Yesss," agreed Prophet. "If we play our cards right, we can align ourselves with Moses by day, and the Pharaoh by night; riding this confrontation all the way out to its naturally bittersweet, blood-soaked, power-up end!"

"Gentlemen!" Ha-satan grinned. "Far be it from us to waste a perfectly good crisis!" He grabbed the nearest shoulder of each cohort and shook violently. "This is our opportunity for the taking! Let's exterminate our pesky Hebrew infestation—once and for all!"

CH22: TRIPLE DOWN
1478:10:15:17:22:17

Moses was flat on his face. Nothing had gone as planned. Not only had they been thrown out of Pharaoh's court, but conditions on the ground had gone from bad to worse.

He loosed a long, emotional sigh.

"Why did y-you send me?" the humiliated ambassador complained. "Ever since I arrived, things have only gotten worse!" Frustrated, Moses reached out, tossing a fistful of dust into the tepid evening air. "My involvement has done nothing to rescue your people. Instead, I have become the c-cause of everyone's troubles."

A gentle breeze began to blow, quietly removing the dust that had just begun to settle upon the back of Moses' neck.

"Have no fear," Elohim's familiar voice whispered. "Now you will see what I will do to Pharaoh! Your forefathers knew me as El-Shaddai, *'God Almighty.'* But you will know my judicial name— *YHWH ('Yud-Hey-Vav-Hey'), Yahweh—'I Am that I Am.'"* There was a brief pause, allowing the heaven-sent breeze to build in momentum. "Yes—when Pharaoh feels the force of my strong, judicial hand, he *will* let my people go." Elohim loosed a light-hearted chuckle. "In fact, he will practically *force* you to leave his land!"

Immediately, Moses' spirit began to lift. He picked up his staff and stood meekly before his LORD, the words and the wind quietly carrying his burdens away.

"Go back to Pharaoh." Elohim smiled. "Tell him one more time, *'Let my people go!'"*

—| 1478:10:00:00:00:00 |—

Thutmoses the Third, was incredulous. *Had he really heard correctly?
'..Let the Hebrew slaves—the children of some lesser, foreign, no-name
god—go?'*

..Really?!

"Don't you know what I'm capable of doing to you?" He
glared at the odd couple, not entirely sure why he'd granted them
counsel a second time. "Show me a miracle," he challenged. "Give me
a sign."

Moses signaled the 'OK' to Aaron. The king's question was
inevitable; their answer, well prepared.

In one smooth motion, Aaron threw down his staff.

WHAAA—the entire room withdrew, Aaron's rod snapping
and hissing before it even hit the ground.

Moses and Aaron stepped back too. Aaron's serpent was far
bigger and far more grotesque than any of the serpents Moses had
repeatedly produced in the desert.

"Magicians!" Pharaoh coaxed his crew of shaman and
sorcerers forward. "Display to them the abilities of Egypt!"

The sinister group wasted no time in following Aaron's lead,
casting down rod after rod, until the entire room was teaming with
reptiles.

Thutmoses III shot Moses and Aaron a killer look. *Was this
age-old parlor trick truly the best their no-name foreign god could do?*

UGHHHH—the spellbound crowd was gasping again.

Pharaoh's attention immediately returned to the show. *What
was this—?* he caught his own gaping jaw. The Hebrew's serpent had
turned on the others and was consuming them methodically, one
after the other.

There was no shortage of murmuring among the magicians
on stage as Aaron bent down and retrieved his original rod. *Was this
some sort of cosmic foreshadowing? A back-handed insult? An indirect
challenge?* They were certainly concerned. *At the very least, Aaron's
rod now contained the powers of ALL their rods combined.* Certainly
that plot-twist was worrisome, *no?* The frazzled group quietly

bickered amongst themselves. *Dare they be so bold as to ask the foreigners to return their ingested belongings?*

On his throne, the Pharaoh stifled a yawn. He was entirely unimpressed. Moses' god posed no real, legitimate threat. After all, his own magicians had essentially done the exact same illusion. *No*—it would take more than a ragtag battle of paltry parlor tricks to change his divinely superior mind. *His complicit, compliant, Hebrew slave-class was going NOWHERE..*

..And so the showdown began:

Pharaoh exits his morning bath in "de-Nile." He dons his super comfy, extra fluffy, complimentary, palace towel and—*Whoa!* there stand Moses and Aaron.
"Let my people go!"
"Mmm—*No?*"
Aaron's rod goes up. Bathwater turns to blood.

Pharaoh is fly fishing in the palace pond. He's not catching much, due to the fact that it's still mostly blood. His wrist snaps back. Then forward. *What the—?!* there stand Moses and Aaron.
"Let my people go?"
"*—No!*"
Aaron's rod goes up. Frogs begin to swarm.

Pharaoh is out on the patio, firing up the old palace grill. Barbecued frog legs—again—*Mmmm*, been eating them all week. Today he's gonna try a new dry rub. He's shaking the seasoning and prepping the frogs when, *How in the—?* there stand Moses and Aaron.
"Let my people go!"
"How 'bout—*No!*"
Aaron's rod goes up. This time it comes back down, striking the ground. Lice infestation explodes.

Pharaoh is in the 'little Emperor's room.' He's shaving at the bathroom sink, thanking the gods that his hairless body—for the most part—remains lice free. He shuts the sink mirror when—*For the love!* There stand Moses and Aaron.

"Let my people go!"

"*NO!*"

Rod goes up. Clouds of buzzing flies arrive..

..And you get the idea:

Pharaoh is in the stables.

    Moses and Aaron are plaguing the livestock.

Pharaoh is in the palace courts.

    Moses and Aaron are spreading the Pox.

Pharaoh is out in the fields.

    Moses and Aaron are calling down hail.

Pharaoh is inspecting his storehouses.

    Moses and Aaron are unleashing hungry locusts.

Back and forth it goes: By day, Elohim is releasing Pharaoh's well-deserved judgment. By night, Ha-satan is hardening Pharaoh's heart. It's a standoff of epic proportions, a cosmic battle of whits. *Will Heaven's sovereign boss best it's two-faced CEO?* Pharaoh is the unsuspecting puppet. The Egyptians, the unsuspecting victims.

Finally the ninth plague, the Plague of Darkness falls.

With a mighty sweep of his staff, Aaron deploys a deep, all-consuming darkness that can only be described as: '*twisted*.' Billowing black clouds blot out the sun. A thick murky fog, rolls up from the Nile. The gates of Hell crack open. Terror claws its way out. Candles, torches, and fire are useless. Nothing dispels the gloom.

For three days nothing moves.

"Summon the troublemakers," Thutmoses III eventually sighs, waving a jewel covered hand blindly in front of his face.

"We're already here!" a familiar voice calls from the dark.

"Shoulda known," Pharaoh mumbles, doing his best to remain calm in his skin. Somewhere in the darkness a creature scurries, its furless tail brushing ominously past Pharaoh's sandaled feet. *My god,* he squirms in his chair, desperate to see, *even a god could go mad in this kind of darkness.*

"*Let my people GO!*" The familiar command rings out once again.

"Fine—," comes the surprising retort. "You win. Go and worship your God. Take your wives, your sons, *and* your daughters.." There was a brief pause, accompanied by an almost audible change of heart. "Only … leave your flocks and herds behind."

Moses had heard enough.

"You *MUST* provide us with animals for sacrifice," he growled, placing a constraining hand on Aaron's already rising rod. "There will *NOT* be a hoofed foot left behind. For we must choose our offerings to our God from among our animals. And we will not know exactly how we are to worship *until we get there!*"

At this, the Pharaoh went livid.

"Get *OUT* of here," he screamed. "How stupid do you think I am?" He waved a violently trembling fist. "I'm warning you … never show yourselves to me again. For the day you see my face—*you will surely DIE!*"

"Very well—," Moses blazed. "May we never see your face again!"

The duo turned to go, but something in Moses had shifted.

"Tonight. About midnight," the smoldering spokesman spun brazenly back around. "*The eternal God of Heaven says*: I will pass through the heart of Egypt. ALL the firstborn sons in Egypt will DIE—from the oldest son of Pharaoh, to the oldest son of his lowliest servant girl. Even the firstborn of all your livestock." Moses' rod pounded the floor in emphasis. "Israel is my firstborn son. And just as you have taken my firstborn from me, so I will take your firstborn from you!"

The room went silent.

"*You stiff-necked, hard-hearted, arrogant DONKEY!* " Moses held nothing back. "Not until your officials run to me and fall on the ground begging, 'Hurry! Please leave and take ALL of your followers with you!' Then—*and ONLY then*—will we go!"

There was a mighty *SWOOSH,* like a staff being swung wildly about in the dark. A screech and a clang, like someone ducking and toppling a vase on a cat. Then, a very red-faced Moses and a very wide-eyed Aaron, turned and casually made their exit.

—| 1477:00:03:15:00:02 |—

"Roast for yourselves, this night, a lamb." Moses was instructing a tight-pressed group of grave-faced, Israeli elders. "But first, collect its blood in a basin." He took a long, deep breath, doing his best to convey the gravity of the situation. "Apply that blood to your doorpost with a brush made of hyssop. And do not let *anyone* go out of that door until morning! For tonight God, himself, will pass through the land to strike down the Egyptians." Moses nodded emphatically, mirroring the solemn frowns of the surrounding leadership. "When he sees the blood on the door of your home, he will *pass-over;* forbidding his death angel to enter your house."

The troubled looks and stricken faces, sparked memories of Moses' own brush with death. The *only* thing that had saved him was following Elohim's instructions *precisely.* He wasn't entirely sure how to adequately covey it, but he knew it was dire they follow God's plan to a 'Tee.' "Gentlemen," he reiterated. "The blood of the lamb, placed on the doorpost of your house, will be a sign to Death itself *NOT* to touch your household. Instruct every Hebrew and every Egyptian who will listen. Make them fully aware—the only thing that can stop Death from pillaging your home this night, is the pure and spotless blood of the lamb!"

—| 1477:00:03:10:16:12 |—

AAaaaAAAAGH—Pharaoh collapsed, sobbing uncontrollably. He lifted the wilted body of his firstborn son and held it motionless against his pounding chest. *His baby boy! His treasured heir!* Only hours ago, so full of laughter and life, now suddenly ... gone. "*Something—,*" they'd said, when they'd roused him from his chambers, "*was terribly wrong!*" He reached down and brushed one cold, unresponsive cheek, his fingers curling into a hate-filled ball. Somehow, he knew *exactly WHO* that "something" was..

"*GO—!*" Pharaoh wept, the moment Moses and Aaron arrived. "Whatever you want.."

He stripped the rings from his fingers.

"Whatever you need.."

He pulled the gold from his wrists.

"Take it, and *go*—!" He clung to the outstretched hands of Moses and Aaron. "But first," he begged. "Bless me.."

The duo warily lifted their voices and rods, calling out to the God above all other gods. But wary prayers do little to rouse the lifeless bodies of the disobedient dead. So, while the plague immediately lifted, the lifeless bodies remained.

The king was wrecked. "Clothes, shoes, silver, gold—." He turned to his counsel. "Give them whatever they want!"

"Please," the devastated counsel begged, piling their compensations high. "Leave—and take ALL of your people with you!"

Moses and Aaron beamed, staring at one another in awestruck disbelief. *This was their sign! This was THEIR SIGN!*

They hurried to comply.

How could they not obey?

And so, with arms and wallets bulging, they set out about the impossible task of moving an entire nation out of captivity in a single night.

—| 1477:00:03:09:06:06 |—

Back at the palace, the throne room slowly emptied; each officer, official, and servant having their own late night tragedy to attend to. Alone in the dark, Thutmoses III wept bitterly, begging his gods to do the impossible.

"..Are you really going to stand for this?" a dark voice rang out, a sudden chill sweeping the room.

Thutmoses III bolted upright in his chair. *What was that?!* He slowly stood, peering intently into the darkness. *This chamber was empty—was it not?*

"Are you really going to stand for this?" the calculating voice demanded again.

This time, Thutmoses the Third replied. *After all—this WAS a voice he'd heard often before, albeit mostly in dreams..* "A-Anubis, g-god of the dead?" He stammered. "S-Show yourself!"

A dark figure shifted in the shadows, moving just enough for Thutmoses III to make out the outline of a jackal's head towering a good twelve feet above his own.

In reality, this was Haylel—reinvented and well-disguised. But for all intents and purposes, and of course to clueless Pharaoh— this was Anubis.

"They've made a mockery of you," the looming figure growled. "Taken your economy. Your health. Your wealth. And now," he motioned to Pharaoh's lifeless son. "Your very future." There was a long, oppressive pause. "Again—I ask you one simple thing ... are you *really* going to stand for it?"

"A choice? Do I have any other?" Thutmoses the Third was indignant. "*—And what of you?*" He flipped the script. "You come to me at night. You disappear by day. You implore, '*Remain steadfast.*' Then you pillage my country, my government ... and now, even my own house?!"

"*—perhaps Moses *is* the bigger man," Anubis snarled, hastily sidestepping the obvious blunder. "It's clear he's bested you in this war of words, AND that his command of the spirit-world vastly out maneuvers your own. However—," his voice trailed off. He was casting his line, gambling on the sudden assault of Pharaoh's insecurities to reel him back in.

"However—?" Thutmoses III cautiously took the bait.

"However, you still command the Physical World. *Do you not?*"

"Of course I do," Thutmoses III grouched. "I am supreme ruler of it!"

"Then prove it! " Anubis snapped. "Dispense with the stick waving trickery, and confront these dogs on *YOUR turf.* Will I not, most certainly, deliver them into your hands?"

At this, Thutmoses the Third went livid. "They have ruined

my kingdom and tarnished my name! They have made me out for a bumbling fool!" He set down his son, and lifted his sword. "Where invisible powers have bested me, their pitchforks and clubs *never will!*" His hands shook violently. "I will *spill their blood before me!* I will *trample them beneath my feet!* GENERAL—," he called, his voice booming down the tempered halls. "Rally my troops! Ready my chariot! *Today—we ride at dawn!*"

Underneath his big doggy mask, Haylel was all smiles. *Mission accomplished,* he grinned, watching Thutmoses III stride hastily out of the room. *The king's blind rage was once again, perfectly misplaced—and BACK under his control!* He raised his chin and loosed a horrible, blood-curdling howl. Things were finally moving in the right direction.

The dark angel bent and lifted Pharaoh's motionless son. Dispelling his guise, he drank deeply from the boy's adreno-filled reservoir of terrorized lifeblood. *Ahhh—still warm,* he wiped his dripping mouth. *Just the way he liked it.*

Cries of grief-stricken mourners were fast approaching the room.

Haylel cocked his head. *It was time to move!* With a sweep of his arm he caught his victim up by the soul; ripping it from its flesh by the scruff of its squirming neck.

Ka-BOOM—the hellbound underlord exited the room; crashing down through the floor in a shower of sparks and ash. He could hear his writhing cargo groan as it raked against the racing rocks below, bouncing from boulder to boulder. *The trip would be quick. The pain wouldn't stick.* Haylel understood quite well that *every* underaged soul had been unarguably legislated to enter Paradise. *Still—,* he glanced down and roared. *That didn't stop him from terrifying it … ALL the way down.*

CH23: THE BITTER END
1477:00:01:07:11:11

Thutmoses the Third tugged hard on the reins, wheeling his chariot to a clattering halt. In his dusty wake, sixteen-hundred Charioteers all did the same. Down the canyon, across the valley, beyond the sandy dunes below—the motionless Egyptian army could clearly see their Hebrew defectors setting up camp near the banks of the sprawling Red Sea. A slow smile spread wide across Thutmoses III's determined face. "They're hopelessly trapped! How can we lose?" he gloated, striking his chariot hard with the base of his shield. "To the gods! ..And to the king!"

All sixteen-hundred warriors struck their own armored rides. "To the gods, and to the king!" They echoed like thunder.

Thutmoses III squinted, waiting as the sound reverberated across the rolling landscape. Even from this distance, he could see clear signs of panic erupting in the Hebrew camp below. *This was going to be easy!* His razor-sharp sword sliced high through the air. "Onward!" he bellowed, snapping the base of his reins.

Then he was off, the massive Egyptian army slowly thundering along in tow.

WhoooooOOSH—what was that? Pharaoh leaned forward, securing his stance. An unusually strong headwind had suddenly picked up. He bent hard against the gusting gale, taking note of the changing world around him: *Billowing clouds were gathering and blotting out the sun. Daylight was fading away. And an all-too-familiar fog, seemed to be rolling in from the sea.* "Stick games," he muttered, peering down the steep canyon slope. No doubt about it—somewhere along that shoreline a staff had been raised.

Visibility dropped to half.

Then it halved, and halved again.

Chariots began to slip and slide, horses spooked and clambered. The king resolutely set his jaw. *Anubis had promised— they would NOT be stopped!* "To the ground," he ordered his scouts, arming each of them with a torch and a shield. They knew this land like the back of their hands. Even in this blinding murk, they could certainly guide the way.

Slowly the army began to move, shields raised high, torches sweeping low. All day and night the Egyptian forces crept along— inch by inch, step by step—relentless; until at long last they broke through the..

Whoa—! Pharaoh stopped dead in his tracks. *The Israelite camp had completely disappeared. Vanished … into thin air!* In its place stood an ominous tornado of tightly spinning fire—roaring like a fiery freight train, stretching high into the heavens.

"What manner of magic is this?" the awestruck king wondered aloud, eyes slowly adjusting to the flickering amber light. *"..Anubis?"* Thutmoses III glanced ahead to the sea, terror striking his core. *Somehow … Someway … the depths of those choppy waters STOOD, frozen in place and parted before him—like some sort of hidden, aquatic, super-highway.* His jaw dropped. He felt weak in the knees. He blinked, and blinked again. *How was this even possible?* He craned his neck. *Yet, there it stood—two walls of neatly stacked water, towering a thousand feet high.*

Then, he saw them.

The slaves. *HIS* slaves. *They hadn't disappeared!* They were simply *standing* on the *OTHER SIDE OF THE SEA!* Anger erupted. *Did they really think they could escape his relentless grasp so easily?* His fists balled. He lifted his sword, eyes darting to the sky-scraping walls of water that stood waiting.

Waiting for what?

Thutmoses III closed his eyes. *Anubis had PROMISED.* He clenched his teeth, growling in royal frustration. *If Anubis had promised then, of course—*the answer suddenly struck him—Anubis *was making a way!*

His eyes flew open. He let out a sinister laugh. *"CHARGE!"* he roared, wildly spurring his ride. "Anubis *WILL* have his revenge!" The Pharaoh raced forward, sword drawn, a dark gleam overwhelming his eyes.

Twenty across, his well-trained troops followed suit. Shields raised, spears held high—they thundered savagely along behind.

Bump.

Boom.

CLANG—

Pharaoh jerked on his reins.

Crack.

Snap.

SCREEEEECH—

Thutmoses the Third spun frantically around. Axles were snapping. Chariots were tipping. Horses and wheels were coming off in the mud.

..In the mud?

The wild-eyed king looked up. The winds had died down. The sun was now rising. And of course, that tornado of fire was burning so hot overhead. *Mud could only mean one thing.* His gaze fell to the dripping base of the towering aquatic corridors. *The walls were beginning to melt..*

..THE WALLS WERE BEGINNING TO MELT!

"ANUBIS—?!" The petrified cry exploded from anxious lungs. *Silence.*

Pharaoh raised two trembling arms. *Where was his god?!*

All around the chaos continued. Chariots careened and skidded. Horses panicked and tumbled. Mountain-sized chunks of ice fell from the walls above.

"Their God fights for them! Their God fights *FOR THEM!*" The cries echoed through the toppling ranks.

Then it happened.

From across the expanse—like a small bearded dot—Moses stepped forward and slowly lifted both hands.

Everything went silent.

Too silent..

CREEEEEEAAK—in epic slow-motion, the walls cracked, broke and caved. From shoreline to center, they collapsed, falling back into place. In an instant, Pharaoh's army was swallowed. The showdown was done. One staff had been lifted: Game over.

God won.

CH24: WALLS, WALLS, AND MORE WALLS

"So—who's right?" Elohim broke the silence. The holy trio was sitting, gazing up at their familiar round table—now hanging precariously, upside-down above them.

"—It's all a matter of perspective," Spirit responded with a giggle. Of course, she already *knew* the answer … she was just excited about the fact that her two ethereal teammates had actually accepted the invitation to join her, midair.

There they all sat, hovering impishly, upside down above their respective chairs. Each staring up at the massive, chiseled table planted directly below them.

"So—who's right?" Elohim casually resubmitted his question.

Spirit furrowed her brow, flashing a cute little pout. *Had she not just stated, it was simply a matter of..*

"No one—," interjected The Word. "No one is right. At least not until, up & down—right & wrong—have been clearly defined."

"Bingo!" grinned Elohim. "It's a bit like gravity." He gestured to the seemingly floating table. "Without the constraints of gravity, how do we know who's upside-down and who's right-side-up?"

"We don't." The Word smiled. "Without gravity—it's *all* just a matter of opinion."

Spirit bit her lip to keep from laughing. This was, of course, *precisely* what she had just said. "Yes—well then, let's clearly define it." The darling deity waved a slender hand. "The right/wrong, up/down, love/hate, light/dark, self*less*ness/self*ish*ness—um, *gravity* of the universe, *I mean!*" She plucked her coffee mug up from the table, holding its brimming contents inverted above her head. "Let's be sure Heaven & Earth know *exactly* who's the one, right-side-up." She produced one large, glowing, curly-cue straw, slipped it into the cup's shimmering contents, and took a sip.

"Oh they'll know," Elohim grinned. "When we give them our Word.."

"..and then make him flesh!" Spirit squealed. "But, oh—," her face suddenly fell, "what happens until then?" She shifted uncomfortably, returning her straw and her beverage slowly to its original post.

"Unfortunately," Elohim sighed, "Haylel will enjoy free reign. *HIS* interpretation will be *THE* interpretation."

Spirit cringed at the dark mental image. "Just look at what he can do with practically no rules at all." She leaned in to Elohim. "Knowing that the strength of Sin *IS* the Law, do we really want to give him an entire, handwritten, step-by-step playbook?"

Elohim raised a calming hand. "It does appear," he reassured, "that, at first, we are playing right into his treasonous plans. However, establishing clear-cut boundaries that we'll be obligated to enforce, does three critically necessary things. First—." Elohim winked. "It establishes clear-cut boundaries that we'll be obligated to enforce!" He stifled a hardy laugh. "Second. It creates a foundation—a baseline gravity—over which we can soar!" There was a moment's pause, to let that thought soak in. "But best of all," Elohim's eyes twinkled. "It will pave the way for our little test.."

"You mean our little *trap*," corrected Spirit.

"—it will pave the way for the perfect scenario by which we can rightly examine the heart of the Serpent," Elohim reframed each word precisely.

"But what of the inverse?" The Word raised a critical eyebrow. "If weaponized, doesn't the playpen become the prison? Gravity, the tether? And our plot to save mankind, the unwitting plot to punish it?"

"*M-hmm*," Elohim nodded, looking up. "It's the age old conundrum every child must face for themselves: *Are the finite arms of a loving Father my protection, or my prison? My launching pad, or my roadblock?*"

"*Violá!* And once again—we've arrived at *perspective!*"

Spirit giggled. "But—what of *our* trap?" She squinted, oddly determined to flesh this thing out. "How do clear-cut boundaries and predetermined penalties—in any way—help *our* cause? By laying out the rules, aren't we just empowering the accuser to punish mankind all the more?"

"So it would seem," Elohim slowed, eyes brimming with emotion. "*BUT—*," he leaned in, "by setting up a rigid system of laws—we have, in essence—established a cosmic loophole in the fundamental requirements of the universe."

"Do tell—," Spirit was literally all ears.

"Simply put, by establishing a governing set of laws, and plainly defining perfection—we have, in essence, created a safety-clause, protecting the *eternal life* of any human in whom perfection remains." Elohim smiled. "In this way, we can safely implant our Word on Earth and allow him to thrive directly under Haylel's control. Continued perfection will keep our Word untouchable and believe-it-or-not, legally aided by Haylel, himself." At this, Elohim leaned back and let out a long, deep, belly-laugh. "If anything happens to our Word while under Haylel's care, assuming that our Word has maintained perfection," he gave The Word a playful nudge, "than by default, Haylel will be held liable. Even as I am liable for the cosmic blunder of Team Adam." He raised a single finger. "However—please remember: our little 'test' is *first-and-foremost* an *OPPORTUNITY. An opportunity* for the *PERMANENT PROMOTION* of our anointed cherub." Loving eyebrows lifted above compassion-filled eyes. "Should Haylel watch over our Word—keeping him forever safe—our governing cherub will have inadvertently solidified his own eternal position, fulfilling his deepest heart's desire to become the sovereign God of Earth." The Father searched his spirit's wide unblinking eyes. "Remember, our test *only* becomes a trap *IF* the Serpent illegally bites."

Spirit's heart sank, her soul moved with understanding. "Oh, he'll bite," she whispered, not quite sure she still wanted to be so matter-of-fact. "But what of the misunderstanding?" She took a deep breath, her final questions tumbling out. "With Haylel fully at the wheel, won't *we* seem more distant, harsh and unloving than ever?"

There was a long, pregnant pause.

"That—dear one—is the billion dollar question. And the catastrophic mess created by a pathological liar." Elohim's words were heavy, yet to the point. "We can be open. We can be honest. We can make the rules plain. We can even create a way to atone, should any rule be broken. But as long as our deceiver remains fundamentally unchanged, accusation and gross misunderstanding *is* the collateral damage we will *heavily* sustain.."

"..Until we bust his charade, catch him red-handed, and try him for treason!" Spirit blurted out, slapping two silencing hands over her still moving mouth.

"Absolutely," Elohim grinned at his petite powerhouse. "But unfortunately the cost of a lie, is that someone must die.."

Spirit froze, she knew exactly *who* that someone would be. Slowly, she turned to The Word, his untimely destruction flashing violently before her wide, unblinking eyes.

"Two words," she mouthed to Heaven's beloved son.

"I'm sorry."

CH25: PREPARATIONS

"Almost time!" Elohim smiled, lifting a welcoming hand.

Haylel stepped forward, snapping a sharp, protocol salute. He waited until he was set at ease, then he strode confidently towards the center of the room, quietly taking in his surroundings. Today, the mighty throne room embodied more of a tactical feel. Its typically soaring walls had shrunk—down, down, down—into a perfect, intimate sphere. Closed, two-way communications, and holographic Intel screens lined its sleek, padded leather walls. An intricate, semi-translucent floor hovered seamlessly above the room's circular equator, overlooking a perfect digital replica of Heaven's countdown clock projected horizontally beneath. The entire room rotated slowly—floor one way, walls another—almost as if they were at odds, weaving the room's overwhelming sense of 'immutable possibility' between lingering strands of 'perpetual vertigo.'

Haylel didn't seem to notice. He moved swiftly towards his commander standing in the middle of the room.

"So—," Elohim smiled, "what do you have in mind?"

Haylel slapped a large, rolled-up parchment down on the lone, center table. With a flick of his wrist, it unrolled—a pale blue, holographic image of Earth's Mount Sinai springing to life several feet above its surface, casually rotating in the thick, energized air.

"Fire. Smoke. Thunder." Haylel began, the rotating hologram depicting each verbalization with pinpoint accuracy. "Lightning. Earthquakes. Fanfare." His arms waved in eloquent wonder. "And of course, an absolutely breathtaking meteor shower to wrap it all up." He grinned, proudly folding his arms.

Elohim wasn't entirely sold.

"Don't you feel this may be a little … over the top?" he gently chided. "After all, this is the first time that *all* of my children will be assembling specifically to see me.."

"Certainly not!" Haylel pushed back. "Everyone knows first impressions set the tone of the relationship." He dropped both hands to the table and looked up. "If your children are to know you mean business, then they must—first and foremost—*see* your grandeur.. *sense* your greatness.. and *taste* of your absolute intolerance for mediocrity." He pounded the table for emphasis. "Is it not the fear of the Lord, which is the beginning of wisdom? Besides—," he smirked. "Are we not here to give them your law?" The deceiver cast a flippant shrug, flashing his most winsome smile. "How else will they know how earnestly you intend it to be kept?!"

Honestly, Haylel couldn't have cared less about first impressions—or about anyone actually fearing Elohim. The master manipulator simply needed a tangible way to generate as much distance as possible between all parties involved, leaving him standing boldly in the middle—with plenty of room to secretly influence both sides.

"Well, if that's truly how you most deeply feel," Elohim acquiesced, staring thoughtfully at the meteor shower now ravaging the base of the spinning blue mountain. "Still, let's go ahead and cancel the burning asteroids."

"Fine.." Haylel rolled his eyes, reaching over and swiping the notes right off of the page.

"But what of dinner?" Elohim cordially moved on.

"A full, six-course meal has been prepared." Haylel activated several ink marks descending vertically down the left side of his parchment. The hologram zoomed in, focusing on a discreet little clearing near the top of the mountain. Two more clicks and it settled on a formal dinner: staged, set, and prepped to feed exactly seventy-five.

"We'll begin with a hearty, leafy green, Shepherd's Salad," the master of ceremonies announced. "Followed by a smooth, brisk, Red Sea Tomato Bisque … fully parted." He flashed a tepid smile. "Course Three will be a modern twist on one of your personal favorites: Fresh Tilapia Sushi Rolls, over hot coals, Tempura style."

Elohim chuckled. "Do go on!"

"Round Four debuts a traditional palate cleanser: Goat Yogurt & Whey, with tangy Mint Oil." Heaven's culinary artist grabbed a much needed breath. "To be immediately followed by the evening's highly anticipated entree: Seasoned Roast Lamb with brazen beets and leeks." He waited for the official nod of approval.

"..And for dessert?"

Haylel smiled. "A sweet, fluffy-white, extra moist and extra light: Angel's Food Cake."

Elohim laughed out loud. Haylel certainly knew his audience. "Sounds amazing," he complimented. "Let's add just one more course to make it a complete seven."

Haylel bit his tongue. Six was clearly a much more balanced number. "..A suggestion perhaps?" He tossed the ball, and the pressure, back to Elohim.

"Let's start with hors d'oeuvres," Elohim proposed. "Perhaps a bite-sized unleavened bread under a Tepenade of sorts?"

"Fine.." Haylel muttered, bending to update his parchment. "Crackers with olives it is."

"Splendid!" Elohim clapped. He glanced down, through the floor, noting the digital clock below. *Click. Set—Whirr. Click. Set—LOCK.* He watched the rotating display snap into perfect alignment—minute, hour, day, month, year—opening the space-time continuum, like a sort of cosmic combination lock.

It was go time!

"Ready the cargo! Call in the crew!" Elohim announced, stepping towards the portal already forming above the lone center table.

Haylel jumped immediately into action. Parchment in hand, he rallied his troops. Musicians, hosts, sous-chefs and cooks began pouring into the throne room; wheeling carts, carrying supplies, and chatting excitedly. Two by two, they entered the ever-expanding portal; eager to host the highly-anticipated, entirely-unprecedented, intergalactic dinner party.

The line moved quickly, but not in a rush. While most portals lasted only a few minutes or hours at best; this portal was different. This portal sourced its energy directly from the throne room itself; and thus, would last indefinitely.

Slowly, the line shrank..

..Until, at last, there were two.

"After you," Elohim nodded to his second-in-command.

Haylel graciously accepted the offer, tipping his hand and disappearing into the spinning ball of crackling light.

For a moment Elohim paused, watching his angelic son go. Then he turned and beckoned his two counterparts. With a flash and flicker, Spirit and The Word materialized, entering into the brilliance of Elohim's presence.

Then, the trio was off—stepping from the maternal safety of Heaven's eternal perfection, and into the barren, untamed wilderness of Earth's Sinai Mountain.

CH26: DINNER IS SERVED
1477:10:11:03:00:00

Elohim was excited! It had been quite some time since he'd traveled to Earth. And the first time, since his daily romps with Team Adam, that he'd attempted any sort of 'extended stay.'

The God above all gods, inhaled slowly, smelling what must have been a million smells. *Ahhhh—the air was much thinner than he remembered.* He stifled a laugh. Of course, the Great Flood was largely responsible for that. Its cleansing downpour had stripped Earth of her heaven-like atmosphere, leaving a perpetual and sterile reminder of just how urgently she had need of a savior.

Elohim surveyed his surroundings. Camp—for the most part—was already assembled: The tables were set. Decorations arranged. Food prep, well under way. Angelic musicians lined its perimeters, busily collaborating in song. Their praise-laden, joy-infused breath released a fragrant, heavenly fog. Thick. Swirling. Energized. Sweet. Elohim watched as it billowed like incense, filling the entire space with the atmosphere of home.

Above the camp, Haylel was actively orchestrating the team's introduction. He circled high overhead, the train of his robe dragging low—walls of holy fire erupting behind. Rapid bouts of thunder and lightning shook the mountain to its core. Forest fires raged hundreds of feet in the air. Powerful seismic tremors ebbed and flowed.

One final touch, the master of ceremonies grinned. He raised his hand, and a long series of trumpet blasts began. Haunting. Ambient. Powerful. Terrifying. The dazzling fanfare enveloped the entire mountain. *There will be no doubt,* Haylel smiled. *Heaven has fully arrived!*

Elohim slowly lowered his gaze. He could see his adorable

kids, gathered at the base of the mountain, shaking like dried autumn leaves. His heart sank. He'd envisioned a warm, personal encounter with each and every child he'd rescued from Egypt. *But after this introduction,* he loosed a long, knowing sigh. *Only seventy-four would actually brave the journey.*

"This way, my Lord." A tall, stately angel—sporting a spotless gray and white tuxedo—bowed low. "Your staging awaits.."

"Please—call me, Dad," Elohim chuckled, moving to the indicated platform and taking his seat at the head of the table.

From his stunning perch atop the thick labyrinth of, Lapis Lazuli, the beloved Father sat in full view of the sprawling seventy-five seat table stretching eloquently before him. His stage—a brilliant blue, clear as the sky above—was magnificently adorned. Waters churned within. Gem stones twinkled like stars. And just a hint of atmospheric fog rolled continually over its rough-hewn edges.

A megaphone of sorts was placed in Elohim's hand, and the facilitating angel who had readied his seat, mouthed that he would go live in, "Five, four, three, two.." Elohim lifted his head, set the megaphone down, and right on cue—unveiled Heaven's 'Top Ten Commands.'

Of course, time in the atmosphere of Heaven moves much differently than time in the atmosphere of Earth. So, even before the commands were halfway finished, a pathway through the surrounding fire opened, and seventy-four frazzled, Hebrew elders stumbled their way into the clearing.

Elohim wrapped up his announcement, gazing fondly at the sea of shifting sandals and mind-blown faces. Haylel's introduction had worked, everyone looked quite ... overwhelmed. In fact, there were only two men sporting anything resembling grins. The first, was Moses. And the second, was Moses' hand-picked assistant, Joshua.

It didn't take long for the other faces to change, however. Not once they saw the decadent feast laid out before them. The facilitating angel gestured, and each man took his seat. It was completely surreal. There, in the mist of the flames, atop a rumbling mountain, on a humble planet called, Earth—sat the God of the Universe and seventy-four well-mannered, well-bearded men enjoying a meal.

Truth be told, it *was* a fairly awkward meal as far as meals go. Let's face it, it's pretty hard to truly enjoy a feast, even an incredibly delicious one, when you aren't entirely sure if you will live all the way through it. Still, somewhere around course four—when the wine glasses were being refilled a fifth time—everyone did manage to relax and loosen up a bit; each dinner guest amazed they were eating, talking, and somehow existing, in the very presence of Elohim.

At long last, the dinner was done; and the plates and utensils taken away. "The King, himself," the guests were informed, "requests the honor of meeting each of you individually."

Terror shook the group.

"We cannot go near," the elders whispered to Moses. "Today we have seen that God can speak—yes, even eat with us and yet we live! Why should we risk death again?" they reasoned. "You go. Then come, tell us everything, and we will obey. For who can hear the voice of God out of the fire, and survive?"

Moses mulled it over. He'd heard Elohim's voice, once from a burning shrub, and then again out of the blaze today. So far, he was two for two. He opened his mouth to say so, but decided to let it go. *There were far worse things than being consumed by Godly fire,* Moses looked around at all the anxious, self-concerned faces. *Things like being chosen to lead this motley bunch.*

"Very well." He slowly conceded. "I will take Joshua. And we will go up, alone."

—| 1477:10:11:01:12:00 |—

The stage where Elohim sat, had seemed so close at dinner— practically at the head of the table. Yet as Moses and Joshua approached, they soon realized it was actually perched atop the very peak of the mountain itself. Seconds turned to minutes, and minutes into hours before the two found themselves stepping into the fiery presence of Elohim.

The scene was stunning. Joshua did his best to take it all in.

Just ahead, the translucent stage—which had seemed to be made of clouds at dinner—was clearly hewn from a single, thick, sky-blue stone. Hovering several feet off the ground, it gently rocked and swayed, peacefully bridging the gap between Heaven and Earth. A thin layer of crystal-clear water bubbled endlessly up, out, and over the highly polished rock—cleansing and energizing all it touched. Gemstones lay everywhere; glimmering, spinning and tumbling in the ever-invigorating flow. Beneath the stage, a strange, powder-like substance covered the entire mountaintop. It was bright and soft and white like … *snow?* Joshua glanced down, nudging a drift with his foot. *Steam and fire erupted.* He jumped back, watching the flames leap high in the pressurized air. A small, high-pitched gasp, eeked its way from his lips. *That was no snow. Those were embers—sizzling, white-hot embers!* His knees began to buckle. His body felt weak. *The entire summit was literally ash in the presence of God!*

THUD—Joshua hit the ground like a sack of dropped rocks, the decision completely out of his control. He could feel the soft white ash settling back down around his unresponsive body. Searing. Burning. Branding him with—*love?* Living waters pooled around him, cooling him back down. He felt so free. So accepted. So powerful. So clean. It was incredible, like being home for the holidays and skydiving without a parachute—all at the same time.

Moses stepped over Joshua's limp body. He'd heard the odd groan and ash-muffled thud—typically, those sounds were his. Just this once, it was nice to be the one still standing.

With a grin and a nod, he left his smitten friend; moving up a flight of stairs and across the floating platform until he was kneeling at the base of the throne.

"You came alone?" Elohim inquired, looking past Moses and seeing only Joshua.

"I sent them back, my Lord." Moses braced for the potential rebuke.

Elohim simply nodded. "I heard what the elders said," he sighed. "Oh, that they would always have hearts to fear me and obey all my commands!" He leaned down and whispered. "If they did, they and their descendants would prosper forever."

Moses nodded.

The King above all kings straightened up. "But of course, you're wondering why you're here."

Moses nodded again.

"I called you up to discuss the details of our new ... arrangement." He gestured to the space around them.

Moses could see the stage had been purposefully laid out like a courtroom—complete with legal bench, witness stand, and Elohim presiding as judge.

"You heard the Ten Heavenly Commands?"

"We did."

"And you agree to the terms?"

"We do."

"And do you accept that the commands should be enforced neither by God, nor by man, but by an independent, mediating third-party?"

"We accept."

"..And that the court should rightfully appoint such a party?"

Moses remembered the angel at the foot of his bed warning him of impending death. The angel had been intense, direct, and intimidating to say the least, but he had been good. Surely Elohim would appoint just such an angel to this critical position. Besides, the terms were more than honorable: even Heaven would be held accountable to the rules.

"We—do," he nodded.

Elohim seemed pleased by the response. He pulled out a very fat, very lengthy scroll—and upon opening it—read some very fine print, very very quickly. When he had finished, he closed and sealed the document, tucking it securely into one of the bottomless folds of his inner robe.

"Well then, gentlemen—," Elohim's attention turned back to the guests at hand. "It's my great honor to introduce you to our mediator, effective immediately." He gestured triumphantly towards the lawyer's bench.

Moses did a double-take. The bench was no longer empty. A large, perfectly manicured, stunningly beautiful angel sat, occupying its lengthy seat. The angel's face displayed a winsome grin, but his eyes were cold as stone. On the table before him sat two large sapphire tablets, cut from the rock beneath Elohim's feet. And in his palm rested a chisel and hammer.

Moses acknowledged the being with a nod.

The angel ignored the greeting, lifting his tools and turning eagerly to the task at hand.

Moses raised an eyebrow, this was certainly *not* the angel he had witnessed at the foot of his bed. That angel had been wholeheartedly for him. This angel seemed more interested in its work. He watched as the flawless being began to engrave the ten heavenly commands. The angel was perfect in appearance. Still, something didn't sit quite right. Had it not been for the unshakable peace flowing from the presence of Elohim, an icy shiver would have certainly shot down Moses' spine.

"The Commandments will be for man." Elohim explained. "And the engraved stones, for man's remembrance."

Moses turned back to the throne.

"If you keep my commands," Elohim assured, "all will go well. I will bless you, protect you, and set you high above the nations of the world." He smiled at his newest Patriarch. "Yes—you, your children, your towns, fields and livestock—all that you have, I will bless. I will crush the hand of your enemy, while everything you set your hand to do will prosper."

Moses grinned. Sounded good so far.

"However, if you refuse to listen to me, and do not obey the commands I have given you today." Elohim's voice grew serious. "You will fall under a curse. You, your children, your towns, fields and livestock—all that you have, will fail." Concerned, fatherly eyebrows shot skyward. "I will set my hand against you. Send you curses, confusion, and frustration. I will afflict you with disease and disasters that will hunt you down til death." He pointed towards the angelic mediator, still busily engraving. "Beware, my son, lest my jealous anger destroy you!"

As if on cue, the mediator angel looked up and grinned. For the briefest of moments Moses saw his face change. It went dark:

Devious. Devilish. Skeletal.

Moses recoiled. How was this being any sort of 'unbiased third-party?' It was absolutely *lusting* for his death.

The conflicted Patriarch turned back to Elohim, silently laying his concerns at the foot of the throne. *No worries,* Elohim's indescribable presence reassured. *The Living God of the Universe was more than capable.*

By this time, the mediating angel had finished his work and was fidgeting noisily. After several, increasingly loud minutes, he was graciously thanked and dismissed. Moses watched as the dreadful being hurriedly went on his way, streaking down the side of the mountain in a flurry of fanfare, wind and flame. Clearly it was moving on to much more important matters.

Moses returned to the conversation with his Father, all worries finally melted away. Time stood still. Moses knelt at the foot of the throne. Joshua listened from a distance. No one was in a rush. There was no need to hurry. In the atmosphere of Heaven, no one needed a thing. Everyone was simply engrossed in the overwhelming joy of one another's company.

Suddenly Elohim's countenance shifted.

"Go down from here at once," he commanded. "Your people, whom you brought out of Egypt, have become corrupt!" Deep concern flooded his voice, he peered regretfully down the hill. "They have already turned away from my commands, and have made for themselves an idol," he grieved. "Heaven's blessings have already been blocked!" The King of Heaven gazed deep into Moses' terrified eyes. "Leave them alone," he ordered. "Let my anger burn against them, to destroy them. Then I will make *you* into a great nation."

"But my Lord!" Moses gasped. "Why should your anger burn against your *own* people—the people *you* just brought out of Egypt?" He threw himself down, his mind racing. "What would the Egyptians say? Wouldn't they claim it was with evil intent that you brought your people out of captivity, just to kill them in the desert?" The words were tumbling out. "Turn from your anger," he appeased. "Do not bring disaster on your people. Remember your servants Abraham, Isaac, and Jacob, to whom you swore, by yourself. Remember your covenant to them, and all of your promises!"

Elohim exhaled slowly. "You have spoken wisely." He reached down and lifted the ten commandments from the table where they lay. "Bring these instructions to my people." He gently placed the stones at the feet of his friend. "Every move I make is just. But for a genuine heart of sacrificial love, I will relent."

Moses was dumbstruck. *Had the God of the Universe just listened to HIM?* Quickly he stood and hoisted the stones. Elohim had changed his mind once, there was no need to wait for him to change it again! With an eternally grateful bow, he turned and made his expedient exit—after all, there was an absolute train-wreck of a mess, with his name written all over it, ready and waiting for him at the foot of the mountain.

—| 1477:09:02:06:06:33 |—

"Come, make us a god who can lead us." A crowd of Hebrew evacuees pressured Aaron. "Its been weeks since this fellow, Moses, disappeared." They pointed to the blazing mountaintop. "He walked into those flames nearly forty days ago and has been gone ever since. By now, anything could have happened to him."

Aaron looked around. *Had these people already forgotten the miracles they'd seen in Egypt?* He glanced at the restless crowd. *What about the Red Sea parting? Or the elders dining with God? Or the blazing mountaintop, still burning bright behind them?* There was evidence of God at every turn, yet these people still wanted him to '*make a god who could lead them?*' He threw up both hands in frustration. He was good with words. But holding down the fort—that was an entirely different story. He had done his best, pushing back against each request, but he was quickly running out of excuses.

Truth be told, Haylel was the one behind the bizarre petition. As soon as he'd been dismissed from his mountaintop, courtroom, yawn-fest, he'd grabbed his personal Power and made a beeline for the base of Mount Sinai. Now he and his Power stood brazenly in the middle of the crowd, directly in front of Aaron. The Mediator of Heaven & Earth flashed a devious grin. With Elohim and Moses currently prattling on, now was his golden opportunity to break those freshly minted commands and place himself back in full control before anyone was the wiser. He glanced from the people, to the mountaintop; then back to the people. *No need to waste time agonizing through the entire list,* his grin widened. *They would simply break commandment number one.*

Deep breath.

Knuckle crack.

"Why not make them a god?" The Deceiver leaned in to Aaron. "They mean you no dishonor. They simply want to worship your god in a way that feels familiar to them."

Long pause.

Slow exhale.

"Why not make us a god?" the crowd parroted. "We mean you no dishonor. We simply want to worship your god in a way that's familiar to us."

Haylel shot Aaron a knowing look.

Aaron stepped back, bending under the sudden pressure, uncertain what to do.

With a growl, Haylel reached down and grabbed the hand of his Power. Drawing back, he plunged it deep into the chest of the conflicted high priest—all six fingers wrapping tightly around Aaron's still beating heart.

Sparks flew as pride connected with pride.

"What's the harm?" Haylel picked up right where he left off. "Let the mice play." He chuckled unassumingly. "These people will still be celebrating in honor of the one true God. Why not let them have a little fun as well?" He shot Aaron a wink. "Your delinquent brother—if he even still exists—will be none the wiser."

The crowd began to chant and cheer as dark energy flooded Aaron's heart. The high priest stiffened, initially resisting the pull. But soon he relaxed, his deep-seated pride and childhood insecurities soaking it up like a sponge.

Why not celebrate the Egyptian way? he reasoned. *We can still sacrifice by our traditions. Besides, this will be an excellent way to bring our cultures together, to heal the rift between slave and oppressor! He* raised a calming hand, silencing the rowdy crowd. "Take off your gold," he instructed. "Bring to me the earrings that your wives, sons, and daughters are wearing if you would like me to do as you say."

The crowd immediately obliged.

Aaron took the metal and threw it in the fire, forging what would become a makeshift calf. In all honestly, the resulting abomination looked *more* like the illegitimate love-child between an orangutan and a doorknob, than it did any sort of 'gilded bovine sensation.' But, of course, the crowd riotously agreed—it was indeed a golden calf.

Aaron held the monstrosity high. "Here is your god, oh Israel," he proclaimed. "Your god who brought you up, out of Egypt!"

The crowd roared its approval.

"Tomorrow," Aaron fawned. "There will be a feast to Jehovah! We will sacrifice and celebrate as one!"

...

The festivities kicked-off at dawn the next day. Aaron was pleased to see the crowd had grown from mere hundreds to several thousand. The weather was beautiful. Spirits were running high. Aaron's ego was soaring.

Haylel and his Power had also returned, bringing with them an army of drooling hordes. Hell had formulated its plans too. And unlike the hopeful party goers, Haylel's troops—and this blasphemous opportunity—were not going to be wasted.

Aaron fired up his altar and the Barbecue began! Brisket, bikini's, and beer bongs were everywhere. Wine flowed freely. Egyptian Top 40 blasted.

As more and more aromas from the day's peace offerings filled the air, the celebration turned from neighborhood block party, to straight up Spring Break.

Then, just as the sun was setting, things got hedonistic.

Haylel's hordes roared with anticipation. This was the moment they'd been waiting for! In only a matter of minutes their breach would begin, and every horde capable was eager to enter in.

You see, in the act—at climax—a human's guard is down. And in this moment of genuine transparency, a window—a sort of 'portal to the soul'—is opened. Like a match, it sparks only for a moment; its intended purpose to allow the spirit of a baby to attach at conception. Of course, if this act is done within the loving confines of marriage—a marriage legally established in the eyes of God—Elohim's own Spirit will guard the portal, assuring safe passage. However, when done promiscuously, outside the proper safeguards, *any* spirit, Haylel found, who is ready and waiting may take advantage!

Granted, the window is often too small, too brief, or not opened at all … and thus, no soul—baby, or other—gets in.

Still, there is always one guarantee. A single, quantum stitch—flung from the soul of one partner and entangled within the fabric of the other—is *always* generated. This subatomic thread binds the two together, so that any spiritual force moving on the one, may now—in real time—also affect the other.

In this way, Haylel found he could easily control entire populations. Knitting them together, into a sort of 'invisible human tapestry.' Stitching and weaving until all he had to do was tug on one tormented soul, and *voilá*—everyone would begin to move.

And so the sounds of music, merriment, and revelry filled the night air. To the carnal eye, this all looked like free, uninhibited fun. But to every eye opened plainly in the spirit, it was the interlocking of shackles, webs, and chains..

..And to those particularly discerning—*it was the very acts of war!*

—| 1477:09:00:09:11:00 |—

Dawn was just beginning to shed first light when Moses finished barreling his way down the mountain—a very loyal, very disheveled, Joshua, careening in his wake. The two came to a screeching halt atop a rocky cliff overlooking the remains of the previous night's debauchery.

Moses paused, plucking the leaves and twigs from his matted hair and beard. He surveyed the damage. Wine vats and party goers lay strewn across the desert valley below. Squinting and squirming, he straightened his clothes, fighting the rage that was rising within.

CRUNCH..

What was that?

Joshua's head popped up in the distance—eyes wide, jaw clenched—he leapt from the center of a large tangle of brush. He had wheeled to a stop some fifty yards back—*right in the center of a thorny briar!*

Back arched, he hopped from one throbbing foot to the other, biting his tongue, desperately trying not to cause a scene. He could see Moses standing before him, towering confidently above the quiet desert valley—one giant stone tablet tucked under each powerful arm. His robe and beard blew fiercely in the wind. His darkened silhouette boldly contrasting the brilliant colors of the rising sun.

Joshua tried not to scream. Shooting pain or no, his heart was moved. The scene was breathtakingly surreal.

Then, reality set in.

Moses began to tremble and shake. Not because his adrenaline had been running largely unchecked. Nor because his anger had suddenly sparked into rage. But because the rarefied energy erupting from the sacred stones he was holding was quickly becoming too hot to handle.

He twisted and jerked, holding on as long as he could.

But it was too little, too late.

The tablets flew from his grasp, up and over the ledge, crashing—down, down, down—to the hard-packed earth below.

BOOM—they exploded on impact, detonating like a heaven-sent bomb, dirt and debris shooting hundreds of feet in the quiet, morning air.

The crowd was instantly on their feet.

Every bird taking flight for miles.

Car alarms, dogs and babies screamed at the top of their lungs, heralding the dark cloud rising ominously above the abruptly awakened nation.

Moses dove for cover.

Joshua threw up both hands—deflecting and dodging debris—still hopping from one throbbing foot to the other.

OK—freeze frame.

You're probably right. Artistic liberty aside, most likely the scene played out a bit more like a stoic, well-lit, Charlton Heston movie. *But you get the point.*

Thankfully, it took several minutes for the dust to settle, leaving Moses and Joshua plenty of time to pick themselves up, gather their whits about them, and stand perfectly poised as if nothing had ever happened.

Then—Moses lifted his staff and sternly called all of Israel to himself.

When Haylel realized he'd been busted, and that his night of debaucherous soul-stitching was ending up a total waste; he quickly turned on Moses in the hopes of salvaging the situation. *After all,* he growled, *there was more than one way to skin a meddling cat.* He buried a hand deep into Moses' chest, waiting for his Power to connect. But the connection never came. Somehow the Patriarch's humble heart-cry for *mercy* was short-circuiting the flow.

Haylel shrieked in frustration. *Someone MUST pay for this hellacious transgression!*

The words pierced Moses' soul. He searched his heart for a better solution, but he knew it to be true: *With spiritual redemption not yet on the table, there was only one possible resolution..*

Eradication.

With a heavy heart, he turned to Aaron, who in turn rallied the troops. This was their mess. Their clan, the Levites, would clean it up. Moses wept as brother turned on brother and three thousand died that day.

The Law had levied a powerful blow. Its first act had not been to bring God and man together, but instead, it had driven them apart. It gave no life to God's Spirit, but instead, upheld Death. Once again Hell had prevailed, perverting Elohim's protection, and establishing Heaven's rule not upon the goodness of God, but upon the shed blood of his beloved children.

CH27: REDO
1477:07:20:04:11:11

Moses was on his face ... *again*. It had been forty days, to the day, since he'd shattered the tablets. Forty days, to the day, since the blood of his brothers had been savagely shed. He hadn't eaten a thing. In fact, he hadn't moved. He lay motionless beside Joshua, face buried in the sandy floor of the makeshift, tabernacle tent. He wasn't waiting on water. He wasn't waiting on food. *He was waiting on God to arrive.*

A gentle wind picked up.

"Chisel two blank tablets, like the first," it quietly began. "Then, return once more to the mountaintop."

Moses froze. For a moment the tent went totally dark. Then the presence of Elohim burst through, hovering directly over the spot where the two repentant leaders lay.

Joshua cracked an eye. *He couldn't help but peek!* The thick, shimmering, iridescent, heaven-cloud was electrifying.

"Make an ark—a box of wood and gold," Elohim heralded. "I, myself, will engrave the new tablets of stone. But you must put those tablets immediately in the ark—for safekeeping." He flashed a winsome, forgiving grin.

Moses let out a deep ragged sigh, relief washing over his desert-dusted frame. For the first time in weeks, he relaxed. If the plan was to, 'redo,' than that could only mean one thing: *Elohim HAD turned away from his anger!* Overwhelming gratitude flooded Moses' soul, filling his heart, full to overflowing. "Teach me your ways," the thankful shepherd beamed. "So I may know you, and continue to find such favor!" His spirit soared. "*Never leave us!* For who else—*but YOU*—distinguishes your people from all the other people on the face of the earth?!"

Elohim smiled at his precious son. "I will do the very thing you have asked, because I am pleased with you and I know you by name."

"*Show me your GLORY?!*" the words erupted like fire.

Moses could barely contain himself.

Elohim dropped everything and smiled. He was deeply moved. It wasn't so much the request, as its brazen audacity which so warmed his humble father's heart. For a moment it was like old times again—two walking together in the cool of the day. No one worrying about, "who was God" or "who was man." It was just pure, raw, uninhibited relationship—heart to heart, friend to friend, father to son.

"I will grant your request," Elohim spoke to Moses directly. "But you must come alone. No one may come with you or be anywhere on the mountain while you are here. Don't even let the flocks or herds graze nearby. There must be nothing with a hijackable soul anywhere around ... understand?"

Moses nodded his agreement.

Elohim exhaled his relief. "Then come up the mountain in the morning," he grinned. "There, you will present yourself to me. And my Glory, I will surely show to you."

Then he was gone, leaving only the train of his aura behind.

With a shove and a grunt, Moses was up and moving, eager to complete the requested tasks.

Joshua, however, remained: The train. The atmosphere. The presence. *It was better than life!* He listened as Moses exited the tent, its slender flap falling quietly back into place.

At last—he was alone.

Slowly, he settled back, immersing himself in wave upon passing wave. Oh, the love.. The power. The freedom. The light. Each swell was better than the last. Each revelation, deeper.

Joshua relaxed, sinking further into the welcoming arms of the lingering spiritual dimension. *On second thought,* he grinned, another mind-bending aspect of Heaven unfolding plainly before him. *Not only am I most certainly NOT alone ... but this is FAR better than life!*

—| 1477:07:19:12:12:12 |—

Hoot-whoo, Hoot-whoo—a hungry, old owl called in the distance.

Moses sat up, instantly wide awake. It was pitch black, the dead of night, darkness all around. He reached out, groping for his staff, careful not to wake the others.

Hoot-WHOO, Hoot-WHOO, the old owl complained again, a little bit louder this time.

Already dressed, Moses stepped from his tent, moving to his workshop outside. Hoisting two freshly cut stones—one under each arm—he silently exited camp.

HOOT-WHOO—the old owl reluctantly grumped, voicing his final wake-up call. It had been a long night of futile hunting, and his belly was still quite empty. He watched as the man with the rocks silently passed by below, dredging the brush with his feet. A tasty morsel went scurrying, and the old owl honed in. With a blink and a snort he abandoned his post, chasing his reward off into the dark.

Moses smiled his gratitude, picking up the pace. As instructed, he was exiting camp in secret. When daylight did finally arrive—no one but Joshua would be the wiser.

The hike up the mountain was considerably substantial—especially with his hefty load. But Moses was determined. Methodically, he moved past the timber line, across the slow burn, and through the piles of dwindling ash, stopping only when he'd reached the clearing at the top. He stifled a frown, glancing around.

Where was the stage?

..the throne?

..the embers?

..Elohim?

With a shrug and a sigh, he dropped his giant paperweights, plopping down beside them. His legs were tired. His shoulders were strained. His knees were beginning to ache. He stretched and turned, nestling back into the cleft of two overhanging rocks.

No worries, he smiled, *he could wait..*

and wait..

and..

Slowly the sun began to rise. Moses watched the residual piles of smoldering ash fade from purples and pinks to rich ambers and golds. He surveyed the abandoned clearing. There was no wind, no fire, no earthquake, no fanfare ... only a thin wispy cloud—inconspicuously gathering. Slowly it grew, enlarging and thickening, until the entire mountaintop was completely consumed. From the outside looking in, it seemed dark, stormy, and gray. But within, it was bright—a cheerful golden light—and actually quite pleasant.

Elohim had arrived!

Moses bowed his head in reverence. "My Lord—," he worshiped. "Show me your glory!"

There was a motion..

A movement..

An anomaly among the trees..

Was that a man? Moses squinted, craning his neck to see. The anomaly had no distinct features. Just motion. Color. Fire. Light. Moses marveled at its developing presence, eager to see God's glory revealed.

"No one may see my face and live," a voice called from the gathering light. "So I will cover you with my hand, until I have fully passed by. Then I will remove my hand and you may see my back."

Instantly, everything went dark.

Moses slumped to the ground—trapped beneath an incredible weight. His eyes were shut tight, yet all of history flashed before them: Earth's creation. The rise and fall of man. Hell's two-faced insurgence. Heaven's secret redemption plan.

From snake to seed, son to salvation—*he saw it all.*

Then he awoke.

Moses leapt to his feet, darting from his makeshift shelter. *Was it too late? Had God's Glory already passed?*

The determined observer blinked repeatedly, forcing his vision to focus beyond the bright, electric auras dancing all around. Stretching to his toes, Moses steadied himself against the trunk of a tree, desperate to catch one more glimpse of those shimmering, fiery robes fading slowly in the distance.

That's when The Word introduced himself.

"I am Jehovah," he smiled. "The compassionate God. Slow to anger. Gracious and abounding in love!" His calming voice seemed to flow—to, from, and through everything—bathing Moses in peace and understanding. "I bring God and man together. I do *not* drive them apart. I am merciful—forgiving their hate and selfish rebellion. But I am also just. I will not leave the guilty unpunished."

The words dropped like bombs into Moses' astounded soul. *Everything was beginning to make sense:* The snake. The fruit. The infiltration. The plan. This wasn't so much 'Heaven *against* Earth' or 'God *against* Man' as this was—*an inside job!* Moses gasped. *No wonder Elohim seemed so distant, scary and aloof—his jealous, rebellious CEO, had hijacked the company!*

A quivering palm planted squarely in the center of his awestruck forehead. Moses' mind flashed back to the night two opposing angels has battled at the foot of his bed. *Of course—,* understanding eyes began to roll, *the Heaven-sent contradiction didn't mean Elohim was bipolar. There was simply a massive conflict-of-interest between Heaven's merciful, man-LOVING President; and its legalistic, man-HATING CEO!*

I MUST tell the world! Moses trembled. *Everyone needs to know: There's a literal snake in the grass—secretly pulling the strings!*

"Oh, Lord!" he implored, suddenly rife with understanding. "*Never leave me! Never leave your people! Your personal presence is the ONLY thing that distinguishes us from any other nation on the earth!*" He raised both hands, sensing the utter urgency. "*Teach us your ways, that we may continue to find such favor with you, that you may always be free to bless us, and to bring us fully into the land that you promised our ancestors!*"

"I will certainly do as you have said," the Grace of God assured. "But you must be careful to obey *all* my commands. If you don't, my law—my wrath and jealousy—my mediating cherub—he, will legally destroy you!"

"We will certainly do our best," Moses cried, dismayed. "But what of the times when we fail?"

The Word smiled at the genuine heart of his beloved brother. "Offerings," he gently replied. "Burnt offerings will provide the temporary grace you'll need, until the time when true Grace can arrive. They will cover your imperfections, appease the Devourer, and protect your generations, until I can permanently make a way where there currently is none." The hope-filled words stirred life and laughter, lightning and thunder.

Flash.

BOOM.

Smiles.

Then God's Grace was gone, vanishing back into the surrounding clouds.

Moses wept out loud, his entire being bursting with the burning light of undeserved revelation. *Could it really be?* That Grace—like Sin—was a *person?*

Thump. Thud. Two freshly inscribed tablets dropped softly to the dirt at Moses' feet. A refreshing rain began. The awestruck son gently lifted the hand-written stones. He could feel the mighty, all-consuming fire burning fiercely within. Standing, he cradled them like two lost, little lambs. These would be forever safe, stored within the heart of the ark—supernaturally sealed within the Savior, himself.

Slowly Moses turned, squinting at the lingering trail of fading heavenly lights. *Guess that begs one last question,* he grinned, thoughtfully starting his way back down the deserted mountain slope. *So—who exactly IS this Savior?*

CH28: GRADUATION
1438:01:07:17:07:07

Wow. The air was brisk tonight! Joshua shook his legs and stomped his feet, blowing on his hands to stay warm. Hood up, cloak tight, he was standing on the side of a mountain—Nebo, to be exact—waiting for Moses to return.

He glanced up the hill, into the thick, murky darkness. Somewhere up there, Moses was meeting with Elohim.

Joshua bent down, quietly gathering grass and twigs for tinder. Waiting was nothing new. Moses had met with Elohim many times over the years. And many of those times, he had been stationed patiently nearby.

Of course, everyone was much older now. The seasoned sidekick turned his back to the wind, expertly stacking a neat little pile of kindling. So old, in fact, that the silver from Moses' 120 year old head had started making its way into his own, 80 year old beard—or so they liked to joke.

Click, click—Joshua struck two stones together, sparks flying from the flint into his small clump of tinder. He blew gently, smiling as smoldering smoke turned to flickering flame.

Had it really been forty years? the astonished protégé shook his head, tending the growing blaze. *They'd been walking 'round this God-forsaken desert for ... forty-years?* He stifled a chuckle. *How many people would have actually left Egypt, had they known this would be the outcome?* He laid a thin piece of timber across his maturing flame.

Truth be told, it really was their own fault. When Elohim had compelled them to leave the desert and take the territory promised them, it was the people who had chickened-out.

"Giants in the land," they'd moaned. "We're like

grasshoppers in their sight.."

Joshua heaved a hefty sigh. Only he and Caleb—Moses' other assistant—had stood their ground, ready to charge.

But the people had made up their minds. And as a result, the entire campaign was stalemated; shelved for nearly four decades, until a new generation of eager participants could willingly step in.

Joshua lifted his staff, stirring the crackling embers, a heartfelt smile spreading slowly across thick, reminiscent lips.

"*You and Caleb will LIVE to take the land,*" Elohim had promised him directly. "A*s will the next generation I raise up!*"

Joshua shook his head. *What an assurance!* There was no denying the unshakable confidence those words had brought— knowing he *couldn't* die until Heaven's promise had been fulfilled! He laughed out loud. It had certainly made life much more exciting, and the drudgery of waiting forty years, much more bearable.

Ahh—, but Moses..

Joshua's thoughts drifted back to *that fateful day*. His stirring slowly stopped. He puzzled, doing his best to remember the details.

"Go—outside the tent!" the order had been given. The people were out of water, and Moses and Aaron needed to speak with Elohim alone.

Thankfully, this wasn't their first rodeo, Joshua ducked through the hanging tent flap, somewhat relieved. The last time this occurred, Moses had simply struck a rock wall, shattering its thin facade and releasing the aquifer of water hidden behind. *But this time*—Joshua's ears perked up—*the instructions were much more peculiar.*

"Speak to the rock." Elohim plainly directed. "At your command, it will pour out its water before you."

The plan seemed simple enough. Yet, when the crowds had gathered, and Elohim's message relaid, there had been some bizarre confusion. Caught between the people's stubborn arrogance and the embarrassment of stuttering before an inanimate object, Moses had snapped.

"Listen, you rebels," he'd bellowed. "Must I bring water out of this rock too?"

He spun to face the wall, lifting his staff high in dramatic fashion. The thought arose, '*Speak to the rock.*' Moses opened obedient lips, every intention of following through. But the rage was so blinding. And the people so *STIFF-NECKED!*

CRACK—his staff came down hard against the shale.

Thunk. Thud. The rock didn't budge.

The thought returned, '*Speak to the rock.*' But frustration had already taken root. This time Moses *CHOSE* to ignore it. He swung his staff again with all his might.

CRUNCH..

Crack.

Splash.

Roar.

A mighty river flowed.

God's follow-up debriefing had been understandably intense, Joshua remembered the scene. Elohim had been quite displeased; Moses badly shaken up.

"My Glory," Elohim had plainly explained. "Had *himself,* become that rock!"

It was all a part of the plan: A foreshadowing. An example. A premonition of the law's fulfillment—demonstrating Elohim's ability to transform stone into flesh, death into life, and rules into relationship.

"My son, *why* did you ignore our relationship?" the Father of Heaven & Earth implored. "You struck the rock, striking *my* Glory and keeping a most spectacular miracle from my children. Now tell me—," he demanded. "How is YOUR stubborn arrogance any less offensive than the arrogance of my people?"

Moses had no reply.

Elohim narrowed his gaze. "Had you, at any point, changed your mind and spoken to the Rock, your consequences would have surely been different," he chided. "However, anyone willing to abuse the living God, forcing him to do what he is *already* willing to do, just to satisfy personal ego? That person," Elohim lifted his voice, redirecting his warning toward *every* spirit listening, "is not fit to enter my promised land. And the honor due him, will be afforded to another."

There was a fizzle and a pop, a strange wind above the trees—Joshua jolted back to reality, the fire he'd been unintentionally ignoring suddenly on the verge of going out. He reached down, tossing a dry log onto the whimpering flames. *Whoosh*—there was a sudden burst of ash, a renewed surge of light. Joshua scooted back, taking refuge against the weathered trunk of a nearby Mulberry tree. He slid to the ground, loosening his cloak, suddenly exceedingly warm. *When would Moses return?* Joshua looked up to the heavens, a chuckle rising from his lips. *From his boss' track record, it could easily be another—thirty-nine days!* Moses' faithful sidekick smiled and settled back, resting his head against the tree, watching the twinkling starlight dancing its way through the twisting branches above. Certainly, he would sleep here for the night. *After all—it might be another..*

thirty..

nine..

"Go down to the people."

Joshua woke with a start.

"Tell them their leader has died." Moses nudged his sleepy successor. "I will return to the mountaintop. From there, I will depart." He flashed a broad grin. "My son, at last—*my time has come!*"

Joshua rose quickly to his feet, a lump instantly in his throat. His knees felt weak. His stomach unsettled. This moment had been a long time coming. *So—why did he feel so NOT ready?*

Moses reached out, wrapping his wide-eyed protégé in a tight bear hug. "With Elohim's direction, and the power of his mighty Spirit," he whispered. "*Everything will be OK!*"

The words filled Joshua's soul like wind in his sails. His heart slowed. His mind settled. Peace overcame.

He stood tall and grinned.

"Tell the people, I love them!" Moses relayed his final message. "And you too, my son—I dearly love you!"

There were more handshakes, hugs and words, before Moses eventually stepped back. With a prayer and a blessing he offered up his staff, sending his emboldened successor fearlessly back down to the people.

It was then, and only then, that Moses turned—and giggling like a perennial school girl—practically skipped his way back up the hill.

...

Moses' best friend stood, waiting for him at the top of the mountain.

"Are you ready for this?" Elohim chuckled, extending a welcoming hand.

"You have no idea!" Moses reached over, grabbing his Heavenly Father's forearm. He hesitated a moment, *how—exactly— would this work?*

'*I pull, you follow,*' Elohim answered the thought with a thought of his own.

Moses shot him a look.

'*No worries,*' Elohim grinned. '*It's mostly painless—I think.*' He flashed a huge smile and tugged.

Moses didn't budge.

Elohim frowned and tugged again.

Then again.

Moses burst out laughing, the look on Elohim's face was priceless. '*Free will,*' he shrugged, still chuckling.

Elohim laughed out loud. '*Well—whenever you're ready,*' he playfully mimed a bow. Dropping both hands, he meekly stepped back.

Moses squared his shoulders, closed twinkling eyes, and with a long deep breath stepped painlessly over into the spirit realm. His body crumpled to the ground behind him like a discarded party costume.

Elohim welcomed his beloved son with a hardy embrace. '*May I unveil to you—your destiny!*' one brilliant hand swept boldly across the horizon.

Moses' jaw dropped. The entirety of the Promised Land unrolled before them—past, present, and future—in a 360 degree display of ravishing spiritual beauty.

For ages they stood. Side by side. Arm in arm. Eager, and fully engaged. They analyzed victories. Strategized outcomes. Debated and role-played results. Until, at long last—and after countless millennia—the all-immersive, mountaintop panorama rolled itself up once again.

Then—like long lost family, finally reunited—father and son linked arms, locked step, and turned to..

"One last thing before we go," Elohim chuckled, reaching out and parting reality like a curtain before them. He casually motioned towards four men laughing and trudging their way up the hill, and a fifth coming down in a chariot. "My son," he finally asked the question Moses had been dying to hear his entire life. "How would you like to meet my Glory, face-to-face?"

CH29: HEAD TO HEAD
1438:01:05:07:07:07

CRA— CRAAACK, two flashes of lightning struck Nebo simultaneously from opposite sides of the mountain. The earth trembled, flames flaring bright; each strike sending a pillar of dirt and ash billowing skyward. Slowly, the dust cleared and the dirt settled. In their wake stood two very stoic, very powerful, very determined Cherubim Angels.

Michael surveyed the mountain's northern face. Tall and true, he stood; dark curly hair cascading down broad, muscular shoulders. A shield of glowing bronze hung securely from his back, a massive flaming sword sheathed vertically beneath it. Like a trained marksman, he held his stance; fiery eyes darting left and right, expertly scanning for hostiles.

Three..

Two..

One..

He was on the move again. Speeding uphill, closing in on his target. Boulders, logs, thickets, ravines—he never slowed down, never broke stride. The special-ops angel was on a classified mission, direct from Elohim: Confrontation was certain. Opposition imminent. *Failure,* he knew, *was not an option.*

On the other side of the mountain, Haylel furrowed his brow, gazing up its rising southern slope. For a moment he paused, calculating gray eyes observing his deserted surroundings.

Five..

Four..

Three..

Two..

He too, turned uphill, moving at an all out sprint. His brilliant blond hair and bronzed, jewel-covered body sparkled in the cool, morning light. Unlike his rival, he carried no weapons—nothing to "needlessly slow him down." *And why would he?* Deception was his shield. Savage whit, his sword. And his crackling crimson aura, all the protection he'd ever need—he touched his left shoulder—as long as he held the keys!

Hell's personified vessel pressed forward, pushing himself to exceed his already blistering pace. Rumor had it, Moses had recently "graduated," and as the rightful owner of Earth, Haylel had big plans for the patriarch's freshly discarded body. Of course, he was taking a bit of a chance showing up completely undisguised. But he didn't care. He needed the option of pulling rank—and to him, this "once-in-a-lifetime opportunity" was well worth the risk.

From opposing sides, the two angels converged, fiery trails blazing in their wake. Both were single-minded. Both fiercely resolute. Each quite certain, they alone, would fulfill their intended mission.

Michael arrived at the body first. It lay peacefully across a bed of dry leaves near the peak of the mountain. The Heaven-sent angel sped to its side, carefully looking it over. He'd been ordered to transport the remains to an undisclosed, secure location—a cozy little catacomb hidden deep within the confines of a neighboring valley, and he needed to be sure nothing uninvited was secretly tagging along. One final glance around, and he bent to retrieve his cargo.

Six powerful fingers, wrapped tightly around his arm.

Michael froze.

"The body, of course, is mine—old friend," a familiar voice purred.

Haylel. Michael stiffened, tightening his grip.

"No need to trouble yourself," Heaven's Chief Executive Officer leaned down, extending a second helping hand. "I'll take it from here."

Michael didn't budge. Slowly, he looked up, peering intently at his unlikely adversary. "I am under direct orders to *bury* the body," he calmly clarified, returning his opposition's steely gaze.

"Whoa. At ease, soldier," Haylel chuckled, turning the charm up full-blast. "Your duties have been formally relieved: I will handle the burial, and all its messy details. Rest assured, *everything* will be well documented and well taken care of."

"My orders come from Elohim, himself," Michael cut-in, not entirely fond of the self-aggrandizing, deceptively-dissuading, smooth-talk.

Haylel squinted, *certainly this was a bluff. Elohim ran everything Earth-related through his department. Would he not have been notified?* He tightened his grip—impatience beginning to rise. "Moses was a murderer." He leaned in close. "He slew a man in Egypt, buried him in the sand." His voice dropped to a whisper as if Michael hadn't heard the inside scoop. "Does he truly deserve such an honorable burial?"

This Haylel said, not because he desired justice, but because he desperately wanted control of the body. Hell's plan was to return the body to the people for mummification, a practice they were well acquainted with. "Forget lumpy, misshapen calves," Haylel had proudly swaggered. "I will make *Moses* their god!"

Properly executed, Hell would once again take full control. And with everyone's focus shifted away from Elohim and back towards a useless mummy; Israel's destiny—along with Earth's salvation—would be perpetually and indefinitely derailed.

Besides, Haylel still wasn't entirely sure whether Moses was the fulfillment of the foretold "savior" or not. And acquiring complete control of the body was the only way he could ensure that good 'ol Moe remained dead, permanently.

"Not worthy of an honorable burial? ..You don't say," Michael looked incredulous, and quite frankly a little bored. "My Lord, we both know the law was not even written, much less in effect, at the time of the cited incident." He shook his head in disgust. "How can Moses be held accountable for something that didn't even.."

"So, what do you want?" Haylel cut him off. "Power? Prestige? Promotion? Control? ..I can make all of it happen," he raised a generous eyebrow. "Just release the body to me. I'll take care of the rest." He looked left, then right—leaning in close. "Elohim will be none the wiser.."

Michael sarcastically mirrored the disingenuous gesture. "All I have. All I need. All I *WANT*, comes from Elohim," he sternly rebuked. "HE is the *ONLY* one I answer to."

Haylel burned red with anger. *Who was this insolent prude?* "The body is mine," he hissed, tugging hard on the corpse. "He grew up in *my* systems. Bowed at *my* altars. Swore oaths in *my* courts."

Michael's grip only tightened. He was both outranked and out-muscled, he knew it. But his actions came on the *direct* word of the *highest* authority. *Besides—, he held on for dear life, if a scuffle did ensue, he had a few tricks up his sleeve he was certain Haylel would never see coming.*

"You brazen, impertinent cuss," Haylel raged. "Release my property immediately!" His eyes grew dark with fury. "This is *MY* jurisdiction, and *MY* responsibility." He jerked the body with all his might. "*I* am the mediator between Heaven and Earth—the *Master of Matter. This body is mine! Give it TO ME!*"

Michael released nothing more than a sterile, half-smile. He was never letting go. "The *LORD* rebuke you," he exclaimed. "The Lord of *ALL* spirits, Master of *ALL* matter, *rebuke YOU!*"

BOOM—thunder exploded in the heavens.

CRACK—lightning rent open the sky.

Haylel's eyes went wide, his protective aura suddenly snuffed out. *This was no bluff!* He shrieked, shooting backwards across the clearing—slamming into the trunk of one very large, very withered tree.

CREEEEEK—the old tree complained loudly, splitting violently in two.

Haylel slid slowly to its base.

Michael raced to detain the implausible insurrectionist, leaping through the air and crashing down upon the disarmed deceiver with a tempest all his own. *Ka-POW*—bark and leaves exploded a second time. The ancient tree let out another piercing whine. Micheal reached out to grab Haylel, but Haylel was already gone—vanished into thin air—fleeing to the safety of his Second-

Heaven Headquarters.

With a frown, Michael rose to his feet. *There would be no accountability held today.* He blinked a few times, poised and alert, waiting to be absolutely sure Haylel wasn't coming back.

Deafening Silence.

He glanced around. *What a scene*—scorched earth, shredded leaves, one giant smoldering tree.

Cautiously he retraced his steps, scooping up his precious cargo, securing the body tight against his own. Long and slow, he exhaled his relief. Then—in a final whirl of wind and leaves—he too, fled the scene.

...

Michael's spirit was deeply troubled as he lay Moses' body gently down across the dimly lit, catacomb ledge. He hunkered over, properly preparing and preserving the remains, his mind hashing and rehashing the day's odd events. For quite some time he stood, working and puzzling, puzzling and working, his sizable presence consuming every nook and cranny of the tiny mountainside grotto.

Was Haylel not completely, unequivocally, overstepping his bounds? The question tossed and turned in his ever-awakening mind, it just didn't compute. *Clearly, the charlatan wasn't following protocol. Certainly, not Elohim's orders.*

The massive angel finished his work, ducking carefully back through the tomb's humble entrance. With a long, hard-pressed sigh he turned, erasing the opening with a simple brush of his hand.

The hillside trembled, rocks and debris falling all around.

Could it really be? He bent—head down, arms in 'starting block' position. *That the very being commissioned to protect the sons of God, was the very being dead-set against them?*

BOOM—he launched himself skyward, rocketing into the cosmos at twice the speed of light. His jaw was set. His fists were clenched. Every muscle tense. He was rattled to the core.

Turning, he adjusted his trajectory, gaining speed as he transitioned to hyperspace, heading for home. *At first opportunity, he would expose this rebellion,* his heart was firmly resolute. *But for now, he would hold his tongue.* He leaned forward and relaxed, Heaven already coming into view.

Yes—for now, he would hold his tongue.

CH30: BACK AGAINST THE ROPES
1437:09:12:09:00:12

Arruuuugh. Aruu-Aruuuugh! Three shofar blasts pierced the early morning air.

Joshua peered silently over his shoulder.

There stood Jericho—city of the moon—massive, daunting … impenetrable. Its double-tiered walls and steep, sixty-degree embankments towered nearly ten stories above the marching Israeli nation.

The novice General lifted his head. In the limited vision of the early morning fog, Jericho's walls seemed to stretch upward forever. *With just us,* he mused, *taking this city is impossible. But with God..*

Aruu-Arruuuugh! another powerful blast sounded.

Joshua broke rank, scrambling up a nearby embankment. From his rocky perch, he could see all forty-thousand of his men marching in perfect unison—wrapping the city like a giant python, silently stalking its prey. He grinned. If someone had told him just seven days ago what his game plan to take Jericho would actually be, he would have laughed that same someone right out of house and home. Yet here he was, marching his fledgling army repeatedly around the most heavily fortified city on the planet—in absolute silence.

Left.. Left.. Left, Right, Left..

Joshua slid from his perch, falling back into step. The collective crunch of Israel's silent cadence reverberated off Jericho's thick stony walls, echoing like the ominous "ticks" and "tocks" of a militant, army-sized, countdown clock.

Slowly Joshua's breathing evened. His arms and legs settled

in. *How incredibly supernatural the past few weeks have been,* he mused, his thoughts beginning to wander. *First, there was the Jordan River:* As soon as his men had stepped foot into its swollen torrents, its waters had completely dried. *Miraculous, was an understatement. More like, completely unbelievable.* One minute, its banks were overflowing. The next, it was a dry, empty riverbed. Joshua smiled, remembering how his faith—like the faith of so many others—had virtually exploded, supercharged by their very own, completely personalized, 'Red Sea,' moment.

Then, there was the angelic messenger: Clad in white. Sword in hand. Golden belt around his waist. The cosmic stranger had surprised Joshua along the road to Jericho.

Joshua could've kicked himself. There he was, in hostile territory, just outside Jericho's gates—caught alone, off guard, and weaponless.

Certainly, it was his own fault. He had slipped out of camp just before dusk to do a little "impromptu reconnaissance." Keeping to the shadows, he'd left his personal weapon behind, thinking it would only slow him down. Now he stood, frozen, some fifty feet away from a fully armed stranger, doing his best to make it appear like he was resting his hand on the hilt of his sword.

'*You and Caleb WILL LIVE to take the land,*' Elohim's forty-year-old promise suddenly pricked his pounding heart.

Joshua paused, the words exploding in his soul. *Of course!* he shook himself to action. *He would NOT die! The God above ALL gods had promised.*

"Are you for us, or against us?" he shifted his weight, renewed boldness rising.

"Neither," came the peculiar reply. "I come as Commander of Heaven's Armies."

Joshua's jaw dropped, he forgot all about bluffing. *This was exactly what he'd been searching for!* "My Lord," he fell to the dirt. "What orders do you have for me?"

Immediately a welcoming palm rested on the back of his head. "See, I have delivered the city into your hands," the stranger spoke, his words so full of life they impregnated the balmy air.

Joshua's heart leapt, a vision flashing before his eyes: It was Jericho—burned and in ruins—its people fallen and scattered beneath triumphant Israeli banners.

"For six days, march silently with your men, once around the city," the visitor relayed Heaven's strategy. "On the seventh day, march seven times. Then blow your trumpets! When you hear the final blast, give a loud shout. The walls of the city will collapse, and your armies will go up, over the embankment and into the city."

Aruuuuug. Arr-Aruuuugh!

There was the trumpet now! Joshua looked up, roused from his own reflections. *One lap down. Only six more to go.* He listened for the shofar to sound again, his gaze drawn to a particular red cord—hanging somewhat conspicuously—from a tenth-story window near the top of Jericho's outer wall.

Then, there was Rahab: Joshua grinned, quietly adjusting his pack. Rahab, a Jericho-born citizen, had put her own life on the line, protecting two of his spies. Of course, being the shrewd business-woman she was, she'd asked for Israel's sworn protection in return. It was a protection they'd gladly afforded. *Still—,* Joshua shook his head, *she'd somehow picked intruder-underdogs over lifelong friends & family?* He eyed the scarlet lifeline. *What a sign! Her bold, unshakable faith was—in this moment—supernaturally building his!*

"Be gone, infidel dogs!" Insults rained down from above.

Joshua glanced up—the town was beginning to stir! High above, men, women, and children gathered like schoolyard bullies, challenging their lowly enemies below. "Morons!" "Simpletons!" "Fools!" they cried from the safety of their lofty walls. "Where are your ropes? Where are your ladders? What makes you think you could ever hope to reach us?" Swaggering, they hurled a steady stream of gestures, insults, and last night's bath water down upon the heads of their tight-lipped opposition.

Israel took it all in stride, marching relentlessly beneath Jericho's flood of perpetual demoralization for six more grueling laps.

In the natural, it seemed Israel had already lost—silently flirting with the very enemy soon to be responsible for their certain demise. Yet, in reality—in the spirit realm—the God who sits above *all* gods was openly stacking the proverbial "deck" on Israel's behalf.

You see, had their enemy's eyes been fully opened—even for the briefest of moments—they would have noticed every venomous, hate-filled word spewing from their blasphemous mouths rising slowly into the atmosphere and hanging like a thick, black cloud above the city. Waiting. Festering. Expanding. Growing.

Aruuugh! Arrruuuuuuuuuuuuuuuuuuuuu—!

The final shofar was sounding!

Joshua lifted his head and sprang into action. "*SHOUT!*" he bellowed, thrusting his sword high in the air. "*For the God above ALL Gods has GIVEN US THE CITY!*"

A thunderous roar erupted, rocketing into the heavens like a primed, ballistic missile. *Ka-BOOM*—it collided with the looming cesspool of festering insults, mushroom cloud instantly rising. For a moment the pool stood still, absorbing the blow, shuddering and trembling violently. Then it imploded, falling back down to earth; crashing down—heavy—upon the incredulous city.

Jericho's walls swelled, buckled and collapsed—unable to withstand the sudden increase in catastrophic, quantum-weight. Bricks melted. Stone ran like wax. Each flowing down upon the other until a perfectly smooth, 360-degree ramp of liquefied rubble led up and into the city. Only Rahab's house remained.

"*CHAAARGE!*" Joshua roared, effortlessly spanning the breach with his men.

Up and over the debris Israel raced, pouring into the city like water over a dam. No one was left alive. Every inhabitant—hybrid or hell-contrived—was put to the sword. Nothing, save Rahab and her household, survived.

It was then—and only then—that Joshua gathered his men, gave them the command, and together they burned what was left of Jericho to the ground.

—| |—

"We've got his back against the ropes!" Spirit leaned gleefully across the table. "The Undertaker's got nowhere to go!" She flashed her most brilliant smile and winked at her two holy cohorts once again seated—right-side-up—around the immutable round table. "Time for a little WWE DDT action," she enthusiastically tapped her raised elbow.

"WWE—DDT?" The Word playfully shot Spirit a skeptical look. "You sure professional wrestling is the analogy we wanna go with?" He held his look of mock disbelief for just a second longer. Then he broke into a smile. "Whatever the event—we'll clean his clock, destroy his giants, and take back our land whether he likes it or not!" A thought suddenly dawned. "Ya know—it's kinda fun, when a generation comes together and actually *follows* our instruction!" he laughed out loud.

"Definitely more fun than walking around all confused and sweaty in the desert!" Spirit giggled. "But—," she paused. "Shouldn't we make it a bit more obvious?"

"Obvious?" The Word raised a questioning eyebrow.

"..As to why we want everything, and everyone, completely eradicated." Spirit was already switching gears, thinking proactively. She *had* to consider the generations to come. "I mean, he's never stopped, not even for a moment." She turned to Elohim. "Why not make it obvious for all to see? Why not show the world—how, even after *all* his ambassadors were jailed, the entire earth scrubbed clean, and we personally selected a human nation to engage with directly—Haylel *continues* to insist upon spreading his twisted, hybrid, serpent seed.."

"When the time is right, we'll make it plain," Elohim exhaled, shifting confidently in his seat. "However, until that time arrives, we want our trickster to remain largely oblivious to our ever watchful eye." He laid a compassionate hand across Spirit's. "Certainly, we'll be misunderstood." He gave a reassuring squeeze. "Certainly, we'll take some heat. However, if we want to fully expose the darkness hiding deep within our Adversary's heart, he must be allowed to think that we are naïve, clueless, and/or otherwise unconcerned about the game he is quietly playing."

Spirit forced a conceding nod. She understood. Haylel was

a lot of things, but stupid was not one of them. He would only fight, if he was confident of victory. Only cheat, if he felt certain he couldn't be punished. Only build, if he thought no one was looking. "Got it," she replied. "No sense in dragging this out any longer than necessary."

She paused a moment. "On the other hand—," her nose scrunched, her sparkle returning. "I suppose a divinely inspired 'Pile Driver' *here* ... with the occasional, supernatural 'Stone Cold Stunner' *there,* could appease my appetite for now." She grinned. "At least until.."

"..until he openly steps into the ring against us?" The Word emphatically finished her overly-analogous sentence.

Spirit nodded, and burst out laughing.

The Word looked confused.

"Sorry," she recanted between snorts. "*Haylel versus Elohim*—probably not so funny to you. But the mental picture," Spirit choked out the words. "It's like a T-Rex versus a toddler—I just keep envisioning a raging battle between two wildly flailing sets of ... little arms!"

Tears were rolling down delightfully quivering cheeks.

A slow, understanding grin spread wide across The Word's otherwise quizzical face. "Maybe try envisioning a battle between Rambo and The Rock?" he suggested.

"You mean, Rambo and ... *A rock!*" Spirit was howling again.

Now The Word was chuckling too. "Sumo and a Samurai?"

Spirit shook her head.

" ..Sumo and a snail?"

Still shaking.

" ..Sumo and a sugar cookie!"

Spirit stopped to catch her breath. "Really?" she challenged her amiable counterpart. "The analogy *you're* sticking with is—*man diapers?*" There was a renewed tempest of laughter. "Oh Word, you slay me!"

"What—? No—," The Word protested. "You started it! It was professional wrestling. *Professional wrestling!*" He turned to the one in charge. "Dad, help me out here.."

Elohim couldn't hide his own grin. "It's called a *fundoshi!*" he laid down the law. "And I'll have you *both* know, they're surprisingly comfortable." He squirmed mischievously in his seat. "Surprisingly comfortable, indeed!"

CH31: THE DAY THE EARTH STOOD STILL
1435:06:12:03:00:00

Joshua looked up, squinting into the midday sun. *Afternoon already?* He stifled a frown. It had barely been seven hours since their sunrise, surprise-attack, and somehow the enemy was already on the run.

He glanced toward the city of Gibeon—peacefully sprawled across the rolling valley below—then back to the troops retreating all around. In a strange turn of events, five kings from the south had traveled many miles north. Not to destroy him, but to destroy the city of Gibeon—a city that, each attacking king felt, had cowardly (and prematurely) surrendered to the advancing Israeli army.

Full disclosure, the men of Gibeon *had* used a bit of trickery to deceive the Israeli nation into signing a treaty with them, pretending they had come from a far-off land. However, they'd humbled themselves once the ruse was uncovered, and willingly become servants of the mighty Hebrew nation.

It was because of this willing servitude, that Joshua had answered Gibeon's cry for help. And upon marching all night, his troops had surprised the advancing southern armies, descending upon them in the wee hours of the morning. Now—barely noon— they had their enemy *spooked, routed, and on the run!*

CRUNCH—Joshua brought his sword down heavy upon the helmet of a passing adversary.

The deserter crumbled to the ground.

Joshua grimaced as nearly half a dozen other defectors raced freely by, headed in as many different directions.

'*Complete annihilation?*' he pondered the Heaven-sent directive, pinpointing his next target and turning in hot pursuit. *These people are virtually disappearing into the woodwork—if they*

*manage to escape today, it could take WEEKS to accomplish the
requested task… if ever!*

"What do we do?" he breathed a quiet prayer, suddenly side-stepping right. *THUNK*—a swift uppercut sent the butt of his sword skyward, catching a second passing opponent squarely in the jaw.

The southerner dropped like a rock.

"Time," Joshua reminded his Maker, "is not *my* problem to solve!"

He spun around, immediately back on the move. *SWOOSH*—a third defector experienced the fury of his blade.

Spin.

Stretch.

CLANG!

..a fourth, the finality of his shield.

Of course—! Joshua rolled his eyes, sprinting to catch a fifth. *If Elohim had given the orders, than Elohim was RESPONSIBLE to ACHIEVE them!*

The sudden revelation sparked a wild burst of hope-filled imagination. "Let the sun stand still over Gibeon!" he skidded to a halt, shouting at the cloud-covered sky. "And the moon over the valley of Aijalon!" He gave a short grunt, like he was only now comprehending the words that had just come out of his mouth. 'Oh well,' he shrugged, 'not my problem anymore.'

Immediately, he turned back to the chase.

Now, had it been given a second's more thought, it would have become abundantly clear, that a prayer of this audacity just wouldn't do. But the prayer had been prayed, and it was entirely too late—because in the cosmos above, God was already making his move.

Bold and bright—and radiating a rose-colored light—Earth's twin-planet, Mars, brazenly stepped into Earth's 'resonate orbital space.' Like a giant red billboard, looming some fifty times larger than the full Autumn moon—Mars crisscrossed Earth's skies in spectacular, "once-in-every-fifty-four-years" fashion. As she passed, Phobos and Deimos—her two closest moons—reached down from the heavens, gripping the tectonic plate upon which Joshua's men stood, dragging it along for the ride.

What resulted next, was recorded in annals all over the world: For the next twelve hours—time, on the surface of Earth, indeed, *stood still*.

Of course, it wasn't so much that the sun, or the moon, or the earth had ceased their respective rotations. Rather, it was the continent on which Israel stood that had frozen in place—locked by the gravitational pull of the passing solar bodies. And while the rest of the world continued spinning freely beneath—for nearly half a day—Joshua's continent remained, skimming across the earth's surface like a runaway water ski, pulled by invisible ropes.

...

Now it was during the flood—Noah's flood—that the 'fountains of the deep' had burst, sending water miles into the stratosphere, and ripping the earth apart like a baseball at the seams. Over the following centuries, the land masses which resulted had slowly drifted apart, forming six distinct continents. Of course, most of these continents had moved no further than a few miles in distance; and for all intents and purposes, still remained one large landmass separated by lochs and keys, lakes and rivers, bays and sprawling waterways.

Such was the case in the quiet village of Casablanca, some two-thousand four-hundred miles away from the pressing Israeli conflict. The village, which was really nothing more than a handful of sparsely scattered houses, lay peacefully along the western coast of what is present-day Morocco. To its west, (another quarter-mile across a freshwater straight), sat its nearest neighbor, the humble town of Biscayne—otherwise known as present-day Miami.

On this particularly fateful day, a well-weathered Casablancan fisherman glanced up from where he sat mending his nets. It had been a long, cold night, but his haul had been bountiful.

He squinted in the light of the warm morning sun and yawned. To him the rising sun meant only one thing—*it was finally time to retire*. The worn-out fisherman quickly finished his work, peering across the sparkling channel to where his closest Biscayne neighbor sat, quietly packing what appeared to be an unusually modest catch.

"Friend!" he hollered, lifting a cordial hand. "It seems the river isn't big enough for the both of us!" He good-naturedly gestured to his own impressive collection.

"I can see," returned the lighthearted smile. "So tell me— when are you planning to move?"

The seasoned Casablancan fisherman laughed out loud, countering as he often did. "Ah, *ha!* You first—my friend! You first!"

There was the customary thoughtful pause:

Three..

Two..

"Well then, old chum—I reckon I'll be seeing you tomorrow!"

The two fishermen chuckled and waved, each retiring to their respective bed on opposite sides of the channel. Today would be another day. And tonight, another golden opportunity to dredge the depths of their abundant aquatic divide.

But something, on this day, was different. Somewhere, far away, a radical prayer had been radically prayed. And what's more, the radical God of that radical prayer had radically answered.

And so, while two fishermen slept, continents and planets— oceans, shores and coasts realigned. And when both men awoke, peering out at what used to be a well-traversed, freshwater straight, they scratched their heads in knee-knocking wonder, horrified at what the other must have done to deserve the unfavorable fate of being swallowed alive—by an ocean.

...

Back at the conflict, the battle raged on. It didn't take Joshua's men long to realize Heaven had actually answered their prayer! Renewed zeal consumed their ranks.

Their enemies were panicked. *Where could they run, where could they hide, if the god of the Hebrews could start and stop time?!*

But stopping the sun was only the start: On that day, Elohim, himself, fought for Israel—raining down fire & brimstone upon the heads of her enemies. Heaven's bombardment was so well designed, that more foreigners died in the Heaven-sent firestorm, than by all of Joshua's men put together.

And so it was, that the obedient Hebrew nation—headed, by Elohim, himself—rose quickly to power, cutting one drop-jawed, hand-tied, increasingly-frustrated, Haylel, perpetually out of the equation. Kings and kingdoms fell before their divinely unhindered hand, hopeless to stand against the God whose heart was wholly with man.

Haylel was stunned. Forced back underground, he secretly regrouped. Going back to the basics and appealing to pride, he slowly and quietly seduced Israel to "go her own way." And over the following centuries, coaxed her out from under the protective covering of Elohim and back into a world where *he* was, once again, calling the shots.

Of course, he used his leadership position *not* as a bridge to heal—spanning the gap between two estranged worlds—but rather as a platform to openly demand, before the Courts of Heaven, that Israel be punished for her rebellion. The very rebellion *he* was inciting.

Elohim did his best to delay the inevitable, sending Israel prophet after prophet to explain the bizarre conundrum:

"I am a jealous God," he would caution with one.

"My Anger burns fierce," he would warn through another. "Obey my statutes. Do *not* let my Anger have his way with you, nor my Jealousy destroy you!"

But Israel would not listen. Her leaders were more interested in interpreting Elohim's mercy as 'indifference,' his delayed justice as 'approval,' and his true prophets as 'false,' than in hearing anything he actually had to say.

"God is not concerned with the trivial affairs of men," they would dismiss. "Does he not have far more important matters to attend to?"

In this way, they would appease their own minds, while continuing to do as they saw fit. They could not comprehend, that the very one leading them astray was the very one eager to devour them.

And so it was, that when the fullness of time had arrived— and Israel was once again sacrificing her own children upon the altars of foreign idols—that Elohim, at long last, was compelled to appease Haylel's demands. And it was with great remorse that he lifted his protection, allowing hell-directed Babylon to eagerly rush in. And once again, Heaven's house, lay in bondage to Sin.

CH32: THE TIDES HAVE TURNED ... AGAIN
0638:06:11:08:01:10

BOOM—the wrought iron door slammed callously shut behind Daniel. From where he lay on the rough cobblestone floor, he could hear the heavy door being bolted, barred, chained and locked—then barred and bolted again. Only moments ago, he'd been kicking and screaming, fighting for his dignity. Now, he didn't bother moving. What was the point? Those sounds could only mean one thing— Ashpenaz (*'Ash-peh-noz'*), the Chief Eunuch and the king's Chief of Staff, had finally had enough.

To be honest, it really wasn't Ashpenaz's fault. At six and a half feet tall, and well over three hundred pounds, he was typically gentle as a teddy bear. Well, maybe a tranquilized panda. But recently, this scrawny, rebellious, sixteen-year-old punk—plucked from the courts of Israel—had managed to bring out his inner grizzly.

"Only when this room is *SPOTLESS* will you get out," he roared. "Go ahead, *TEST ME*," espresso-brown eyes blazed through the thick door's sliding peephole. "It would be my absolute *PLEASURE* to let you rot in here *FOREVER!*"

He slammed the peephole shut, doing a sharp about-face. *As far as he was concerned, he was done with this smart-mouthed, stiff-necked headache.* Motioning to his assistant, he took off, storming his way back to higher ground.

Daniel lay motionless on the cold stone floor long after Ashpenaz's footsteps had died away. He was devastated. *How had his life come to this?* As a brilliant young mind, flourishing in the courts of Israel, he'd had it all: Power. Prominence. Position. Wealth. Not to mention his smokin' hot fiance, and the handsome family which was sure to follow. He winced. That was, until the day his life had suddenly jumped the tracks and become one huge, blistering, dumpster-fire of a train-wreck.

So what. Let me rot, he brooded. He didn't care. Life was worthless. *He was worthless.*

Accusing thoughts pounded his young psyche, bringing him repeatedly back to the cruel twist of fate which had triggered his current downward spiral:

He'd been taken.

Yes, *taken*—along with several dozen other prominent youths. Kidnapped from the courts of Israel and forced to join the courts of Babylon in what had been diplomatically termed, 'a good-will gesture..'

Daniel shook with anger. *Goodwill gesture? He would rather have died at the end of a Babylonian sword!* The thought ravaged his mind, drudging up visions of his fiance's final moments on earth.

Suddenly, he was choking back tears.

Her life had been taken in exactly that way.

Hatred flared, he cringed in disgust. *Why would he ever join the world of the very people who had so brutally dismembered his?*

Aaaagggghh—an inconsolable groan erupted from the depths of Daniel's belly, hanging heavy in the motionless air. Taken from king and country had been hard enough. Losing family and fiance, even harder. He shifted tenderly, wincing in pain. *But being made a eunuch?* His hand instinctively moved to the disturbing vacancy of his freshly bandaged wound. *It was almost too much.*

A second groan erupted. *How could he possibly survive the reality?* Never would he hear the delighted laugh of a lover, wife, and mother. Or the innocent giggles of his very own children. Never would he hear loving voices call him, "Daddy, Husband, or Grandpa." Nor would he ever be afforded the satisfaction of leaving his own legacy to future generations. He whimpered softly. Not to mention the daily prejudice—and relentless humiliation—that came with living such a ... 'sterile' lifestyle.

Daniel quietly convulsed, it wasn't *almost* too much ... *it WAS too much!* Anger exploded. Blood began to boil. His future had been brutally erased, taken from him in a moment—*and it was eating him alive.*

For a long time Daniel lay motionless on the ice-cold floor, drowning in a pool of his own self-hatred. He lay so long that the midday sun began to poke its way into the isolated, basement room—squeezing through the thick wooden slats of a solitary window overlooking the two-story, underground chamber. Silent, it danced, flickering playfully around Daniel's still frame, quietly vying for his undivided attention.

But the boy never noticed. And while the light outside, danced brighter and brighter, the darkness within, grew darker and darker.

Then—just as the depths of Daniel's depression peaked with internal rage—Haylel stepped in. Entering the room, he bent down and placed a single comforting hand on Daniel's right shoulder. Leaning close, he quietly whispered two little words.

"It's time.."

Daniel cringed, he could feel the weight of the world in that simple, dark phrase. It was crushing. Suffocating. Completely overwhelming.

It WAS time, he agreed. *Time to end it all.*

A wicked grin flashed across Haylel's twisted face, what a pleasant surprise to be so quickly—and so warmly—welcomed! He breathed in deep. He could feel the pull of Daniel's soul, tugging irresistibly at his core. He had to let go.

Negative energy flowed.

With renewed vigor, Daniel looked up. For the first time he took note of the room. It was large, spacious, and roughly hewn. Thick, exposed timbers lined its gracefully curved ceiling. There was a heaviness in the air which smelled of dust and mold, and an eerie chill that seemed to shoot persistently down one's spine. Every so often a pair of unsuspecting feet would walk busily by the underground room's tiny, second-story window, causing the few rays of penetrating sunlight to flicker frantically throughout.

Daniel rolled to his stomach, hands instantly clammy against the slick, damp floor. He lifted his head. Long wooden shelves lined white-washed brick walls, spanning the room's circumference. Even in the dismal light, Daniel could see the shelves were stacked from floor to ceiling, piled high with loot and plunder. In fact, he craned his neck, mountains of loot lay in towering piles *everywhere.*

"Clean this room?" he muttered. "What a joke."

Pushing up, he gingerly moved on hands and knees, digging relentlessly through the unending paraphernalia. He was looking for something, anything he could use—*like a rope.*

Coins went flying.

Pottery was tossed and smashed.

Weapons and scrolls, flung aside.

As he dug, a realization slowly dawned: *This wasn't just a room full of random treasure ... this was treasure, taken from Israel!*

Taken from—HOME.

His stomach dropped. Daniel felt ill. *What had they done? Priceless, sacred artifacts—most belonging to the house of his God—had become nothing more than dust-catching piles of ... barbarian's plunder.*

Bitter tears stung blushing cheeks. He shook with rage. *'Barbarian's plunder' ... that's EXACTLY what HE'D become!*

He collapsed on the floor beside a jumbled collection of broken pottery, lost and tossed aside. *Like him, these jars belonged in here forever.* Daniel dropped his defeated head, letting every ounce of life go.

..That's when he found it.

Coiled beneath one very large, very smashed ceramic vessel—lay a very long, very thick, scarlet cord.

This will do, he mused, hoisting the discovery to his shoulder.

He scanned the ceiling, rafter after rafter, searching for a sturdy beam with which to toss it over.

Mission accomplished! he scurried up a nearby pile of tapestries and literature. At the top, he secured the hefty rope— pausing only a moment to mentally prepare for his sudden, imminent descent into the welcoming arms of sweet, sweet death.

He bent down, every muscle tense, ready to leap:

In three..

Two..

Whaaa.. What was that? Something peculiar caught his eye.

Encapsulated in a single ray of glimmering sunlight—*was that a ...
book? ..An actual book? Not a single, rolled-up parchment like—*, he
looked around, *—every other manuscript in this place?*

Daniel reached down and gently retrieved the unusual
suspect, turning it over carefully in his hands. It was well made,
hand-stitched and leather-bound. Its pages painstakingly
handwritten. The book's cover, while ornate, seemed oddly faded and
worn; as if it had been both well used, and well preserved.

Strange, he puzzled, it almost seemed to glow, even after he
moved it out of the direct sunlight.

A short blast of breath revealed the dust-covered manuscript
was actually dyed a very deep, dark red. *I-s-a-i-a-h,* Daniel squinted,
running his fingers lightly down the book's spine. His heart skipped a
beat. *Could this really be the book of Isaiah?!*

As one of Israel's most infamous Seers, Isaiah's writings had
regularly foretold of Babylon's imminent takeover. Love him or hate
him, everyone had heard of his prophecies. In fact, it was Isaiah's
well-known, highly accurate writings which had caused Israel's king,
King Jehoiakim *('Jay-hoy-ih-kim')*, to so fearfully, and easily, cave.

Wait a minute, Daniel's jaw clenched. *Didn't that sorta make
Isaiah the SOLE party responsible for ALL of his current problems?* He
reared back, ready to toss the book.

*BUT—*still*—there was just something about it.*

Daniel peered down the slope of his current "artifact-
mountain." *Oh well*, he shrugged, *death would just have to wait a few
more minutes.*

Plopping down, he placed the book on his lap and flipped
it open. The text fell to a portion he would later come to know as,
Isaiah 56:3-5:

> *..And don't let the eunuchs say, 'I'm a dried-up*
>
> *tree with no children and no future—,'*

*Whaaa—*Daniel shot backwards, dropping the book like it
was on fire. *That odd phrase had practically LEAPT OFF the page!* He

gripped his chest, attempting to calm its thunderous pounding. His mind was racing. *How could a single line of text make such a tangible impact?* He was deeply disturbed. *Was it even possible?* Outstretched fingers trembled. *That a book actually existed—which could so palpably read its reader?*

"It's just a book. J-Just a book," he stammered, feeling the need to audibly address the creepiness of the situation.

Still, why was his heart so captivated?

With a long, slow breath, he regrouped, locating the sprawling text and gingerly flipping his way back through its delicate pages.

Wide-eyed, he continued:

> *..For this is what the Lord says: I will bless those eunuchs who keep my Sabbath days holy, who choose to do what pleases me, and commit their lives to me.*
>
> *I will give them—within the walls of my house—a memorial, and a name far greater than sons and daughters could give. For the name I give them is an everlasting one. It will never disappear!*

Wow. Did that really just—? How was this—? What in the—? Daniel's blown mind was off to the races. He was still trembling, but it was no longer with rage. Suddenly it was 'wild amazement' which rattled his bones.

What just happened? he marveled. In only a few short lines of text, *every* answer to *every* question he was currently battling, had just been answered!

Hope flooded his exhausted frame.

He felt so relieved. So accepted. So … *LOVED.*

Dropping his head, he sobbed uncontrollably. *Who was he, that the God of the Universe, should look down from Heaven and single him out? Mmm—*it was hard to believe. Yet, somehow he'd found Isaiah's book in *exactly the right room,* on *exactly the right day,* at *exactly the right time*, on *exactly the right page..*

What were the odds? he marveled. *It was a mathematic impossibility.*

..And yet, it was!

Big tears ran down thankful cheeks, gathering in tiny pools across broken relics below. For the first time in months, Daniel smiled. It was as if the words of Isaiah had lifted off the page and somehow wrapped themselves around his soul. He felt warm. Safe. Secure. Loved. Insulated from the brutal Babylonian reality so revoltingly set on destroying his.

With new life, Daniel sprang to his feet, lifting the scarlet cord from his neck. His heart felt light. His mind felt bright. He whistled a merry tune.

Sliding down his 'artifact mountain,' he dropped to the floor below, setting his entire being to the task of cleaning the surrounding mess. Tirelessly, he worked, all day long—until, with the final flickers of fading sunlight, and the most beautiful "nails-on-chalkboard screech" Daniel had ever heard—the wrought iron door, slowly swung open.

Ashpenaz's face said it all. The king's Chief of Staff just stared..

And stared..

And stared..

The room was unrecognizable. Daniel was unrecognizable. Asphenaz didn't know what to think. *Clearly this was NOT the same boy he had locked inside ... was it?*

For a long time he stood, puzzling ... while Daniel stood, grinning from ear to ear.

Slowly, Asphenaz extended a bewildered hand. It was dinner-time—and Daniel was desperately needed in the kitchen. *Come*, he motioned, pressing an apron-wrapped, peeling-knife into Daniel's open arms.

In the distance, through the twisting cellar corridors, they could hear the evening's Prep Chef calling their names: The kitchen was short-staffed, and the king was demanding a feast—they were desperately needed.

Ashpenaz stepped aside, allowing Daniel to squeeze by.

"I'm sorry," Daniel genuinely apologized.

Ashpenaz didn't respond. Tugging at the massive door, he barred and locked it once again. For a moment he paused, arm absentmindedly pressed against its cold metal frame. *This couldn't be happening... could it?* He shook his head in disbelief, reviewing the day's unusual events. *Yet somehow, it was.* With an almost defeated sigh—he acknowledged the unexpected peace offering. "All is forgiven," he breathed, letting the morning's offense go. "Now come." He gripped the young exile's shoulder. And turning around, he moved up the stairs, returning his still grinning enigma back to the land of the living where he belonged.

...

Ashpenaz wasn't the only one left scratching his head, Haylel was completely baffled. He stepped from the shadows, silently watching them go.

..That book! he spun around. *What on Earth could have possibly been etched into that crust-covered pile of psycho-babble?* His hands shook with rage. They had literally been seconds away from victory—Rahab's thick, scarlet noose draped emphatically around Daniel's scrawny little neck. *How in the world did six lines of text, from a delusional prophet's soiled memoir, spark such a complete emotional 180?*

Haylel hunched over the small carpenter's bench where Daniel had carefully stored the document. He too, flipped it open, staring defiantly at its flickering pages.

In the light of its own aura, the book was surprisingly hard to read. Haylel shifted uncomfortably, the text was definitely alive— rising and morphing before his very eyes. He squinted and blinked, fighting to focus, impatient eyes darting down the moving page:

> *You have committed adultery on every high*
> *mountain. There you have worshiped idols and*
> *have been unfaithful to me. You have put pagan*
> *symbols on your doorposts and behind your*
> *doors. You have left me and climbed into bed with*

*these detestable gods. You have given yourselves
to them..*

Blah, blah, blah..
Haylel flipped the page.

*..Is that why you have lied to me? ..forgotten me
and my words? Is it because of my long silence
that you no longer fear me?*

*Now I will expose your so-called good deeds.
None of them will help you. Let's see if your
idols—your "good works"—can save you when
you cry to them for help. Why a puff of wind
could knock them down. Don't you see? Whoever
trusts in ME will inherit the land. They alone, will
possess my holy mountain..*

What a load of CRAP, Haylel slammed the book shut. He
shook his head, attempting to clear the hodgepodge of blazing
words still spinning before his eyes. Had he been privy, he would
have realized the portion of text he'd just viewed had not only been
penned for backsliding Israel, but more importantly, it had been
penned for The Backslider, himself. In fact, inside scoop: the entire
book had been written as a wake up call for Haylel. *Hello—,* "only
those who *trust* Elohim would possess his holy mountain?" *..Could it
be any more obvious?*

Haylel brought a frustrated fist crashing down. "*Gibberish,*"
he snarled, clawing the table. "*Complete GIBBERISH!*" He grabbed at
the book, attempting to fling it across the room. But the book was
frozen to the table beneath.

ARRRRRAUGH—Haylel swept an arm across the rebellious
surface, knocking everything else to the floor. The noise echoed
loudly through the underground corridors.

Haylel didn't care. He was furious.

He turned and burst through the wrought iron door, tossing

it effortlessly from its hinges. With a blood-curdling scream, he launched himself into the air. Lightning and thunder erupted. His countenance transformed. *Tonight, he had a meeting to attend—dark energy crackled—and aside from being late, he loathed arriving empty handed.*

How dare he do both!

With a savage roar, he dove through the ground; corridors and catacombs trembling in his wake. He was headed straight down—deep underground—thundering to the depths of Hades.

—| |—

Wet fur—that suffocatingly, all-too-familiar stench filled the balmy cavern. Prophet looked around, doing his best not to gag. From where he sat—alone at the square table—there was just enough light to glimpse the tiniest flickers of movement before BEAST came bursting from the shadows—sopping wet and grinning broadly.

"Let me guess," Prophet frowned condescendingly. "You took the scenic route again?"

"YEP!" roared BEAST, steam already billowing from his broad, dripping shoulders. "TOTALLY MISSED THE PORTAL!" He paused, head cocked, almost as if he was having an actual thought. "Why, old man?" he grinned. "Did you think I wasn't gonna make it?"

"I was holding out against hope," came the dry reply. "But your stench announced your arrival long before you actually showed up." Prophet hesitated, letting the dig fully entrench before he probed. "Any reason you didn't take advantage of the ferry I personally installed after our last missed-portal blunder?"

For a long moment BEAST stood, brow furrowed, carefully retracing his steps. "*Oh—,*" it finally clicked. "Is that what you call the crusty piece of driftwood I saw docked by the Styx?"

Prophet gave a curt nod.

BEAST shrugged. "Didn't wanna pay the toll."

Prophet gagged. Had there been something in his mouth— anything at all—he most certainly would have spewed it. "*Didn't wanna pay the toll?"* he choked, fighting for composure. "But you own *EVERYTHING!"* Frustrated hands wanted to flail, indignant vocal chords wanted to rise. "Currency and commerce only happen because of *YOU. You're* the Master of Trade. The spirit of Mammon. Mister, Money Bags himself," he glanced feverishly around. "You mean to tell me—you couldn't part ways with enough scratch to incur a *SINGLE FERRY TICKET?!"*

"Nope," spat BEAST, matter-of-factly. There was nothing in his mouth, yet he spewed liberally. "Cuz, if I'd given that god-forsaken, money-grubb'n, mostly-dead, Mr. Ferry Master even a single gold coin—I wouldn't own it *ALL* anymore. *Now would I?"* He cleared his throat, quite proud of his 'economicals.' "Besides," he sent forth a fresh supply of frothy slaver. "The swim just feels good." BEAST was winding up. *"AND BEAST LOVES TO SWIM!"*

Spit went flying.

"Speaking … of swims," Prophet wiped his dripping brow.

"LIKE I ALWAYS SAY—," BEAST continued to froth. *"Why say it? ..WHEN YOU CAN SPRAY IT!"* The brazen ox extended one long, hairy arm and self, high-fived—*himself.*

The cavern thundered violently.

Prophet cringed, dodging the fresh downpour. It was official, *the elevator didn't go all the way to the top.* What's worse, there seemed to be several floors, multiple lights, and an ungodly number of rocking chairs missing as well. The disenfranchised enchanter reached down, feeling for the cavern floor. As far as he was concerned, this charade was over. Grabbing a fistful of grime, he muttered a quick incantation, tossing the filth in the air. There was a sizzle, a fizzle, some loud pops and a giggle. *FLASH*—hanging midair, a wicked looking gas-mask appeared. Prophet smiled, donning the dark veil. *Ahhh*—he sighed, *he could breathe freely again!* His head rolled back, his shoulders slumped, his eyelids drooped to half-mast. For the first time—in probably, *ever*—Prophet looked visibly relaxed.

Silence filled the steamy cave.

BEAST began to chuckle.

And chuckle.

And chuckle.

Slowly, his laughter grew louder and louder—until he was at an all out, roar. "You mean … you've had," he pawed at tear-filled eyes. "That ability … all along? And yet … you wait—until NOW—to … use … it?" BEAST was absolutely howling.

Immediately, Prophet was back to tense. He lifted his staff and opened his mouth, preparing to release the harshest of muffled retorts.

SWISH, tha-Thump—the sound of a large winged-creature landing heavily, put a sudden halt to the amorous bonding experience.

All attention turned.

A very dark, very empty-handed figure stepped boldly from the shadows.

"What—no portal, *AND* no loot?" Prophet promptly pointed out both elephants in the room. He shot his cohorts a pious and patronizing look—*what could he say, he was good with elephants.*

"There's been a change of plans," Ha-satan hissed, dropping to his seat at the head of the table. He plopped his big, helmeted head into his big, empty hands—and sulked.

BEAST opened his mouth, ready to loose any number of massive verbal blunders. However, Prophet's well-aimed prod under the table, caused him to rethink things.

He closed his mouth again.

"So—the Hebrew kid—how are we going to take him out?" Prophet cautiously ventured.

Everyone shared a 'knowing' look. After the damage Moses had levied in such a similar scenario, it was well understood—this round, there would be no taking chances.

Daniel had to go.

"We could question his sexuality," BEAST jumped in. "That's always a sure-fire way to isolate and dehumanize. At least—until we can arrive at a more permanent solution." He made a subtle 'cut-throat' gesture, which was anything but subtle.

"Really?" Prophet shot him a dirty look. "Over-sexualize a eunuch? ..is that truly the best idea you've got?" He squinted. "Need I remind you: that NOBODY has *NEVER*—in ALL the ANNALS OF

HISTORY—*EVER,* felt threatened by a eunuch … no matter how "sexually deviant" that eunuch was "perceived" to be." He pounded his staff emphatically. "Cuz, he's a *EUNUCH!*"

BEAST stared blankly.

Prophet shook his head.

"What about his ethnicity?" the smoldering ox continued. "..Or his loyalty?

..His sanity?

..Civility?

..Taste in draperies?"

Prophet glared daggers, now BEAST was just being … BEAST.

"We'll use Jujutsu.."

Jujutsu? Every head turned.

"..the art of using your enemy's own momentum against them," Ha-satan looked up.

BEAST stared blankly.

Prophet shook his head.

"Of course, we'll use it in the form of—*ill will.*"

"Ill will?" Prophet reluctantly picked up the ball.

"*Ill will,*" Ha-satan was coming alive. For one, he loved being the center of attention. For two, he loved being the *only* one in "the know." And for three, he absolutely *LIVED* for the moments where he was *BOTH.*

"Gentlemen, do you not see?" the life-sucking narcissist slurped up the energy in the room. "We'll take his momentum—his new-found, sunny-side-up attitude—*and we'll twist it!*" he smirked. "We'll assign it, *dark motive.* We'll assign it—*ill will!*"

The silence got awkward.

"Gentlemen—we'll make evil appear good, and good appear evil!" Ha-satan finally spelled it out. He eagerly slid to the edge of his seat. "We'll make our target appear so happy in the face of adversity—that clearly, he *MUST* be up to something!"

Finally—light bulbs began to flicker on.

"You mean, like, he's so happy about cleaning the king's treasure room, he MUST have pocketed some plunder?" A wicked grin spread slowly across Prophet's masked face.

"Or—he's so happy about being an exiled eunuch, he MUST be a paid foreign spy?" BEAST lifted his head and an eyebrow.

"Now you're over the target!" the underworld overlord was already nodding. "Envy, suspicion, and insecurity are powerful tools when placed in the right hands and hearts—boys," he flashed a wicked grin of his own. "Especially when masked by genuine concern."

"It's ... *brilliant!*" Prophet admitted. "If we can't get him to bend around his world, we'll simply bend his world ... around him!" An unsettling giggle escaped. The perpetual schemer was totally smitten: *Turning day into night, and night into day? It was sheer genius!* After all—who in their right mind, would ever believe that something as irrational, illogical, and 'diabolically conspiratorial' as genuine, heaven-inspired, heart-change would EVER actually occur?

"BUT—," BEAST twitched, still struggling to catch up. "HOW do we actually ACHIEVE such a feat?" He half-closed an eye, belched uncomfortably, and began to noisily chew his cud. "How do we ACTUALLY turn treasure into trash? And make that which is legal, illegal?"

Ha-satan lifted both hands, planting them securely behind his big, helmeted head. *He already had a plan ... a beautiful, breathtaking, barbarous plan!* "Watch and learn, boys," he grinned, settling comfortably back. "Watch ... and learn."

CH33: UNKILLABLE
0571:08:27:21:36:36

THUD. Daniel hit the ground like a royal sack of potatoes. He rolled to his back, gasping for air, clinging to the stitch in his side. With a gulp—and with every fiber of his being—he slowly forced the wind back into his empty, eighty-year-old lungs; gingerly checking himself for any collateral damage.

He glanced up. From where he lay, at pit's rugged bottom, he could see the last of the king's royal guards—some fifteen feet above—sealing his fate with a stone.

THWUMP, the half-ton cover slid firmly into place, plunging the pit into darkness. For a moment, Daniel flashed-back to the first time he'd been locked in a dark, cluttered room. Much younger, much more rebellious, he'd barely made it out alive.

What would become of him now? he peered futilely into the surrounding gloom. *That room contained little more than aging artifacts, this room was filled with..*

Mmmeerrrrr—a disheartening growl jolted him back to reality. Daniel pushed up, poised on all fours, instantly ready to move.

Gggeerrrrr—the growl grew closer, much more defined.

Daniel's hair bristled. Blood pounded in his ears. He fought the urge to run.

Slowly, a pair of beady yellow eyes opened.

Daniel's heart lodged in his throat. He gasped a silent prayer. *Those eyes were right in front of him!* He could feel the beast's warm breath. Smell, its musky odor.

Suddenly, there was another pair.

Then another, and another..

Daniel bowed his head, and silently waited. *What else could he do?* The pride of lions—into whose den he'd been thrown—had him completely surrounded. *It was only a matter of time,* he swallowed hard. *Until he was—DINNER.*

'*Curse God and die..*'

What—? Who said that?! Daniel physically shook. *The thought had been so loud it was almost audible.* Fear exploded all around, the air tangibly thickened—the undeniable chill of death descending slowly upon him.

'*Curse God and DIE!*' the thought came again.

Instantly, Daniel was back in that cluttered basement, decades ago, his soul swirling with negative emotions.

'*..CURSE GOD AND DIE!*'

There was no holding back now, the demonic phrase had somehow hijacked his mind. Daniel covered both ears and sunk to the ground, the pressure relentless. He could feel the darkness crowding in, demanding he, 'throw a fit in the face of the uncaring God who had surely left him here to die!'

It was almost too much—*he had to give in!*

Dropping all pretense, he stood to his feet; his entire body shaking with uncontrollable ... *laughter?* He lifted both arms, joy full and overflowing. *How fortunate was he—to, once again, have an enemy who had so OVERPLAYED his hand!*

"Do you not know?" Daniel challenged the darkness. "That no weapon formed against me will *EVER* prosper!" He hugged his heaving sides, attempting to catch his breath; praising God with what he assumed would be his final two words on earth.

"*THANK YOU!*" he bellowed, bracing for the roaring repercussions.

FLASH. FLICKER ... BOOM!

W-What was that—? Daniel staggered back, forearm instinctively shielding his face. A light—pure and white, fiery bright—was suddenly flooding the cave.

The disoriented patriarch dropped to the ground, every beast around him already scattered and gone. He pursed trembling lips. Wiped his running nose. The only opposition he had now, were his own, lion-sized tears.

Daniel lifted both eyes. He could feel volumes of Heaven-sent love engulfing his soul, washing away impurities with wave after unconditional wave. It was inexhaustible. Unrelenting. Spectacular. Refreshing.

It was completely overwhelming.

'*Get up,*' a figure stepped out from the midst of the blaze.

What—?! Daniel moved to obey, fighting to rise with every ounce of his being. But the love, the life, the weight of the surrounding light—*it was all too much.*

'*I-I—can't,*' he slipped back to the ground.

'*You can,*' the stranger was suddenly beside Daniel, answering his internal monologue with an internal monologue of his own. '*Come,*' he bent down, placing a strong hand on Daniel's furrowed brow. '*I want to show you something.*'

Instantly they were gone. Pit, pride, rocks and walls—eyes, claws, cats and all—quickly fading away.

—| 0636:09:19:07:47:00 |—

Uncanny! Daniel could hardly catch his breath. *The buildings. The grounds. The sights, smells and sounds. The perfectly manicured shrubs.* He lifted welcoming arms, nostalgia flooding his soul. *From the theaters and halls, to the stables and stalls—*these were the sprawling corridors of his unlikely Babylonian Alma Mater. This was *The King's University*, buried deep within the educational courts of, *King Nebuchadnezzar.*

"Atten—tion!"

Daniel spun around.

Across a narrow plaza, beyond a bed of budding sprouts, under the distant colonnade, he could see a group of well-dressed, ruddy-faced teens, scrambling to line up. Ashpenaz—his old friend and the king's Chief of Staff—was actively leading the charge.

"Ten, hut!" the stout foreman directed, anxiously pacing back and forth, eyeing the long line of smiling, robust faces.

Daniel gazed down the boisterous row, his focus landing on

one young man in particular. Clean cut. Fresh shaven. Eyes alert and bright. This particular student stood out like a grinning sore thumb, confidently standing at attention.

Immediately, Daniel was moving across the plaza, motioning for the stranger to follow. He forged his way across the knee-high sprouts, making a beeline for his intended target. The smile on his face said it all: *Clearly, this young man was a leader among leaders, a man among men. And—dare he say it—looking particularly handsome on this mighty fine morning!*

"Belteshazzar! *('Bell-tuh-shah-czar')*" Ashpenaz continued to pace. "*Front and center!*"

The young man stepped forward, immediately snapping back to attention.

Daniel, and the stranger, wheeled to a stop beside him.

My God, Daniel chuckled, peering out of the corner of his eye. *Was the resemblance not striking?!* He shook his head, amusement coursing his soul. *How could it be, that on this fine, time-traveling morning, he was—*oh, how should he put it—*so literally beside himself!*

Ashpenaz spun and stepped through Daniel as he returned to the front of the line. Daniel winced, fielding the sudden wave of unsolicited emotions. Ashpenaz was certainly unsure of himself— even more than his anxiety-ridden, abnormally-shifty exterior portrayed. Daniel closed his eyes, a torrent of faded memories suddenly roaring back to life.

Today's crossroads had begun nearly two weeks prior, when he—err, Belteshazzar—had issued Ashpenaz a challenge: Why not allow the Hebrew exiles to consume the "fresh water, whole food diet" outlined in the Torah *('Tore-uh')*—their ancient and holy cannon?

Of course, the modest request was in no way intended to interfere with any other student's enjoyment of the tasty delicacies assigned them from the king's table. Nor was it a way for the exiles to reposition themselves above anyone else. It was simply an opportunity to exercise their own religious convictions, while partaking in the blessings and culture of home. Furthermore, should Ashpenaz have any further reservations, Belteshazzar assured, "A simple, side-by-side comparison at the end of the month could easily be arranged, to see who was—in fact—healthier."

Ashpenaz agreed, but only for ten days.

Daniel shifted his focus, peering back down the line to where his former professor was still going strong—apparently following some sort of internalized checklist. It was almost comical. Ashpenaz would raise an arm here, pinch some fat there, inspect nails, teeth, hair, and breath. Then, just when it seemed like he was wrapping things up, he would shake his head and start all over.

Whoosh—a shimmering hand dropped firmly across Daniel's wide eyes, covering them completely. *What the—? Daniel tried to pull away. Now was not the time for games.*

'Look,' the stranger directed.

Daniel sheepishly obeyed, his jaw dropping slowly to his chest. Looking *through* the hand of the stranger was like looking through a pair of interdimensional glasses. *Nothing was hidden!* He could see clearly across the *entire* spectrum of light, making him privy to everything going on—on-stage, off-stage and everywhere in-between.

The unlikely eavesdropper swallowed hard, reanalyzing the world through his brand-new, full-spectrum, 12-dimensional, multi-ocular lenses. Angels, entities and energies moved freely throughout the space before him. To his surprise, he could see another likeness of the stranger moving about as well. This stranger was keeping pace with Ashpenaz, mirroring his every move: Ashpenaz would stop, the stranger would stop. Ashpenaz would turn, the stranger would turn. Ashpenaz would poke, the stranger would poke.

The only time things shifted was when Ashpenaz would step back to calculate. Then, and only then, would this stranger step forward, place a hand over his eyes, and point. (Much like he was doing right now). Without a word, Ashpenaz would nod and look, then nod and look again—occasionally muttering some sort of exploitative under his breath.

This went on for quite some time until Ashpenaz came to his full and final stop—right in front of Belteshazzar.

"I wouldn't have believed it, if I hadn't seen it with my own two eyes," he addressed the entire group. "But clearly, the Hebrew boys are in far better shape ... *far better shape!*" He leaned forward, nervously dabbing his brow with a large, linen cloth. "Gentlemen, I see no way around it," his hands—and his cloth—shot up in surrender. "In light of the undeniable facts, I have no other option but to assign *each* of you—a similar diet."

The groans were bountiful as the Babylonian boys watched their daily rations of steak, wine and crème brûleè evaporate into water, lintels and carrots in a literal instant. Even young Belteshazzar showed mixed emotions. His desire had been to create a space where he and his friends were free to follow their God personally; not a space that forced everyone else to follow suit.

"From this day forward," Ashpenaz drove the nail deep into the coffin. "It's fresh veggies and spring water for everyone!" He breathed a huge sigh of relief, his heart finally settled—no question about it, he had to do what was best for his boys.

Faces fell like dominoes.

Daniel glanced down the line.

Now that he could see his former classmates' full, unfiltered reactions, it was quite clear just how unpopular the sudden turn of events had made his younger self. He stepped forward, his heart begging to intervene.

'Come,' the stranger grabbed Daniel's arm, their world fading quickly away. *'There's more.'*

—| 0635:06:06:11:07:57 |—

Daniel squinted, Nebuchadnezzar's throne room was packed. Warm bodies and torchlight were everywhere. The hidden observer silently surveyed the surrounding crowd. Thronging the floors, lining the walls, and filling the halls was a veritable, "who's who," of Babylon's self-proclaimed elite—every scientist, sorcerer, and sage in the kingdom, involuntarily crammed into the lofty, narrow space. Daniel flashed a fearless grin, making little effort to hide his growing amusement. *The petrified looks on ashen faces said it all ... King Nebuchadnezzar was in rare form.*

"STOP STALLING—I KNOW WHAT YOU'RE DOING!" the Babylonian king indignantly raged. "If you don't *TELL ME MY DREAM—AND IT'S MEANING,"* he shook a large meaty fist. "I will tear you apart, limb from limb, and turn your houses into *HEAPS OF SMOLDERING RUBBLE!"*

Daniel peered through the crowd. Clearly, the king was livid. His face was red. His eyes wild. His bedhead, off the charts! It was quite apparent that Nebuchadnezzar's current state of affairs was the direct result of a very disturbing, very vivid dream; from which he had very recently awakened.

"N-No one on Earth can tell the king his dream," his intellectuals pleaded. "A-And no king, h-however great and powerful, has ever demanded such a thing!" They frantically conferred with one another. "The king's petition is *impossible.* No one except the gods can tell you your dream, and they do not live here among your people."

As expected, the self-preserving, lackluster reply went down like a cold rat sandwich. Daniel could feel the room instinctively brace as the king took another deep breath.

BOOM—his tempest raged on.

Once again, the stranger's hand dropped securely over Daniel's wide eyes. This time, Daniel was ready. He peered keenly into the unseen realm, the room instantly bursting with invisible life. *Wow.* He scanned and rescanned the crowd, *Nearly every person had at least one otherworldly, interdimensional being communicating with, to—and/or through—them!*

The king was no exception.

Daniel shifted his gaze. Breathtakingly beautiful and compellingly charismatic—Nebuchadnezzar's tall, interdimensional friend was by far the most impressive of all. Its spellbinding skin flickered with millions of nanoparticulate gemstones. Colorful bands of fiery light radiated from its core. Every word the being spoke, the king would immediately parrot and exaggerate, decreeing them visibly into the atmosphere like a sort of amplified rebroadcast.

At first glance, it was clear this was a powerful being of light. Yet a closer look revealed its countenance was surprisingly dark like that of the king's. It seemed irritated and disturbed, almost confused by the dream. Worst of all, it was merciless—demanding answers as if it were a matter of life or death. It didn't seem to fully comprehend how no one in the room knew anything about the dream.

Daniel turned back to the crowd. There were literally hundreds of voices, all frantically speculating as to what the dream could have been. Yet, not one seemed able to answer the king's outrageous demands. Daniel couldn't help but chuckle at the chaos. He didn't mean to be insensitive, he just knew exactly how the story would end. And that end was scheduled in:

Three..

Two..

One towering throne room door slowly opened, several disgruntled attendants forcing their way inside. With shushes and shoos, they parted a path, making their way towards their disheveled, sleep-deprived king. In their wake, shuffled one equally disheveled and sleep-deprived—*Belteshazzar.*

The verbal dissent was immediate; the entire room—visible and invisible—taking audible note of the sudden unannounced competition.

Daniel smiled at his younger self—he was in way over his head, and everyone knew it. Yet, there he stood—cool, calm, and collected.

Slowly, the throne room door began to close, but not before the stranger—*his stranger*—strode boldly through. The heaven-sent messenger walked right up to Belteshazzar, placed a hand on his shoulder and spoke quietly into his right ear. Like Nebuchadnezzar, Belteshazzar simply spoke what he heard. "Oh king," he bowed. "I don't have all the answers. But my God, the God above all gods, does. If the king will permit, I will return in twenty-four hours and resolve all of the king's demands."

The invisible world went silent—eager to hear the response of the king. Oddly pacified, Nebuchadnezzar agreed. He was, in a strange way, honored by the frank discourse and honest conjecture. It was a welcomed change to his dog-eat-dog world of perpetual excuses, one-upping half-truths, and shameless self-aggrandizements. With a grin and a nod—and seeing as this was his only real option—he granted the bold request.

The room let out a collective sigh of relief, at least for the moment they were finally off the hook.

Daniel also stood enraptured, awestruck by his new, third-party perspective. He slowly shook his head, his mind reeling from having just experienced both sides of the coin, *simultaneously*.

Inching forward, he moved to take a closer look.

'*Come,*' the stranger gripped his shoulder firmly. '*There's one more stop to go.*'

—| 0571:08:28:05:06:56 |—

The sudden clatter of hooves against cobblestone, rattled Daniel from his daze. The introspective extrovert lifted his eyes, glancing attentively around, immediately back engaged. They were standing at the mouth of a wide-open plaza, in the center of a bustling street. Above the hustle and the bustle of the cobblestone noise, Daniel could hear the energetic cries of the local street-merchants passionately peddling their wares. He breathed in deep, his skin tingling with excitement. Turning a slow 360, he inventoried his surroundings. Government buildings stood tall before him, lining three sides of the circular plaza. To his rear—and intersecting the mouth of the plaza—lay a wide open, six lane, thoroughfare. Tents, carts, and peddler's shops ran along either side of the busy highway, narrowing its lanes to four. Daniel puzzled only a moment. The regalia, the architecture, the accents and flair—*he knew exactly where he was*—these were the courts of King Darius! He took another long gaze—if his calculations were correct—this was actually a recreation of the day's earlier events.

Daniel spun to face the entrance of the King's High Court. *Yep. There he was—out on the courthouse steps—moving among the pillars!*

For a moment, Daniel froze, watching himself engage with the people. It was as plain as the permanent grin on his face—*he loved his job*. As one of Darius' top three officers, he oversaw many of the king's affairs throughout the land. But his absolute favorite thing to do was to plant himself there, atop the courthouse steps, greeting the locals, fielding daily problems, and keeping a compassionate thumb on the pulse of the general population.

Today was no different. It was business as usual. Daniel watched himself greet two argumentative newcomers, and immediately begin to diffuse the situation. Nothing seemed out of the ordinary. In fact, everything appeared very ordinary. That was— until the stranger's hand dropped securely over his eyes, one last time.

Wow. Daniel lost his breath, there were no words. *The sight was epic!* Above, beside, below, behind—as far as the eye could see— *angels were everywhere!*

Jaw agape, he took it all in. There were angels striking up conversations. Angels striking down conversations. Angels smoothing over conflicts. Angels instigating confrontations. There were angels calling from rooftops. Angels whispering in doorways. Angels beckoning from windows. Angels waving from carriages. There were angels walking, flying, flickering, crying, following, leading, falling, riding, playing, hovering, praying, shouting, scooting, sliding, fishing, and pouting. There were warrior angels, watcher angels, business angels, and bodyguard angels. Helper angels, healing angels, messenger angels and minstrel angels. There were primitive, personal, patriarchal, passionate, preaching, purple angels. Not to mention the occasional: Host, Virtue, Power, Ruler, Principality, and/or Authority.

<Deep breath>

A-And—what was that?

Daniel glanced skyward, his eyes open wide—*there, circling overhead, was the largest snake-like dragon he'd ever witnessed.* Twisting and turning, surfing and soaring, it rode across the winds, filling the entire space with its ominous red presence—watching, lurking, recording, influencing—orchestrating everything below.

Daniel watched for what seemed like ages.

Then, he felt a hand on his shoulder. Slowly, he turned his gaze back to the crowds.

Once again, the stranger was present, this time moving playfully among the people. Daniel watched, genuinely amused, as the stranger pantomimed and waved, stirring each patron's attention towards the courthouse—showing off what clearly appeared to be his best friend on the steps. Daniel chuckled. He couldn't help it, it was comical. If, by some chance, the stranger's outrageous performance failed to capture the intended target's spiritual eye, the undaunted jokester would kick it into overdrive, clowning around—influencing the surrounding scene—until, at some point, the unsuspecting patron would *have* to acknowledge Belteshazzar's existence.

Then it would happen.

A single emotion—like a little, lone bubble would trigger, deep within the viewer's soul. At first, it would stir. Then, it would grow, and inevitably rise. In time, it would release—most often through the lungs—via a cough, sneeze, laugh, wheeze, a sigh, snort, or burp. As it released, each emotion solidified, materializing as a color and a fragrance all its own. Endearing emotions—like affection or joy—appeared a sweet-smelling, amber-honey gold. While negative emotions—like envy or hate—appeared a nauseating, stomach-turning, pale-green. As more and more emotion was released, it would gather and pool—combining with other 'like' emotions—clustering together in little floating patches of polarized, 'emotional fog.'

To Daniel's amazement and chagrin, these pseudo-atmospheres began attracting people of similar heart and mind. Like sharks to chum, those who carried jealousy gravitated toward the clouds of gelatinous pale-green, while those with copious affection, congregated nearest the clouds of shimmering gold.

A polite tap to Daniel's shoulder, redirected his gaze toward a particularly thick cloud of jealousy nearby. Over the course of the morning, three very like-minded men had been attracted to its unusually opaque gloom and were now actively conspiring deep within its protective emotional cover.

Daniel looked them over.

The first was Mostanphanus (*'Moe-stan-fan-us'*), a high officer in the courts of the king. Daniel interacted with him daily.

Thick white hair. Unsettlingly thin. He looked like the unfortunate mishap between a brilliant German scientist and a mop. Thankfully, he had the personality to match. Very few could accurately pronounce his given name, even less his last, so he often went simply by, 'Stan.'

The tall guy beside him was Xavier Narcistcah *('Nar-sist-kuh')* Potrich the Third. Standing a mere six foot twelve, the up-and-coming Governor towered over most Babylonians by well over a foot. There wasn't a crowd, a court, a cart or a chair that he didn't stick awkwardly out of—*and he loved it!* He was the sideshow's main attraction and he made sure everyone knew it, multiple times, every day! He was super personable, able to talk to anyone for hours—as long as the conversation remained, *all about himself.* He was unusually conceited and fully convinced that the world existed to revolve around *him*—not that anyone could totally blame him, since 'narcissist' was sorta his middle name.

The third guy was Hayzel *('Hah-zel')*. Short. Selfish. Completely obnoxious. He was a total piece of work. Towering a whopping, "five-foot none," he had little man's syndrome to the MAX. Not to mention that he was just flat out mean. Rumor had it, that on the day of his birth a forcep had slipped, and he was literally born with a stick up his backside. Been that way ever since. To compound matters further, he was actually quite hilarious and completely unintimidating—inadvertently perpetuating his adorably-funny, yet totally-serious, "No really, I'm gonna cut you!" 'tiny-man tantrums' to no end.

Another quick tap to Daniel's left shoulder, and the stranger moved within earshot, motioning for Daniel to follow.

"Did you hear the latest?" Stan, the high officer was probing. "Our foreign friend over there is up for another promotion."

"*Promotion?*" snorted Xavier, eyes glued to their target. "The king practically *invented* the position that traitor's being awarded."

"..Chief Administrative Officer!" Hayzel loudly complained. "That's—the official title." He waved tiny, wild hands. Daniel was least familiar with him, but the little man seemed very familiar with Daniel. "That means he'll be second in command—like some sort of,

'Vice-King,'" the disgruntled employee sputtered and coughed. "Who ever heard of a … *'Vice-King?'"* A fresh puff of hunter-green haze rose from his belly, thickening the already murky air.

"Look at him," Xavier hunched over, waving a subtle hand in Belteshazzar's general direction. "So smug. So into himself. He's probably cutting some sort of backroom deal as we speak."

Daniel turned and saw himself smiling and shaking hands with the two men he had intercepted earlier. He remembered the dispute he had just helped them settle, saving them the trouble—and the cost—of going through the official court process. It was, of course, at no benefit to himself. *I suppose—from so great a distance—that is a clear-cut case of projected bribery,* he squinted. *But only if you really, really want it to be.*

"Are we *actually* going to let him get this promotion?" Stan prodded."Giving 'Second-in-Command' to a foreigner—*is that not clear-cut treason?*" He seemed genuinely concerned. "I mean, how can we ever fully trust *an outsider?*"

"We took an oath," Xavier agreed. "Protect the motherland at all cost." He raised his right hand. "We would be worse than infidels if we let this traitor slip through—and up—our ranks." His left hand wiped his troubled brow. "He *must* be exposed. He *must* be stopped," he was clearly distraught. "Even if that means protecting the king—*from the king, himself!*"

No one had ever put it quite like that before. And as another puff of puke-green haze muddied the mid-morning air, everyone nodded in solemn, heartfelt solidarity.

"Now, wait a quick minute—," Hayzel piped up. "Why not let me handle this?" He adjusted the blade on his belt. "All this traitor needs is one faulty step off Potiphar's Peak. One unfortunate spike to his pomegranate punch," a furious little fist smashed down into a furious little palm. "One roasted coconut to the back of his head. One cross-eyed cobra in the commode. One misplaced toaster in the bathtu.."

"No.. no.. no," Stan cut him off. "Everything we've tried— every trick, every trap, every test—he's navigated them all."

"H-He's faultless," Xavier whined. "Faithful, honest, friendly, outspoken. Fiercely loyal to his God."

"He's a traitor.."

"A tyrant.."

"An evil genius.."

"A eunuch!"

Green clouds and snickers ensued.

"Faultless … to a fault," Hayzel concluded the conversation, throwing two little frustrated hands high in the air.

There was a long, thoughtful pause.

The wind picked up.

For the briefest of moments, the surrounding clouds shifted and moved, the dragon overhead breezing slyly by.

"Then that is our way," Xavier whispered, mostly to himself. "Gentlemen," his eyes lit up. "*Then that is our way!*" He was trembling with excitement. "If we can play the laws of *his* god against the laws of *our* king. Then certainly, will he not follow the laws of *his god?!*" The scheming governor gave a thunderous hand clap, quite delighted by his own wicked epiphany. "My friends—'*being faultless to a fault*'— that very irony will be his undoing!"

Everyone agreed, *it was brilliant!* There were smiles, high-fives and handshakes, all around.

"Follow me gentlemen," Stan immediately urged. "It just so happens that I already have a meeting with the king on the books for this *very* afternoon." He tugged at his cloak, lifting a tightly bound scroll. "We'll simply add one final silver-bullet-point to our newly perfected hit-piece … and *boom—we can finish the cleansing today!*"

The three men headed off, gathering numbers and steam as they went. Their intentions were no longer a secret. They wanted everyone—save Belteshazzar—to know: There would be a public audience with the king today, held within the highest court of the land, and everyone loyal to the crown *must* attend.

CH34: THE FOUR ONE ONE
0571:08:28:02:25:36

There was one thing that stuck out like a glittering sore thumb the moment Daniel stepped into the king's private court: Nebuchadnezzar's angel—the sparkly, flawless one—*yea, it was there again.* But this time, it stood at the right hand of *King Darius!*

Daniel peered intently through the hand of the stranger. In the spirit, the intimidating, glittering angel hadn't changed a bit; it was just as shrewd, beautiful and intense as ever. But through the fleshly filter of the new king, it seemed much more calm, cool and collected.

Daniel marveled at the newly unveiled reality: *The man had changed, but the spirit behind the man had not!*

"King Darius—*may you live forever!*" the unlikely entourage eagerly greeted the king. "In *your* honor, and during the coming month's holiday festivities—we governors, officials, and high officers unanimously demand a law, irrevocable under any circumstances, that for the next thirty days anyone who asks *any* favor of god or man—except from you, Your Majesty—shall be thrown to the lions."

Daniel watched as the angel beside the king whispered into his ear, shamelessly stroking his ego, and repeating—nearly word for word—what the conspirators had spoken only moments before.

"That is highly flattering," the king admitted. "However, is there any reason—other than my own, personal ego—by which I should grant your endearing request?"

"Your Excellence—several concerns have been raised," came the pre-scripted reply, "as to the allegiance and loyalty of some of your—*uhm*—so called, subjects. Particularly those taken in exile and/or born under previous administrations." There was a short, sly pause. "This law, great king, will be a thirty-day audit of sorts. A way to publicly vet the loyal from the disloyal within your kingdom."

Darius nodded slowly. He was well aware of the polarizing unrest which could so easily beset a fledgling kingdom. Especially a kingdom captured in battle like his own. Such unrest could foster shadow-governments, deep rooted deep-state headaches—and much, much worse. A strange pang of fear pierced the pit of his stomach. *'Remember—misunderstandings left unchecked are the breeding grounds for murder,'* the cryptic warning silently erupted in the back of his mind.

Darius shifted uncomfortably in his chair. He didn't want his intentions to be misunderstood. And he certainly didn't want any political misunderstandings to result in—*murder*. He grimaced. The unusual tag-team of 'emotion *and* intellect' was making him strangely uneasy. He fought to keep a level head as his perception clouded with self-concern. *The last thing I need right now, is to worry about treason,* he reasoned. *Besides, this might actually be a brilliant ploy to proactively expose anyone in opposition to the throne..*

"Mmm, you make a good point—," he deliberately conceded.

As soon as the words had left the king's mouth, Daniel watched the beautiful angel lift his hand from Darius' head, and remove a finger from the pit of his stomach.

"—You have my blessing to proceed as suggested," concluded the king, feeling much better already.

Emboldened by the king's response, Daniel's conspirators pressed further. "Your Majesty, may we also request your personal signature backing this law? Sign it, so that it cannot be changed. It will be as a law of the 'Medes and Persians,' which cannot be revoked."

"Why the need for such finality?" the king immediately pushed back, leaning forward in his chair. He might have become king overnight, but he hadn't become king *last night.* The unusual request sent red flags flying sky high. He recognized a hidden agenda when he saw one.

"We—*uhm*—fear that without your personal, irreversible seal, this law may not be taken seriously by all subjects," the conspirators backpedaled. "E-Especially by those subjects who are well aware, that without your signature, the law may still be changed, overlooked or even removed." This they said, not because they wanted to be taken seriously, but because they didn't want the king to be able to revoke the decree, once he discovered it was Belteshazzar they had trapped.

Again, the beautiful angel placed a hand on the king's head and plunged a finger deep into the pit of his stomach. The king turned white, shifted uneasily, and quietly gave his consent.

Daniel watched in stunned silence as the law—already constructed—was signed, sealed and decreed.

Then, it was over.

Everyone filed out of the courthouse swiftly.

Daniel fell into step alongside his three jovial conspirators. As they left, the king's angel exited among them, placing triumphant arms around both the governor and high officer's shoulders.

Daniel paused to watch his accusers stream past Belteshazzar on their way out of the building. Several cohorts stopped to greet him warmly—the governor and high officer warmest of all. It was all so strange. They almost seemed giddy. Inebriated. Intoxicated. They had just sentenced a colleague to death, yet it was as if they had just won the lottery.

A hint of sadness welled up in Daniel's soul. He knew exactly how the following hours would play out, and for little more than a few 'strokes to their own personal checkbooks and egos,' these men were willing to destroy arguably the best thing that had ever happened to their country. Willing to commit murder and treason, in the name of thwarting it. Willing to destroy a man—perhaps the only man—who had quite literally given up everything to do what was best for Babylon's citizens, her future, and her king.

It broke Daniel's heart.

'Do you want to know why?'

The question jolted Daniel back to reality. He blinked rapidly and looked around. The crowds, the conspirators, the clatter, the courts were all gone. He was back. Back in the dark eerie shadows of the unusually quiet, lion's den.

'Do you want to know why?' the stranger silently reiterated, placing a hand on Daniel's heartbroken shoulder. *'Why you were made a eunuch? Why you were routinely singled out? Why you alone, were given the interpretation to a dream that was intended to destroy you? Why you were betrayed by your peers? ..hated and despised? ..tested in every possible way? Why I took the time to revisit each of these scenarios with you?'*

Daniel stole another look around. He was beginning to hear the heavy breathing of big, hungry cats and honestly, in this moment, he didn't particularly care. He opened his mouth to say so—albeit, much more politely—when..

BOOM—it all made sense.

Total sense.

Daniel dropped to his knees. The constant barrage—physical and emotional—robbing him of everything he'd ever held dear … no doubt, it was an attempt to disable and destroy him. *BUT* … in reality, it had been his opportunity—*his golden opportunity*—to move past his own self-absorbed love for his own self-absorbed life, and to sell-out to the only one in the universe who would *never* sell him out.

Gratitude, like a river, began to bubble up from his belly.

Likewise, being routinely singled-out, had—on one hand—been a relentless attempt to keep him isolated, scrutinized, and hated. *BUT* … in reality, it had been his opportunity—*his golden opportunity*—to rise up, distinguish himself from the crowds, and perpetually showcase the marvelous, miraculous, supernatural yet practical God he claimed to know and serve!

Daniel shook his head in disbelief, liquid love invading his heart, redefining every painful moment and freeing him from a lifetime of emotionally-charged, soul-crushing, traumatic and toxic events! He bowed to the ground, amazed. In a single instant, he'd been gifted the gift above any gift he could ever be gifted—*a bottom-line understanding of his life's twenty-thousand-foot world view!*

But there was one last thing.

Daniel trembled in the dirt, an unerasable smile spreading irreversibly across his humbled face. *How was his current predicament any different?* This den of lions was simply one more hellish attempt to permanently remove him from the picture. *BUT*… in reality, it was nothing more than his opportunity—*his golden opportunity*—to become, *unkillable!*

CREEAAAAK—the stone sealing the den was suddenly moving. Daniel rose to his feet, turning his attention upward. The growing beams of sunlight—streaming past the ashen faces of the awestruck guards—was the perfect punchline to the evening's hair-raising, heaven-ordained events.

Daniel threw his head back and laughed. The tumbling dust, in the golden morning air, gave each intruding ray of light a sort-of ethereal, 'other-worldly' glow. It was as if Heaven itself was invading his hopeless prison cell.

Disheveled hair appeared.

Followed by a disheveled face.

"Belteshazzar, servant of the Most High God," King Darius called from above. "Was your God—whom you worship continually—able to deliver you?"

"May the king live forever!" Daniel called in a voice bolder than bold. "*Yes!* My God sent his angel, and he shut the mouths of the lions." He motioned to the peacefully sleeping beasts. "They have not hurt me, because I was found innocent in the sight of my God." Daniel bowed low. "May I also be found innocent in your sight as well, my King."

"Lift him out!" Darius wasted no time. "And bring to me his accusers, *and their families!*" The king himself joined in with the guards, pulling Belteshazzar quickly to safety. He clung fiercely to his loyal servant like a long lost brother. "For, I am most curious to see," he grinned, arm locked immovably around the shoulders of his newest, Chief Administrative Officer, "if *their* gods will be as well able—*to protect them.*"

CH35: DETAINED

"Hmm—let me see here," an orange-haired, heavyset angel muttered, hoisting one rather large clipboard onto one rather large hip. "The Word.. The Word.." she cleared her throat authoritatively, adjusting her horn-rimmed glasses and rescanning her clipboard database for a third and fourth time. She looked like a Debbie—perhaps, a Doris or a Marge—but her name-tag clearly read, Celeste.

The Word stood patiently. He was being detained at one of Second Heaven's many checkpoints, waiting on the proper clearance to enter Earth's orbital subspace. For anyone without direct portal access, this was standard protocol. Two heavily armed, angelic guards waited silently behind him. This was Haylel's territory. The rules were different here. Not just anyone could come and go. A tight air-space was meticulously maintained—an airspace that reportedly grew tighter and tighter with each passing decade. Of course, this was all of little consequence to The Word, as his orders had come directly from Elohim, himself. A simple confirmation, and he would be well on his way.

"The Word.. The Word.." Celeste ran a pudgy, well-manicured finger down the list one last time. Slowly, she shook her head. "You sure you don't go by any other name—Jambreese? Clandestine? ..Jeff?" she half-jokingly offered.

Silence.

"Never heard of anyone called, *The Word,*" she was muttering again. "Usually the word *is* Jambreese, Clandestine, or Jeff.." She tapped her clipboard impatiently. " 'Course there are billions of you strange fellers running around these days—named all sorts of strange things." She loosed a loud, throaty laugh. "It was only a matter of time until one of ya's turned up.."

Silence.

She looked up, over her glasses. "Say—what's your business, anyways?"

The Word lifted a leather satchel from his shoulder. He motioned to an attached cylindrical container. "Delivering a message," he replied.

"To—?" Celeste's eyes probed the case.

"Daniel—of Babylon."

The look on Celeste's face was priceless. You would have thought she had just sunk her new Prada pumps into a freshly made cow patty. "Daniel, of—oh, my.." she muttered, backing up and lifting a nearby phone. "Please have a seat, while I make a quick call."

She motioned to a nearby chair.

The Word said nothing. He took a seat as Celeste talked in hushed tones to whoever it was on the other end of the line.

"Looks like you'll be stuck here a while," the flustered gate-keeper hung up. "My boss wants to speak with you, personally."

Silence.

"Gentlemen." She turned and addressed the guards. "Escort this nice young feller to the waiting room."

The guards motioned for The Word to stand. He obediently complied. Each grabbed an arm and the three headed down a flight of stairs, back a short hall, and into a tiny, unmanned guard shack. At the door of its modest, 8x10 waiting room, they stopped. No one spoke a word. The guards pushed their detainee inside, tipped their hats, and left him standing alone.

Slowly, The Word glanced around, taking in his new found living space. A single table sat in the middle of the stark, tiled room. Two complimenting chairs, one on either side, were its only additional furnishings. He chuckled. The waiting room seemed to be suited a little less for waiting and a little more for—interrogation. All that was missing was a low-hanging light. He placed his satchel on the table, and took a seat.

Superiors came and went, each touting their own set of questions, their own confusions to be cleared: *Why was The Word nowhere to be found in the database? Where did he come from? Who did he work for? What business did he have with Daniel of Babylon?* Each finding The Word's direct, throne room appeals frustrating, and his simple descriptions highly unsatisfactory. Each passing the buck on to their superior, and to their superior, and to theirs.

And so The Word waited, and waited—and waited. With each passing hour the red tape thickened. Hours turned to days, and days to weeks, until things were so hopelessly tied up, he wasn't sure if he would ever get out. In all the confusion, only one thing was certain— no messages, to or from Daniel, were being delivered.

—| |—

Back, at the center of the multiverse, the throne room had, once again, been transformed into a war room. Elohim stood at the room's lone, center table, hovering intently over a single bowl of smoking incense. Its sweet-smelling aroma filled the intimate space. Today it was the Archangel, Michael, who had been summoned. He stood silently before Elohim, patiently waiting to be addressed.

"The Word was sent some time ago," Elohim finally spoke, his focus remaining on the strange smoking bowl. "Yet Daniel's prayers, requesting My Word, continue to steadily rise." He motioned towards the incense. "It's troubling. Something's not right," Elohim looked up, addressing Michael directly. "My friend, you must go and see what is the cause for delay."

Michael nodded, he understood. In fact, he believed he already knew. "Permission to speak," he respectfully requested.

"Permission granted."

"News concerning your prophet Daniel is all over the heavens. Ever since your undisputed favor was given to him in the lion's den, he has been highly esteemed and closely watched."

Elohim nodded.

"Which means, your delay is most likely a Second Heaven issue," Michael shifted anxiously, frustration lacing his voice. "Seems like every year communication becomes harder to get through, sir. More and more red tape. More and more bureaucracy."

Elohim nodded.

Michael shifted again, he *knew* what the problem was. But Elohim didn't seem concerned. Apparently, hinting wasn't going to be enough. "Permission to speak freely," he persisted, the request practically bursting from his lips.

Elohim paused, looking Michael over carefully. He knew what was coming, but he wanted Michael to be absolutely sure that Michael wanted to speak freely. "Permission granted," he slowly conceded.

"*It's Haylel!*" The pent-up accusation erupted like a volcano. Its force caught even Michael by surprise. Immediately, he wished he hadn't spoken. But it was too late, there was no going back now. He took a deep breath. "It's Haylel, sir. He's your problem. He's your troublemaker. He's the one calling the shots. All the bureaucracy, all the red tape—it's him. He's using it to silence your voice, to strangle your influence on Earth. I've seen his dark side firsthand, sir. On the mountainside of Nebo—he forced me to appeal to you. He does not honor your word, your voice, or your commands. Behind your back, he does as *he* wills. Confront him, sir. Clear up the confusion. Put an end to all of this.." Michael stopped, suddenly feeling very sheepish. *What was he doing? Was he actually giving THE God of the Universe orders?* It had all spewed out of him so abruptly—so impulsively. As a leader and a warrior, the sudden lack of control was embarrassing. His face flushed. His eyes dropped. He shut his mouth and stood down.

Once again, Elohim thoughtfully paused. Everything Michael said, he already knew. If only Michael understood what Heaven already had in the works—what had been planned since the very beginning. A slow smile spread across Elohim's face. He threw his head back and laughed—a long, hearty, belly laugh. "Michael—for a second there, you totally had me going," he chuckled, stepping forward and affectionately embracing his friend. He lifted the mighty angel in a huge, all-encompassing bear hug that left Michael's feet dangling. "No need to worry your pretty little head," he smiled, ruffling the mighty angel's flawless hair. "Everything—my son—is under control."

Michael's heart sank. Elohim wasn't getting it. Apparently, he had let his emotions take over, clouding his communication. He opened his mouth to clarify.

"No need," Elohim whispered, holding up a silencing finger. He flashed another dazzling smile and winked. "All in due time, my son, all in due time."

That was when the wave of terror smashed into Michael like a speeding tsunami. From the core of his being, he trembled and shook. Not for himself, but for Haylel. *The wink had said it all.* In that moment, Michael understood: *Nothing had gone unnoticed.*

The mighty angel fought to catch his breath, *Elohim knew—everything. Every lie, every temptation, every trick, every intimidation, every selfish word, selfish motive, every hidden resistance, every angel who had—or ever would—succumb.. Elohim knew it all.* The thought made Michael sick. *How foolish was Haylel? How dark was his future? And if he continued in his dead-set ways, how hopeless?* The thought— let alone, the outcome—was almost too much to bear.

Elohim grabbed Michael. Another powerful embrace, and the terror was gone. Love flooded back in. Once again, Michael could feel Elohim's appreciation and affection. He understood how thankful Elohim was that he had taken the hard road and stood up against Haylel. He felt a sudden strengthening of their interpersonal bond, created by his decision not to let anything, or anyone, draw him away from Elohim's pure and perfect relationship.

Michael wiped the tears from his eyes.

Elohim wiped the tears from his eyes, too. His heart was thrilled by the fact that Michael had pushed past personal ego—even to his own detriment & inconvenience—in order to protect *their relationship* above all else. The display of unshakable loyalty was like a breath of fresh air.

The Creator of the Universe took a short step back. "But, you must go *now*," he smiled at Michael. "For Daniel's sake."

This time it was Michael who nodded. He bowed and turned, a new fire in his belly. He would never breath a word, but the new revelation electrified him—*Elohim knew!* He was supercharged. Pumped. Ready for war. It was as if the soundtrack to his life had just started playing, and the 'floor-stomp'n,' 'butt-kick'n,' 'hell-crush'n' hook was almost ready to drop.

Game on! He grinned. *The world seemed bright, and shiny and new.* Not a thing had happened, yet everything—yes, *EVERYTHING*—had radically changed.

—| |—

"Got here as quick as I could."

The Word looked up as the latest boss, in a long line of bosses, squeezed his way into the tiny waiting room. The new boss reached over—extending one great big, furry paw.

The Word smiled and shook his hand.

It was BEAST.

"Head of the **B**abylonian **E**xcursion **A**nd **S**ojourner **T**eam," came the curt introduction.

"Pleased to meet you," came the genuine reply.

"My 'official' title is, Prince of Persia," BEAST continued, taking his seat. "So you can call me, POP." He glanced up mischievously.

Silence.

BEAST cleared his throat and tugged at his collar. *Tough crowd,* he shifted uncomfortably in his seat. "Uhm—have you been fully briefed?" He buried his gaze deep into a clipboard of his own.

The Word shook his head.

"Daniel, of Babylon," BEAST clicked his pen disapprovingly, "he's on our ... 'Short List.'" He raised only his eyes. "Which means—," he continued, diving back into his paperwork, "we watch him closely. We check, triple check, and/or chaperone all activity surrounding the guy ... Elohim's orders."

The Word nodded. BEAST was correct. Elohim *had* ordered special protection surrounding Daniel. *He was not to be touched.* But the red tape, the hold-ups, and the unnecessary babysitting? —that was Second Heaven's own initiatives, entirely. The Word observed the look of forced concern plastered across BEAST's face. On the surface this charade certainly looked diligent and thorough, even downright noble. But in truth, it was nothing more than control-freak bureaucracy at its finest—a brilliant excuse to screen, rescreen, manage, and micromanage any and all activity surrounding Daniel, and more importantly, Earth.

"Which brings us back to … *you*," BEAST flipped to the next page and tapped his clipboard. "It says here, you're delivering a message from Elohim, himself?" He raised a doubtful eyebrow. "Yet you're nowhere to be found in the database. In fact, as far as I can tell—you are nowhere to be found, anywhere.."

The Word nodded politely. Of course, he wasn't in the database. He was top secret. As far as Heaven was concerned, he didn't exist. As far as he was concerned, he didn't either. And for this little excursion—he wasn't about to blow his cover. Elohim would send help if help was needed. Besides, his unofficial secondary objective was to unbiasedly observe exactly how Second Heaven would treat the infallible word of Elohim (double meaning intended). So rather than reply, he simply slid a sealed document slowly across the table.

"What's this?" BEAST took the document, turning it over in his hands. He examined it closely, continuing until he was thoroughly convinced of its legitimacy. With that, he broke the seal, observing its classified contents—a living, breathing, twelve-dimensional, holographic message straight from the mouth of Elohim.

When he'd finished, he folded the document and slowly slid it back across the table. "It certainly looks legit," he admitted. "From seal, to interactive content." He scratched his head. "But herein, lies our problem," he was tapping again. "Daniel is my personal responsibility. His—*uh*, safety rests squarely on my shoulders.." He paused. "So … without you displaying some sort of personal credentials—we are unfortunately at a standstill." This he said, not because a genuine problem truly existed, but because he was in no way going to allow an unfiltered, unpreviewed message travel unchecked between God and man. *Not on his watch.*

There was a sharp rap at the door. The Word smiled. *His credentials had arrived—right on time!*

Michael turned the handle and poked his head in. "Heard there was trouble," he flashed a broad grin. "Gentlemen, I'm here to clear things up!" He nodded respectfully, addressing BEAST directly. "Sir, I can assure you—this messenger *is* who he says he is. In fact, I was sent here directly from the throne; just to verify that this messenger's orders are indeed, legit." He stepped into the already crowded room, filling what little space was left. "My personal credentials," he slapped his identification down on the table. "Feel free to verify them as well."

"No need," BEAST growled, grudgingly returning Michael's nod. "I'm well aware of who you are." He stood and painstakingly gathered the sprawling credentials. "I apologize gents, but even I must follow protocol," he cleared his throat, attempting his best, sympathetic look. He wasn't letting them go that easy—not when he still had rolls of red tape at his disposal. *It was simply time to initiate a new delay sequence.* He reached to his left and punched the wall, smashing a thin piece of glass labeled, '*emergency.*' Lifting what appeared to be a red, toy phone, he punched in a number and was soon mumbling profusely. Several long minutes passed before he ended his call, reluctantly returning the fluorescent receiver to its tiny, toy holster.

"Unfortunately gentlemen, it seems everything must be documented and signed by at least two senior officials," BEAST sighed, squeezing past Michael. "Only a few more minutes of waiting while I finish the necessary paperwork and persuade my associate, the Prince of Greece, to co-sign." He lifted a parting hand, ducking through the narrow door, locking it securely behind him. Then, with absolutely no intention of returning any time soon, BEAST was gone.

As soon as the door clicked shut, Michael turned to The Word. "*Go!*" he urged, stepping to the wall and touching it. "*Go*—or Daniel may *never* get his answer." He smiled as a doorway, courtesy of Elohim, appeared.

The Word needed no further prompting. Scooping up his belongings, he moved to the exit, ducking through the angel's makeshift portal.

"Do not worry," Michael called out after him, scooting the

the lone table up against the locked guard shack door. "I will stay behind and make certain everything is properly handled."

—| 0570:00:22:22:44:48 |—

"DAAANIEL—," the voice pealed like thunder, rolling eerily across the banks of the Tigris river.

Daniel alone froze while his students and colleagues scattered. He would have gladly joined them, but all the strength in his body had fled as well. His rubber legs were useless.

"*DAAANIEL!*" the voice boomed a second time.

Trembling, Daniel looked up, his awestruck face ashen and pale. There, standing before him—hovering midair—was a man, glowing like the son of God. The man was dressed completely in linen, a brilliant gold belt fixed around his waist. His countenance shown like lightning. His arms and legs, like burnished bronze. His eyes burned with an all-consuming fire. And his voice pierced to the marrow of one's bones. He was both terrifying and—*strangely familiar?*

Daniel swayed, teetering on the brink of consciousness until the realization, like the ground below, suddenly hit—*this was the stranger from the lion's den!*

"Daniel, highly esteemed," a fiery hand pressed firmly against Daniel's cold, clammy forehead. "Consider carefully my words and stand up, for I have been sent to you directly."

Daniel struggled to open his eyes. The voice of the angel was still roaring around him like a mighty rushing wind. He reached out, taking the fearsome angel's forearm. *No wonder they had only spoken spirit-to-spirit during their adventures in the lion's den.*

Still trembling, Daniel slowly arose.

"Do not be afraid," the angel thundered, touching Daniel's pursed lips. "Since the first day that you determined to pray relentlessly, your words have been heard. I have come in response to them." His hand moved back to Daniel's forehead. "However, the Prince of Persia resisted me for twenty-one days. So Michael, one of the Chief Princes, came to my aid, because I was detained." He paused as renewed strength flowed into Daniel's weak frame. "Now I have come to explain to you what will happen to your people in the future."

"Speak, my Lord." Daniel bowed his head, letting the angel's power fill him. "Because your life is giving me strength."

Then, the angel spoke: He spoke of kings and kingdoms. Of conflicts and armies. Of disaster, distress, and disease. He spoke of predetermined events and of predetermined times. Of great and terrible things.

"Daniel," the angel lifted his satchel, revealing its precious cargo. "Seal up the words of this scroll." He removed the delicate parchment, plunging it deep into the recesses of Daniel's heart. "Hide them here," he instructed, "until the end of time has come."

A sudden warmth spread throughout Daniel's entire body. He bowed low, accepting the manuscript and the responsibility. Immediately, he was aware of two things: *One*, these sacred words had been very safely hidden. *And two*, he would never be able to forget them.

"How long will it be, before these astonishing and dreadful events are fulfilled?" The question rang out boldly across the Tigris.

Daniel lifted his head with a start. Two more heavenly beings had just joined the mix. One—a flaming, warrior—stood silently, only a few yards away. The other—a tall, thin, hooded figure—stood defiantly on the opposite river bank.

"I swear by Elohim, who lives forever," the angel lifted his hand from Daniel's head and stepped back into the air. "It will be fulfilled for a time, times, and half a time, *after* the power of Elohim's people has fully been broken."

The being on the far bank bowed with a smirk, lifting his staff in acknowledgment.

"My Lord—," Daniel gasped, sensing the dire opposition. "Of what will the outcome be?" He looked up, surprised by the words of his own lips.

The angel turned and smiled. He would have gladly answered the question had his audience with Daniel remained private. But having the Prince of Greece within earshot changed everything.

Besides, this information was intended for another—a future, prophetic, unkillable disciple, whom he loved.

"Go your way, Daniel," he gently instructed. "Those words are rolled up and sealed until the time of the end. Until then, many will continue to be purified, made spotless, and refined—but the wicked will continue to be wicked. None of the wicked will understand, while those who are wise will understand."

Ka-BOOM—from across the river, the Prince of Greece brought his staff down, disappearing in a thunderclap of pale, yellow smoke. He had heard enough. *"The power of Elohim's people WOULD BE BROKEN!"* He needed nothing more, his Square Table cohorts would relish the news. By the word of Elohim, himself: *They would win!* Of course, the fatal irony was, that the very same word had also warned, *"none of the wicked would understand."*

But, of course, Prophet had not understood.

On the heels of the odd and sudden departure, Daniel also turned to go. His heart was full and overflowing. Now was the time to go and write it all down.

"As for you, Daniel," the angel called after him. "Go your way. Live your life. These things will not affect you. You will rest, and then, at the end of days, you will rise to receive your allotted inheritance."

Then, the vision was gone.

Daniel wasted no time. He took off running, heading for the decaying corridors of the former Babylonian catacombs. He had to get this on paper, and there was only one place to properly record a message of this magnitude.

CREEEAK—the heavy door swung open. Daniel lifted his lantern, lighting the thick twisted candles lining the old, underground chamber. The well-seasoned sage looked fondly around. The room was exactly as he remembered—everything in order and put away. A thick layer of undisturbed dust confirmed Daniel's suppositions—that aside from his own, increasingly frequent visits— the room had remained largely untouched since his first, fateful stay.

Daniel moved swiftly down a cobweb-covered path to the simple writer's bench where the book of Isaiah lay perfectly preserved and tucked away. Its weathered cover the only indication that it had ever been read, reread and studied a thousand times over.

Daniel bent and lovingly retrieved the priceless manuscript.

Opening its familiar pages, he took a seat at the table, placing the book gently before him. Flipping past the writings of Isaiah, he settled on one of the many blank pages near the end of the book. With quill and ink, he carefully penned his own name. Then, with all the wisdom, favor, and vigor of Heaven, he began the meticulous task of recording the stories, visions, insights and revelation that had somehow, supernaturally become his own crazy, amazing, living adventure.

CH36: INTERMISSION

Unfortunately, dear reader, there is no time to tell of Joseph and Pharaoh, David and Saul, Ruth and Boaz, Jacob and Esau—nor of Solomon, Samuel, Deborah, or Esther—Elisha, Elijah, Eli or Ezra; of Micah, Jonah, Nahum or Malachi. Of Enoch, Jehu, or Samson the Nazarite. Nor of the judges, priests, prophets and kings who lined the long halls of Pentateuch history. Suffice to say that throughout each new age—Haylel's war, *The War of the Heavens*, relentlessly raged.

It was a silent war. A vicious war. A war of wills and quills, lies and deceit. A war that—with each passing century—progressively unfolded, as Heaven's 'secretly disgruntled' CEO, battled its 'seemingly oblivious' Presidential Board for complete control of the company. The name of the game was espionage. Its playbook, sabotage. Its unfair advantage, secrecy. Its ultimate goal, *total acquisition.*

For those closest to the Presidential Board, it was an endless source of frustration. Especially for those who could see no good end. Like an invisible cancer, the perpetual corruption posed an ever-festering problem to which there was no known cure. At least, not as long as the passive-aggressive offenders remained safely hidden behind their impenetrable walls of lies and ever-shifting blame. Even for the eternally-patient, brilliantly-strategizing Presidential Board, the relentless redundancy of the increasingly malignant situation could have easily become maddening.

But today—today marked the dawn of a brand new day. Heaven was ready, and it was time to invade. And what had yesterday seemed only impossible; *was suddenly—all about to change.*

CH37: GAMETIME

Elohim's war room was completely abuzz, last minute preparations in full, unfettered swing. A tight-knit group of hand-selected, heaven-directed, secret operatives were excitedly scurrying about, diligently at work, putting the finishing touches on a millennia of carefully constructed plans and objectives. It was showtime. Go time. Game time. Pain time. Time for a covert sting.

Along one wall stood the Heavenly Host—a savage tribe of angelic warriors. Their barbaric, oversized weapons lay in a heap—carelessly cast aside—as they eagerly put the finishing touches on a soaring, harmonious, forty-eight-part, choral arrangement.

Along another wall, an attractive superstar was literally beaming with anticipation as she was meticulously fitted with the perfect crown and evening gown for her debuting role in the twinkling heavenly lights.

A third wall boasted several stately beings, all milling about, diplomatically rehearsing their prescripted soliloquies. They motioned and moved, postured and posed—honing each presentation until they were flawless.

Gabriel, Heaven's Chief Messenger, stood silently among the fray. He was ready, stationed at attention beside the War Room's lone, center table, patiently waiting for the holy trio—currently huddled around it—to give him tailor-made, detailed instructions. He had a good hunch as to what they would be, but the trio was turned—backs to him—lost in deep conversation.

For now, he would wait.

"Are you ready?" Elohim nudged The Word playfully, leaning in with a questioning elbow. The query was lighthearted, the smiles genuine, yet there was an air of seriousness surrounding it. Soon, there would be no going back.

"Without a doubt!" The Word grinned. "I was *made* for this!"

Elohim waved a commanding hand over the table. There was a click and a whir as a secret compartment lifted. Rising high in the air, it exposed a cabinet packed with transparent golden vials. Many of the vials were full of a thick, black liquid. The strange, dark substance twitched and breathed, moving with a life all its own. The Word stifled a shiver. It was almost as if the liquid was attempting to escape the corked confines of its airtight restraints.

Elohim selected the nearest empty vial. Opening the lid, he plunged it deep within his own chest. After a few moments he pulled it out, swirling its contents and checking its overall level. He then repeated the process until he was wholly satisfied—the vial was full. Corking and sealing it, he placed it back inside the cabinet, where it quickly began to rattle and shake like the others.

"Are you sure?" Elohim nudged The Word a second time. "You're completely willing to absorb my wrath?" He gestured towards the angrily clattering rack. "All of it?"

The Word looked at the vials—row upon row upon row. This was all the pain, turned to wrath, that mankind's continued sin was creating in his father. He winced. He understood the gravity of the question. As a perfect, eternal being, Elohim's wrath couldn't just be ignored or discarded. No, it was far too late for that. It already existed. And once it existed, it would always exist … unless. Unless, it was properly disposed of. The Word smiled. Fortunately, there *was* one way to get rid of it—something had to absorb it. *Someone* had to absorb it. *Unfortunately*—he swallowed hard—*that someone was slated to be him.*

"Dad—you know that I am … right down to the very last drop," he smiled again, firing back a reassuring nudge of his own. Difficult as it was, there was no way he was backing down from this fight.

"But what about your Power?" Spirit stepped in, pushing the conversation further. "Are you willing to lose that?" She lifted an eyebrow and a finger. "How about your position? ..Your wisdom?

..Your understanding?" She let out a terse giggle, marking each new point with a separately raised digit. "Oh, and don't forget—your dashing good looks!"

The Word chuckled. "Two things," he shot back. "One: It's only temporary. And two: Soon I'll have absolutely no memories of anything I've lost!" He threw one arm around Spirit and the other around his Father, pulling them close. "Besides, the one thing I *won't* lose is my connection to both of you." His tone grew serious. "And that is what really matters." He gave them both an affectionate squeeze. "You will be my Power. My wisdom. *And* my dashing good looks!" A twinkle flickered across both resolute eyes. "Honestly," he relaxed, "it's gonna be fun. I'm totally off the hook. All I have to do is what you *tell* me to do—you guys have to do all the work!"

"And work we will," Elohim chuckled. "To make sure you're the perfect example of what mankind can be." He leaned in and hugged his fearless son. "Fully God and fully man. Capable of bypassing Second Heaven's interference, and manifesting Heaven directly on Earth, wherever you go!"

"A second Adam," Spirit chimed in. "Slipped into the world under the cover of skin." Her face lit up. "Operating on all cylinders, as mankind was originally intended!"

"That sounds—totally off the hook!" The Word grinned again.

"Yes—well—speaking of hooks," Spirit shifted gears. "Don't forget—you're about to become the squirming, helpless worm at the end of a very large one." She grabbed The Word's face with both hands, squeezing soft, satiny cheeks. "Oh, it's gonna be so hard for our almighty serpent to resist a poor, lowly, nameless man who cannot be controlled." She pulled his face close. "It'll be like Team Adam, all over again! But this time with a secret so simple, so unstoppable, so unprovable—Haylel will never see it coming," she smiled, eyes dancing with delight. "Oh—it's gonna drive him ding-dong, bat crazy!"

"So crazy, he'll bite?"

"Oh, he'll bite—*hard.*"

"And that's when we've got him?"

"That's when we've got him!"

The Word laughed out loud. "No more lies. No more excuses. No more gaslighting or blame shifting. Just his hand, in our cookie jar … *BUSTED!*" He flashed a dazzling smile, prying his face from Spirit's ever-loving squeeze. "Come on Mom—let's go catch us a devil!"

He lifted his head and stepped back, taking one long, last look around. A sigh rattled his muscular frame. *He would miss this place.* His family. His friends. Everything he'd ever known. It was all here. He didn't bother to hold back the tears. Slowly he made his way around the room, embracing each and everyone in it. He took his time, soaking up the moment. Enjoying every hug. Every connection. Every emotion.

Then, he was done.

The Word stood tall, lifting his hand high in one final, "good-bye" to all. With that, he turned, and with the widest of grins, stepped fearlessly into the center of his Daddy, Elohim.

The room held its breath, watching as the Son of God's transformation took place. First, there was a flicker. Then a flash. Then, The Word began to vibrate. Slowly at first, then faster and faster—glowing brighter—until the entire space was filled with a blinding, pulsating light. Like dust in the wind, he began to dissolve, his spirit reverse-engineering back into its original, most basic form.

One more blinding flash, and The Word, as they knew him, was gone. All that remained was a tiny ball of blazing blue light about the size of a marble—his heavenly, DNA blueprint. The tiny blue flame wiggled and wriggled—like a baby—full of life, full of light, full of joy.

The Word had become seed.

Out of Elohim's heart it squirmed, making its way joyfully into his Daddy's outstretched hand. Elohim raised his palm gently to his lips and blew, sending it sailing like a ship on the sea towards a ready and waiting, Gabriel. The seed wriggled and giggled, tumbling in a shower of shimmering lights towards the stoic messenger. For a moment, it paused, quivering with excitement, hovering near the mighty angel's chest. Then it disappeared, into a small, ornate incubator, hanging from Gabriel's neck.

Everyone paused, wondering what was next.

Elohim shifted his gaze downward, noting the ticking clock below. When the time was right, he took a deep breath and blew again. Long and steady, it swirled around the room, filling it with color and life. As it moved it picked up speed until it became a mighty, rushing wind. Out of the deafening roar, a portal began to form, burning like a fire in the center of the ever growing gale.

Elohim turned to Gabriel. "Go!" he bellowed over the howl of the wind. "Bring my Word to Mary of Nazareth. She is Heaven's chosen vessel—pure and undefiled—the perfect ground in which to cultivate my seed." He pulled something like a scroll from the recesses of his whipping robe. Reaching over, he plunged it deep into Gabriel's chest. "Speak to her the words I have placed in your heart. When she agrees, release to her my seed."

Reaching out, Elohim gently took Spirit's hand. She stood, effortlessly poised in the mighty gale, her gown and hair swirling elegantly about her graceful frame. There was no doubt about it—she was a mighty queen, fit for a mighty, matchless king.

"My Spirit and my Power will go with you," Elohim smiled at Gabriel. "To ensure that my seed is properly planted within Mary's womb."

Gabriel nodded and bowed low. Then, pressing hard against the gale, he moved towards the open portal.

"Do not forget his name," Elohim raised his voice one last time.

The entire room froze, listening intently. This was the mystery hidden from the beginning—the name they'd been longing to hear.

"His name means, Savior," Elohim began.

"Salvation..

Deliverer..

Redeemer.."

Everyone strained above the sound of the wind.

"His name is ... Yeshua (*'YEH-shoe-uh'*)."

There was a collective gasp. Resounding squeals and cheers.

Gabriel nodded his understanding. Bending once more against the wildly whipping gale, he stepped forcefully through the open portal, disappearing in a flash.

Spirit delicately followed his lead, holding onto Elohim's powerful, outstretched hand. Unlike Gabriel, the wind nor the weightiness of The Word's revealed name seem to phase her. She walked effortlessly to the edge of the portal. Hair and dress whipping about her. Pausing, she glanced back, playfully blowing the room a farewell kiss. The gale intensified, the portal expanding slightly, beginning its collapse. Spirit grinned mischievously, pausing until the very last moment. Then, just as the portal caved, she fell in backwards, cannonball tucking her legs and blowing one last farewell kiss to the room.

CH38: INSURGENCE

Four hundred years. That's how long it had been since anyone had received a fresh word from Elohim. Certainly, it wasn't that Elohim had stopped talking. No, it was a well-known fact, his Spirit was a bit of a chatterbox. It was just that Haylel had done his job well. Too well. His constant barrage of subtle lies had dulled Israel's ears. His endless supply of passing temptations had captivated her heart. Truth had become relative. Image was everything. Virtue signaling, the new norm. And over time, the narratives of tradition, skepticism, shame and pride had grown so loud they'd drowned out Elohim's voice, altogether.

In the light of his sustained success, Haylel was beginning to flaunt his arrogance. His uber-control-freak, micromanagement methods were finally paying off. In fact, they seemed to be working out in spades. Israel's slow implosion had already caught the jealous eye of nearby neighbor, Rome. And in 63 BC, Rome pounced on its prey, taking Jerusalem as its own.

Haylel couldn't have been more pleased. Once again, he was on top, with Israel fully submitted to his dominant, oppressive rule.

Elohim, however, was deeply disturbed. *How long would this cycle continue? ..this pattern remain unbroken? How long would his people continue to just sit back and take it?* It was heartbreaking. Gut-wrenching. Sickening. Still, he hadn't broken a sweat. He understood that Haylel's growing confidence meant Haylel's guard was also dropping, and whilst soaring at the current altitudes of his new-found superiority, Haylel would never see it coming.

In fact, at this very moment, in a lowly house, in a lowly town, among average, everyday, lowly mundane people—*Heaven's insurgence had already begun.*

—| 0034:04:04:08:04:44 |—

"Hail—highly favored one!" Gabriel's bold greeting rang out in the quiet little Nazarene home, echoing loudly off the white stone walls. There was a flicker. A flash. The distant sound of ... *chimes?* Instantly, the one-room bungalow was alive with bright and shimmering lights.

Mary gasped, letting her bowl of partially kneaded dough slip through startled fingers. It fell to the ground, skidding wildly out of control, clanging loudly across the hard-packed floor. She sprang to her feet, spinning to face the intruder. Her long, dark hair whipped frantically around behind her, revealing big brown eyes—wide and brimming with concern. *Who was this?* She squinted through the glowing lights, now dancing playfully off the walls and low thatched ceiling. *And what sort of greeting was it?* She took a precautionary step towards the nearest exit. *Only a man with the best—or the worst—of intentions would have the audacity to address a younger woman in this manner. What did he want from her? Didn't he know she was engaged?* Her teenage hands trembled, instinctively balling at her sides. Her shoulders tensed. Her jaw clenched. She glared daggers, almost daring him to make the first move. If he was going to take something from her, the very least she could do was return the favor. She wasn't too proud, or too afraid to go 'spider-monkey' all over this guy.

"Mary." Gabriel broke the tension. "Do not be afraid. For you have found favor with God." He smiled a kind, genuine smile, nodding a short, respectful nod.

Mary instinctively softened. She sensed the truth in his words, the kindness in his voice. Slowly she bent to retrieve her morning's work, her hands relaxing as they went back to their familiar task. She scrunched her nose, carefully studying her unannounced guest. He was a peculiar man—tall, dark, and ruggedly handsome. He seemed of African descent, although his glowing, bronzed skin made it particularly hard to tell. His head was clean shaven. His ears masculinely pierced. A beard—full at the bottom, faded at the top—clung like that of a Roman Soldier's to the lower portions of his chin. His eyes flickered, burning with a sort of unrelenting tenacity. And for a fleeting moment after each wholehearted smile, his face remained noticeably more aglow.

Mary grinned, she liked him—there was a hardness about his countenance, yet a gentleness about his soul. Besides, it didn't take dancing lights and glowing skin to perceive ... *this man was other-worldly.*

"You will conceive, and give birth to a son," Gabriel continued in a soothing baritone. "You are to call him, *Yeshua— meaning Savior;* for he will save his people from their oppressor." He cleared his throat, raising the intensity of his voice once again. "He will be called *The Son of the Most High.* And *The Most High* will give him the throne of his father, David, where he will reign over Israel forever and ever!"

Then there was silence.

Long. Awkward. Joy-filled. Silence.

Mary hesitated, searching for the words. *This was where she was supposed to reply,* she knew that. *But how could she?* She was still trying to take it all in. One minute ago she was making lunch, and now she was being—*propositioned by God?* Her teenage mind was reeling. She needed a moment to process ... *surrogate mother of the foretold Messiah—ruler of the universe, savior of the world? That was kind of a big deal, right?*

Suddenly a thought hit.

..but, How—? Her cheeks flushed. *God/human.. Human/God.. there were serious compatibility issues, no?* She didn't even want to speculate. Still, the elephant had just walked into the room and it needed to be addressed.

"*H-How* will this be?" she blurted out, understandably a little flustered. "Seeing that—*I'm a virgin?*"

Gabriel smiled, *fearless and to the point*—he liked this girl.

"Elohim's own Spirit will come upon you," he answered. "And The Power of the Most High will overshadow you. So that the special one to be born will be called, *God's own son.*" Nostalgia hit his voice. "Even Elizabeth your relative is going to have a child in her old age, and she—who was said to be unable to conceive—is already in her sixth month." He smiled broadly. "Be assured, no word from God will ever fail."

Mary's heart leapt. *Elizabeth pregnant? No way. Not in a million years!* She fought to control her excitement. *If that was truly the case, than surely this was a message from God!*

A long-forgotten memory suddenly bubbled to the surface. She almost giggled. Strange as it may sound, she had once prayed for a day like today, never dreaming that it might actually happen. She glanced back to her angelic visitor, renewed hope rising. If Elizabeth was all in, so was she. "I-I too, am the Lord's maidservant!" she clamored. "Let it be done to me according to your word."

At the sound of Mary's consent, Spirit entered the room.

Immediately, the home was bathed in rainbows of living color—moving and breathing—flickering gleefully around Spirit's delicate frame. Mary gasped. There were pinks and blues, purples, greens ... shimmering golden iridescents. Not to mention the countless bands of heavenly chroma defying all logical description. Mary squinted, looking deeper. Music flowed within each band like cytoplasmic lava. Bubbling. Burning. Shimmering. Streaming. Releasing periodic bursts of melodious light in perfect orchestral composition.

A holy hush fell.

All eyes followed Spirit as she moved about the room. Dancing. Flowing. Beaming. An enthralling union of power, melody and light.

Suddenly, a bell rang. Strange and long. Like a timer going off.

Somewhere, deep within Spirit, a Power began to rise. Like a vapor, it emerged. Wafting and whirling. Spreading and swirling. Filling the entire space.

Mary watched in awe. This Power was unique, unlike any other. Its body—while it had a form—seemed to have neither beginning, nor end. It was larger than life: spanning eternity and overflowing the depths of time. Yet strangely, it rested comfortably within the confines of her tiny, singular abode. Over its head drooped the customary veil. Yet, this Power needed no guidance, since the cloth which veiled its face, was itself, covered with eyes. It was both dreadful and delightful, comforting and chilling all at the same time. Mary sighed, there was no need for introduction—clearly this was, *The Power of the Most High.*

Then the dance was done.

Spirit slowed to a stop beside Gabriel, placing one hand on his shoulder, and one on his chest. Hoisting herself to her tippy-top, tip-toes, she gently removed the cherished seed from the angel's protective necklace. For a moment she paused, delighted beyond words, lovingly watching her little seed squirm. Then, with a giggle, she pushed off, pirouetting effortlessly to Mary's side.

Hugging Mary tight, she swung her arm down, planting her hand securely into Mary's untouched belly, tenderly positioning the wiggling seed, just so. With her free hand, she slowly raised a dainty, golden-threaded needle. There was a moment's hesitation. A second of heightened anticipation. Then, quick as a flash, she stitched the giddy little seed to one of Mary's hand-selected eggs. A solitary spark flashed as the stitch took hold. Spirit stepped back, watching the tiny seed wriggle and squirm, trying its best to make its way back into her open hand. *Too late,* she blew it a kiss, *the deed was done*—God and man had just become one.

Wow. Mary flushed, dropping to the ground, waves of liquid love coursing through her being. She felt complete. Full. Totally overwhelmed by the goodness of God. She tried to catch her breath. But everything in her longed to burst from her skin and run free, unfettered, forever. Her face tingled. Her heart pounded. It was as if she could literally explode. She had never felt anything like it, and never would again—not until she had departed from this world and moved on to the next. It was as if the fullness of Heaven had momentarily invaded her home—*momentarily invaded her.*

She cradled her stomach, hugging the tiny spark that had just become a baby within her belly. Already, she would do anything for it. Anything to protect it. She didn't even know it, yet she already loved it. *Her baby. Her son. Her savior?*

Then, they were gone—Spirit, the Power, the dancing lights,

the music. Gone.

All gone.

Only Gabriel remained.

The angel bent and helped Mary to her feet. With a huge smile and a heart full of joy, he kissed the top of her head. *What a treasure!*

Grateful, Mary reached out to thank him one last time. But it was too late, the angel had disappeared—translated, far away—suddenly surrounded by ancient Babylonian artifacts in a moon-lit, dust-covered, all-too-familiar room. He smiled, looking up from his itinerary, the exposed beams and aged timber were exactly as he remembered. *Mmmm*, he breathed deep, the unique musk of timber and cobblestone arousing fond memories. For a moment he paused, listening as excited footsteps wheeled to a stop outside the room's large, wrought iron door. There were *clicks* and *clangs*, *pops* and *bangs*, as locks and bolts flew open. *Creeeeeak*—several well-dressed, well-bearded sages spilled into the room.

Gabriel smiled. *One. Two. Three wise men—that was his cue.*

Pocketing his instructions, he stepped briskly to the edge of a nearby desk—the wandering rays of a puzzlingly bright star showering its supremely dusty contents. He stared fondly at a certain red leather-bound book, gauging with supreme accuracy the desired landing page.

Then, with a flutter and a flurry—and a somewhat startling breeze—he spilled its precious contents open and onto the floor.

CH39: FAST FORWARD
0003:11:24:04:30:55

A refreshing spring breeze blew cool on The Word—now, Yeshua's—face. He slowed to a stop, enjoying its passing relief. His olive complexion and robust, thirty-year-old frame stood out conspicuously against the surrounding, sun-bleached landscape. He raised a strong, calloused, carpenter's hand, shielding his brow, squinting into the dusty, mid-morning light. His striking blue eyes scanned the plains of the distant valley below. Through the haze, he could faintly make out the swollen banks of the Jordan River. Beside them, a crowd was quickly forming, gathering around a uniquely dressed man he knew to be, John. Yeshua smiled, *sun-baked leather and course camel's hair—certainly not your typical, mid-eastern attire.* Still, fashion statements aside, he knew why the crowds had come. Rumor had it, a revolution was on the rise. And Elizabeth's son, John—Yeshua's crazy-dressing, fearlessly outspoken, often hot-headed, tell-it-like-it-is cousin—was single-handedly spearheading the movement.

Yeshua took a deep breath. Yes, change was certainly in the air. It was almost tangible.

Dropping his hand, he pressed onward, picking up the pace. He too was eager to hear his cousin speak. The tall prairie grass bent willingly beneath his sandal clad feet. Well saturated, cumulus clouds billowed majestically overhead. Desert Larks and Trumpeter Finch darted and danced from tree to low-lying tree, singing brightly, proclaiming his soon arrival.

Yeshua took little notice. He was lost, deep in thought—reflecting on the lifetime of events which had miraculously brought him here.

A smile pursed his lips. He had grown up like any other boy—well, any other boy with a direct, unbroken connection to God. He chuckled. He was thankful for Joseph and Mary, the strong earthly parents Elohim had chosen for him. He had not been an easy child to raise by any stretch of the imagination: His vivid dreams, frequent visions, and deep insights into the Torah; his ability to hear thoughts, perceive motives, and regularly bend the laws of physics; not to mention that he could plainly see into the spirit realm, often meeting with Elohim and Spirit face to face—it was all so strange, so foreign, so out of left-field. It gave his parents endless fits. Dead pets rarely stayed dead. Oil lamps never burned out. Food often multiplied. And he was constantly disappearing for hours on end, interacting with what he called, "his heavenly family." Oh, and then there was the summer he took the infamous "shortcut," walking conspicuously across the middle of the very unfrozen, very well-attended, neighborhood, community pond.

That fire certainly wasn't easy to put out.

Furthermore, he was shamelessly outspoken. And of course, he was never wrong (although he often apologized for it). It was almost maddening, there was no training manual on how to handle socially awkward, unpunishable perfection. For Joseph and Mary, everyday felt sort of like trying to field a pop-fly marble at high noon and then, just for good measure, taking an unanticipated, Chuck Norris, roundhouse kick to the face.

Yeshua burst out laughing. He couldn't help it—the mental image. He was pretty sure he looked like a crazy man, stumbling down the hillside—eyes tearing, nose running, laughing so hard his sides hurt—but he didn't care. He wiped his face, and cleared his nose. From Bethlehem to Egypt, Egypt to Nazareth—he was pretty sure the degree of difficulty in raising him was one of the main reasons Elohim had moved them around so much. Certainly it was to fulfill prophecy, and throw Haylel off his scent—but mostly it was for his own family's sanity. They definitely needed the mulligans.

Yeshua slowed as he regained composure. Sadly, there were several years where he had inadvertently embarrassed Joseph so much that he wasn't sure if his dad's natural skin color was brown or faded maroon. But over time, his parents had become accustomed to his strange ways—even grown to appreciate them. And in time, they learned to use honesty to address the steady stream of elephants he constantly dragged into the room, and humor to dispel the awkwardness. Thankfully, this led to an endless supply of laughter growing up—with Yeshua's personal love for practical jokes only adding to the hilarity.

Ultimately, Yeshua did learn to bridle his ways—to speak only when he heard Elohim speak, to do only what he saw Elohim do, and to use his gifts only to the advantage of others. Yeshua's heart welled. His parents had been a surprisingly good covering, taking a great deal of societal beat-downs on his behalf. They had handled the pressures of life well, all the while maintaining a protective greenhouse family environment—a safe place for him to grow as he learned, practiced, and interacted with Heaven on Earth. For that, he was exceedingly grateful.

Of course, it hadn't been all fun and games. His life had been shrouded in controversy from day one. *Son of God? Immaculate conception? Virgin birth? —yea, right.* The truth was just too far-fetched, too unbelievable. Even his unified, overprotective parents couldn't shield him from the sting of being labeled 'illegitimate.' The looks from neighbors. The whispers of classmates. The distance maintained by family and friends. Yeshua could still hear their silent, collective voice, screaming loud and clear—*he didn't belong.*

Heaven's darling son, chuckled. Certainly, he knew he was an outsider. It just never bothered him. He couldn't explain it. He just never had the desire to appease or deny the label. Besides, there was always another voice, booming deep within, telling him how all the labels and misunderstandings were for a reason, a greater purpose, a purpose far bigger than himself. A slow smile spread across his fearless face. He could still picture the exact moment when it had all made sense—his parent's stories, the quiet persecution, his perpetual, supernatural, 'Twilight Zone' of a life, Heaven's constant interactions..

He had been studying the Psalms and the prophets, when suddenly scripture after scripture began flashing their way across his mind's eye. Hundreds of little, seemingly disconnected pieces of truth falling together into one, big, fully completed, jigsaw puzzle of a revelation. Suddenly, it had dawned—*I'm the ONE! The Promised Messiah! —born of a virgin, born in Bethlehem, taken from the tribe of Judah, descended from the line of David, called out of Egypt, called a Nazarene, made to suffer outside the camp, destined for the salvation of Man. That's me! All those scriptures are about… me.*

Even for him, it had been a tough pill to swallow. While he loved the ultimate reward and immediate sense of purpose it had brought, passages like Psalm 22 and Isaiah 53 held his unbridled excitement in gut-wrenching check. Knowing the pain he was destined to endure in order to make his future a reality—it was beyond sobering. This was Earth. The supercharged atmosphere of Heaven was gone; the electrifying boldness felt in the presence of his all-powerful, heavenly father, long forgotten. And while he still had that all-powerful, internal connection—he was now on the front lines, in enemy territory, alone.

Yeshua immediately chased the unpleasant thought from his mind. No need to dwell on that today, he needed his strength for the present. Besides, he wasn't the only one who had suffered. His eyes softened as he thought of his mother—so pure, so willing, so fearless. Mary had been at the heart of this whole supernatural misunderstanding from day one; risking everything—her life, her marriage, even her reputation—to make Heaven's truth, and his life, a reality.

Yeshua winced, feeling his mother's pain. She had lived the perpetual Catch-22 nearly her entire life. To those around her, she was at best, 'a fornicating liar,' and at worst, 'a schizophrenic adulteress.' There was no way around it. Virgin birth, Son of God—it wasn't even on the radar of possibility.

Thankfully, Mary had one saving grace. Her relentless focus on Elohim had slowly cultivated an unshakable peace within her own soul. Because of it, she understood—with Elohim on her side, she was destined to walk *through* her dark valley. She was not destined to remain there. And even on the days when she felt overwhelmed or stuck, whenever she looked back over the months—and eventually the years—she could clearly see that her inner, spirit-woman was only growing brighter and brighter and brighter.

The story, however, was a bit different for Joseph. Although he had been hand-picked by Elohim and emotionally empowered to walk through everything Haylel would bring his way, a little piece of his heart always felt as if he had been thrown into the fire, tossed to the wolves and forced into a fight he hadn't chosen to fight. This left a tiny little door of doubt buried deep within his soul, a door Haylel often took advantage of. As a result, the constant paradox of his firstborn being either, 'the crazy man's promised Son of God,' or a, 'pathetic infidelity cover-up,' plagued him to no end. Even his own insider information did little to dispel the outward social stigma. Angels in dreams, rumored shepherd's tales, strange stars, distant wise men, outrageous gifts, child-killing decrees, self-proclaimed virgin births—it was all of little use for easing the minds of "concerned" onlookers. To Joseph—it was beyond frustrating. Move after move, he watched it play out over and over again, like the repetitive plot of a low-budget movie. Every time he thought the slate had been wiped clean, something would 'tip' his new world off. If it wasn't his son's uncommonly blue eyes and highly unpredictable ways, it would be a loose-lipped relative, an old shepherd's story, or a marriage/birthdate not quite lining up. Immediately the distance would begin—the whispers, the shifty eye-contact, the avoidance and uncomfortableness—the distrust. Thankfully, the Babylonian wise-men had given him more gold than he could spend in several life-times, because—truth be told—the gossip did affect business. Joseph did his best to forgive and overlook the daily offense. He threw himself full-throttle into his carpentry work, becoming one of the best craftsmen around. He did gain a level of victory and comradery due to his superior artistry, but truth be told, he never fully got past it. Yeshua blinked away a tear. He knew what he was about to do would launch his dad once again into that unwanted spotlight of intense social scrutiny. Yeshua whispered a heartfelt prayer, but he already knew—this next move was going to put Joseph in an early grave.

"REPENT, FOR THE KINGDOM OF HEAVEN IS NEAR!"

The booming voice caught Yeshua off guard. He looked up, snapping back to reality. There, perched atop a large limestone rock, stood his fiery, full-bearded cousin—staring directly at him. John's thick, stocky chest was heaving. His eyes piercing. Sweat dripping liberally down both sides of his beard, running down his robe, and pooling near the top of the thick leather belt girding his full-figured waist.

John called out again, this time directing the crowd's attention toward Yeshua. "After me comes one more powerful than I—the straps of whose sandals I am not worthy to stoop down and untie!" He gave a respectful nod. "I baptize with water, but he will baptize with the fire of pure, relentless love."

Yeshua quietly returned the welcoming nod, continuing towards his fearless cousin, never breaking stride. The crowd, now fully engaged in the exchange, parted instinctively between them.

"Friend," he called out. "Baptize me."

Now it was John's turn to be caught off guard. "I-I need to be baptized by you!" he managed. "How is it that you are asking me?"

Yeshua laughed out loud. He reached the oversized rock and grabbed his cousin's outstretched arm. "My brother, if even so much as a 't' is left uncrossed—all will be counted as null and void in the Courts of Heaven." He leapt up onto the rock, and embraced his cousin. He so loved the heart of this man. "It must be done," he continued. "It is required to fulfill all righteousness."

John nodded. He understood—even the son of a king must be officially sworn into office before his authority is legally recognized.

"I will do it," he agreed.

Grinning, Yeshua slapped his cousin heartily on the back. "Come then!" he urged, leaping from the rock and making a beeline for the heart of the river.

Discarding his outer garment, John quickly followed. The two men waded in waist deep. And there, in front of a captive, captivated audience, John did the deed.

Then things—even by John's standards—got a little strange.

As he lifted Yeshua from the chilly, murky waters, the clouds above them parted. A living light, brighter than the noonday sun and more colorful than seven rainbows, streamed down upon them.

John could feel its comforting warmth descending slowly downward. It floated and fluttered, settling quietly on Yeshua.

The crowd whispered and murmured. *Who was this man? What was this sign?* Some could see the strange supernatural phenomenon, while others saw simply a dove.

Yeshua just smiled and closed his eyes. Breathing deep, he soaked in the familiar presence, enraptured by Heaven's intimate embrace. At long last, he whispered one word. "Spirit!"

That's when Elohim spoke.

"*You* are my beloved son. With *you* I am well pleased." His voice thundered from the heavens, publicly affirming his approval.

It was official—*this was the man for the job.*

Yeshua didn't even flinch. He was already gone—lost in the loving arms of Spirit. Overjoyed that she had finally come down to be with him, *permanently.*

The crowd, however, most-certainly flinched, their reactions quite mixed. Some plainly heard a voice and saw Heaven's Spirit descending *like* a dove. Others swore they heard thunder, observing an actual dove. In the days that followed, it was cause for many a heated debate—each side certain of what they had personally experienced.

John was of the camp who'd heard the voice and witnessed the spirit. He had also recognized the significance of the heavens parting. This was the exact spot where, centuries earlier, Joshua had parted the Jordan River, just before launching his unstoppable 'Promised-Land' campaign. John couldn't help but wonder. *Was his cousin being empowered to do the same?*

By now the crowd was lining up, eager to be baptized themselves. Each excited for their own "thunder and lightning" experience.

John turned to his cousin, but Yeshua wasn't budging. Everything in him had suddenly come alive. It was difficult to describe. All the promises, all the scripture—every supernatural word he had ever ingested in the first thirty years of his life—it all went up in the flames of love. Like a match tossed on jet fuel, his soul ignited.

His inner water turned to wine. It was as if Elohim's words were no longer just words. They had become a real, tangible experience, that he was physically experiencing.

They had become life.

As soon as John realized his cousin wasn't going to budge, he simply stepped aside and began to baptize the eager crowd.

In the back of his mind, Yeshua could hear the commotion going on around him. He knew the inconvenience he was causing, but he didn't care. Elohim. Spirit. That familiar, supercharged atmosphere. They had all come and set up camp *inside* of him! He didn't fight it, he didn't want to. He simply slipped deeper and deeper into their amazing, expanding presence. It was ecstasy. He was back in the fullness of Heaven. *He was home!*

All day Yeshua stood.

All day the people displayed their hunger for true repentance.

Finally, as the sun began to slip quietly away behind the surrounding hills, Yeshua came to himself. Opening first, one eye. Then the other. He managed a sloppy, euphoric, "Goo-bly!" before he stumbled on his way. Up and out of the water. Off, into the sunset. Off, into the desert. Staggering like a drunken sailor. Smitten with unconditional love.

—| |—

The cave, like its dark cohorts, had begun to visibly change. Its walls had been expanded. Its floors, polished and paved. Exposed ducts and vents lined the ceiling. A rather impressive cooling system hummed steadily in the background. Even a clock, mirroring Heaven's countdown clock, loomed ominously in the distance.

There was a flash of light, then another, as two shadowy figures stepped quietly into the dimly lit space. BEAST—now master mechanic—glanced up from the turbine he was tinkering with. He growled a halfhearted "hello" and was back to work before the tardy arrivals could even respond.

A grunt, a twist and a curse, and the turbine roared to

life. BEAST sat back on his haunches and looked around. The new, streamlined grotto was largely his handiwork. He wiped a greasy glove across his coveralls. He was proud. When he had finally realized that meetings were becoming 'increasingly regular,' and that his uncomfortabilitly at those meetings was 'regularly increasing'—he'd taken matters into his own claws. A few months and several general contractors later, he had carved out for himself a much bigger meeting space. Into which, he'd promptly installed, one very large, very loud cooling system. He hadn't gotten it 'to work,' per say, but a few taps from Prophet's staff and some enchanted muttering seemed to do the trick. It had run continually from that day forward, doing its best to keep up with the room's blistering demands.

BEAST pushed up off his knees and stood. He glanced toward the table where his two counterparts now sat. *There,* behind them—out the new, arching, floor-to-ceiling window—stood the clock. It was impossible to miss. Built into the mile-high, vertical-drop cliff of the neighboring plateau, it dominated the surrounding landscape—tracking Heaven's time for all of Hell to see.

BEAST paused, admiring the rumbling, monolithic structure. The clock's stone face resembled that of a combination lock—the kind commonly found on a briefcase. It was comprised of fourteen massive, cylindrical wheels, each standing nearly a hundred stories tall. The wheels had been placed side by side, with numbers vertically etched into their towering, rotating faces. They were forever moving—counting down the seconds, minutes, hours, days, months, and years until … well, that was the problem … until, what? Nobody really knew. Ha-satan definitely had his suspicions, and he had certainly done his best to find out. But when no satisfactory answer could ever be obtained, he had practically demanded that BEAST install the stone monstrosity. 'He—err *they* needed a way to monitor what little time remained. And to be perpetually reminded that time—for whatever reason—was of the essence.' At least, that was the expressed reasoning behind it. The irony of the entire situation was that as much as Ha-satan ignored the heavenly clock above, here below, he could hardly turn away. Its meaning, its significance—it plagued him. And as its time continued to dwindle, it became increasingly clear—there would be no rest for *anyone* until a resolution was found.

    BEAST refocused. Clock and confusion aside, the new window's view was remarkable. Breathtaking actually. All of Hell was visible from its vantage point. The clock, of course, stood opposite the cave. Its neighboring plateau clearly visible from the cliff in which the cave was embedded. A narrow expanse, housing a deep valley—uh, wasteland—separated the two.

    BEAST looked down. The wasteland, although narrow, was long and flat. Rivers of molten lava, fed via lavafall, ran along either side of the desolate ravine. He smirked. He could clearly see the millions of hoodwinked souls held captive in those fiery waters. *Simpletons.* He shook his head in disgust. *So easily deceived.* He had no pity for them. Most had eagerly traded their eternal future for nothing more than a few moments of heightened pleasure.

    Slowly, BEAST turned and stretched, making his way towards the square table. Ha-satan and Prophet watched from their seats as he effortlessly tossed aside his superhero-sized wrench. It landed with a resounding thud, shaking the entire space. Prophet would never admit it, but he was secretly impressed. The cave wasn't the only thing undergoing a facelift. BEAST had changed too. The steady stream of misplaced worship, flowing from an ever populating Earth, was starting to visibly take its toll. BEAST's teeth had become razor sharp. Several new, fierce-looking horns had sprouted. His once disheveled coat had become sleek, clean-cut, and spotted like that of a leopard. Even a strange row of headlike nubbins had taken root across his upper back. Yes, mankind's continued compliance had left BEAST more powerful and more intimidating than ever.

    The mighty ox flexed, he enjoyed the attention. Besides, if he was going to be sized-up, he might as well put on a show. He made a few calculated moves, giving his critics something to chew on while he secretly did some sizing-up of his own. Truth be told, he was equally impressed. Both Prophet and Ha-satan were taller and more muscular. Their disguises darker and more cryptic. However, unlike himself, it wasn't their exterior physic which had undergone the biggest changes. It was their hearts—which had grown hard as stone, cold as ice. And their power—which had increased exponentially.

A dark shiver ran down BEAST's crooked spine, he welcomed its murky presence. It was abundantly clear, this wasn't a game anymore: the desire for control, the lust for power, the need to consume every ounce of worship—to squeeze every last drop of life from mankind ... it had become insatiable.

"You look different," Prophet called out. "Manny? Peddy? Breath mint?"

"New coat," BEAST growled, dropping heavily to his seat. He squinted condescendingly at his cohort. "Fortune teller, you've changed too."

Prophet loosed a wicked grin. BEAST was right. Aside from the obvious cane and cloak upgrades, he'd tweaked his gas-mask so his eyes—which were more piercing than ever—were clearly visible. "Communication is only ten percent verbal," he tapped his goggles, firing a sharp glare.

BEAST paused, summing up the intensity of Prophet's non-verbal firepower.

"Congratulations, you got your other ten percent back," he snorted.

Prophet glared harder.

"..make that eight percent," BEAST retracted.

Prophet reached for his staff.

"Gentlemen—the news?" Ha-satan interrupted. Even as he spoke, he was turned sideways in his chair, eyes fixed on the distant clock, fingers methodically rapping. It was quite clear, his own set of gears were spinning. "I hate to impose upon such a delightfully entertaining lover's quarrel," he hissed. "But tell me, have you heard the latest news?"

BEAST stared blankly, all he'd heard in months was the endless roar of his makeshift AC.

Prophet leaned forward to fill him in. "There's a new man on the scene," he whispered. "Some average Joe, construction worker named—*Yeshua.*"

BEAST didn't even twitch. Why should he? Sure, *Yeshua* meant 'savior,' but ever since Joshua's unstoppable, Promised-Land campaign over fourteen-hundred years ago, nearly every third kid in Israel was named 'Yeshua' in his honor. That name was 'common as rock.' Hardly noteworthy. Certainly nothing to get anyone's panties in a wad.

Prophet waited for a response. When he got none, he continued. "Seems he had a paranormal experience in full view of several hundred witnesses—and now rumor has it, he's the promised seed."

Finally, BEAST rolled his eyes. "So what's new?" he grumbled, eager to get back to work. "There's always someone, boasting some strange experience who fits the bill."

"It's not that—," Ha-satan interjected, his focus still on the clock. "It's the timing." His foot tapped impatiently. "I don't like the timing."

BEAST and Prophet followed his gaze. He was right. The clock did seem to be winding down. In fact, according to it, there were only about three more years to go. *Until what? The promised-seed take over?* BEAST fidgeted subconsciously. If that truly was the case, then 'right now' would certainly be a great time for the so-called 'seed' to reveal himself. *Wouldn't it?*

Still, he wasn't sold.

"So—?" BEAST sneered. "He's a blue-collar worker's apprentice—a nobody." He rolled his eyes again. "What's there to be worried about? He's human. We simply find his deepest insecurity, use it to drive his pet sin, and *voilá*—we control him. Just like we've controlled every other human since Adam."

Ha-satan turned toward BEAST, he wasn't so sure. "I've seen his light," he faltered.

BEAST waited. He understood the lingo. In the spirit-world, especially the spirit-world on Earth, each being had both an 'aura' and a 'light.' An aura was more of a surrounding glow. A covering of sorts. Used mainly for attraction or repulsion. But a light … a light was different. A light referred to an individual's aim—their current trajectory in life and their eventual destination. It was almost like a spotlight. In the dark, a spotlight could shine ahead, illuminating the unknown—allowing one to see where one was going even before one arrives. In the same way, it was easy to spot any human's potential—even see their future—simply by observing the direction in which their light was currently pointed. Both the path, and the targeted destination would be clearly lit up. BEAST nodded. This is what Ha-satan was referring to when he said 'he'd seen his light.' Ha-satan had gotten close enough to see the future that this human's light was illuminating. *And obviously*—he glanced at his nervously rapping boss—*it had troubled him deeply.*

"I've seen his light, and it's pointed at.." again Ha-satan lost the words.

BEAST waited. Honestly, he was a little weirded out. He had never seen Ha-satan struggle for words—ever.

"It's pointed.."

Silence.

"—at.."

"..it's pointed *at him*," Prophet whispered loudly, leaning all the way in.

At him? For a moment BEAST was confused. Then it hit: *This man's light wasn't pointed at a place, a position, or even at some sort of 'ideological future.' No, this man's light was pointed at a person! A spirit person. Whoa*—the fur on BEAST's neck bristled. *Was that even possible? … that this man's destiny—for lack of a better way to say it— was Ha-satan, himself?*

BEAST looked quizzically at his boss. "Really? A replacement?!" he smirked. This type of direct challenge was entirely unprecedented, and BEAST wanted to know. *What was Ha-satan going to do?*

Even before he could fully form the words, the room grew wickedly cold. BEAST knew the strange sign had nothing to do with his clattering AC. Rather, it was the deep, wretched darkness of Ha-satan's cold, dead soul clawing its way to the surface. Indignant. Self-righteous. Fatally offended. It would not tolerate *any* insecurity exposed. The walls quaked violently, distracting from the quaking in their dark Lord's soul.

BEAST cringed. He could feel the darkness pressing in, pushing down, crushing him. *How dare he even THINK of questioning such things?* The air grew thick and heavy. The room bowed and bent. One by one, lights began to pop and shatter. BEAST could feel their piercing shards raining down upon his neck and shoulders. Beams and girders began to twist and wine. The floor began to bend. Everything shuddered.

Gasping, BEAST struggled for breath, desperate to fill his lungs with anything besides Ha-satan's thick, suffocating, bottomless rage.

Then, it was gone.

BEAST slowly lifted his head. The room, the lights, the floor, his boss—everything was back to normal—as if nothing had ever happened. *Creepy.* He looked around. Nothing seemed out of place. Not a light. Not a nail. Not a square-inch of tile floor. The stunned ox lowered his arms, giving his coat a rigorous shake.

There was no glass.

"So—?" he growled, still not sold. "We'll just get him to adjust his light, shift his focus, and change his destiny." He glanced around one last time before cautiously settling back. Changing a human's light wasn't a big deal. Over the years, he had redirected, realigned—even replaced—countless personal illuminations. It wasn't rocket science. It was simply a matter of convincing an individual to shift a core belief—any belief—and then watching that individual's light shift as well.

Ha-satan frowned. "He's not like the others," he complained. "The reports for this one are … unique." He hesitated, almost unwilling to continue.

"All his watchers swear … he can't hear them," Prophet filled in the gap.

"Can't hear them?" BEAST shook his head. "*Impossible—.*"

"That's the report."

"Maybe he's a good actor."

"Nope."

"Strong-willed?"

Prophet shook his head.

"Slow upstairs?"

"Not even close."

"Maybe he.."

"..has no pride," Ha-satan cut in.

Both, Prophet and BEAST stopped dead in their tracks. BEAST raised a confounded eyebrow. *How was it that Prophet had not spotted this elephant?*

"So, no darkness? No door within?" BEAST puzzled out loud. "Every son of Adam is born with original sin." Suddenly he was second-guessing, reconsidering, "Maybe he *IS* the promised seed—the perfect son of God."

"..And beyond our control," Prophet nodded.

"*NO ONE* is *beyond our control!*" Ha-satan snapped, slamming down a furious fist. For a second BEAST thought the crazy, suffocating, room-rage was about to come roaring back. He ducked his head. But Ha-satan stopped. The underlord took a long, slow, deliberate breath—in through his nose, out through his mouth. "No," he settled himself. "We will handle him like we handled all the others," the atmosphere quieted. "We'll offer him a new light, an improved light. A fast-tracked, short-cut, "better" destiny—*beyond* his current destination."

He paused midthought, a dark smile creeping slowly over his brooding, hidden face.

"It just seems," he turned back to the clock, "that we'll have to deal with him as we dealt with Adam." His gears were turning, fingers drumming again. "I will have to go. I will have to talk to him—*myself.*"

CH40: DUAL IN THE DESERT
0003:10:13:05:00:11

He was hot. He was weak. He was hungry.

Yeshua plopped down on a dead patch of grass—rocks and sand stretching as far as the eye could see. He smiled. *Mmm, nothing to eat and nowhere to go—same as yesterday!* An affectionate grin lit up his thin, gaunt face. The newly affirmed Son of God glanced slowly around. Over the last forty days this desert wilderness had quickly become his home. A hearty chuckle shook his wind-chapped frame. *And from the looks of it, it certainly seemed, that his one-of-a-kind baptism experience had simply been a fast-tracked promotion to—sweet, desert living.*

His stomach growled, obnoxiously butting into the conversation. *Forty days, no food.* It wasn't exactly happy. Yeshua grinned and looked down, silencing it with an affectionate pat.

That's right baby—he was livin' the dream!

With a yawn and a stretch, he slowly settled back, resting his sweat-drenched head on a particularly uncomfortable rock. His eyes closed. He relaxed, *no worries—he had plenty to do to keep his mind off his stomach.* Life out here was a perpetual circus of supernatural activity, and truthfully—all heat and hunger aside—he was having an absolute blast!

"If you are the Son of God, simply tell these stones to become bread.."

Whoa, Yeshua opened one eye, *that voice had spoken almost immediately.* He looked up. A being—easily mistaken for a man—stood tall and confident before him. Yeshua squinted, peeking inquisitively at his newest Heaven-sent guest.

The visitor was strikingly handsome—perfectly manicured

and well spoken. Like the surrounding sand, his skin sparkled and shone, twinkling from head to toe. He wore a compelling smile, and his gray eyes seemed to dance playfully in the bright sunlight—that was, until Yeshua looked deeper. A second opened eye revealed the startling truth. The only thing staring back at him from behind the visitor's dazzling facade was—*stone cold, death.*

Yeshua nodded a respectful 'hello.' He'd been expecting this one. This was his personal angel. His covering. His destiny. His opposition.

This was the Watcher over all of Israel..

This was Haylel!

Haylel spoke again. "If you are the Son of God, simply tell these stones to become your bread." He motioned helpfully to the veritable buffet of rocks littering the surrounding landscape. His suggestion was unassuming. His tone, almost sincere. Almost as if the sole purpose of his visit was to offer this simple, divine solution to Yeshua's greatest unmet need—*food.*

Yeshua rolled to an elbow and casually sat up. His stomach was already revoicing its opinion. He stifled a grin. Certainly, shifting a rock's subatomic vibration to satisfy his personal, physical need *was* a brilliant solution. One easily achieved by any legitimate son of God. And true, in time, he WOULD turn the law (engraved in stone), into the bread of life. *However, he hadn't come to Earth to spend his supernatural abilities on himself, nor to put his physical needs above the spiritual. His abilities had all been given BY Elohim, FOR Elohim.* He lifted bold eyes, defying the selfish twist. *And as far as he knew, Elohim only intended on using his gifts to ease the burdens of OTHERS.*

"It is written," he quietly countered, gazing at his most ancient creation. "Man shall not live on bread alone. Nor by the bread that comes from his own mouth. But on *every* word that comes from the mouth of God!"

A laugh and a smile kept the exchange pleasant. A nod, kept it sincere. Still, Yeshua could read between the lines … and the fleshly self-indulgence Haylel was selling, he wasn't buying.

Haylel stifled a frown, a bit put off by the whole lackluster exchange. Still, he took it in stride. Even he had to admit, after four thousand years, the whole 'forbidden food' ploy was becoming a bit overused. Not to worry, he had anticipated as much. He reached down and extended a helping, six-fingered hand.

Plan B was already underway.

"Come," Haylel grabbed Yeshua's outstretched elbow and lifted him to his feet. Immediately they were in Jerusalem, standing at the highest point of the temple. Yeshua stepped forward, resting his hands on the narrow stone railing before them. He could feel the warm summer wind swirling playfully about, lifting the sounds of the bustling crowds below: The bleating of goats. The squawking of chickens. The banter of hard-working merchants. The laughter of children at play.

Yeshua looked around. The city, its fields and hills—they all stretched endlessly before him in full, panoramic view. He inhaled deeply, doing his best to embody the surrounding experience. He could feel the prayers of his brothers and sisters rising from the walls below, engulfing him in a growing, blanketing hug. The Son of God smiled. He so loved this city. He so loved her people.

"If you are the Son of God," Haylel casually nudged. "Give these people a show they'll never forget—throw yourself down. For it is written: Elohim will command his angels concerning you, and they will lift you up in their hands, so that you will not strike your foot against a stone."

Yeshua shut his eyes and took another deep breath. *An attention-getting, crowd-gathering spectacle to instant stardom, huh?* He paused as he mulled the invitation over. Indeed, he *had* come to Earth to occupy this very spot. And yes, Elohim's unwavering protection *was* guaranteed until that occupation had fully arrived. He thoughtfully nodded. No doubt, a well timed publicity stunt would speed up the process. But—*Ahhh, therein lay the catch.* The proof of his authentic, bonafide relationship with Elohim wasn't in Elohim's ability to prevent his injury or death. Nor was it in Elohim's ability to promote him overnight. No—it was in the simple reality that nothing—and no one—would ever be able to stop his Heavenly Father from raising him up, *in due season!*

Yeshua smiled as he mentally connected the dots.

Besides, 'Death & Injury,' wasn't that Haylel's department? He shot Haylel a sideways glance, noting the striking set of keys hanging from his lapel. Yes—and if he was to *willingly* throw himself down, than wouldn't that mean he had *willingly* submitted his body to 'Death & Injury?' ..to Haylel, himself?

He closed his eyes again. *Yea—so what were the odds that Haylel would actually catch him up?*

A scene flashed across the window of his mind:

"But your Honor," Haylel purred, standing meekly before the Courts of Heaven. "He threw *himself* down. It was *his* choice. Of his *own* volition. Who am I to catch him, against his *own free will?*"

Yeshua shook his head and smiled. *Was that not exactly how it would ultimately go down?* He inhaled deeply, one last time, his mind fully resolved.

"It is *also* written," he slowly replied. "Do not put the Lord your God to the test."

He stopped, letting the strong words sink in. He could have sugar-coated this rebuke with a smile, but making Haylel sweat was just too good to pass up. He graciously kept his eyes shut. He could tell his reply had gotten a rise, and he didn't want to blow Haylel's cover. *Not yet.*

The underlord's dark scowl was as plain as the daylight around them. This human wasn't easily hooked, not even by pride, and that was deeply bothersome. He glared at Yeshua's peaceful face. *It irked him.* "Come," he snapped, his patience suddenly worn thin. "It's time to make you an offer, you'd be an absolute fool to refuse."

WHOOSH—an icy blast of arctic wind caught Yeshua completely off guard. His eyes flew open. His hands fell to his sides. The railing, the temple, the city were gone. Replaced by a thousand-foot drop into a patchwork of clouds sprawling far, far below.

He gasped, instinctively stepping back.

Haylel smirked. *Did he detect, Fear? —what a pitiful sign of mortal human weakness. Maybe he HADN'T met his match.* He spit the disgust from his mouth, watching as it slowly fell towards the clouds a thousand-feet below. *After all—between two supposed gods—what was the edge of a snowcapped mountain, or a hundred-story vertical drop?*

Yeshua quickly regrouped, securing his whits—and his footing—about him. His Father *would* catch him up, should someone *else* cast him down. He grinned, resting again in that comforting truth as he gathered his robes tight against the blistering gale.

Moving back to the edge, he glanced fearlessly down. The noonday sun blazed bright across the sprawling cumulus clouds floating lazily below, making them shine like a thousand tiny, floating, ice-capped mountains. Birds, trees, and towns lay below that. And beyond them—spread out in glorious array—lay all the kingdoms of Earth ... past, present, and future.

WHOOOSH—Another arctic gust sent a shower of loose debris shooting past the onlookers; out, over and down the mountain's sheer vertical face. Yeshua braced himself against the unexpected shove, glancing questioningly at his clearly unconcerned guide. This time it was Haylel who seemed to be enjoying the moment. Gravity, wind, and cold weren't elements he had to contend with. And death—well, he held the keys. Casually, he swept an open hand across the majestic landscape below.

"All this, I will give you," Haylel purred, putting the splendor of each city on visible display. "If you will simply bow down and worship me." Slowly he turned, staring straight into Yeshua's wide, unblinking eyes.

All gloves—and masks—were finally off.

Yeshua sized up his brazen opponent. This *was* the ultimate shortcut to do exactly what he had come to Earth to do—to take back *every* Kingdom of Man. He let out a long, slow sigh. *Brilliant as he was, Haylel just didn't get it.* It didn't matter the cost. It didn't matter the price. The offer could have been *EVERY* city across *EVERY* galaxy ... *EVER*—his loyalty wouldn't change. His heart was for his father, *and that would ALWAYS remain.*

A righteous anger rose.

"Away from me devil!" he burned. "Is it not written, 'Worship Elohim, and serve *him, ONLY?*'" Yeshua's eyes flashed. His soul was livid. *The rumors were proving true!* The very one created to uphold Elohim's heart, *was* the very one defiling it. And the very one claiming to 'protect and serve,' *was* the very one delivering the abuse. The beloved son of the most high God raised a rebuking right hand, his mouth already forming the words, "The Lord.."

KA-BOOM—Haylel made his immediate exit, knocking his adversary to the ground with the seismic aftershock of his sudden departure.

Yeshua rocked and reeled, his mind racing a mile a minute. Like Michael, he had plainly seen Haylel's dark side. He now knew, by name and by face, who Heaven's traitor was. He lay in the snow stunned. *What could actually be done?* His brow furrowed. He fired a quick frown. While many of the laws of the universe had been irreparably bent, none had actually been broken. And while it was wildly inappropriate for any god to tempt a man, technically nothing had been done wrong. Resolute, he set his jaw. His only solace lay in the fact that in this pivotal moment the tables *had* been turned. And for the first time since the fall of Adam, the devil had gone head-to-head with a man—and lost.

At least for the moment.

Yeshua lifted his head, hope beginning to rise! Bottom line, from this moment forward, as long as he never misspoke, never mis-stepped, never openly or secretly sinned—as long as he knew who he was, and never transgressed any part of his own, spoken or written Word, *ever*—the devil *had* to answer to him!

It was just like old times.

Of course, the deceiver still held one distinct advantage. Both *the law* and *time*—at least for now—were on his side, and both demanded perfection. Yeshua whispered a quiet prayer. As long as he remained an "earthbound man," there would always be a chance that he could slip up. Not to mention the fact that 'actual perfection' vs. 'perceived perfection' would be a frustratingly tough tightrope to walk.

The Son of Man clenched two icy cold fists, and grinned. It would certainly be tough, but the greatest thing about being the *actual*, perfected Son of God—was that all he had to do to never mess up—was to simply be *himself.*

Yeshua relaxed, his internal light shifting, shrinking from

full-scale spotlight to pinpoint, laser focused. *Whatever it took. No matter the cost.* He *would* expose Haylel. Heaven's traitorous, Second-in-Command, now stood *alone* in the crosshairs of his laser-sight, internal light ... *and time was winding down!*

A tangible peace flooded his unwavering soul.

Yeshua opened his eyes. Eternity settled, his attention quickly turned back to the matters at hand.

Warmth, he needed warmth. He scanned the treacherous peak. *Not a stitch of shelter in sight.* He heaved a disheartened sigh. His only option would be to use the snow's natural insulation to trap what little body heat he had left. He picked himself up, moving to a nearby drift packed against the side of a jutting vertical boulder. With all his might, he tunneled into the frozen mound. He needed a moment of warmth, just to gather his thoughts. But the snow was mostly ice, and his hands were beginning to throb. Soon his vision blurred. Shivers overwhelming him.

He was so cold.

So spent.

So weak.

"Father, help!" he gasped, his world going black. He could feel himself falling forward, towards his half dug shelter.

Swoosh—a pair of powerful hands caught Yeshua's worn out body, a supportive arm cradled his neck. "Bring blankets. Robes. Clothes. Warmth. Command those stones into bread," Michael orchestrated a flurry of activity as he lifted his King like a child in his arms. Already a portal was beginning to open. "Stand by for immediate transport—," the mighty angel directed, carefully readjusting his cargo to pass through. "Come—," he motioned to the others. "In Galilee, we rendezvous.."

CH41: TRAPPED
0000:03:12:05:00:07

"Teacher, even the *demons* submit to us in your name!" The cry rang out across the rolling Judaean valley. Yeshua turned, watching as Peter and Matthew, two of his star students, sprinted up the dirt-packed road. He grinned. It had been three whirlwind years since his baptism & wilderness experience and much had changed. He was no longer unknown. Twelve full-time students, hundreds of devoted followers, and relentless, thronging crowds had put him permanently on the map. In fact, his overwhelming popularity was surpassed only by the endless supply of supernatural phenomenon surrounding him. He had obtained Heaven's ringing endorsement, and Earth's was close behind. Like it or not, Yeshua was on the rise. And each new day was quickly becoming another step closer to the top.

It was enough to make any lesser god jealous.

Until now, Yeshua had managed to dodge, dismiss, or deflect most of the hype. It had proved a brilliant strategy. Flying under the radar kept him a step ahead of Haylel's accusing, limiting finger; allowing him to remain elusive and laser-focused on his preliminary objective of, 'bringing Heaven to Earth.'

But recently, all that had changed.

In a bold marketing move, Yeshua had sent seventy-two of his most trusted followers into towns all across the region. He had given them authority, instructing them to, "Heal the sick, raise the dead, cleanse the lepers, and proclaim to everyone they meet: 'The Kingdom of Heaven is here.'" The plan was to give each town their own 'wake up call,' including a small 'teaser,' of what it would be like when he, the teacher, finally arrived. Truth be told, this was also a well calculated, muscle flex. A flex, Yeshua knew would grab Haylel's undivided attention.

The response had been nothing short of miraculous.

Yeshua watched fondly as Peter and Matthew moved closer. Like the others, they were clearly excited, talking a mile a minute. He glanced up to Heaven, mouthing a heartfelt, "Thank you!"

Pop. Crack. FLASH—ka-BOOM!

Yeshua froze, momentarily overwhelmed by the sudden, brilliant light. *What in the—,* he did a double-take, staring at … *a rip in the clouds?* He paused, curiously transfixed, blinking away his temporary blindness. Slowly, the rip expanded. Stretching. Puckering. Splintering. Bursting into a thousand shimmering lights.

There, midair, behind the unzipped veil, stood the arch-angel, Michael—peering down on Earth through the freshly opened portal. His right hand gripped a sword, blazing and drawn. And in his left, hung a dangling, panic-stricken, Haylel. There was a moment's hesitation. A pause just long enough for Yeshua to catch the disappointment clouding Michael's countenance. Then, in a cosmic burst of light, Michael cast Haylel through the opening and screaming down to Earth.

Immediately, Yeshua understood. He threw his head back and full-on, belly laughed. *It was done!* The scales were fully tipped! In a paradoxical turn of events, their relentless actions—and his relentless perfection—had actually managed to shift *Haylel's* light, not the other way around. Yeshua shook his head. He had seen the future, Haylel's future, and Haylel had taken the bait. Heaven's potential, and its current unchecked liability, had so flustered Hell, that Haylel had already made his decision. It was done, set in stone. Should the trajectory of their current collision-course remain, it *would* end in Haylel's heavenly termination.

Ahh, young grasshopper, Yeshua chuckled to himself, *it seems the student has become the master.* He smiled. There was no doubt about it, the seed of offense, flourishing in Haylel's hard heart, was finally blossoming with murder. *And it would be his undoing.*

"Teacher, even the *demons* submit to us in your name!" The cry rang out again.

Yeshua turned his head, snapping out of the vision and back

into the throes of physical reality. Peter and Matthew were all over him now, eagerly relaying their amazement of the past month's supernatural activities. *The demonic, supernatural world, was actually obeying mortal men!* They were ecstatic.

"I know—I know," Yeshua laughed, jovially returning Peter's repeated 'high-fives' and giving Matthew's shoulder a rigorous, 'Atta boy' shake. "I saw the Deceiver fall like lightning," he grinned, basking in the moment's deserved celebration. "But," he cautioned, looking Peter square in the eyes. "Don't draw your self-worth from the fact that demons obey you." He cocked his head and smiled. "There may well come a day when they do not. Instead," his voice softened, "rejoice that your name is forever inked in Heaven's Book of Life—where no one can remove it."

Yeshua took a short step back. *Demons*—the term was only recently coined. As currently trending, it referred to the disembodied spirits of those half-human, half-angelic, hybrid-giants, so common during the days of Noah and Joshua. *Nephilim ('Neh-fuh-leam')*, as Heaven called them. They were troublemakers. Cold-blooded. Hard-hearted. Terrorists. Their earthbound, physical bodies having passed away long ago, it was their rebellious, destructive spirits which remained. However, unlike Haylel's angels, who were forced to maintain Heavenly appearances and positions, these illegal, illegitimate creatures already knew they were sunk. As a result, they didn't give a rip about following the rules of *any* universe. This, of course, was music to Haylel's ears, as they made for the perfect minions. Useful patsies, who handled *all* of Hell's dirty work and accepted *all* of Hell's blame. For Heaven's appearance-driven, hopelessly two-faced CEO, this was a virtual dream come true.

"Master, even the *demons* submit to us in your name!"

Peter and Matthew froze mid-conversation. Yeshua lifted a questioning eyebrow. *Was this déjà vu, all over again?* Simultaneously all three heads turned toward the sound—bursting out laughing.

This time, it was James and John running up the trail.

Next, came Philip and Andrew.

Then Thomas and Judas.

Each duo touting the same unbelievable experiences. *Hell*

was finally beneath their feet.

Yeshua listened intently, his heart overflowing with gratitude. *Heaven's invasion had begun!* He set his jaw, all the more resolute. The stage was set. There was no turning back. Each new story was a joyful confirmation of what he already knew, *it was time.* Passover was only months away and they *must* be in Jerusalem to celebrate. No excuses. These were the days predetermined since the foundation of the world.

"Come," he directed the boisterous crowd. "We shall finish our circuit, and head for Jerusalem." Turning, he stepped out, moving down the path that would take them through Samaria—the most direct route.

"Master," it was Judas. "Thomas and I have just returned from the village which lies at the end of that path," he smiled, almost as if he was somehow pleased to relay the information. "They have denied us access, because we do not believe as they do."

Yeshua paused, recalculating. If this was true, they would have to go around, costing precious time. *Could they make it up?*

James and John were quick to speak. "Master, perhaps we should call down fire from Heaven—to consume them in their insolence?"

Yeshua cringed. *Taking a life, just because one is truly right*—it was wrong on so many levels. He looked at them sternly. "You do not know the manner of spirit by which you speak," he reprimanded. "Who do you think actually benefits from human death? Is it I? My father? No—I tell you the tuth. I was *not* sent to destroy life, but to save it."

The pindrop silence which followed reassured him they were taking his words to heart. He flashed another smile to ease the tension, then waved them on to a new path. "Come my friends," he was already moving forward. "We will gladly pass through another village."

CH42: WRATH OF GOD

Purposefully Elohim stood, his back turned towards the War Room door. There was a click and a whir as the door slid open. Haylel quietly entered. In the dim, intimately lit space, he could see Elohim leaning over the War Room Table, swirling a vial of thick, dark liquid. Elohim corked the vial and placed it on a rack next to hundreds of similar vessels. Haylel watched as the entire rack shook, each container rattling violently. The whole room smelled. Haylel did little to hide his disgust. *The old man was spending more and more of his time standing at that table, collecting and swirling his putrid liquid. He was wearing down. Becoming old. Aged. Obsolete.*

It was pathetic.

"Have you seen my servant Yeshua?" Elohim broke the silence.

Startled, Haylel dropped to a knee. He was surprised that Elohim was even aware of his presence. He bowed low—although not as low as if Elohim had been looking. "Y—Yes," he managed a purr, quickly regaining composure. "I have seen him."

"Is he not perfect in every way?" Elohim continued, still not turning around. He reached for another empty vial.

Haylel grimaced. The words were so—giddy … so naive, so full of—*unconditional love*. A jealous anger flared. "Of course he is—," Haylel snapped, his indignation poorly disguised. "That's because your Spirit has never been far from him. Remove it, and like Job, he will rail against you."

Elohim smiled to himself, *the lies just kept on coming.* Certainly Job had railed, but never had his heart turned. Besides, Yeshua wasn't a second Job, he was more like a second—Adam. Still,

Elohim knew exactly what Haylel was getting at. And oddly enough, he couldn't have agreed more.

"Well—you do hold the key," he replied, raising an eyebrow as he let the statement settle. He casually motioned to the contents of the clamoring cabinet, then went back to his task of filling the new vial. He would let Haylel connect the dots.

Haylel raised an eyebrow of his own. He looked down at the key ring hanging from his left shoulder lapel. *He did?* Slowly, he flipped through the keys, their familiar metal clanking quietly in his hands. *Death, Hell, The Grave ... Death, Hell*—he'd done this a million times.. Suddenly, something prompted him to look more closely. *There,* embedded in the key marked 'Grave.' *What was that?* He turned the relic over in his hands. *Amazing,* a small, simple, heart-shaped, skeleton key seemed to be etched into the center of one of its larger, inlaid gemstones. Haylel puzzled. He knew these keys like the back of his hand. Strange, he hadn't noticed it before. He popped the stone lose and held it up, examining it inquisitively. The skeleton key was flawless. Expertly carved out of a single, blood red ruby, it seemed to be perfectly sized for a vial cabinet ... *or any cabinet, for that matter.* He glanced toward Elohim, then back to the key in his hand. A dark grin flooded his face as he turned the key around one last time. *Who knew—he was literally holding the answer all along!*

The crafty serpent shot Elohim a sideways glance as he carefully replaced his new discovery. For a moment his heart almost softened. *Maybe the old man wasn't as dumb as he seemed after all.* He glanced back at the multitude of quaking vials—evidence of the pain Elohim had endured since the beginning of mankind. *All for those impudent, ignorant, worthless, creatures.* He shook his head, letting his keys fall noisily back into place. *No—the old man was far dumber.*

Haylel stepped backward. He was done here. Little thanks to Elohim, he'd found what he'd been looking for. He nodded curtly, tipping an invisible hat. Then without a word, he spun around and disappeared back through the War Room door.

CH43: THE FINAL STRAW
0000:01:23:02:03:07

Like a stallion at the gate, Michael stood, poised, ready for action. He was restless, eager to move. It was go time and he knew it. He inhaled slowly, every muscle tense. He was chomping at the bit—yet he held perfectly still.

He was waiting on a word.

Yeshua stood before him, weeping. Four days ago a dear friend, Lazarus, had unexpectedly slipped into the afterlife. The tragedy had, of course, temporarily derailed Yeshua's beeline for Jerusalem. Now he stood weeping, staring at the gaping entrance to Lazarus' tomb. To his right wept Martha and Mary, the sisters unfairly left behind. To his left huddled the friends and relatives forced to endure death's unexpected sting. Yeshua glanced around, their tear-stained faces said it all; this was a hellish reality for which they were never intended.

A renewed torrent of tears assaulted Yeshua's cheeks. He couldn't stop them. They flowed relentlessly—almost with a mind of their own. His nose was running. His cheeks were flushed. He could barely breathe. But he didn't care, his heart was completely broken ... *for them.*

He wept, long and hard, until something arose, roaring like a lion within.

No! This would not happen—not on his watch.

"Lazarus, come forth!" he bellowed, the words bursting from trembling lips, exploding like dynamite off the walls of the cold, stone tomb.

Michael sprang into action. *That was his cue.* He launched himself skyward. For a moment, time slowed, his wings expanding majestically—unfolding in a breathtaking ripple of light, energy, and sound. For the briefest of moments he hung, midair. Then, with a single formidable flap he spun, 180 degrees, diving head first—down, down, down—right through the ground.

A powerful blast of air engulfed the mourners as he thundered through their midst. At the speed of light, he raced, unhindered—down through the earth's crust, nearly four-thousand miles to its fiery core.

Almost instantly he arrived, bursting through the compact sediment and out into the vast, spherical expanse of Middle Earth. He slowed. Below him lay Paradise, a thriving, domed metropolis built atop a large rocky plateau in the uppermost part of Hades. It was a temporary residence, a holding tank of sorts—almost a Purgatorial-type of afterlife—manifesting in the form of a self-sufficient, Earth-like, mega-city.

Michael tilted his head and refocused. Far below, he could faintly make out the smog infested, ever smoldering, ruinous gates of Hell—the entrance to Hades' other, more permanent, holding-tank. Poorly lit and wickedly uninviting, Hell sat well below Paradise, across an immense ocean of spherically spinning lava. A chill shot down Michael's spine. Just by looking, he could sense the deep darkness consuming that place. *Uggh*—he shuddered, it pierced him to the bone.

Paradise, on the other hand ... he flipped around, feet first. *Now that was a party waiting to happen!* He raised a hand, shielding his eyes, doing his best to scan the gently rolling countryside below. *Lazarus, where was Lazarus?* He frowned. The thick, electromagnetic dome made it almost impossible to see. He shifted impatiently. *This was pointless,* he needed to get inside. Looking up, he quickly scanned his surroundings. *There!* ... a narrow section of the dome was thinning. It wasn't ideal, but it would suffice.

Michael raced to make his entrance.

Skillfully, he maneuvered through the dome's strange, quasi-stable atmosphere. Too quickly, and the air would become thick like molasses. Too slowly, and the dome's electromagnetic energy would begin to interact wildly with his own spirit body. *Hmm—trapped indefinitely or disabled permanently—neither sounded particularly pleasant.* Michael grinned tersely, it was little wonder why most avoided this place altogether.

Agh—sharp pain!

Michael stifled the urge to flinch.

There it was again ... *like a million burning pin pricks.* It was already beginning—the unfortunate side-effects of the dome.

The seasoned warrior tucked his head, increasing speed.

Woosh—an intense flash of heat.

Swoosh—then another.

Sweat began to drip from his brow. He could feel the air thickening around him.

The pricks intensified.

He shuddered involuntarily. His stomach began to tremble. There was a sudden dropping sensation. He shifted uncomfortably, instinctively moving a hand to steady his belly. *Oh yea,* he grimaced. He had completely forgotten the best part ... *the overwhelming sensation to purge everything from one's bowels!*

The mighty angel gritted his teeth. A few more seasoned moves, and the profound discomfort began to subside. He breathed his relief as the suffocating dark of Middle Earth melted into gorgeous, noonday. *He was through!* He shook himself rigorously. Discomfort aside, the dome was totally ingenious. Not only did it block Middle Earth's intense heat, but it also generated its own light and wind. He slowed, a pleasant breeze tousling his hair. *Hmm,* he glanced around—waving green grass, lazy white clouds, a distant metropolis city—everything seemed so ... *normal.* Even the familiar blue of Earth's sky was perfectly mimicked by the massive, protective covering. *Wow,* he whistled his amazement. From this perspective, it was absolutely impossible to tell that he was actually located deep within the recesses of Middle Earth.

"Lazarus, come forth!" Heaven's diligent messenger echoed exactly the word he'd been given. The command visibly left his lips, racing towards the thousands upon thousands of souls below. He watched as it washed over them, rippling around them, breaking into millions of tiny, concentric, ever-expanding circles.

Within seconds it had reached its intended target. As it did, it began to resonate, multiplying and glowing brightly. Michael moved towards the increasingly luminescent glow, easily closing the gap with the aid of his 'visual sonar.' He chuckled. He could already see Lazarus talking with a strangely dressed, highly animated, heavily bearded man. *What were the odds?* he grinned. *A beard of that caliber only grew from the face of one mortal in particular.*

He slowed to a stop, pausing overhead.

"Cousin John!" the angel's wings dissipated as he dropped the remaining thirty feet to the soft, lush ground below. With a playful grin he landed perfectly between the two men, bowing low, waiting to be addressed.

"My good friend, to what do I owe the pleasure of this overwhelmingly unexpected salutation?" John didn't miss a beat, extending a welcoming hand. He flashed a broad, toothy grin, as if angels dropping from the sky unannounced were an everyday occurrence.

Michael stood and gestured to the somewhat dazed, and clearly confused, Lazarus. "This one's being recalled," he fired back, nodding his apology for the unconventional interruption. "However," he flashed a quick grin. "I suppose I could ask you the same thing."

John jovially rolled his eyes. "Sorta lost my head," he dragged his thumb across his throat. "The Queen—not a fan." He tugged mischievously at his bristled beard and motioned to his mismatched clothes. "Of course, I've never been very good with the ladies.."

Michael smiled as he tucked one hand under Lazarus' armpit. "The beard, I could help with—," he wrapped another hand securely around Lazarus' chest, "but the clothes.."

"..hopeless," John cut in, lovingly smoothing his duds. "I know—hopeless." He grinned, eyes twinkling as he watched the angel finish securing his cargo. "Are you sure you're not here for me?" he ribbed. "It would give the Queen quite a start." His smile shot ear to ear as he mimicked the return of his head to his shoulders.

Michael paused. Clearly, John was joking. But truth be told, the fearless forerunner *had* wrestled, rather intensely, with why Heaven had remained so passive about his untimely—and rather barbaric—death. Incarceration, abandonment, decapitation—any one was a tough pill to swallow ... but all three? A strange empathy flooded the warrior angel's soul, followed by nine heaven-sent words.

"Friend," he gently replied. "You are right where you're supposed to be." He bent slowly, casually taking a knee. "You'll see—." The powerful angel hugged Lazarus to his chest. Then, with a wink and a nod, he rocketed skyward, his unsuspecting cargo gaping like a deer in the headlights.

Lazarus tried to shut his mouth. He watched as John, the ground, and his stomach dropped simultaneously beneath his feet. Within seconds he and the massive angel were high in the sky, beginning to enter the hazy dome.

He managed to look up, towards the brilliant blue into which they were heading. Bewildered, was an understatement. This was all brand new, he felt completely out of the loop. All he knew was the simple understanding that had come the moment Michael had wrapped his massive arms around him—*he was going home!*

He felt Michael's grip tighten, and soon understood why. *Ouch.. ouch.. OUCH!* His body was literally becoming a pincushion. His skin was burning like fire.

A dry heave came. Then another.

His bowels felt like they were scrambling.

Slowly, a cry began to force its way up his throat ... past his lips ... and out his mouth..

Aaaaaaaaaaauugh—!

Then, it was over. *They were through!* Bursting out of the dome and into the expansive darkness of Middle Earth. A wave of relief washed over him, followed by a wave of incredible heat. *And ... was that the sound of a grown man screaming?*

Lazarus sheepishly shut his mouth.

Michael slowed.

Silence. Beautiful silence. Only the faint sound of churning lava far, far below.

Lazarus rubbed his blinking eyes, desperately trying to look ahead.

Darkness.

He glanced back down to the light of the dome. It no longer seemed to be shrinking. *Were they moving at all?* He leaned back, hoping to attract the massive angel's attention.

No luck, Michael's gaze was intently up.

Lazarus frowned, *wasn't the angel the least bit concerned that they were hanging out in pitch black—burning hot—Middle Earth?*

Michael furrowed his brow and shifted his hold, noting his cargo's obvious discontent. He didn't respond. It wasn't that he wasn't concerned, he was just busy recalculating the trajectory of their ascent—the smallest miscalculation could land them miles away from their intended destination.

"HALT!" The sudden command exploded around them.

Michael tensed. *Jurisdictional discrepancies.* He was well aware this might happen. For a moment he entertained the possibility of a race to the surface, but with the added weight of his cargo, it didn't put the odds in his favor. He hesitated, his mind reeling. He was out of his jurisdiction, with nowhere to go, and no real plan B. A frustrated sigh escaped his lips. For now, it looked like he would have to sit tight and engage.

"Give him to me," the voice continued, calm and straightforward, but vehemently intense.

Michael peered into the darkness. His confronter was in full disguise, and in the low light, almost impossible to see. *A visor, some dreads,* that was about all Michael could make out. Still, the negative energy being emitted was unmistakable. Michael instinctively braced—*it was Haylel.*

"Ahh, old friend—we meet again," the mighty angel engaged.

Haylel froze. Michael's reply was not exactly what he had anticipated, especially considering he was decked out in full devil disguise. *How could he possibly know?* Hatred shot through Haylel's bones. *A fool's bluff,* he reasoned. *There was no way this second-string, throne room wannabe would speak like that if he actually knew who he was talking to.*

"I said, *give* him to me," Haylel snarled.

The atmosphere instantly thickened, negative energy spiking off the charts. Michael could literally feel it crushing his skull. He shifted uncomfortably against the weight. His mind felt sluggish, almost confused. Everything seemed to scream, *Comply!*

"Never—," the fearless angel leaned in, gritting his teeth and loosing a supercharged snarl of his own. "I have orders from a higher authority."

"I'm the highest authority here," Haylel raged. "It's day four. *He goes nowhere!*"

Michael understood Haylel's anger. The 'Four Day Rule' *was* basic protocol. Standard operations, really. For three days, a soul could stay near its body, hoping for the chance to return. But come day four, *every wandering soul belonged to Haylel … permanently.* Everyone knew it: *Nobody, but nobody returned after day four. Nobody.*

Still, Michael didn't budge.

Haylel pressed his helmet right up against Michael's face. He could sense the angel's thoughts. Michael knew the Four Day Rule, and he knew it well. Haylel scowled. *There was no confusion.. no precedence.. no extenuating circumstance.. So what made this poser punk think that he alone could break protocol?*

Michael felt his nose being irrevocably crushed, and his pinned cargo beginning to squirm. The atmosphere was now crackling with the supercharged energy of both relentless angels and it was becoming quite clear that Haylel would *never* back down. If Michael didn't comply, things were going to get ugly.

But Michael could have cared less. He already had his orders. And like it or not, those orders came from the *highest authority.*

The air buzzed with electricity. Michael held his ground, pushing right back, driving his face hard into the uncomfortable helmet. His eyes blazed. His muscles flexed. He so wanted to beat the life outta this meddling, two-faced charlatan. Silently, his left hand dropped to the hilt of his sword.

Slowly, he began to draw..

Movement.

He shifted focus, continuing to lift his blade..

More movement.

Lazarus gasped.

Above, below, left and right—something seemed to

be..

Michael froze. He saw it too. Circling them, like sharks in the water, were five of the biggest demonic thugs he'd ever seen. He clenched his jaw. These creatures were easily thirty times his size, brandishing all manner of brutality. Clubs. Chains. Barbaric looking blades. Some weaponry he'd never seen before. Michael's hand instinctively tightened around the hilt of his sword. *The stakes had just gotten significantly higher. Way higher.*

Haylel leaned in.

Michael pushed back.

Lazarus struggled in the middle.

Then it happened … Michael snapped.

Letting go of his sword, the archangel moved back, throwing his face skyward, and howling with laughter. His sword dropped back to its sheath with a thunderous click. The strange sound and bizarre behavior stopped Haylel and his thugs dead in their tracks. Michael didn't even notice. He laughed until long after he had captured Hell's full and undivided attention. Then, and only then, did he slowly wipe the tears from his eyes, secure Lazarus to his chest, and chuckle his two final words. "Father … help."

Immediately a pillar of blazing blue light shot down from the heavens, penetrating all the way to the streets of Paradise. Its fiery shaft surrounded Michael, instantly separating him from his tormentors. The thugs lit up, suddenly exposed for the feckless lowlife wannabes they really were. Middle Earth began to tremble, quaking so hard that even the mourners waiting outside Lazarus' open tomb felt a disconcerting rocking, deep beneath their feet.

With shrieks and squeals, the demonic thugs fled screaming. This was the kind of light that altered darkness permanently and they wanted no part of it. Haylel hesitated—but only a moment before he too disappeared into the thick, expansive darkness.

Micheal waited. Astounded. Watching as his Creator absolutely crushed his opposition. Secretly he had hoped to do a little hell-crushing himself—but he understood, considering the circumstances.

Then it was gone. The light, the quake, the screams—all the

drama, gone. Nothing but hot and dark all over again, and the sound of churning lava far, far below.

Lazarus opened his mouth to speak, but Michael was already on the move. A quick flap of his wings brought them up to speed and within seconds, they were back in the tomb.

The massive angel hunkered over, his twelve foot frame more than filling the limited space. He shifted slightly. In the catacomb's dim light he could see the physical body of Lazarus, tightly wrapped, and laying on the thick burial slab. He bent, gently returning spirit to flesh. He could hear the crowd outside growing restless. It had been several minutes since the first command and the doubters were beginning to doubt.

"Lazarus, come forth!" Yeshua called a second time. This time Lazarus heard it too. With a muffled shout, he began to move, attempting to free himself from his trappings. Michael smiled. "A little help, my friend?" He lifted Lazarus from the slab, standing him near the entrance.

Instinctively Lazarus headed towards the sound of the crowd. He bit at the cloth covering his face, hopping and inching his way forward, moving slowly into the light. "A little helph?" he mumbled, stumbling and leaning against the mouth of the tomb.

The crowd went silent, terror and disbelief shooting through its jaw-dropped ranks. One mourner took off running.

Was this—for real?

No one dared move a muscle.

"Unwrap him," Yeshua chuckled, a twinkle in his eye. "Indeed, he lives. Go—set your brother free!"

CH44: BEGINNING OF THE END

"Boundaryless, piece of trash!" roared Ha-satan, shoving himself back from the square table and loosing a long string of blushworthy expletives. "It's time for that panty waste-of-space, carpenter's son to finally ante-up."

BEAST glanced knowingly at Prophet. Ha-satan was in a mood, and there was no calming him down. The Dark Lord had called their meeting immediately upon returning from his failed face-off with Michael. Yeshua had proven his superiority, Lazarus' resurrection was the talk of the town, and to put it mildly—Ha-satan was livid.

"So ... what's the game plan, boss?" BEAST was stepping carefully.

"We call this mortal's bluff," Ha-satan hissed, "—we torture him until he bows."

"And if he doesn't?"

"Then we nail him to a tree—and leave him hanging," a new voice entered the mix.

Every head turned. *Who was that?* The new voice was cold, calculating and—feminine?

"Gentlemen—Belle. Belle—Gentlemen," Ha-satan stood for the introduction.

BEAST and Prophet nodded their hellos. They were well aware of who she was.

Jezebel smiled curtly.

Ha-satan dropped his head. "I finally called in the big guns," he sheepishly conceded, flopping to his seat like a spoiled adolescent.

Jezebel flashed a sultry smile. She *was* the big guns, and

she knew it. "No more worries, boys," she immediately took control, defiantly flipping her hair. "The rhinestones and reinforcements have arrived."

Parading to her seat, she flaunted everything she had with every step she took. All eyes were on her every move. They couldn't look away. Hell's rebellious queen wore a long-sleeve, thumbhole, shoulderless, halter top, layered above a smart looking, perfectly starched, black collar shirt. A plunging neckline and leather miniskirt completed her stunning allure. As she moved, darkness surrounded her. Ebbing and flowing, it crept throughout her being, trailing behind like a sort of twisted bridal train.

Prophet shook his head, it was nearly impossible to tell where guilty pleasure ended and abject depravity began.

"Love what you've done with the place," she cooed, stroking BEAST's chin as she overbent to take her seat.

BEAST purred. His "mom" *was* a stunning creature—professional yet provocative, cordial yet calculating, smart yet seductive. He deliberately looked her over. She had all the right curves in all the right places, and she wasn't afraid to use them. Externally, she was sleek and sophisticated. Internally, she was a pit of destruction. She was a master manipulator. Narcissistic and self-absorbed. Completely insecure. Rarely would she hold anything back if she knew she could get what she wanted, and what she wanted was control. There was not a doubt in her mind, that you existed *to serve her.* She was a poisonous spider—all legs and eyes—compelling you to join her in the confines of her web, wrapping you in the comfort of her lies, and gently stroking your ego until she had sucked every last drop of life from your blood. She was bitter. She was brash. She was breathtaking.

She was Belle.

Belle slid smugly into her seat at the foot of the table. A wave of her hand revealed a sizable crystal ball. Another wave brought a lifeless, twisted tree, flickering into focus. "We'll leave that big talker dangling between Heaven and Earth," she smirked, tossing the ball mid-table. "Wallowing in the wrath of our perpetual indifference!"

The ball landed solidly yet silently, levitating several

centimeters above the table's rough surface. All eyes moved with the large glowing orb, staring transfixed at its glimmering interface.

The picture flipped and changed, flickering again, this time resting on a clip of Yeshua raising Lazarus.

Ha-satan flinched.

"We leave him wallowing," Jezebel leaned in, "—until the truth is *plainly* revealed to us."

Prophet nodded his full agreement. *Nail him to a tree*—it *was* a good plan. If Yeshua was bluffing, then like any man, he would eventually die—*game over*. And if he was telling the truth, then like any god—he would hang there unable to die, *forever*.

Either way, they would get their answer.

"It's a win win," Belle purred, enjoying the sound of her own silky-smooth voice. "If the troublemaker dies … he's finally out of our hair. If he lives … our suspicions were confirmed and we simply leave him there, suspended between Heaven and Earth until he either gets himself down, or curses the humanity who put him there." She looked deliberately at each pair of eyes around the table. "Boys, without our help, the only way off that cross is for him to orchestrate his own salvation." A wicked grin ignited two flickering flames in her glowing red eyes. "The instant he does, he will have broken Elohim's trust," she cackled. "Perfection will no longer be his. He will have chosen the path of self-reliance and least-resistance, joining our ever-enlightened ranks." She paused, breathing deep, commanding their full, undivided attention. "And when we allow him to succeed— *he will owe us his soul!*"

Hearty grins broke out all around.

"Boys," she continued her roll. "You work for me now. Get that brash-talking show-off into my hands." She reached out, patting the arms of Prophet and BEAST like good little puppies. "Your only job is to instigate the betrayal—you can leave the leaders, the crowds, and all the heavy lifting *to me*."

Ha-satan leapt to his feet. *He absolutely loved what he was hearing!* Slamming both hands down on the table, he leaned in, his face only millimeters away from the hovering crystal ball. "Die, or hang forever," he defiantly spewed at Yeshua's flickering image. "It makes no difference to me!" He smashed a heavy hand down on the ball, pinning it to the table. "Let's see who you bow to when your own skin is on the line," he squeezed with all his might, shattering the crystal into a million glowing pieces.

"Either way—," he growled, "your inheritance *is mine!*"

FRIDAY
CH45: COUNTDOWN, FINAL WEEK [DAY6]
0000:00:08:20:08:08

Heartfelt wails reverberated through the otherwise peaceful neighborhood. Yeshua looked over his shoulder at the sobbing prostitute washing his feet with her tears. *Awkward.* Well, it would have been, if he hadn't been the son of God, and the woman hadn't been Lazarus' sister, Mary. He glanced around at the wide eyes, gaping mouths, and untouched food surrounding him. He couldn't help but chuckle. *It certainly appeared to be awkward enough for everyone else at the dinner party.*

Yeshua's eyes scanned the tightly packed room, looking for one face in particular. His entire crew was back in Bethany, hometown to Lazarus. They were dining at the house of a prominent religious leader affectionately known as, 'Simon the Leper.' Yeshua smiled, he was pretty sure Simon had asked him over to see if he was, in fact, legit. And perhaps to cure a particular case of leprosy that was personally troubling.

A jostle. A shove. A guest pushed past. Yeshua nudged Lazarus—very much alive and seated beside him. They chuckled about the crowds spilling out of the house and filling the streets. *It was crazy,* word of Lazarus' resurrection had spread like wildfire. Even with Passover only days away, many had traveled from nearby Jerusalem, just to see this 'walking dead man' for themselves.

Yeshua turned back to the commotion at his feet and puzzled. *If everyone knew about the miracle of Lazarus … why then, was his sister's display of gratitude causing such a stir?*

Mary looked up from where she had just finished drying Yeshua's feet with her hair. For a moment their eyes locked. *Liquid love*, pure as the driven snow, washed over Yeshua's being. There was no other way to describe it. *How was it possible, that this prostitute could be so full of his own heavenly Spirit?* Yeshua physically shook, it was a radical energy—unbridled, uncohersed, completely free. His eyes filled with tears. *This was the very reason he had come to Earth.*

The energy doubled, multiplying as it returned to Mary. Immediately she was weeping again. Almost uncontrollably. She pulled a large vial of perfumed oil from her cloak, and trembling, began spilling its contents onto her savior's beautifully calloused feet.

By now, all eyes were on them, the oil's spicy fragrance filling the modest home. Yeshua surveyed the crowd once more. This time his gaze landed on that 'someone in particular.' He grinned. Finally, everyone was watching—*including Haylel.*

The Son of Man closed his eyes, breathing a quick prayer, inhaling the musk-scented fumes. With both Lazarus and Haylel present, it was the perfect time to make another bold statement. *But what?* A one-two punch would be nice. Maybe even something along the lines of a round-house kick to the face, *you know—Chuck Norris style.* He shook his head. It didn't particularly matter, he would take whatever Elohim was sending—*but what to do?*

His ears perked up. Nearby, he could hear Simon, Judas, and several others among the religious crowd murmuring. "What's wrong with her?" they criticized. "Why is she wasting that oil? She could have sold it for well over a year's wages and given that money to the poor. Why is she here? Why is she touching his feet? Doesn't the teacher know what kind of woman she is?" On and on they went. Completely blind. Completely bound. Completely bitter..

Completely offended.

That was the moment Yeshua understood—*he didn't have to do anything, because Elohim had already done it!*

He turned back to Mary, everything suddenly so clear. *Mary WAS his one-two punch!* One, she was publicly honoring him above all others in attendance. Two, she was openly preparing his body for burial, and thus his face-to-face, heaven-destined date with Haylel. Furthermore, she was breaking all the rules by refocusing her love directly on him, leaving all devilish middlemen out. But most, and "worst" of all—she was anointing him, King, in Haylel's presence.

Ouch, Yeshua grimaced. *Haylel stuck watching his own replacement's inauguration? How embarrassing for him.* He stifled a grin, this was far more than a one-two punch. This was a left jab, a right hook, a round-house kick to the face AND—the final knockout blow!

As usual—*Elohim had more than delivered.*

Mary lifted her head and smiled. It was as if she could read her savior's thoughts. She reached up and poured the remainder of that earthy smelling liquid over the crown of Yeshua's head. Yeshua shut his eyes. He could feel the oil flowing—thick, like honey—down his scalp, over his face, and through his well-worn beard. He breathed in, deep. He could sense Elohim's Spirit all over the costly offering, crowning him like a King, covering him like a robe. It was settled, he *was* the undisputed, anointed 'King of Earth.'

His heart overflowed.

Quick as a flash, the final veil lifted, revealing the full gravity of the situation. Yeshua saw the betrayal. The defilement. The shame. The torture this simple gift would trigger within only days. He saw the whips. The thorns. The nails and scars. The hopelessness of the cross. But he didn't care. All he felt in this moment was a broken woman's radical, selfless love—and he knew, that he knew, that he knew: *He would go to the very depths of Hell—if only to save this one wayward daughter.*

Yeshua turned to the group of naysayers. "Leave this woman alone," he scolded. "She has done a good thing for me." Tilting his head, he looked directly at Judas, his heart breaking for his appearance-driven, money-bound friend. Judas was his personal accountant, who truthfully, had only suggested selling the oil as an excuse to line his own pockets. "The poor you will always have with you," Yeshua's voice softened. "But you will not always have me. Surely, I say to you, that wherever my story is told, what this woman has done will also be told as a memorial to her." He took a deep breath. "But what, I wonder, will be said about you?"

Immediately Haylel was beside Judas, whispering in his ear. Judas' cheeks flushed. His face reddened. Shame flooded his soul.

Why was he being singled out in front of everyone? he fumed. *Were his words not equally note-worthy? Did the Torah not command the aid of the poor, the widow and the orphan? Was one mere man more important than all of they?* A barn door of offense swung wide open in Judas' bitter soul.

Haylel smirked. *This was almost too easy.* He sidled through, putting a comforting arm around Judas' bruised ego. "Let's see if this carpenter from Nazareth really has what it takes," he whispered. "Return the favor, call *him* out in front of the crowd. Offer *him* up. If he really is who he claims to be, he will walk away unscathed—just like he's done every other time. If not, you will have outed a conman and a liar. Go ahead. Put *him* to the test. End this charade, once and for all."

Yeshua watched the transaction conspire. Watching as Haylel whispered in Judas' ear. As he stepped into Judas' soul. Earth's anointed champion slowly finished his meal, folding his napkin neatly beside his plate. Rising from the table, he placed a loving hand on Mary's head, stooping to whisper his gratitude. Then he moved through the dining crowd, out into the waiting yard.

Pandemonium ensued as miracle after miracle flowed. *It was so much fun!* Laughter and joy filled the evening sky, grateful hearts full to overflowing. The guests loved Yeshua. And Yeshua loved the guests. Dinner's social awkwardness was quickly forgotten as the crowd reveled in the merriment of Heaven's outrageous love.

There was, however, one downcast face. One indignant heart, still nursing an irreparably bruised ego.

Judas paused to fire a bitter glance his master's way. Unrest scoured his heart. Betrayal troubled his mind. *The game was on,* he scowled, *and there would be Hell to pay.*

Another miracle.

Another ruckus roar of laughter.

Judas flinched and stifled a growl, already moving on. With a flip of his cape, he slipped quietly away. *He would get his revenge. He would get his due payday.*

SUNDAY
CH46: COUNTDOWN, FINAL WEEK [DAY4]
0000:00:06:01:49:48

"Master—your ride has arrived!" Peter enthusiastically threw his cloak over the back of the skittish donkey he held securely by the bridal. "She was back in town, tied to a tree, exactly as you said!" He marveled, offering Yeshua the reins.

"Of course!" Yeshua laughed heartily, throwing a confident leg over the shifting colt. "Just as my Father showed me!" He secured the reins, handing them over in turn. "Judas? Will you do the honors?"

"Gladly," Judas grinned, taking his place at the head of the procession. *He wouldn't have it any other way!*

Then they were off, moving down the hardened trail, making their way into the midst of the annual Jerusalem Seder celebration.

Passover was only days away, and news of Lazarus' resurrection was still the talk of the town. Yeshua gazed in amazement. Both sides of the dirt-packed trail were lined with spectators, chanting and cheering, watching and waving, spreading palm branches and personal cloaks on the road—*paving the way for a king!*

Behind the scenes, the spirit world was equally abuzz. Messenger angels were spreading the news. Powers and Virtues were gathering crowds. And Principalities shot to and fro, leading spirited cheers.

Yeshua closed his eyes. Lining both sides of the path, he could see a long line of Heavenly Hosts standing shoulder-to-shoulder, swords and shields raised, sent to protect his winding, preordained trail. Even Haylel was in on the action. Levied with the strictest of orders, he was walking beside Judas, calling out through ever clenched teeth, "This is the way in which Elohim honors those who truly please him!"

The procession continued until Yeshua came to a stop beneath a particular tree, atop a particular hill, overlooking his beloved city. There he paused, slipping from the back of his donkey. The energy here was palpable. Off the charts, electric. He let it sink in. This was the spot where Abraham had offered up Issac. The hill where David had buried Goliath's skull. And the tree, under which, the serpent had tricked Eve.

Yeshua grinned, a vision of the next 24 hours bombarding his unblinking eyes. *Yes*—tomorrow he would publicly curse this tree. Everyone would see. It would be the final blow in a long line of final blows, paving the way for Wednesday's unprecedented, extracurricular activities.

Tears welled. *Things were coming full circle.* Yeshua turned to face Jerusalem. "Oh, how close you came," he whispered to his beloved Alma Mater. "Eternal peace, within your grasp—and yet you turned it down." Big tears rolled down rosy red cheeks. "Now your enemies will encircle you and crush you to the ground," the words seemed to thunder as he slipped the bridal-reins over his donkey's furrowed brow. "For you have rejected the unbelievable opportunity Elohim so graciously afforded you."

One slap of his noble steed sent it galloping for home.

He turned, reins still in hand, braiding them as he moved steadily down the sprawling hillside. With only three days to go, Heaven was making its boldest move yet. Yeshua released his makeshift whip. There were tables to turn. Scripts to flip. He fixed his gaze upon the shimmering temple dome. *Like it or not, he was going inside—where the heart of his Father was about to be made known.*

MONDAY
CH47: COUNTDOWN, FINAL WEEK [DAY3]
0000:00:05:04:00:11

"Teacher—good TEACHER!" The pious cries rang out across the crowded Jerusalem valley.

Yeshua stopped mid-lesson and turned toward the strangely sterile greeting. Near the base of the mountain, about a quarter mile downhill, he could see the culprits—a small band of lemon-faced, overly solemn rabbis, earnestly heading his way.

Immediately, Yeshua's thoughts returned to the prior day. *Oops, had that 'madman' trashing the temple courts—driving out merchants at the end of a homemade bridal whip—been him?* He chuckled. It was a simple misunderstanding really—an attempt to 'drain the swamp, put an end to temple corruption, and reestablish Heaven's authority over every hijacked systemic Power,' nothing more.

He surveyed the surrounding hillsides swarming with the holiday masses straining to hear his every word. *Clearly, the people approved.* 'Making money off of required religious practices,' they were as sick of it as he was.

Yeshua turned back to the sour little mob, now pushing their way uphill through the crowd. This time Haylel wasn't just among them, *he was driving them*. They were furious. *Templegate*, as they had coined it, had deprived them of their most profitable week of business. It was akin, only to having somehow cleared Christmas from the fiscal, Gregorian Calendar. This kind of shenanigan was unheard of. Inexcusable. Downright criminal. It demanded repercussions.

"Good teacher.."

They had arrived.

"..could God create a rock so heavy that he himself could not lift it?"

Bang—shot one, already fired.

They wheeled to a stop.

Yeshua turned, sizing up his adversaries. *Arrogant and smug?* Check. *Cordial, yet calculating?* Double-check. *Their question, a catch twenty-two?* Triple-check, trifecta. *Clearly they had come to trip him up.* He grinned. *This was gonna be fun.*

"See here," he replied, motioning them close. "The Son of Man stands freely on this rock you call Earth, no more capable of lifting it than you or any other man." He winked and lowered his voice. "Yet, that very same Son of Man—millennia ago—spoke this rock into existence.."

The mob leaned in, straining to catch a mistake.

"..and is, at this exact moment, *holding it all together.*" Yeshua stepped back, slapping the nearest slouching shoulder and laughing merrily.

Clang—shot one, deflected.

A look of contempt swept over his questioners. *Lucky guess,* they were certain. They quickly reloaded, conferring among themselves. Haylel roamed ravenously between them—whispering, offending, instigating, provoking.

Another rabbi came forward.

"Master," he challenged, feigning sincerity. "Since it's obvious no question is too difficult, can you rightly explain the Holy Trinity?" He set his jaw proudly. "For the Torah—our sacred text— plainly tells us that God is *one.* Yet, in Genesis—the first book of that same text—it reads: *'let **us** make man'* ... and later ... *'let **us** go down.'*" He paused, letting the contradiction sink in. "How is this possible?"

Yeshua inhaled deeply, his eyes dancing with delight. He too paused, letting the contradiction fester.

Nearby, a wandering minstrel group played sweetly in the background. Finishing their song, they started another.

Then another.

Still, Yeshua waited. He waited so long that the band eventually stopped playing altogether.

The crowd began to murmur. *What was this? ..had the Teacher already met his match?*

Casually, Yeshua turned.

"What's your name?" he called to the band.

"—p-pardon?" the minstrel playing the guitar seemed taken aback.

Yeshua grinned. "My friend, by what do you call yourselves?"

"Oh—," the minstrel laughed. "*Jerusalem's Pride.*"

Yeshua turned back to his arrogant interrogators. "God is like this band—like any band, really." He stopped, letting the sudden outburst of snickers die down. "*God,* is the band name. The Father, Spirit, and Son are the band members." He held up a finger. "*One* band," he flipped up two more. "*Three* distinct members. Each playing in perfect harmony. All playing as *one.*" A grin spread wide across his jovial face. With a masterful pivot, he turned the spotlight back on his challenger. "And you sir, are you part of a family?"

"O-Of course—," the rabbi stammered indignantly.

"By what name does your family respond?"

"Kohen," he answered proudly, beginning to catch on. "For we are a family of priests."

"Likewise," Yeshua grinned. "God is a family of gods. One family. Three family members. *God*, is the family name."

A quiet gasp washed over the crowd.

Yeshua chuckled and stepped forward. "Friend, a better question would have been: *How does a family of Gods, manage to make up one God?*" He smiled warmly at his questioner's quickly melting demeanor. "Not to worry—I'll tell you." He smiled again. "The *secret* is for each family member to make *every* decision with the best interest of the family at heart," he confided. "When each family member truly does this, then no matter how big the family becomes—that family … or that band … flows as *one.*"

Now the crowd began to stir. *Who was this man? And how could he explain such unexplainable mysteries so easily?* "He *must* be God's very own son," they concluded in awestruck whispers.

One by one, the rabbis stepped forward.

One by one, Yeshua answered each claim.

It was maddening. Instead of exposing and humiliating, their questions seemed only to be solidifying and authenticating.

Tensions mounted.

Frustrations grew.

Still, try as they might, they could find nothing wrong. Somehow, they had found a pure and spotless lamb. And so—at risk of floundering irreparably in front of ever-awakening crowds, or drowning in the ever-widening mire of their own embarrassment— they eventually fell silent.

When Yeshua realized the interrogation had ended, he immediately turned to the root of the problem—*Haylel*.

"You say 'Thou shalt not commit murder,'" he charged, looking past his physical contenders, and deep into the spirit realm. "But I say 'if you even hate your brother in your heart, you have already committed murder..'"

He watched the lower half of Haylel's left eyelid twitch, ever so slightly.

"..And if *anyone* does *anything* to keep so much as *one* of these little ones from me," Yeshua gestured towards the thronging crowd. "It would be far better for him to have a millstone hung around his neck and be drown in the sea.."

A flinch.

Another twitch.

"..I tell you the truth," Yeshua raised his intensity. "If your right eye offends you, *pluck it out.* And if your right hand causes you to stumble, *cut it off.* Better that one of your members perish, then for your entire body to be cast into the fires of Hell."

Haylel growled, tightening a fist.

Yeshua pressed on. "Again, I tell you the truth, there will always be temptations to sin, but oh, what sorrow awaits *the one who does the tempting.*"

BOOM—a spiritual shockwave erupted. Haylel could feel the carpenter's words drilling like ice-picks into his soul. *Who was this blue-collar punk, to tell him how things worked?* He nearly lost it. *This was HIS world. It ran by HIS rules. HE would dictate how things would go around here!* He started to lunge, but caught himself—resulting in a sort of awkward lurch forward.

Too late, Yeshua saw his move. Matching the step, Yeshua stepped forward too, stopping just short of his adversary.

For a moment the two stood face to face, nose to nose, eye to eye.

Haylel bristled.

Yeshua flexed.

The pressure to cave was immense.

The Son of Man leaned in. He could almost smell the bitter-sweet stench of Haylel's twisted breath. *There was no way he was backing down*. This was his final warning—*a screaming wake-up call*. Haylel *was* the watchful eye of Elohim. He *was* Elohim's right hand man. He must know—in no uncertain terms—that if his current self-absorbed trajectory wasn't changed abruptly—he was going to find himself cut off, plucked out and cast into the sea.

Haylel stared daggers. If looks could kill, only carnage would have remained. He didn't move, but truth be told, it was only because he was railing against his own raging temptation to put a permanent end to this charade, right now.

Yeshua wasn't swayed. He waited for a response ... *any response*.

Haylel stiffened. He couldn't take the bait. *Not now*.

He spun to face his retreating, elitist mob. "Do you not hear what this clown is *SAYING ABOUT YOU?*" he bellowed, brilliantly projecting the blame. "First in your temple, and now in *YOUR FACE?*" Gas-lighting lips quivered. "This half-breed, hack—in front of all these people—is practically demanding YOUR DESTRUCTION!" His rage was palpable. "*HOW LONG ARE YOU GONNA PUT UP WITH THIS BLASPHEMOUS CHARLATON'S THREATS? ..HIS BLATANT LIES? ..HIS PUBLIC DISREPSECT?*"

One by one, his religious patsies agreed. *They didn't deserve this undue shame. Not when the carpenter was clearly to blame.*

Haylel waited impatiently until his indignant, self-righteous mob was blindly back on track. Then, *poof*—he was gone—disappearing in a brilliant cloud of glitter-bombed smoke.

The rabbis, having suddenly lost their incentive to remain,

began to slink away as well.

Yeshua watched them go. No need to re-engage. Heaven's point had been abundantly made. *He* was the Spotless Lamb, in which no blemish could be found.

The fearless son of God turned to readdress the crowd. There was still so much to say and time was quickly winding down. After all, on the heels of today's public pummeling, he was fairly certain they would crucify him now.

WEDNESDAY BEGINS
CH48: COUNTDOWN, FINAL WEEK [D-DAY]
0000:00:03:21:00:00 [6 PM, SUNDOWN - DINNERTIME]

Tonight was Passover—the eve of that unforgettable meal, first celebrated nearly two thousand years ago. It was a celebration of Israel's greatest exodus, when death had been defeated, Egypt's oppression lifted, and their tormentors led to destruction. In short, it was that miraculous night when, 'the blood of a lamb,' had rescued them all from 'death, hell, and the grave.'

For this reason, Passover meals were often a joyful celebration. Tonight's was no different. Still, there was an unusual energy in the air, an eery familiarity, as if the clock had somehow been set to replay, and once again, 'death, hell, and the grave,' was back on the prowl.

Yeshua's gaze was long and steady—out the second story window.

John leaned back against the chest of his teacher, glancing up fondly. From where the two reclined, side-by-side at the sprawling dinner table, John could sense something was troubling his master. He followed Yeshua's concentrated gaze out the darkened window—*nothing.* He looked again—*nada.* Still, Yeshua seemed transfixed. Clearly, something was holding his undivided attention.

A frown and a shrug released John from the struggle, his attention quickly turning back to the dinnertime ruckus. He'd often seen his teacher move to the beat of a different drummer. That was nothing new. *Besides,* he nestled back against his friend and mentor, *as long as Yeshua was here, everything would be OK.* He glanced one last time at the empty window. There was no way he could have possibly known—*Haylel had just arrived.*

Yeshua eyed Haylel, the archangel was gazing in on their

unsuspecting party. Cold eyes, pale skin, blood-thirsty lips—his face was the very picture of death. For what seemed like an eternity, he stood unnaturally still—his focus laser-like, his posture ready to pounce. A strange chill engulfed Yeshua as he suddenly understood. *Haylel was stalking his prey.* Slowly, he followed the Death Angel's gaze ... *Ughh,* his heart sank, *it was—Judas.*

"Friends, one of you will betray me," the warning practically leapt from Yeshua's lips, instantly quieting the room. "But woe to the man by who I am betrayed," he continued, ignoring the sudden silence. "It would be better for him, had he not been born." He paused until Judas made eye contact. "Tho, I tell you the truth, it is *not* necessary."

Pandemonium broke out. *What did the teacher just say? Betrayal? One of them? Certainly not!* What had been an evening of lighthearted banter, suddenly shifted to one of alarm, dismay, and confusion. "Is it I?" each student began to ask in turn. "Master, is it I?"

Methodically, the question passed, seat-by-seat, around the table. There was a pregnant, almost awkward pause as it inevitably landed in Judas' treacherous lap. Judas hesitated, hoping in all the confusion, it would simply pass him by unaware. "Is it I?" he finally asked.

Yeshua cocked his head and smiled, his cheerful demeanor didn't skip a beat. Judas truly was one of his favorites. He was brilliant, and witty, and charming, with an infectious laugh that could often be heard clear across the room. He was a gifted speaker and capable businessman—well organized, yet compellingly personable. However, Judas' insatiable need for approval, frequent delusions of grandeur, and over-exaggerated love for himself were quite literally leading him down a dead-end road.

Sorrow flooded Yeshua's heart, he flashed an empathetic smile. Judas' constant self-comparisons and situational ethics weren't helping matters either. In fact, they had pretty much stunted his growth. While the other students were learning from their mistakes and working through personal challenges—growing by leaps and bounds—Judas' inexhaustible supply of excuses had allowed him to remain comfortably *stuck.* Of course, that hadn't stopped him from noticing the preferential treatment Yeshua gave to several of the others. Others who took responsibility, put self-interests aside, and didn't continually pass the blame. The perceived "injustice" had certainly aroused Judas' jealousy, although not his desire for self-growth. Even when Yeshua pulled him aside and warned him in no uncertain terms, that it was his *own* lack of personal growth which was holding him back—it had been met by a barrage of "legitimate" excuses, enabling things to remain conveniently unchanged. Sadly, it was becoming increasingly clear that Judas had only joined the group for his own personal gain, and little else. *Still,* Yeshua smiled warmly at his betrayer. *This was a man he dearly loved.*

Lifting a dinner roll from his plate, Yeshua tore off a generous portion. Eager to clear up the misunderstandings, he dipped his 'peace offering' into a nearby bowl of sop, allowing the oil and blended-spice mixture to fully saturate the tasty morsel. He lifted the sop for all to see. Then, smiling ear to ear, and brimming with unconditional love, he handed it to Judas. Everyone in the room understood, by 'receiving the sop' Judas had just become the party's most honored guest.

"Friend," Yeshua finally replied. "You have said it."

Rage exploded as Judas' guilty conscious flipped the extended olive branch into a backhanded compliment. *How dare you?* he fumed. Yeshua's reply had neither confirmed nor denied the question. He flinched, everyone knew that basically meant, *"Yes."* Judas struggled to control himself. He could feel his ears turning red. The honor of Yeshua's gesture had just fallen flat in the shame of its warning.

There was almost an audible snap as something broke in Judas' soul. All he wanted was the same respect as the others. A little love. A little grace. A little pat on the back. Yet here he was, publicly humiliated once again. Never mind that it was because of his own selfish actions. Never mind that his Master was truly trying to make amends. From Judas' perspective, it was *all* Yeshua's fault.

The betrayer stared at his master still holding the dripping

Trojan horse. *Honor above all others in the room?* He grudgingly took the sop, *no—this felt more like rape.* His eyes darkened, for a moment pure hatred surged through him. *He was so done here.* He longed for what was to come as he choked down the piece of oil-dipped bread. It made little difference if it turned to death in his mouth, he was already busily basking in the pleasures of revenge.

In that instant, Haylel vanished from the window. Of course, only Yeshua noticed. And of course, only Yeshua understood—*Haylel had just entered Judas' soul.*

Tears filled Yeshua's eyes for his irreversibly offended friend. Haylel's disappearance could only mean one thing—Judas had just rejected his best attempt at true reconciliation. "What you do, do quickly," the master spoke as Judas rose to make his exit. Judas tipped his hat and grinned, whistling as he walked out into the night. To everyone outside the loop, it was as if he was off to save the world. No one could have fathomed what was actually about to come.

Yeshua lifted his cup and the meal was underway, the room quickly forgetting all about the odd pre-dinner exchange. Spirits soared. Laughter roared. Conversations, sprung to life. By all accounts, it was a Seder of Seders. Yet as the evening progressed, the weight of the world began to press down—right on Yeshua's shoulders. For the first time *ever*, he felt 'oddly unsettled.' Unsolicited doubts began bubbling to the surface of his mind. *He needed to shake them off. He needed to get alone with Elohim.*

But first—a distraction.

Yeshua reached for his napkin, folding it as a token of his dinner appreciation. He chuckled to himself. The playful, after dinner gesture had sort of taken on a life of its own. Over time, it had evolved into a type of 'calling card,' with everyone looking to see what he would create next. Tonight he was attempting a brand new design, something he had never created before. A rose. He allowed himself to fully engage in his work, resting in its temporary reprieve.

"What's that?" A familiar teenage voice piped up.

Yeshua gently placed the masterpiece on his plate, dusted his hands, and rose to one knee. Eye-to-eye, he smiled warmly at the boyish face of John.

"What is it?" John asked again. The question was less about an answer and more about a heartfelt connection. For the first time ever, trouble seemed to be clouding his master's fearless face and everything in John screamed to clear it away.

Yeshua's grin widened. "It's origami," he replied.

"Or-eh—graah, what?" John's reaction was priceless—Yeshua's response might as well have been in Klingon, it was completely off his radar.

Yeshua laughed out loud, he'd forgotten that origami wouldn't be invented for another, oh, six hundred years or so. "Don't worry," he chuckled. "Your great-grandkid's great-grandkid's great-grandkids will understand."

"Oh—," John smiled, allowing his master to help him to his feet.

"But thanks, dear one—," Yeshua grinned, motioning for the room to follow them out and into the cool spring night. "I definitely needed that."

WEDNESDAY CONTINUES
CH49: COUNTDOWN, FINAL WEEK [D-DAY]
0000:00:03:15:00:00 [12 AM, MIDNIGHT]

"Pray.." Yeshua's voice cracked.

Peter, James, and John dropped quickly to their knees. Yeshua had taken them to their favorite late-night, hangout, hot spot—the well manicured, and always peaceful, Garden of Gethsemane. John looked at his counterparts. They had already complied. No one, not even he, dared question the unusual request; they could sense the urgency in Yeshua's voice. John closed his eyes. Like the others, he simply obeyed.

Yeshua nodded his gratitude as he stumbled away into the darkness. A few more yards and he too, fell to his knees. Agonizing, he clutched at his head. From the moment Judas had exited the party, dark thoughts had begun bombarding his mind. Steadily, they had grown more and more frequent, more and more intense. He couldn't shake them. They were all around. "Abba—Daddy," he cried into the midnight air.

Do you know what they're plotting, RIGHT NOW, against you? the thoughts almost screamed. *They're going to strip you naked, mutilate you, and NAIL YOU TO A TREE.* Gruesome images flashed across the theater of his mind. *Son of God,* the thoughts sneered. *Are you just gonna sit back and take it? Stand up. Do what you came to do. SAVE YOURSELF. SAVE THIS WORLD.*

Yeshua groaned. He was torn. His spirit knew what it would do, his flesh did too. That was the problem. He was left stuck, waffling in the agonizing middle. His head pounded. His stomach churned. He was completely overwhelmed. It felt like he was being ripped apart. Divided in two. Great drops of blood dripped from his brow as capillary after capillary burst under the intensity of the pressure. Everything within him felt like mush. A wail escaped his lips, he couldn't stop it. He wanted out.

"Daddy," he cried again. "It's too much! If there's any other way—*take it*. Let me off the hook." He gritted his teeth, bracing against the physical pain. "But … not my will, only yours be done," he forced the words out and waited.

No reply.

He lay for what seemed like ages before he compelled himself to check on his men. Their hearty Passover meal, complete with four large glasses of wine, had done them in. They were sound asleep. Yeshua roused them. "Pray with me, friends—I beg you," he pleaded.

Again he went off alone. Again he repeated his prayer.

Nothing.

He awakened his crew a second time. "Pray with me," he urged. "For where two or more agree, *anything* is possible." He watched their lackluster attempts at rolling to their knees and his heart sank. *Didn't they get it? He needed their agreement. He needed ANYTHING to be possible.*

A third time he withdrew. "Daddy," he pleaded. "You can do anything. If *at all* possible, take this cup from me.."

He waited for the reply.

Nothing.

His mind flashed back.

A vision. Almost like a memory surfaced. Two men. One altar. *A ram?* Yeshua glanced around the scene. He could see himself seated—Indian style, mid altar—elbows on his knees, grinning from ear to ear. "Not my will.." he re-witnessed the words, watching the son be tied, Abraham's blade swinging down.

Thunk—he saw himself catch it mid air.

It wasn't pretend. It wasn't for show. Isaac had willingly laid his life down. Yeshua stirred. His heart moved deep. If a mortal man could do this … *then so could their God.*

"..not my will," he breathed a broken whisper, embracing the coming pain. "Only yours be done."

Suddenly, a powerful hand gripped his left shoulder. An

obedient hand grasped his right. All torment ceased as life began flooding his soul.

Yeshua rose to his feet, an unshakable peace surging throughout his entire being. He breathed deep, his courage returning. He felt completely renewed. Ready for anything. Eternity once again in his sights.

With fearless resolve, he strode towards Peter, James, and John—the archangel, Michael, to his left, Gabriel to his right—their wings stretching majestically above him, like the foreshadowing of an empty, garden tomb.

In the dim moonlight, Yeshua could see that his men were once again sound asleep. His heart skipped a beat, a powerful insight bombarding his soul: *The events of the next three days were as much for his men, as they were for himself.*

Ohh, he breathed, his heart leaping in the understanding of the 'aha' moment. *How had he been so blind?* Of course his men couldn't stay awake, they had no *reason* to. His death *was* their wake-up call. It would be the loss of everything around them, which would compel the awakening of everything within them. He grinned resolutely. *And awaken, they must!* It was brothers and sisters—sons and daughters—he had come to save. Not friends, fans, or followers. There *was* no other way. *This was his cup, and his cup, alone.*

"Are you still sleeping?" He called to his men, no longer troubled by their mediocrity. He motioned to a conglomerate of lanterns and torches bobbing in the distance. "Look, here comes my betrayer. Rise, let's go to meet him!"

Peter, James, and John leapt to their feet, embarrassed by their obvious lack of resolve. Anxiously, they roused the others, questions flying between them in harsh, hushed whispers. *Who was coming? A mob of soldiers? Why was no one warned? Was this the beginning of the insurgence? How could John have let them fall asleep again? Weapons, did anyone have weapons?*

No one seemed to have answers, only more questions. Slowly they quieted, turning once again to their leader.

"When I sent you, and the seventy-two out," Yeshua began, beckoning his men to follow. "I sent you without purse, bag, or sandals—," he paused. "Yet, did you lack for anything?"

"Nothing," they replied, not entirely sure what this highly unorthodox pep-talk had to do with the quickly approaching mob.

Yeshua followed their nervous gaze. The clubs, spears, torches and chains—they were the least of his concerns. It was Haylel, commanding Judas like a puppet. Jezebel, orchestrating the impending confrontation. And the thought of his students left entirely alone, which arrested his attention.

He turned back to his men. "But now I tell you," he updated his advice. "If you have a purse, *take it*—and *also* your bag. If you don't have a sword, *buy one*," he chuckled. "Even if you have to sell your coat to get it." The group picked up the pace. "For what is written about me is soon to be fulfilled. And everything as you know it, is about to change."

Heartily, his men agreed.

Peter drew his sword, eager to begin what he had already coined, the 'Imminent Insurgence.'

But Yeshua wasn't speaking of physical battles. He was addressing the coming spiritual war. The war that would surely ensue once Haylel was cut-off and his cohorts exposed. Yeshua sized up his motley crew. They were willing and eager—but they were clueless. So clueless. *The rules were about to change.* No more one-sided stand-offs, uncontested confrontations, or passive-aggressive inside jobs. The CEO of Heaven was about to get fired. This would escalate into— all out war. Money. Supplies. Armament. Unity. That is what Heaven would need to mount any sort of lasting invasion.

A cheer went up from Yeshua's men. They were eager to watch their leader once again defy the odds and finally establish his Kingdom on Earth.

Yeshua sighed. There was no time to explain. The battalion of soldiers—eh, mob—was already upon them.

"Whom do you seek?" a quick grin flashed across Yeshua's face as both groups came to a tentative halt.

There was a moment of semi-awkward silence as one of the soldiers fumbled for a response.

Somewhere a cricket chirped.

"Yeshua of Nazareth," came the hesitant reply.

"I am he," a blast of blue flame exploded from Yeshua's mouth, consuming Jezebel standing quietly in their midst. With a shriek, she toppled backwards, the entire battalion of soldiers toppling with her like little, time delayed dominoes.

Yeshua waited.

One by one, the mob slowly picked themselves up, doing their best to gather their thoughts, courage and personal belongings.

"Have you come to betray the Son of Man with a kiss?" Yeshua offered a hand to Judas, his question quietly spotlighting the treason still ruminating in his friend's troubled soul. He helped his betrayer to his feet, then graciously stepped aside, offering Judas a final path of escape—one last free exit. *It need not be.* Compassion welled for his friend. He longed for Judas to understand—*this was a fight between he and Haylel alone.* No betrayer was actually needed.

For a minute the two exchanged glances, Judas somewhat confused by the offer. There was still a chance he could be spared? ..if he would simply walk away?

Yeshua swallowed hard, waiting, fighting back tears. But his betrayer's resolute glare said it all—he was going nowhere.

Haylel, on the other hand, was anything but confused. He read the offer loud and clear. Immediately, he exploded. Even afterwards, Judas couldn't quite justify why Yeshua's question had angered him so much. All he knew was he suddenly felt like snapping both Yeshua's legs at the knees, and then crushing every bone in his smug little body. The betrayer didn't hesitate. As if possessed by the devil himself, he grabbed Yeshua with both hands, smiled his most winsome smile, and with a hint of insanity lacing his laughter— betrayed God's own son with a kiss.

Immediately, the games began: Haylel upping the ante. Yeshua refusing to fold.

Haylel had him arrested.

Yeshua went willingly.

Haylel falsely accused.

Yeshua held his tongue.

Haylel beat him once.

Yeshua turned a second cheek.

Haylel stripped and mocked.

Yeshua embraced the shame.

Haylel beat him again.

Yeshua crucified his flesh.

Haylel twisted Yeshua's words.

Yeshua surrendered his reputation.

Haylel sentenced.

Yeshua remained silent.

Haylel sentenced again.

Yeshua refused to save his own skin.

And so, at long last, when it became abundantly clear that Yeshua would never bow—and most certainly never fold: The hammers fell. The ropes were hoisted. And at precisely nine AM—just in time for Wednesday morning's Passover sacrifice—Yeshua found himself bloodied and beaten, nailed and hanging from a tree.

CH50: CRUCIFIED
0000:00:03:06:06:06

The tree stood, gnarled and weathered, its barren branches twisting heavenward, devilishly clawing at the gray skies above. Once upon a time, this great tree had been a beacon of wisdom and understanding, towering in the midst of Eden. But after mankind foolishly ate of its fruit, everything had changed. Slowly, the surrounding garden had wasted away, its soil eroding, its atmosphere thinning. Eventually, the tree too, fell victim to its own curse, finding itself alone—the sole survivor of what had once been a budding, bubbling paradise. And while it had endured the great flood, outlasted the ice age, and remained unscathed for centuries, it had not survived the single curse of a lowly carpenter's son. And so it stood, in shambles—a mere shell of its former self, barren and shadeless, barely recognizable, devoid of fruit and foliage.

That was until today—when a new fruit hung from its lifeless branches.

G-ahhhhh, Yeshua struggled to pull himself up, desperate to fill his lungs with air. Blood gurgled noisily in his throat as he inhaled. Determined, he devoured all the oxygen his lungs could handle. His body shuddered, the pain was relentless, it took everything he had not to waste his hard-fought commodity on a scream.

Trembling, he lowered himself again. The neurotic burn, terrorizing his outstretched arms and legs was almost unbearable. He squinted into the nine AM sun, taking little notice of its warmth against his badly beaten body. He was suspended atop Golgotha, the Hill of the Skull, hanging between two thieves, nailed to the trunk of a tree called, *Knowledge.*

In the distance, he could hear the sounds of the morning sacrifice ... the bleating of lambs, the prayers of temple priests. Yeshua cocked his head, listening. A moment's nostalgia washed over him as visions from his childhood flooded his memory. He experienced them fondly. They were a welcomed reminder that Passover had arrived, and although his own little world had come to a screeching halt, the larger world around him had not. That world was still celebrating past victories and making future plans, even as the savior of the universe hovered helplessly between life and death.

Beauty from ashes, the thought pounded his psyche. He clung to the contradiction. After all, it was the very reason he was here. He blinked rapidly, a futile attempt to clear the steady stream of sweat and blood dripping from his thorn pierced brow and down into his one good eye. His other eye lay warm against his cheek, dangling precariously from a single, unsevered optic nerve. From its new location Yeshua could clearly see his broken body below. Ripped and torn, bruised and swollen, it didn't appear human. Skin was hanging in shreds. Everything was raw and red. He shook his head. Blood splattered everywhere. He was weak. Dehydrated. Naked. Alone. Tongue glued to the roof of his mouth. He was beyond repair, but he didn't care. The coming attack would be far worse. He smiled through gritted teeth. His body had done its part, it had held together. Now it was time to prepare for the assault on his soul.

"Come down off that tree—*if you can.*"

The barrage began.

Yeshua turned, acknowledging the mouthy heckler. For the briefest of moments their gaze met. There was a flicker, a flash of pure, distilled hatred. Then it was gone. Yeshua exhaled slowly, that glimmer was unmistakable ... *Haylel.*

Leaning back against the tree, he closed his one good eye. Haylel and Jezebel finally had him right where they wanted him— humiliated, ravaged, helpless and alone. But most of all, they had him stuck. Stuck, with nowhere to go. To them, this was the greatest of fun. He was their sitting duck, the fish in their barrel, unable to avoid any part of the upcoming emotional onslaught.

"Son of God, save yourself! ..Or let your *God* come and save you!" the haunting jeers of passing hecklers began the new barrage. "King of Israel. Come down off that tree, and we'll believe!" the attack quickly spread throughout the onlooking crowd. "He saved others, but he cannot save himself? Certainly, if he was the promised Messiah, he could easily save himself!" Even the thieves hanging next to him were getting in on the action.

From nine until noon, Yeshua's soul was their punching bag. They hit him fast. They hit him hard. They hit him often. Everyone took a swing. Nothing was off limits. Mercilessly they brawled, until every word had been said, every jab had been thrown, and every punch had been painfully landed.

Yeshua felt completely alone. He surveyed the crowd, even those who loved him most were keeping their distance. It cut him to the core. He had every right to stand up for himself, to reveal the truth, to crush the injustice. Still, he would not take the bait. "Father, forgive them. For they don't know what they are doing."

Insult after insult, he accepted them all. Refusing to be offended, he chose love. And so, for the first time in all of human history, innocent blood began to breathe a brand new narrative— no longer was it one of vengeance and justice, but *of mercy and forgiveness*.

For three long hours the barrage continued, until at last, Spirit had had enough. Moving through the thief to Yeshua's right, she silenced the crowd.

"Do you not fear God?" the thief bellowed, his front row seat to Yeshua's unconditional forgiveness suddenly pressing hard on his soul. "Someday, you too will be checking out. Will you not deserve your judgment? Most certainly, I deserve mine. But this man," he nodded toward Yeshua. "He has done no wrong. Master—," he faltered, turning to the one who seemed to be at the center of it all. "Remember me when you enter your kingdom.."

Even the birds went quiet as Spirit burned the conversation deep into the hearts of every man, woman, and child present—each falling silent under the weight of their own personal conviction.

"Today, you will be with me in Paradise," Yeshua didn't miss a beat. With the biggest smile he could muster, and the meekest of all nods, he completed the unlikely connection.

There was an audible gasp as Jezebel fled the shell-shocked scene, heading back to the safety of Second Heaven. *Who was this man, to speak like this?* the crowd murmured in utter amazement. *Demonstrating such authority in the midst of such chaos?* They suddenly felt drained, convicted, ashamed. Many turned away. There was nothing left to say.

When Haylel realized Yeshua would neither bow nor break, and was somehow still *gaining* followers—a rage filled him like no other. Throwing back his head, he roared. It was time to pull out all the stops, to demand submission and end this charade, once and for all.

With a mighty thunderclap, his summons went out across the heavens. The skies darkened as every demon, prince and power under his authority answered the call. A chilling wind began to blow. Clouds billowed. Lightning flashed. Darkness blanketed the land. The crowd began to tremble, somehow they knew—*Hell's hordes had just arrived.*

Then the portal opened.

Directly above the tree, as in days of old, Haylel unlocked Second Heaven's front door. It burst open with a thunderous—*BANG.* Spinning wildly, like the vortex of a tornado, it descended, encompassing the defenseless hill. Fear danced, electric in the air. Lightning split the skies above.

The crowd shrunk back, terrified. Anxiously they searched the heavens. Bewildered. Amazed. Looking for anything that would explain away the bizarre events.

Yeshua raised his head. Through the swirling clouds, he could clearly see Haylel looming over the ancient spiritual pathway. He squinted. Something was off. Outwardly, Haylel remained an angel of light. Yet, his countenance had clearly changed. His eyes were dark. His teeth were barred. His face appeared cold and hollow.

A chill shot down Yeshua's spine. *Could it really be?* Earth's Royal Prince. Heaven's CEO. The one who controlled it all, seemed almost—*ravenous?*

Truth be known, Haylel *was* ravenous. Rabid really. The taste of Yeshua's blood was fresh on his lips and he wasn't about to stop until he'd gotten more. He laughed, long and hard. It wasn't full-fledged maniacal, but it was definitely borderline.

The gathering hordes quieted as he plucked a vial of strange, dark liquid from a rack nearby. It trembled as he held it high. "Per Elohim's request," he gloated, his tongue flickering, almost serpentine. Painstakingly, he popped the cork, going out of his way to ignore the man on the cross below. There was a peal like thunder. A murmur rippled through the hellish crowd. *What was their master doing?* Haylel beamed from ear to ear, contemplating exactly how he would play to his adoring audience. This was his show, he was the ultimate Puppet-Master, *and he loved it.*

For a moment he paused, basking in the grandeur of his own ingenious. Then, with the sort of over-the-top showmanship that only he could pull off, he slowly emptied the contents of the trembling vial.

Down, down, down ... over the hill, over the tree, over Yeshua, it flowed—thick, writhing, eager to devour everything in its path. The hordes watched, spellbound. All eyes followed its decent. It was like nothing they had ever seen. Haylel licked his lips in anticipation of the carnage to come. There was no way anyone could know—*this was the very wrath of God.*

Yeshua convulsed as the dark liquid hit. Everything about his life had been preparation for this day, yet nothing had prepared him for this moment. The horror of the experience was indescribable. It was as if a tidal wave of liquid death had come crashing down upon his soul. Ruthless, suffocating, bitterly cold, it slammed against him, shaking him to the core. Instantly, he went numb. He couldn't think. He couldn't breathe. He couldn't move. He was completely at its mercy, and it had none. Like sandpaper it grated, stripping his soul, layer by layer, desperate to infiltrate his innermost being, to hijack the very essence of who he was.

He shuddered as it clawed and squirmed, everything in him wanted to fight back. But he knew the force of the wave was too big to oppose. So instead, he fled inward, focusing on the light and life he had hidden inside.

Quietly, he let the wave run its course, crashing down around him—cold, dark, empty. He could feel its magnetic pull, dragging him back into an ocean of uncertainty. He knew how it worked: A little doubt, a little suspicion—one harmless thought—and he would be swept away, caught in an undertow of distrust, anxiety, and fear. His heart pounded. His body trembled. He fought to keep his peace. The tiniest of slips and it would be over—*everything would be lost.*

With a roar, the first wave passed. Yeshua gasped. Air never tasted so good. He looked up, watching the wave's slow retreat back into the heavens. He gulped again. He could feel new life entering his soul, power returning to his spirit. He watched as Haylel uncorked a second vial, emptying its contents directly into the first. The liquids combined and grew. Yeshua cringed, his eyes scanning the racks of vials still to come, *this was gonna be a rough ride.* He snatched another breath, bracing as wave two—new and improved—began its descent.

From noon until three, the gauntlet raged. Wave after wave, vial upon vial. Each pass growing progressively worse—pounding harder, lasting longer, driving deeper. Yeshua groaned, he was beginning to wear dangerously thin. His body had all but given up. His inner light was all but diminished. He shook uncontrollably. Like it or not, the torture was taking its toll. Even his soul was turning against him. *Curse God and die,* it moaned. *Reject mankind, save yourself—you can always start again.*

Yeshua bit his tongue, grateful it was plastered to the roof of his mouth. He shifted his weight, grateful his hands and feet were nailed down too. He couldn't afford to lose control. Not now. Not yet. The results would be nothing short of catastrophic.

He squeezed his eye shut tight, fixating on his personal light. A mere pinprick was all that remained of his once blazing inferno. *What would happen if he let it go out? Did he really want to find out?*

He braced as another wave thundered past.

In retrospect, he'd done quite well. Survival, thus far, had been extremely hard fought. Any other man would have caved long ago. That alone, spoke volumes for his character. He glanced up, his gaze drawn to the single, remaining vial. *Wha—?* He did a double-take. *One last vile? —was the end, truly in sight?*

He turned back to his speck of inner guidance. *Uh-oh,* his heart skipped a beat. He could almost hear the sound of screeching breaks. He was barely hanging on by the thinnest of threads—and there was still ... *one last vial.*

Yeshua swallowed hard, stealing another glance at the sole, remaining offender. This vial, innocent as it seemed, was no ordinary vial. This was the wrath of *all* future generations—condensed and then recondensed into a potent, tar-like sludge. Its contents alone, were more powerful than that of all the other vials *combined.*

BOOM—the realization hit him like a speeding freight train. *It was over.* His heart plummeted in his chest. *There was no way he could win.* This wasn't Moses versus Pharaoh, Joshua versus Jericho, or even David versus Goliath. This was every drop of wrath stored up against *all* of mankind *ever,* versus his one sputtering speck of inner light.

Yeshua squinted his disapproval at the vial. There it sat, like a tiny, corked, Mount Everest, looming silently in his way. This vial was nearly impossible to beat fresh, out-of-the-box ... never mind having scaled every other mountain in the Himalayas first.

His eyes dropped. His shoulders slumped. *He had come so close.* That was noble, right? ..'E' for effort? ..Anyone? ..Anyone? He wracked his spirit, *was there no way to escape the final wave?*

Silence.

..jarring silence.

"Eli, Eli, lama sabachthani?" The cry exploded from the depths of his shattered heart before he could even stop it. It thundered through the heavens, booming in a language so ancient, so rare, that only Elohim, Haylel, and the oldest of angels understood. "My god, my God," it roughly translated. "Why have you forsaken me?"

Jezebel stopped dead in her tracks when she heard the strange cry. *'Eli, Eli..?,'* She poked her head out, through Second Heaven's front door. *Was that not a delusional man's cry for Eli-jah—the dead prophet's help?* She rolled her eyes in blatant misunderstanding. *Whatever the pathetic case, it was obvious the carpenter was breaking. Hallucinations were a sure sign he was ready to talk.*

Immediately, she sent an onlooker running for something to drink, cackling as Yeshua accepted the young boy's fermented refreshment. Far be it from her, if the carpenter's voice wasn't strong enough, and his tongue loose enough, to enunciate the clearest of curses when the final wave hit.

Elohim froze when the cry reached his ears. Unlike Belle, nothing had been lost in translation, and the words tore through his soul like shrapnel. Paternal instincts erupted. He rose from his throne. It took everything he had—and the unyielding hand of Spirit—to keep him from ruining everything and saving his baby boy.

At long last, he slowly turned away.

To Haylel, the cry was almost magical. *Finally, confirmation that he was getting through!* This carpenter had been one, monumentally tough nut to crack. But joy of joys, even the uncrackable was finally beginning to break under the pressure of his relentless thumb. A savage grin exploded across his wicked face, he could barely contain himself. He felt giddy as a school girl. This moment was like winning the lottery, unwrapping Christmas, and depopulating earth by 99.6 percent all rolled into one. *Oh—* and how about this for the big, fat cherry on top? The seemingly indestructible bond between this nut and Elohim was showing strong signs of fracture as well! Haylel laughed out loud. He couldn't help himself, he could almost taste the depopulation. Stupid human, didn't he know, The Destroyer *always* won?

'*Eli, Eli..*' as soon as Yeshua heard his own words, he wanted them back. Not that they weren't true. They were. Or that they didn't need to be said. They did. In fact, they were a much needed, point-blank appeal to both Haylel and Elohim. Both of whom he had lived perfectly before, both of whom were obligated to rescue him, and both of whom were ignoring his plight. Still, this was war—and in a war, one must never show the enemy his true hand. Yeshua cringed. *What had he just done?* In one fell swoop, he had managed to expose his position, vulnerability, *and* current state of mind. *Oops—had he really just taken his first misstep?* He scrambled to gather his thoughts.

He needed an appropriate countermeasure. *Was there an appropriate countermeasure?* He could feel doubt creeping in. Why had he opened his mouth? He had all but guaranteed this wouldn't end well, and nothing had changed. All he had managed to do was level the playing field and stack the odds against *himself.*

With a sniff and a snort, he burst out laughing.

Then again … he swallowed hard, quickly forcing the sudden smile back off his war-torn face … an ill-fated ending was *exactly* what he had in mind.

Unfortunately, Haylel had been too busy being "incredibly pleased with himself" to notice his victim's odd, and somewhat revealing, expressions. And why would he? Victory was imminent.

There was only one more thing to do.

With great satisfaction, he lifted the final vial from its perch. It was surprisingly heavy. Gripping it tight, he brought it to his chest, its spinning, unbalanced weight lurching sporadically in his hand. He shook his head. *'My god, my God. Why have you forsaken me?'* the wretched translation was still ringing in his ears.

For a moment he paused, actually considering the statement. *Was this an appeal to him?* He wondered if it might not be wiser to save the last vial as insurance—should insurance be needed. Slowly he shook his head. This was a golden opportunity, *his* golden opportunity, he wouldn't get a second chance. Shame on him if he let it slip away. He popped the cork, a renewed fury washing over his soul. Besides, if the cry truly was an appeal to Heaven, *then let Elohim save him.* He glanced at his helpless prey, trembling before him like a little lost lamb at the slaughter. Pathetic. There was no way he was backing down now, this battle was only his to lose. He hoisted the vial, more certain than ever—*it was time to go for the kill.*

A deafening silence erupted as Haylel emptied the final vessel, down to the very last drop. Yeshua watched as the combining waves rocketed upwards, billowing majestically into the atmosphere. Stratosphere. *And beyond.* It was disturbingly beautiful to behold; an ocean-sized cesspool of radioactivity—glowing, climbing, swelling, swirling—racing endlessly into the heavens.

Yeshua stared, riveted by the expanded fullness of Elohim's

wrath. It was every hurt, every offense, every selfish deed ever done by all of mankind, *ever* ... past, present, and future.

It was breathtaking.

For a moment the dark wave seemed to stop, towering ominously like the calm before a storm. Then it collapsed, caving back in on itself, crumbling, tumbling, cascading its way back down to Earth, thundering towards the tiny, insignificant hill.

BOOM—the wave hit Yeshua like a tsunami, an insurmountable wall of filth and devastation.

Immediately, his light was gone. Everything went black. Blacker than black. Yeshua went reeling, head over heels, his soul completely separated from his body. He twisted frantically, searching for light—his light, any light—anything to give him a sense of his bearings.

There was nothing. Absolutely nothing.

The darkness was overwhelming.

Yeshua stifled a scream. He could feel the darkness pressing in—cold, rotten, clammy—squirming its way into his soul. Like a fungus, it permeated everything. He couldn't keep it out. Insanity gripped him. Terror overwhelmed him. He fought back, struggling with all his might. But the harder he fought, the more it consumed. Frustration sparked. Panic burned. Rage exploded. He could feel himself giving in. Soon he would come down off this tree and destroy everything he had ever loved. He couldn't stop it. He was self-destructing. It was only a matter of time.

A devilish grin hijacked his face, blood and drool spilling down his quivering chin. Everything inside screamed to let go, to curse this world which had so callously discarded him. He tugged on the nails that were holding him down. They were nothing, like mere wax beneath his fury. He could sense an odd sort of comfort in the terror. He was losing control. His mouth began to open, the darkest of all curses forming on his trembling lips. There was no stopping it now.

Slowly, he inhaled.

It would only be a moment.

Suddenly, in the midst of the chaos, something caught

Yeshua's attention. A flicker. A flash. Like a friendly little nudge. *There it was again.* A fleeting glimmer. Moving. Almost playful. Almost irreverent, considering the circumstances. *What was it?*

Yeshua spun to face the anomaly.

His jaw dropped.

There, dancing before him, twirling without a care in the world, was a light. His light. *His hope remained!*

For a moment, sanity returned. Yeshua hesitated, watching as his light approached. Casually, it drew near, slowing to a stop no more than an inch from his nose. For what seemed like ages, it hovered, patiently waiting until the surrounding pandemonium had reached its fullest. Then it dropped, like the smallest of seeds, silently into his soul.

There was a flash and a rumble as it took root, springing vibrantly to life. Yeshua's spirit trembled violently, instantly propelling him into the very future he was fighting for. It was a world free of oppression, fear, and hate. Free of corruption and lies, and the devastation that follows. A world free of torture and chaos, sedition and selfishness, of depravity and every foul thing that separates.

It was a world free of Haylel!

An elated smile exploded across Yeshua's pursed lips. *He was there! In that world! Right now!* Oh the peace, the joy, the depth of life which remained. It was staggering. Unexplainably good. Almost too good to believe. His heart pounded. Adrenaline rushed. *The mood swing had been nothing short of epic!* He wanted to laugh and cry, all at the same time. For the first time in his endless eternal existence, he was truly beginning to grasp just how wide the infinite expanse between life and death truly was. It was unexplainable. Unimaginable. Mutually exclusive. They were nothing alike. *This was life unhindered! Relationship uninhibited! On Earth, as it was originally intended!*

Then, it hit.

Ka—BOOM.

Unconditional love—exploding like a nuclear bomb. Yeshua beamed. It was captivating. Intoxicating. Astounding. Unstoppable.

Ohh—it was gooder than good!

He closed his eyes, every other emotion paling in comparison. *It was … how to describe?* Like a deep embrace, everywhere, all the time. It surrounded him. Flowed through him. Radiated out of him. In it, he felt completely secure. Completely free. Completely celebrated. Completely fearless. There was no time, no distance, no beginning or end. It was just intimacy beyond intimacy. Turbocharged existence. Unending fulfillment. Forever.

Ahhh, he breathed in deep. *It was pure ecstasy.*

Somewhere deep inside, a switch flipped. It was as if an understanding he had always known had somehow reignited. Maybe the crushing darkness had somehow pressed all the right buttons. Maybe his light was reviving his soul. Maybe he simply remembered. All he knew, was the floodlights had come roaring back on, and suddenly he understood.

It was worth it.

He looked around. What had him—only moments before—teetering on the brink of self-destructive insanity, now had him brimming with overwhelming excitement. And he knew, that he knew, that he knew: All the darkness. All the torture. All the pain. All the misunderstanding, and undeserved shame. Even drowning in this totally lame wave..

It was worth it.

He smiled, his soul once again at peace. *For the future that could be. For the family that would be.* He was all in.

And it was worth it.

"*AhhhhhuuuUGAHHHHHHHHHH—!*" the sound of his own half-formed cry snapped him back to reality. Yeshua clamped his mouth shut, hoping to avert the release. Too late. The trauma-fed curse he'd been previously preparing was somehow, still spilling out.

All of Hell watched as his cry catapulted into the air. They could sense the gravity of the situation, the carnage his cry embodied, and they loved it. It was everything they had hoped for. Eagerly, they licked their lips, waiting for the proverbial shoe to drop, waiting for the cry to detonate with nuclear proportion.

But it never did.

Instead, it began to boomerang back around. *What in the—,*

Hell stared in wide-eyed wonder. *Was this even possible?* Confusion plagued them. This man's curse wasn't aimed at the world around him. *No,* somehow it was targeting—*himself?*

Yeshua calmly raised his head to meet his cry. No longer was there an air of suffering about him, only unshakable peace. After all, this is what he had come to do. His spirit wouldn't fail him now. Unblinking, he watched as his cry barreled towards him, the smallest of smiles tugging at the corner of his lips. He leaned forward, eyes narrowed in anticipation, every fiber of his being on edge.

Ready..

Set..

BOOM—the cry slammed into his chest, his body reverberating from the impact. Yeshua winced as he felt it rip through his soul and pierce his inner man. Immediately, all defenses dropped. *Intruder alert. Intruder alert.* Security had just been breached. He closed his eyes, assessing the damages, confirming what he already knew. There was no possible way to fill in the gap.

By his own cry, he'd been hacked.

The surrounding wave rushed in. Yeshua could feel it— thick and cold—eager to destroy anything that resisted. But this time, rather than fighting the darkness, Yeshua embraced it. In a completely unanticipated, total jujutsu move, he didn't push back. He didn't wall off. He didn't walk away or try to hide his light. Instead, he simply relaxed, letting the battered door to his heart swing wide, wide open.

Like a screen door on a submarine the mighty wave rushed in, the force of its own momentum driving it relentlessly. Yeshua grimaced. He could feel everything: Every sideways glance. Every hurtful whisper. Every broken heart. Filthy thought. Unspeakable act. Depraved existence. He spared himself nothing, not even the tiniest of inconveniences—feeling, receiving, becoming *everything.* With arms wide open he welcomed the pain, taking it as if it were his very own. Ingesting it, until every ounce of wrath had been consumed.

Not a drop remained.

Back on the hill, the mystified crowd could see none of this. All they could see was Yeshua beginning to tremble. Slowly at first, then faster and faster, until he shook so violently it seemed he would be flung from his perch. Transfixed, they stood, petrified by the ghoulish clatter of bone against metal, unable to do anything but pray to the gods that this man's nails would hold.

Then, it stopped. The wind, the rain, the clatter ... everything. Only silence remained. The crowd breathed a collective sigh of relief, *their prayers seemingly answered.*

Somewhere, a pin dropped.

Somewhere else, a melody rang out.

Everyone listened, spellbound, as the Y'varech'cha *('Why-vair-ek-cha')*—the prayer of priestly blessing—drifted up from the courts of the nearby temple. The afternoon sacrifice was now underway, and the lone rabbi's Gregorian-esque chant signaled as such.

Like the crowd, Yeshua listened intently, the rabbi's haunting melody stirring his soul. He laid his head back against the tree, a peaceful smile settling across his lips. He no longer cared that every nerve in his body was screaming in pain, he was certain he had never heard anything more pleasing. He closed his eye, listening to the melodic prayer in its entirety, a silly little grin plastered across his unrecognizable face. *He had done it! The Passover sacrifice was over. This moment marked a culmination. An accomplishment. A renewal. Nothing would ever be the same!* Joy began to spark in his soul. He had just taken on the weight of the world, but to him it felt as though the weight of the world had been lifted.

Haylel stared, dumbfounded. He could hardly believe his eyes. How stupid was this nut? ..to consume the entire wrath of God? Did he seriously think that drinking poison was somehow safer than swimming in it? A sneer began to rise in his chest. No way could one man ingest an entire ocean of nuclear waste and not incur some sort of catastrophic repercussion.

..Could he? Suddenly, he wasn't so sure.

He spun around, pacing his heavenly floor. *But what would that repercussion be? And how long would it take to occur?* He wracked his brain for answers. Waiting for something—anything—to happen.

Tick-tock. Tick-tock. Tick.. he could almost hear the sound of heaven's countdown clock growing louder in his ears.

His face fell. *There was still the question of that pesky clock.* He closed his eyes, shifting his focus. There it was, plain as day, towering over eternity with less than seventy-two hours to go. *The clock,* he cringed. *Countdown to what?* A growl rumbled from his conflicted belly. *If only he'd..*

Wait a second! laughter suddenly erupted. *Did it even matter?* His eyes flew open. This nut was as good as dead. He was nailed to a tree with nowhere to go, hanging in shreds. Heaven *couldn't* take him. And Hell *wouldn't* take him. *What was he going to do in the next seventy-two hours besides ... absolutely NOTHING?!*

A monstrous grin gripped Haylel's face as he finally let go. With a ravenous howl, he threw his head back, giving himself full permission to laugh maniacally. And maniacal laugh, he did. *At long last, victory was his!* For the first time in ages, he felt like he could actually enjoy the entirety of the moment ... *his* moment. *Clock or no clock,* he smirked, *for all he cared, this nut could hang on that tree— forever.*

"*IT ... IS ... FINISHED!*"

The carpenter's cry stopped Haylel dead in his tracks. *What was this?* He was instantly sober. The authority that cry carried was unprecedented. It reminded him of an energy he'd felt once, long, long ago—*hadn't it been attached to some sort of belt?* He gasped, his breath suddenly caught in his throat. His face felt flushed. The god who always had an answer for everything, was suddenly unsure of how to respond.

With unsettling boldness, Yeshua turned to the heavens. "Pater, eis cheiras sou paratithemai to pneuma mou," he bellowed. Which, when translated, means, "Protector, Upholder, Patriarch, Founding Father ... into *your* hands, I entrust my spirit."

Then, before Hell could even bat an eye, he bowed his head— and with a most mischievous grin—gave up his ghost.

CH51: ONE-WAY TICKET TO PARADISE
0000:00:02:23:59:59

Oh, he felt good! Yeshua lifted his head and moved around.

Deep breath—*no pain!*

Full body stretch—*no pain!*

He lifted grateful hands. *No pain—anywhere!* Two loose sleeves dropped to his elbows. *And clothes?* He let out a small, celebratory, "Whoop!" *He had clothes!*

Instinctively he began straightening his duds. They were strikingly familiar, a white linen robe with a complementary gold belt. Of course they looked like they had been tie-dyed in a septic tank—and smelled even worse. But he didn't care, he was more than stoked. After all, *he was free!* He spun around, a complete 360. He couldn't help it. He was like a kid in a candy store. Everything around him was colorful and inviting—the sights, the sounds, the smells—all vying for his undivided attention. He surveyed his surroundings. Even the bleak, cloud-covered Judean landscape reverberated in a sort of high-definition technicolor.

A giddy grin shot across his face. He wanted to sing. To dance. *To bust a move! ...* BUT ... he caught himself—*not now.* He straightened up, regaining composure. There would be plenty of time for that later. Right now it was of the upmost importance that he remember: He was bodiless, hovering midair, and for all practical purposes—*deceased.*

Deceased, the unsettling thought brought him to a standstill. It seemed like such a "harsh" word ... especially considering how good he felt. In fact, he'd never felt better. He glanced down, his eyes settling on his lifeless body below. Naked, abandoned, beaten to a bloody pulp—it looked awful. He squinted. No, it looked worse than that.

A snort escaped him. Then a chuckle. He burst out laughing. He wasn't exactly sure why it was so funny. Maybe it was the absolute freedom he currently felt, or the overwhelming peace. He pawed at tear-filled eyes. Maybe it was the sudden rush that came with having actually accomplished his mission. He shrugged. Whatever the case, the peculiar disconnect between his present world and the world he had just stepped out of suddenly hit him like a fat rubber chicken ... *and it was hilarious!*

He cocked his head, *how to describe?*

It was sort of like watching a horror flick on mute. Or better yet, to a comedic soundtrack. The scene below had lost all emotional credibility. The nails, the thorns, his bitterly ravaged body. From his new perspective it was so obviously overkill, it just seemed ... silly.

Suddenly he was laughing again. He couldn't stop. His sides shook. His belly quaked. His very essence began to vibrate. Slowly, the creation around him began to respond. His energy contagious. His laughter going deep like medicine. Matter began to tremble. The earth began to shake. In the light of such life, death could no longer remain. Up, up, up, it began to rise, until the earth was literally heaving, coughing up its dead—regurgitating the bones of every ill-gotten saint it had ever swallowed.

No one on the hill fully appreciated the irony of the situation. To them, the groundbreaking perspective-shift felt less like 'tickled-pink victory' and more like 'dawn of the dead.' Overwhelmed, they scattered like rats. Toppling over one another as they frantically scrambled for cover.

SHHH-rARR! A ripping sound, like a mighty peal of thunder, reverberated across the dark hillside. A great cry arose. Inconsolable, it emanated from the temple's innermost courts. *The veil is torn! The veil is torn!* 60 feet high, 30 feet wide, 4 inches thick—the curtain isolating the Holy of Holies had just torn from top to bottom.

Impossible, came the reaction from the hill. *This was the temple's most intimate of chambers, guarded by Elohim himself. There was no way the curtain had torn—unless..* Terror flooded their fainting hearts as the realization suddenly dawned ... *surely this man WAS the*

Son of God!

The spectating hordes felt it too, the thunderous rip serving as a haunting confirmation: *They had made a mistake.* Shrieking, they fled in terror. Not one remained. Even Haylel took a step back, quietly closing Second Heaven's front door. He was more than content to watch the remainder of the scenario play out through the safety of its cosmic peephole.

Belle alone, rolled her eyes in disgust. *How short was their attention span? Had they already forgotten?* She squeezed through the shrinking portal, shaking a defiant fist at Hell's cowardly retreat. This mortal had consumed *the very wrath of God.* He was not getting off that easy. *Not on her watch!*

With a flick of her wrist she evoked Yeshua's sentence, summoning to herself the weight of the sins of the world. From the farthest corners of the globe it came, anxious to do her bidding. She cackled with delight as she indicated its final destination. No longer did it belong to all of mankind—but by the deepest laws of the universe, it now belonged to this poor, unfortunate soul.

Swwiiiiish—CLICK. CLICK. The sound of locks and chains brought Yeshua's giggle-fest to an end. He looked down, a rugged set of shackles snapping fast to his wrists. *Clink. Clink.* Links interlocked with links. *Click. Clack. Clink.* Locks attached to weights, attached to locks, attached to links.

Yeshua sighed, heavy hands dropping to his sides. Already he could feel the growing pull of his burden dragging him down. The hill was rising around him, slowly moving past. Like it or not, he knew what it meant; his time had come—*he was starting his descent.*

For a moment he gazed at what was left of the crowd. *Did they even realize, it was their burdens he carried?* He glanced heavenward, to where the protection of home awaited. A wistful smile washed over his face. Had he remained innocent, the natural buoyancy of his guiltless soul would have simply lifted him to its safety. *But instead—*, he swallowed hard, his eyes returning to the passing crowd—so fearful, so judgmental, so easily deceived. *Would they ever realize? ..he had done all of this, for them?*

Then he was gone, rocketing towards Middle Earth.

Mach one. Mach two. Mach Ten. One hundred. His weights gathered speed as miles of dirt, rock, and layered sediment streaked furiously past.

Mach seven hundred. Eight hundred. Nine.

Suddenly, he broke through the crust and out into Earth's hollow core. A blast of sweltering heat slapped him in the face. For a moment everything seemed to stand still. He glanced down. He could see the multicolored, semitranslucent glow of Paradise far below. Rainbow iridescent, shimmering bright—its unmistakable dome shone with a sort of, quiet comfort. He marveled at its beauty, completely captivated, drawn like a moth to the flame. From the look on his face, it didn't seem to matter that within seconds *he would go tearing straight through it.*

Then he was there.

SMACK—he entered the dome with a resounding thud, its thick atmosphere engulfing him like molasses. He could feel it pushing and pulling, twisting and stretching, tearing him apart. Still, his weights wouldn't be slowed. To them, it was as if the dome didn't even exist. At nearly two hundred miles a second, they shot through the atmosphere like a torpedo shooting through water—dragging their floundering prisoner along for the ride.

Far below, the citizens of Paradise began to take note. More and more eyes turned upwards as the strange phenomenon plowed across their manufactured sky. Like a meteor to Earth, it blazed. Electric yellow against a brilliant, sky blue. Glowing bright. Spewing an ever growing trail of rainbow-colored ash.

Closer.

Closer.

Ka-BOOM—the impact was deafening. A shock-wave went racing, mushroom cloud rising. Paradise rippled and shook, trembling to the core. *Its savior had finally arrived.*

For a moment Yeshua laid there, gasping for air, a thick cloud of glittering gold dust settling silently around. He fought to clear his mind, attempting to pull himself together. Slowly, he forced himself to his feet, squinting to see. The weights and chains, which had bound him, were completely gone—decimated on impact, scattered across the plains of Paradise. He massaged sore wrists, fumbling his way through the dust and debris. There wasn't a moment to lose. Already he could feel the weights calling, eager to return. It was only a matter of time until they regrouped and came looking.

"Quite the entrance!" a furry arm shot through the haze, nearly smacking him in the face. Yeshua ducked and glanced up, hoping to catch a glimpse of that familiar voice. *No such luck.* The arm retracted and fired again, this time resulting in much better placement. Yeshua reached out and took the furry lifeline. He smiled as it lifted him to safety—*cousin John!*

"Are you hurt? ..shaken? ..broken? ..in pain?" The questions flew, rapid fire, as John pulled Paradise's newest arrival up and out of the smoldering crater.

Yeshua rose from the ash like 'order from chaos.' Standing tall, he stretched—tendons realigning, bones snapping back into place.

He was perfectly backlit. Robe and hair billowing in the breeze. For a flicker of the briefest of moments, he looked like the perfectly risen Christ, rays of manufactured sunlight streaming ethereally around him; gold-dust mushroom-cloud billowing majestically overhead.

John's jaw dropped. Except for the dirt and grime—and that overwhelmingly rotten smell—Yeshua was the picture of perfection.

The dumbfounded forerunner fell to his knees. "Master," he whispered, in awe of the figure he'd just pulled from the wreckage. "Have you come to save us?"

Yeshua paused, slowly brushing himself off. *How to respond?* He glanced around. For the first time he could truly see his surroundings: The colorful fields, the towering city, the distant mountains, the gathering crowd. He shifted focus, bringing it back to the man humbling himself before him. There was a moment's hesitation as he weighed all his options. Then he just shook his head: one quick, curt little shake, '*No.*'

John chuckled at the obvious joke. This was the foretold Messiah. The son of Elohim. *The savior of the world!* Of course he was here to set the captives free ... *wasn't he?*

Yeshua's expression didn't change.

John glanced again.

Not so much as a blink.

Not a joke? John was instantly scratching his head, it didn't compute. What about the baptism? The ministry? The miracles? The virgin birth? There was no way Yeshua was serious. *Unless*—his heart began to falter—*the smoke, the smell, the soiled clothes.* His mind flew into a tail spin. *No, no, no—it couldn't be.* It just didn't make sense. He glanced over Yeshua's shoulder, across the abyss, towards the distant gates of Hell. His stomach dropped. *Everyone who ever showed up dressed like this, ultimately ended up entering..*

"Is he the One?!"

John felt a tug at his sleeve. He glanced down. A young boy, about ten, head shaved and well tanned, stood fearlessly by his side. The boy fired a wide, confident grin, eyebrows high, eagerly awaiting John's reply.

John opened his mouth. *Nothing.* All he could think was—*smoke, smell, clothes.. Smoke. Smell. Clothes..*

He turned to the crowd. They too, stood attentive, wide-eyed, awaiting his response. Beads of cold sweat erupted across his forehead. He had nothing. No confirmation. No sudden burst of faith. No reassurance from Yeshua. *What was he to say?* Hard pressed, he dug deep—speaking solely from what he had believed all of his life to be true:

"—*yes*," he forced the whisper. "*This is the savior of the world.*"

For a moment the birds chirped.

Then the crowd roared with laughter.

It wasn't in jest, or mockery, or even disbelief. It was in the simple fact that, at this moment, this man looked more like a chimney sweep.

John tried to play along. He tried to force a grin. But in the misunderstanding of the moment, he couldn't help but feel the fool.

"Wait!" a voice boomed above the fray. "Let's have a look at 'cha."

The crowd fell silent as a bull of a man stepped forward.

Pushing past John, he studied his mark, scrutinizing every detail. For a moment he puzzled, one hand stroking his well-groomed beard, the other folded securely across his broad, barreled chest.

"Indeed—," he chuckled, carefully choosing his words. "This is the Angel of the Lord who saved my son!" Abraham lifted both hands and bowed low. "My Lord."

The crowd was roaring again.

"Insufficient evidence—," a voice objected above the fray.

Again, the crowd faltered ... *Really?*

"Let a thing be established by the mouth of *two*, or three witnesses," Moses grinned, playfully raising a silencing, law-abiding hand. "After all, I *am* the only one who has seen both his face, *and* his backside." A raise of his staff parted the crowd. He circled around behind, purposefully exaggerating his analysis. Even he had to admit, he was making a bit of a show. After all, the evidence was quite conclusive. They had met at least twice before. And one of those times had been up close and transfigured.

"Savior!" he grinned, dropping the charade and throwing welcoming arms out wide.

The crowd erupted as everyone, all at once, suddenly saw the truth for themselves. The boy questioning John threw himself at Yeshua's feet. Patriarchs and kings fell to their knees. Children danced. Mothers and Fathers hugged. Daughters twirled for joy. Sons shouted with laughter. Within a matter of moments, the entire crowd was fully engaged, celebrating the arrival of their new king.

Even Thutmoses III came forward, dropping meekly before his true Master. He wore none of his previous Pharaoh trappings. Only a simple white linen garment, lined in a brilliant cobalt blue. After all, it was he—who with his dying breath—had begged for mercy from the very God he was oppressing.

He bowed low, face to the ground, hand resting on the back of his beloved, first-born son. *My, how that mercy had been granted!* He knew the death they truly deserved. *How good was this God—who saved not only his enemies, but their entire households.*

Yeshua's heart was stirred, burning as he watched the bubbling crowd. He knew each soul intimately. After all, he was the potter who had molded and shaped them, cultivating their lives relentlessly behind the scenes. To him, these were lifelong friends. But for many of them, this was the first time the veil had been lifted, and they, in turn, were only just beginning to recognize the stark reality of their newly manifested king!

Yeshua refocused on John—the voice calling in the wilderness, paving the way for it all. *What a friend. True to the end!* He laid a grateful hand on his cousin's bowed head. "Rise," he whispered, "—and prepare the way of *your* Lord.."

The familiar request shot through John like a jolt of electricity. These were the very words spoken over him as a baby. They had guided his life. Defined his destiny. Led him to his death.

His mind flashed back to his final days on Earth: Abandoned in prison. Murdered in cold blood. The unexpected betrayal had conjured some of the toughest questions of his life. Questions he still wrestled with.

He glanced up, Yeshua's words ringing in his ears like thunder. *'Prepare the way.'* A long, slow gasp escaped his lips. *How could he 'prepare the way,' unless he actually went on ahead?* He froze, taking in the sights and sounds of his new eternal family. What were the odds that he would land in Paradise mere months before the arrival of his Lord—unless his death had been carefully orchestrated and *planned to perfection!* John felt his boldness return. *He wasn't forsaken or forgotten.* He lifted his head. In fact, it was just the opposite. He had been predestined. Trusted with his calling on Earth, and in the ever-after!

A big, silly grin washed over his bushy, beaming face. *He was back!* With one word, his entire world had been righted. He climbed eagerly back into his boat. What had felt like betrayal, was now suddenly promotion. And what had seemed like abandonment, was now divine repositioning. His soul soared. *How good was his God—to time his death with such painstaking precision!*

John leapt to his feet, spinning to face the virtual 'sea of humanity' spread out before him. *It all made sense!* Each face was a unique story, testifying to the unrelenting goodness of Elohim. *And his own story was no different!* He raised both hands, life and joy exploding through every fiber of his being.

This was his family.

This was their King.

He longed to grab each by the hand and join them together as had always been intended. "The King of the Universe may be *my cousin,*" he bellowed, searching for the words. "But—he is *your brother!* All hail to the God who demanded no sacrifice, *but became the sacrifice for you!*"

The crowd exploded. Surely, their God was the God *who changes everything!*

John spun around, throwing a grateful arm around his cousin's strong shoulders. He glanced at Yeshua's soiled clothes. He wasn't one to judge—but if he was to properly prepare the way, there was still much work to be done!

Yeshua beamed at his cousin, and then at the crowd. Things were coming together! He surveyed the scene, eyes settling on a particularly tall and well bronzed young man.

"Dad!" Yeshua rushed to greet him.

The young man rose quickly to his feet, catching his son by the shoulders and pulling him close. For a long time the two embraced, tears streaming down ruddy cheeks. This was the first time Joseph had ever embraced Yeshua simply for 'who Yeshua was,' accepting his son's deity without so much as a second thought to how it affected his own reputation. It was glorious. "Go—," Joseph eventually prompted. "Do what you came to do. For indeed, you are, *the savior of the world!*"

That blessing was all it took. Yeshua stepped forward, and for the first time since his highly unorthodox arrival, directly addressed the crowd.

"Beloved," he grinned, a twinkle in his eye. "Don't move a muscle—." He paused, as if he had something profound to say. "Uhm—I'll be right back." He grinned and winked, laying a silencing finger across his lips. Then, stepping to the front of the crowd, he flickered like a match catching flame—*and was gone.*

CH52: INCIDENTAL CONTACT
0000:00:02:02:45:13

Whoa—, Yeshua did little to stifle his amazement. The gates of Hell stood towering before him. Jagged and rusty, they jutted menacingly from the smoldering landscape, stretching endlessly upward, piercing the thick layers of swirling darkness above.

Yeshua craned his neck, straining to see. *How to get inside?* The gates were securely wedged into the treacherous face of a looming, vertical cliff. There was no way over, no way around, and not so much as a doorman—much less a doorbell—to be found.

For a moment he paused, pondering his predicament. In the distance he could hear the boisterous crowds of Paradise chanting and cheering, eagerly egging him on. He cast a fleeting glance in their general direction. Pressed hard against the dome, they were peering out across the abyss, arms and voices raised. The simplicity of their enthusiasm brought a smile to his lips. So innocent. So undefiled. There was no way they truly understood the profound significance of what was about to happen.

Suddenly the earth was trembling. Yeshua dropped to a knee. There was a creak and a crack. A long, eerie groan as the gates of Hell shuddered and began to slide open. Slow and steady, they scraped their way across the barren terrain like fingernails across a chalkboard, clouds of soot and ash billowing in their ever-widening wake.

Yeshua turned to face the opening. Already, he could see the flickering flames. Feel the sweltering heat. And the stench—*oh, the stench.* He covered his mouth with a hand, fighting the urge to gag.

Then, it stopped. Except for the steady hum of churning lava, and the distant sounds of cheering, everything was quiet. *Too quiet.*

Yeshua felt his blood run cold. It was as if the gates—and all of Hell—*were expecting him.*

woosh—*Woosh*—*WOOSH,* wings flapped close overhead, beating the air impatiently. The hair on the back of Yeshua's neck skyrocketed. He could sense a dark presence moving swiftly above.

First one.

Then another ... and another.

Demons—, Yeshua froze, the wind from their wings whipping around him like the turbulence beneath a landing helicopter. Fear exploded, blanketing everything, making it difficult to move. There was an insidious roar, and a blood-curdling scream. Out of the darkness flew a badly beaten body. Smashing into the ground, it tumbled end-over-end like a helpless rag doll. Yeshua cringed. He could hear joints popping, tendons ripping, bones splintering.

Then the demons were gone.

Yeshua breathed a sigh of relief. Through the darkness, he could see the faint outline of the badly beaten body. Limp and lifeless it lay, crumpled in a broken heap.

He moved quickly to help, closing the sizable gap within moments. Already the body was struggling to stand, eager to be on its way, almost willing itself to run from the tormentors it was certain would return.

Yeshua arrived just in time for the broken body of a battered young man to fall squarely into his outstretched arms. The King of Heaven gripped him tightly, sinking to the ground. Even in the dim red light, the man's present condition was painfully obvious. Both legs were shattered. His clothes, like his flesh, hanging in tatters. Remnants of a broken noose hung from his bloodied neck, swaying like a sort of morbid necktie. Tooth and claw marks littered his swollen body. He breathed heavily, clutching his stomach, protruding entrails spilling out between hard-pressed fingers.

Despite the vulgar condition of his present state, Yeshua recognized the man immediately.

"My dearest Judas," he whispered.

Immediately, Judas went stiff, all color draining from his blood-soaked face. It was as if he'd seen a ghost. *How was this even possible?* Ravaged by demons, taken to Hell, *and now left helpless in the arms of the very man he'd destroyed?* It was his own worst nightmare. Terror consumed him. He shook uncontrollably.

"Y-Y-You—," he chattered. "W-Wa-What are you doing here?" He lifted a broken finger, shaking like a leaf. "S-Shouldn't you be up th-there?" He motioned toward the distant glow of Paradise.

Yeshua bent close, his perfect peace spilling into Judas' hollow soul. "I'm only here momentarily," he smiled reassuringly.

Judas sensed the flicker of hope. "Master," he pleaded, white-knuckling Yeshua's collar and pulling him close. "T-Take me with you!"

Gently, but firmly, Yeshua pried away bony fingers. "My friend," his heart broke. "You walked with me. Talked with me. Sat in my inner circles. Was not your window for repentance back on Earth?"

"B-But I didn't know they would kill you," Judas squealed like a trapped rat. "You're the Messiah. The chosen one." He gestured wildly to their gruesome surroundings. "H-How could I possibly know that it would come to—*this?*" He rushed to continue. "I figured we would expose their hypocrisy, play them for fools and secure a few extra bucks while you waltzed effortlessly out of their trap!" Judas paused, eyes frantically searching Yeshua's face, desperate to make a 'good 'ol boy' connection. "Besides—when I saw what they did to you, I gave the money back. *I threw it in their faces.*" He lifted the broken noose like a badge of honor. "Master, I-I took my own life for you.."

"Dearest one—do you not understand?" Yeshua quietly cut in. "If you were truly remorseful, you would not have purchased this rope. Instead, you would have pled with my Father and my friends for another chance." He gathered Judas' head in his hands. "Do you really think that murdering yourself makes up for murdering me? Does chopping down your own tree truly make up for chopping down your neighbor's?" He pulled Judas close. "In what twisted universe does matching death for death actually result in a better life for anyone?" He wracked his heart, desperate for Judas to understand. "My friend, is life not found in relationship, in pure unmanipulated heart-to-heart connection? Certainly, it has been this way since the beginning." There was a break, a troubled breath, a heavy sigh. "Death and justice are powerful equalizers, but they can never restore relationship. Should you not have approached my Father with this truth in mind? Willing to give your life *for* the relationship, instead of taking your life *from* it?" Tears began to well. "But now, Beloved—your decision has been made. Have you not chosen your own fate?"

Judas wept bitterly.

Yeshua hugged his betrayer tightly. Through his own tears, he studied the face of his former disciple, searching for even the tiniest glimmer of genuine remorse. *Nothing.* It was as if his words had sailed right over Judas' head. There was no attempt to drop the excuses or to take responsibility. No attempt to relinquish control. The disciple who often sided with Pharisees, skimmed the company pocketbook, and regularly seated himself at the head of the table was still attempting to manipulate his own destiny. Yeshua's heart ached. Judas was so completely self-absorbed, that even with his head resting in the lap of the one who still had the power to save him, he couldn't—no, he wouldn't—bring himself to lift so much as one sincerely repentant finger.

For a long time the two men wept. Judas loathing the fact that Yeshua seemed completely unwilling to rescue him. Yeshua desperate for Judas to reach out and simply take hold of the life-line he was offering. But reconciliation, it seemed, just wasn't in the books. Slowly, Yeshua's heart sank. As long as Judas continued to play the victim, there was nothing more he could do. Big tears began to fall, spilling down his face and over the shell of the man he so longed to call, "Friend." Even as those tears landed, they loosed new life—mending bones, cleaning cuts, healing bruises—yet strangely they remained powerless to penetrate the hardness of Judas' self-absorbed soul.

Then it was time to go.

Yeshua rose to his feet. Lovingly, he lifted the noose from his betrayer's neck, tenderly kissing his rejuvenated cheeks. Judas rose as well—physically whole, yet spiritually bankrupt. For a moment, he clung to the man he had once called, 'Master,' reluctant to let the moment fade. But procrastination, he knew, would only delay the inevitable. And so, at last, he turned—and straightening his clothes as if nothing was amiss—walked slowly into the raging fires of Hell.

Yeshua turned to watch him go, patiently waiting until he had fully disappeared. Then, with a salute to his Paradise crowd, and the broken noose still in hand, he stepped forward, eager to make his own entrance through the dark, yawning gates.

WHAP—he was hit hard from behind.

Wha—? Yeshua crashed to the ground. Face first. Noose flying. Spitting out dirt, rocks, and blood.

Whap. Whap-whap. Whap.

More hits sent him tumbling helplessly out of control. He fought to regain composure, struggling to rise, but there was an all-too-familiar weight pressing him down.

Click. Clink. Chains slid tight around his neck.

Clink. Click. Shackles snapped around his ankles and wrists.

Yeshua strained to lift his head. *Click. Clack. Clink.* Links twisted menacingly around him, pulling and squeezing, binding his entire being. A slow sigh eeked from his lungs. He glanced down, chains sliding and constricting. *His weights were back—and they were tighter than ever.*

Whir. Swish. Thump—THUD.

What was that? Loud. Behind him. Like drunk buzzards landing. Strange and curious sounds.

Two shadowy figures approached. Arguing. Jeering. Pointing.

Yeshua stirred. Armed with a grin and a kind word, he opened his mouth.

One reared back.

WHAM—everything went black.

CH53: SHOWDOWN AT SUNSET
0000:00:00:22:48:05

"Elohim's son? ..helpless in the hands of the Hidden One?" the rumor spread like wildfire across the infinite expanse of Heaven. It was polarizing. Some called it, 'gospel truth.' Others swore it was, 'fake news.' There seemed no end to the stir it created. All of Heaven was abuzz. It was sorta like trying to understand the thought process behind Uncle Jim's Christmas sweater collection. Things were either going brilliantly right or horribly wrong. No one knew for sure. Still, somewhere amidst the growing confusion, a new voice began to rise. "It's the dawning of a new order," it boasted. "Don't be left out. Showdown starts at sunset. Come, see for yourself who Earth's rightful heir will be."

Michael, the archangel, was exiting the throne room when he heard the news.

"Planning to attend?" two underlings chattered excitedly. "It's certain to be a showdown for the ages."

Michael shook his head. "It's a trap," he replied, matter-of-fact.

Their faces fell. "Maybe—," they paused, listening intently to an internal narrative update. "Or maybe, it's a new era? A chance to be forever free? A ticket to permanent notoriety?!" They were snickering again.

Michael overlooked the twisted response, openly frowning his disapproval.

"O-Of course—*if* we go—we'll stick to the fringes," they quickly back-tracked.

"We'll hide out."

"Keep our distance."

"Until we know exactly what's going on," they nodded responsibly.

"—if we go.."

'If we go?' Michael could hardly believe his ears. *How could they even consider such an infidelity?* He shook his head. Clearly these two were intoxicated by the grandeur of their own delusions. "Don't fall for it!" he implored. "You have no idea what you're in for. Don't you remember what happened to those rebellious ambassadors of old? Or the judgments that were levied on their offspring?"

"You mean the judgments levied by a God not 'god-enough' to keep his own son alive?"

"..who spends the majority of his time literally bottling his own anger?"

"..who practically believes anything he's told?"

"Enough—!" Michael silenced them. "My allegiance lies with Elohim, and Elohim alone." His voice was stern. "Say what you like, but there's no way I would ever attend such a treasonous affair." He looked at their incredulous faces. "And I advise—with every ounce of persuasion I can muster—that you do the same."

"Oh—uh, yes of course!" they assured. "We wouldn't dream of it.."

But the lure of a lottery-ticket, easy-street life, was too hard to ignore. How could they—in good conscience—pass up such a golden opportunity? This was their chance. Their shortcut to the top. Why should they heed the 'prudish' words of an 'out of touch' archangel already seated in high places? Didn't he have some sort of vested interest in keeping himself there?

Disheartened, Michael turned away. He could read the looks on their faces. His words had made little difference. They were bewitched. Transfixed. Overwhelmed by the allure of forbidden fruit. Soon their work here would be done. Soon they would be on their way. Soon they would be standing, front and center, at the very place they had promised not to go. Michael heaved a heavy sigh. Soon they would be in for the shock of their lives.

—| 0000:00:00:00:44:44 |—

Bzt. ZZ-Zzzzzz, the sound of electric shears jolted Yeshua awake. His eyes fluttered open as several long locks of thick dark hair drifted lazily past his nose. He stared blankly, watching them fall some fifteen feet to the smoldering ground below. Groggy, he shook his head, his tunnel vision widening. *Wait a minute,* it slowly dawned. *Wasn't that his hair?!* Instinctively, he reached for his head. His arm wouldn't budge. *What—?* He shifted his weight. *Neither would his legs!* He glanced down. Heavy chains, locked in place, were wrapped tightly around his body. He squinted. Focusing. Confused. The chains seemed to be threaded through the wounds in his hands and feet, hanging down through the ground, and resting in the heart of the earth. He took a deep breath, choking on toxic air. Suddenly it was all rushing back—the tree, the weights, the fist, the gates … that air—*he knew exactly where he was:*

He was back on a cross..

Smack dab, *in the center of Hell.*

For a moment he paused, eyes growing fully accustomed to the surrounding darkness. Best he could tell, he was perched in the middle of a hard-packed, barren wasteland, baked red clay and dried men's bones sprawling as far as he could see. In the distance, a towering, horseshoe shaped plateau stretched nearly 360 degrees around the wasteland's perimeter. A river of molten lava flowed lazily along the inside edge, along both sides of the plateau's base. He craned his neck, straining to look around. Directly in front of him, maybe a mile ahead, stood the now opened gates. In the distance behind, a mile-high lavafalls. Above him to the right, the newly renovated grotto. Over his shoulder to the left, the infamous count-down clock—now dangerously close to zero.

Something flickered, white along the horizon, falling like the occasional snowflake. *Snow?! Not snow—,* Yeshua furrowed his brow. *Souls! Those 'snowflakes' were souls.*

He watched as one tumbled aimlessly to the red-hot floor below, propelled solely by the weight of its own sin. For a moment it just lay there, unattended and alone until—*pop*—it burst into flames.

Yeshua shifted uncomfortably, deeply moved. It wasn't so much the spontaneous combustion that tore at his heartstrings as the hopeless wail which followed. No wonder Hell employed Collection Teams, working 'round the clock to keep the grounds free of such—oh, how did they put it— 'unpalatable debris,' gathering the writhing remains in large bins and tossing them into the fiery rivers where they belonged.

CLICK—powerful lights suddenly illuminated the dark valley. *What—?* Yeshua's jaw dropped. *How had he missed that?* Throngs of anxious spectators were already packing the hard, parched plains. He gaped, in awe. Beneath the sound of the buzzing shears he could hear them, murmuring and mingling, eagerly waiting for the show to begin.

The show. Yeshua squeezed his eyes shut tight. He could feel the energy of a thousand lightbulbs beating down upon him, blazing from the grotto above. Slowly, he looked up, squinting into their overwhelming brilliance. Dark figures moved among the beams. A beast. A witch. A warlock. The unmistakable silhouette of Ha-satan. Yeshua studied them all. They seemed entirely focused on the action below. Watching. Waiting. Wondering.

Then, the clippers stopped.

CRASH—their owner sent them clattering across the hard-packed ground, squealing as he too, scurried into the shadows.

In the distance was a '*pop.*'

Another hopeless scream.

Yeshua scanned the crowd. Something was coming—an angel, head and shoulders above the rest, making his way slowly towards the makeshift cross. Yeshua watched, tracking with him as he pushed his way through the sea of gawking spectators. He was solid. Well built. Clean shaven from head to toe. Wire-brushed armor—loosely resembling football pads—adorned his muscular frame. A loincloth clung to his waist. His skin, semi-transparent, boasted 3D holographic art, spinning ever so slowly within the exposed portions of his body. Self-adoring tattoos, like graffiti, tagged every square inch of his armor. He had no eyes, only a crude metal visor with vertical welder's slats embedded into his skull, and many of his countless body piercings dripped with the ink—not blood—that flowed through his veins.

Yeshua smiled, he knew this angel well. Sehret, meaning 'marked,' had been created specifically to populate the books of Heaven. Most specifically, the *Book of Life.* Keeping "The Book," as Sehret called it, was a job he had originally taken great pride in. But as the years toiled on, and his frustration with mankind grew, he too had succumbed to the grandeur of his own abilities, joining Ha-satan in using his powers to secretly do as *he* saw fit—labeling, controlling, and destroying anyone foolish enough to linger in the center of his, or Ha-satan's, crosshairs for too long.

"Look what the cat drug in," Sehret snorted, coming to a stop at the foot of the cross. Muscles rippled beneath clanging armor as he plunged the body-length, titanium torch he often carried deep into the petrified ground. "What should we label you?" he growled, reaching across his chest and removing the rather large, rather barbaric-looking tattoo gun he kept tucked away beneath his left shoulder plate. "..Son of satan? ..King of nobody? ..Royal pain in the ash?" He threw his head back and laughed a loud chainsaw of a laugh. No, those were all too simplistic, too prepubescent. He glanced to the overlooking grotto. *Did not his Dark Lord deserve a more formidable foe?* He paused, dipping his gun into several of the multiple ink streams flowing freely down his body.

How about, 'King of kings, Lord of lords?' The carpenter's own words suddenly sprang to mind.

Sehret raised an eyebrow, intrigued. *That certainly made for a worthy opponent,* he mused. Besides, was there anything more shameful than the irony of being 'irrevocably damned by one's *own* self-inflated labels?' He sank to a knee, placing the tip of his well-inked gun against the top of Yeshua's thigh. A sarcastic chuckle bubbled up, slowly crescendoing into full fledged laughter. *Yes,* it was settled, he would let the carpenter's *own* words do the damning. He flipped open a switch, fired up his gun, and pressed down hard.

Hiss. Click. POP. The grotto lights flickered and went out—plunging the entire assembly into darkness.

Sehret paused, glancing around for the 'center-stage

entrance' he was certain would follow.

Nothing.

No matter—, he shrugged, redipping his gun. *He'd worked by the light of his torch before.* There was a click, a breath and a pause, then the whir of spinning needles as he returned diligently to his work.

Kick. Snare … Kick. Kick. Snare—a deafening beat ripped across the hellish valley. Bullets and bombs, sirens and screams riddled the stagnant air. A violent melody began to arise. Something thundered overhead. Savage and circling—it rumbled like the lumbering engine of a mighty freight train, stirring up fear, applause and dust.

The crowd erupted, their excitement electric. This was exactly what they had been waiting for.

It was showtime!

WHAM—out of the chaos, Ha-satan dropped, slamming into the ground with bowel-loosing force. His disguise, custom tailored for the occasion, was lined with nanotech optics—all glowing and growing, moving and morphing—animating in perfect time to the music. Ha-satan was moving and morphing too. Each choreographed step more impressive than the last. Each metamorphosis more monstrous.

The crowd ate it up. Insidious. Amazed. Fearsome. Engaged. They couldn't get enough. From lethal start to wicked end, it was wildly entertaining.

Then it was over: The wind. The effects. The music. The show. It all stopped. Only Ha-satan remained—towering above Yeshua, a great and mighty dragon.

CLICK—a single spotlight illuminated the scene.

The crowd inhaled—waiting, bated breath.

Yeshua exhaled—entirely unimpressed.

The clock ticked on, only minutes to go.

Sehret finished his task, grabbing his torch and exiting the show.

Slowly Ha-satan bent—down, down, down—until predator and prey were literally pressing head to head. Yeshua could feel his skull cracking beneath the force of Ha-satan's unforgiving snout. Undaunted, he stared through the illusion, watching the glowing optics of Ha-satan's mask deep within the dragon's being. It was still blinking—flipping from image to demonic image. A chill shot down his spine. He could sense the intensity of Ha-satan's spirit: The power. The darkness. The envy. The hate. To his very core, he was deeply depraved.

"Son of Man," Ha-satan whispered into the uneasy silence. "Why should we fight? Your earthen vessel is well embalmed. Your flesh, still fresh in the ground. Let me resubstantiate you. Pluck you from this rusty pike. Eradicate your bondage. Give you back your former life." He pulled back, ever so slightly. "I will grant you instant fame. Credibility. Success. Give you a hundred times recompense." He laid it on thick, extending Hell's personal olive branch, making Yeshua an offer he couldn't refuse. "I will make you invincible. Immortal. A god among men. Give you charge over every nation. Every government. Every part of my Earth.." For a moment Ha-satan hesitated, eyeing the clock, allowing the temptation to settle.

Then he pulled the trigger.

"All this, I will do," he purred, Yeshua's chains suddenly loosening like magic. "If you will simply drop to your knees, and worship me as the God you already know me to be."

KA-CLACK—right on time, and with a bit of a whine, the massive combination clock rolled—like a big, fat exclamation point—to all zeros.

Everything stopped.

All of Hell waited.

Even Ha-satan hesitated.

Slowly, Yeshua leaned forward. "Tell me," he quietly demanded. "What right have you to hold me? Who has given you permission?" He glanced around, as if looking for someone. "Are you the Creator? The Designer? The Owner or Architect? Are you the Source? The Life? The Author of all of this?" He took a deep breath. "Perhaps I was absent the day you were granted supreme authority. Or perhaps, I didn't get the memo." Sarcasm rolled like butter off his tongue, cutting long and deep. " Let me go," he commanded. "And I will beg for your forgiveness before my Father. Hold me any longer," he leaned in further, pushing back with all his might. "And all you have—*will be given to me.*"

RoahhhhoarRRRRRR—, Ha-satan recoiled as if Yeshua's words had literally stung. Rocketing skyward, he flipped around backwards, hovering mid-air, wings beating furiously against the swirling, charcoal sky.

"*YOU ARROGANT, INCOMPETANT CUSS,*" he roared. "Free yourself. *I dare you—!* Call down for yourself whatever you want. Twelve legions of angels. A bus full of Oompa-Loompas. Your Daddy God, himself!" Fire flickered from trembling lips. "*Go ahead! Save yourself!* Or was that late-night, garden-exaggeration just another part of the act? You piece of trash. How dare you question my right. *I have every right!*" he snapped. "The entire earth is *mine*. It was given to *me. And I do with it, as I please!*" He spit venomously in Yeshua's face, sulfur mixed with acid. Smoke billowed from his flaring nostrils. With a mighty cry he came crashing to the ground, dust and debris flying.

"Where were *you* when I directed the creation of the heavens?" he bellowed. "When I inhabited the all-consuming fires of Elohim?"

Yeshua held his tongue.

"Where were you when I was given charge over all of mankind? ..Or when I *took* charge over all the earth?"

Yeshua didn't speak.

"Did you chisel the laws of Moses out of stone? Or collect the firstborn sons of Egypt? Did you flood the earth with waters from the deep? Or preside over The Assembly of the Almighty?" Ha-satan lunged forward, instantly himself again. "You *MAGGOT—,*" he raged, "you were placed at *my* door. Set before *my* feet. *I* set the weight of the world upon you." He turned to Yeshua, palming his face forcefully. "*I* am your judge and jury down here. Your executioner. Your *only* hope." Trembling violently, he slammed Yeshua's head back against the jagged, iron cross. "Say one word, that without my personal acquittal, would vindicate you in the slightest. One word, that could even begin to set you free—."

Yeshua paused, waiting for his head to stop reeling. Slowly, he raised both eyes, gazing deep into the Underlord's dark, murky soul. The corners of his mouth inched upward, forming the tiniest of mischievous grins.

Poor devil ... just because he said nothing, didn't mean he had nothing to say.

Ha-satan seethed. *That kamikaze confidence. That air of superiority. That revoltingly sloppy grin. THIS WASN'T A BLEEPING GAME.* He barred his teeth, snarling like a guttural beast. *Enough was enough.* It was time to pop this mortal's bubble once and for all.

"YOU WRETCH," he thundered. "You feckless piece of filth. Look around you. *Who do you think owns your soul?* You sack of excrement and bone. It's over. *Day three is done.* The clock has stopped ticking. No one is coming. *You belong to ME now!"* He was pacing. Processing. Stewing. "Do you really think Elohim will come to your rescue?" he spun on a dime. "*YOU FOOL.* You're in *MY* world. *I* run this show. *I* call the shots. Your time is up. Your destiny is bankrupt. Your inheritance HAS just been forfeited ... *to ME!"*

Thunder erupted all around, tremors shaking the death engorged ground. *This was personal.* The Lord of the Flies raged. He could feel himself slipping past offense and giving into ego—sweet, bitter, indulgent, *EGO.*

Then he was gone.

"You *WORM—,"* he shrieked. "*I* will ascend to the heavens above the heights of the clouds. *I* will sit on the mount of The Assembly on the farthest sides of the north. *My* throne will be exalted above the stars of God. *My* footstool will be the earth below," he whipped around, arms raised, pandering to the crowd. "*I will BE LIKE the Most High!"*

The crowd roared.

Ha-satan fist-pumped the air. *"I will BECOME the Most High!"*

The crowd roared again.

"I will BE the Most High!"

The crowd came unglued.

For a moment Yeshua just watched, absorbing the glee-filled pandemonium with a sort of nostalgic regret. Then—when he'd seen enough—he dropped his head, whispered a prayer, and began to make his move.

Had Ha-satan paid even half as much attention to Yeshua as his own, self-aggrandizing, narcissistic rage, he would have noticed a particular ember—bigger and brighter than the others—falling, fluttering, alighting—almost like a dove—upon the head of Yeshua. He would have noticed Yeshua's countenance beginning to change: His muscles strengthening. His aura brightening. A spark returning to his eye. He would have noticed the ground beginning to tremble. Chains beginning to bulge. And the cross beginning to torque and bend. Yes, had he paid even half as much attention, he would have noticed all of these things *BEFORE* it was too late.

CREAAAAAK—the countdown clock suddenly rumbled back to life. Wide-eyed. Confused. The crowd turned with a start.

Heaven's clock was moving again?

Unfathomable.

One. Two. Three. Four.. The count-down clock was no longer counting down—it was beginning to count ... *up?*

"Look—," a raspy voice screamed above the commotion. "I-It ... MOVES!"

Confusion turned to chaos as Hell's collective attention swung back to the peculiar figure on the cross. Like the clock, Yeshua too, was moving. Head down, eyes closed, he was straining at his chains, sweat dripping from his brow. He should have been spent, but he felt electric—as if the blood in his veins had been replaced by the supercharged Power of Elohim, himself. He flexed, muscles bulging, Spirit all over him. He could feel a shift taking place, power flowing to him, draining from the crowd. His chains bent mercilessly beneath the strain of the strange new force, whining and creaking like a ship caught in a storm.

Bewildered, the crowd just stared, frozen in place.

Tick.

Tick.

Tick.

KA-BOOOM—Yeshua exploded from the rust-covered cross, his chains shattering and falling away like dust. A shockwave of light erupted from his innermost being, radiating across the plane—burning, melting, marking everything it touched.

All hell broke loose—every demon, angel, overlord and underling desperately attempting to make their escape. But it was too late. For a moment, the entire valley lit up like the sun. Boulders crumbled from surrounding cliffs. Lava rocketed into the air. The recently renovated grotto exploding into a billion shards of molten iron and glass.

The crowd fell, toppling like dominoes beneath the force of the blast.

The earth shook.

The gates rattled.

The clock came unhinged.

WHAM—Yeshua landed with a resounding thud, dust jetting up around him, miles into the listless air. Slowly he stood, his body blazing a piercing golden blue-white, clothed in the energy of a brand new light. His tattoo, now suddenly alive, rotated in ferocious technicolor. Holy fire raged within his eyes. Passion surged within his being. He breathed in deep—the oceans of ingested wrath poured out from his Father ironically fueling his new, unquenchable flame.

Throwing his head back, he roared like a lion. Shards of blazing light exploding from his core.

All of Hell quaked, terror rippling through the crowd.

Yeshua spun around, heading back towards the iron cross now some five hundred feet away. The ground shuddered beneath his feet, trembling under the magnitude of his resurgent weight. He accelerated to an all-out run, passing quickly through the crowd. Blood dripped freely from his hands and feet, hissing like acid across the molten floor, giving life to everything it touched. Heaven's Champion didn't seem to notice. He was completely focused. There was only one thing on his mind. One target in his sights.

Ha-satan pushed himself to his feet, forcing septic air into stubbornly resistant lungs. He twisted his helmet—40, 90, 180 degrees—scrambling to reconnect the wires. His fingers felt fat and lethargic. His body felt numb. He shook himself, fighting for clarity. Like the crowd, he was still reeling from ... whatever-it-was that had just steamrolled him.

One final adjustment..

..and—Done.

His vision cleared. His breathing stabilized. *What the—,* he glanced at the empty cross. *Where could the carpenter be?* He spun around, scanning the crowd. *There*—the bonfire with legs— impossible to miss—*running right at ... him?* Ha-satan furrowed his brow, the sudden realization colliding full force with the unusual terror that was gripping his soul. "*No, no, NO*—stop him," Ha-satan gasped, choking down a gulp of freshly filtered air. "*STOP HIM!*"

The order thundered across the lethargic plain, instantly rousing the toppled crowd back into action.

Yeshua skidded to a halt, his path suddenly blocked by a sea of limping, melting, nothing-left-to-lose traitors.

"W-Who are you?" that all-too-familiar, rasp-of-a-voice screeched.

Yeshua grinned through gritted teeth. "I AM," he began, picking up speed, racing towards an exceptionally large pair of melted, mangled demonic contenders.

He lifted both hands, lightning flickering from the words on his lips, manifesting as a midsized saber in each.

The demons couldn't move fast enough.

CLANG. Yeshua darted between them, thrusting his blades simultaneously through each devil's belly, pulling up and back as he hoisted his victims effortlessly into the air.

They squealed like stuck pigs, clawing desperately at the unwelcome intruders. *Too late.* They exploded, dissipating like dust across the universe, turning back into the quantum soup from which they came—a murky trail of ink-like energy, all that remained.

Yeshua nodded his condolences, already moving on. His blades raced back down, criss-crossing through the center of his next combatant's quivering chest.

POP. Fizzle—Yeshua burst through the watery remains.

Another stride and he swung up, scissor-slicing the next devil just above the torso and just below the head, instantly separating the two.

POOF—the hellion was gone.
Giant to his right?
Gone.
Ogre to his left?
Gone.
Trio of demons blocking his path?
Gone.
Gone.
And … gone.
Yeshua drop-slid beneath their rancid trails of swirling dark matter. *No worries,* he grinned, *these beings weren't dead—*at least, not for long—*it would only be the matter of a few short centuries before each particle had pieced itself back together … almost good as new.*

Popping up, he skidded to a stop, surveying the crowd of troublemakers before him. He lifted both sabers, his natural follow-through piercing the skulls of two dark figures racing up behind. He waited for the *'pop, fizzle'* and *'pop,'* before flicking his wrists forward, and sending his sabers airborne. Rows of opposition dropped like flies, vaporizing before the spinning blades.

For the briefest of moments, Yeshua's heart welled, a sudden flash of sorrow assaulting his soul. There was no sugar coating it, his resurgence had maimed and marked a third of Heaven's best and brightest, *permanently.*

Still—this was war, and they had chosen their fate. That mark was a necessary transgression if all 'plausible deniability' was to be removed in the Courts of Heaven.

He dodged a fist.
A chain.
A wooden spoon?
"THE—," his voice thundered again, still responding to Hell's original question. He lifted a hand, his word manifesting as an exquisitely ornate, body length, broadsword.

Yeshua grinned, *right on time!*

He snatched the weapon from the air in front of him, gripping it tightly and wielding it expertly above his head.

Spin, step.

Spin, step.

POW. Fizzle. POP.

Spin, step.

Spin, step.

He watched his enemies drop.

Spin, step.

Spin, step.

He was moving on. Nearly to his target now.

"*—I AM,*" his final words thundered across the plain.

Yeshua paused, waiting for the words to manifest—two small, curved blades—wrapped neatly, like brass knuckles, around his already closed fists.

Don't need this, he grinned, punching up on the handle of his broadsword. It beeped and blinked, activating for self-destruction. Yeshua spun one last time, hurling the weapon like a helicopter blade gone rogue. It sailed through the air, devastating the opposition, mowing them down like weeds in a blender.

Yeshua didn't miss a beat. He fell into step close behind, slicing and dicing, eliminating all stray opposition as he closed the remaining gap between predator and prey.

Ha-satan stood trembling, watching the spinning blade and the blazing golden-blue light barreling toward him. He wanted to move. He wanted to fight. To summon his 'mighty inner dragon' and initiate the epic battle he was certain would take place. His mind raced. He thought of a thousand ways to defeat his adversary. Ten thousand ways to bring this carpenter to his knees. But it was as if he had lost all power to respond. Something was holding him back, holding him in place, literally. He struggled against it, willing it to back down. *No use,* all motor ability had been removed. Panic erupted. His knees went weak. He felt like giving up. For the first time ever, Ha-satan was completely..

BOOM—the sword detonated inches from his face, liquid napalm spewing in every direction. Ha-satan flinched, bracing against the explosion and then the inferno that raged—hotter than hot. *What was this?* He could feel himself melting, his essence devolving, dissipating back into the corners of the universe.

There was a hiss.

A crackle.

The smell of decay.

Ha-satan gasped, struggling to hold himself together. His world began to fade. He was beginning to separate.

Soon it would be too late.

WOOSH—strong hands shot fearlessly through the flames. Ha-satan could feel them gathering up either side of his cloak. *Rrrrrip*—they yanked him like a stale bandage from where he stood, rescuing him to meet a fate … *worse than death?*

Ha-satan blanched, all color draining from his already pale face. He could feel that same Power—the Power that had been holding him in place—only it was a hundredfold now. Surrounding him. Crushing him. Pinning him. Coursing through his being. He swallowed hard, struggling for air. With all his might he cracked an eyelid. Then two. *Curses. He knew it,* heavy eyes snapped shut. *He was stuck. Held firmly in the embrace of the man he hated most.* He went rigid. Livid. Reeling. *How had this happened?* He wanted to look again, to confirm the impossibility … but there was no need to waste the effort. He knew it. Everyone knew it.

The carpenter had arrived.

"To what do I owe the distinct displeasure—," Ha-satan opened his lips to speak, eager to manufacture his own escape.

But *nothing. Not a sound came out.*

He tried again.

Not so much as a whisper.

He licked dry lips, tongue heavy as lead. *What was this?* His mind went blank. The god who always knew what to say, was suddenly rendered … *speechless?*

Then it was Yeshua's turn. He pulled his adversary close, the all-revealing light of his aura washing over them both, drowning out the surrounding inferno. He leaned in, eager to reveal who was hidden behind the mask. Slowly, the mask began to fade.

A face took shape.

..Haylel?

No—it couldn't be! The crowd began to stir. *That was Elohim's right-hand man. Heaven's second-in-command. Mr. C.E.O. himself.*

Murmurs rose. Even in this light, the troublemaker was stunning. The beauty of his face marred only by the hideous expression which clung to it—*he was busted and everyone knew it.*

Yeshua leaned closer, pushing past looks, past outward appearances, allowing his light to do a deeper, more extensive work—revealing not what '*seemed to be,*' but what '*actually was;*' revealing how things looked through the lens of Haylel's *own* darkened heart.

A gasp escaped the crowd as beauty and perfection faded away, revealing the rotten remains of a festering, blistering skull—chipped, broken, and diseased. Stiff and scared, it stared, wide eyes shifting uncomfortably in their sunken, hollow sockets.

Haylel let out a dead man's cry, the ever-exposing light striking terror to his core. *What had he done? Had he really killed the son of God?* His jaw dropped just long enough for a familiar red serpent to exit, creep up around his skull, and disappear back inside, behind his right eye.

The crowd watched in stunned disbelief.

Yeshua breathed a sigh of relief, Hell had been exposed. No need for idle chatter, grandiose arguments, or further confrontation. There was only one thing left to do.

He tightened his grip, pressing his head hard against Haylel's helmet. With everything he had, he whispered one little word.

"..boo."

Whoosh—in that *INSTANT*—Haylel was gone, bolting for the nearest exit. *No need to stay, he could return to fight another day.* Right now, all he wanted to do was ... *RUN.*

He spun around, already mid step, time standing still. His signature dreads whipped around behind him, stretching out long, parallel to the horizon.

Yeshua didn't budge. He simply waited, watching his nemesis move. At the last possible second, the resurrected son of the Most High God swung his arm out wide, windmilling around those lingering extensions. Quick as a flash, he snapped his arm down.

SWISH—up in the air, went Haylel's body.

SWOOSH—out in the air, went Haylel's feet.

For a moment he hovered, completely horizontal, the keys on his lapel rising slowly in their moment of zero gravity.

With a grin and a flurry, and a little bit of flair—Yeshua dropped to one knee, head down, fist to the ground.

CRACK—went Haylel's neck.

CRUNCH—went his listless body, slamming hard against the well-packed earth.

Something glinted in the air, hovering a split second longer. Three keys: *Death, Hell,* and *The Grave*—spinning ever so slowly, suspended for all to see.

Yeshua thrust out a hand, snatching his prize mid-flight. The chain binding them to Haylel's lapel exploded—vaporizing on impact—clouds of twinkling, metallic dust falling slowly over their former owner's limp, lifeless body.

A roar erupted in the distance.

Yeshua looked up, almost startled. *Paradise?* In the midst of battle he'd completely forgotten—*Paradise was still watching!* A huge grin flooded his face. He raised his fist, keys in hand, acknowledging their praise.

The roar grew louder.

Then, louder.

Suddenly, it was thundering, quaking, exploding all around.

Yeshua craned his neck, hoping to catch a glimpse.

The clouds rolled back.

The skies divided.

Lightning scorched the barren ground.

Yeshua leapt to his feet. Above him. Behind him. Beside him. Below him. Heaven was bending down. His heart surged. He laughed out loud. Streaming through portals. Breaking through clouds. Rising from the steam and the dust. The Hosts of Heaven were flooding Hell with light, life, and *a spectacular war cry!* Yeshua too lifted his voice, joining the insertion with a cry all his own.

His Daddy had finally arrived!

Hell, on the other hand, wasn't nearly so thrilled. In fact, they were already scattered and gone. Tumbling down cliffs. Diving beneath rocks. Racing up vertical walls. There was no plan B. No measured counter-attack. Their goal was simply *to not get caught.*

Heaven followed in hot pursuit, rounding up traitors by the thousands. Little mind was paid to those who did escape. After all, Hell could run, but it could never hide. It had been permanently marked, it was only a matter of time.

"Take charge—," Yeshua motioned to the Captain of Hosts, handing Michael his captive's long dreads.

"With pleasure," the massive angel grinned, gripping them tight and stepping aside to let his commander pass by.

Yeshua reached up, giving the angel's shoulder a hearty, 'attaboy' squeeze.

Power arched between them.

Michael dropped to a knee, energy running wild down his spine. He fought to maintain consciousness, struggling to balance until the touch had done its full work.

When he did eventually rise, he could scarcely believe his eyes. It wasn't just an upgrade, it was an entire redo. He flexed new muscles and wings. Admired new weapons and armor. He couldn't wait for the soonest opportunity to test them out! Ablaze with life, he turned to thank his fearless leader—Heaven's newest C.E.O. But it was too late, the Son of Man who had just defeated Death had already disappeared.

CH54: JAILBREAK
0000:00:00:03:11:03 AD

WHAM—Ancephaneese (*'Ann-sef-n-ease'*) hit the ground like a speeding locomotive; so hard, he could feel the dirt give way around him. Instinctively, he winced. It should have felt like a solid brick wall, but strangely it felt more like feather pillows on a comfy water bed. For a long time he just laid there, looking up at the sky, watching his trail of smoke and multicolored dust slowly disappear. *The impact should have shattered every bone,* he felt gingerly down his body. *Yet it hadn't even left him winded.*

Slowly he stood, amazed. *What great fortune,* he chuckled, stepping out of his body-shaped crater and scratching his still smoldering head. One minute ago he was nailed to a cross, writhing in pain. *Now he was in..* He looked around—lush green grass, tropical winds, radiant sunlight—this couldn't be anything less than *... Paradise?* His heart skipped a beat. *He'd made it? He'd actually made it?!* He threw both hands in the air and spun around, his feet performing a jig. He chuckled, he couldn't help himself. *A thief in Paradise! Who would believe it?!*

But—, he slowed to a stop, suddenly aware of how very quiet and empty it seemed, *if this was Paradise ... where were the people?* He scanned the surrounding plains, the distant mountains, the nearby city.

Nothing. Nobody.

He clambered up a nearby hill.

No one. Nada.

His stomach sank. *Maybe this wasn't—*

Wait—in the distance. *What was that?!* A noise caught his ear.

Over a ledge.

Down a ravine.

He was running, moving fast.

Across a gorge.

Through a crop of trees.

He skidded to a stop atop a yawning bluff. *There, below—an ocean of people!* Relief washed over him. *He was not alone!*

Scrambling, he slid to the valley below, running to join them, making his way through the crowd. *What was happening? Why the gathering? Was this normal Paradise etiquette?* He was so full of questions, eager to engage, yet the crowd seemed strangely preoccupied, almost distant.

Ancephaneese followed their gaze.

They seemed focused on a man standing tall in their midst. Buzz cut. Clean shaven. Dressed in robes of flowing light. *Who was he?* Ancephaneese racked his brain. The man's voice, his mannerisms and features—they were all so strikingly *familiar.*

"What's going on? Who is that? What's he saying?" Ancephaneese couldn't help himself, he had to know, his lips gushed torrents of questions.

"Mister," a small boy piped up. "Haven't you heard?" He was giggling, eyes closed, head back, spinning. "Hell's been defeated. Heaven has won!" He flung his arms out wide. "We're free of this place. We're going home! Back to Elohim!"

Home? Elohim? Ancephaneese stopped. *This wasn't—? How could they—? Didn't he..* He was trying to compute.

"Everyone gather by family," the man's voice boomed across the plane. He lifted a sizable ring of keys from his shoulder. "Travel begins, immediately."

The crowd began to separate, instinctively forming two lines.

Ancephaneese watched as the man hoisted the keys, tossing them one by one into the thick, honey-sweet air. One by one, they burst in a radiant display of shimmering golden light, leaving glowing, orb-like doorways—one, two, three of them—hovering just inches off the ground, and towering several stories high.

Slowly the crowd began to move, passing through the far left and right portals.

"..and the third?" Ancephaneese questioned as they grew closer.

"For the prophets, priests, and kings!" the young boy exclaimed. "Weren't you listening at all?"

Ancephaneese shook his head.

"They have a few stops along the way."

Already a large group of men and women had gathered near the center door—a veritable 'Who's Who' of Historical characters. Ancephaneese could hear the crowd buzzing about the likes of Abraham and Issac, Moses and Joshua, Esther and Rahab, Elisha, Daniel and David. He strained to see, studying them closely, eagerly watching them enter their portal.

"Say—you're not a king, are you?" The boy questioned.

Ancephaneese smiled, shaking his head.

"Prophet or priest?"

"No.."

Thoughtful pause.

"Where's your family?"

Ancephaneese shrugged. "Not sure, son." He glanced around, then down. "Reckon I'm the first one to make it."

The boy's face grew troubled. He suddenly stopped. "How 'bout you tag along with my family then ... until you find one of your own?" He flashed a brilliant grin, turning and scampering off.

Ancephaneese nodded, ambling along behind, smiling and shaking hands, taking his place in line. He could still see the man, now standing at the split in the crowd, talking, laughing, and directing traffic—greeting everyone like old friends and family.

Ancephaneese scratched his head. It was so bizarre, yet oddly endearing. *Who was that man?*

Then it was Ancephaneese's turn. He tensed. For the first time since arrival, he felt completely alone—like a fish out of water—all the evil he'd ever done playing back in his head like a bad 'B' movie. He closed his eyes, but he couldn't shake it. It was a well-known fact, he'd never cared much for God, certainly not for others. All he'd ever been good at was looking out for good old, 'number one.' *Maybe a bit too good.* Shame settled. He felt exposed. This was all a mistake. He really wasn't supposed to be here, *was he?* He dropped his head, hoping he could just scoot by without being noticed.

Too late. The man placed a hand directly on his chest, "Halt—," he ordered.

The entire line stopped.

Ancephaneese froze, everyone was looking.

His face went red.

Then purple.

Then red again.

The man paused, not at all concerned with the moment's overwhelming clumsiness. "Ancephaneese!" He grabbed him by the shoulders, pulling him into a ferocious bear hug. "My dear brother, have you already forgotten? *'Today you will be with me in Paradise?!'"* He threw his head back and laughed a long, hearty laugh.

Snap, the tension broke.

Ancephaneese cracked a silly little grin, returning the hardy hug. *Of course! This was the man hanging beside him on the cross! The one he'd defended. The one he had dared to put his trust in..*

The one who had promised him Paradise!

He squeezed his brother fiercely. Tears beginning to flow. *God's very own son? The promised Messiah? Savior of the world?* He looked from his brother to the crowds, then back to his brother, savior and king. *He was home!* With a song in his heart and new praise on his lips he dismissed the boy he'd been following. No need to tag along any longer, he was an orphan and thief, *no more!* Finally, he'd found his own family—*and oh, what a family it was!*

—| 0000:00:00:13:33:33 AD |—

The walls had just finished shaking when Moses sat up. He opened his eyes, squinting into the surrounding darkness. It was pitch black—except for the strange dim glow, outlining *everything.*

He rubbed his face, breathing deep, taking his first breath of surface air in centuries.

Mm-Ughh—wet rat! He choked back a cough. *That's what it smelled like—wet rat.*

Pivoting, he dropped his feet to the floor. Cold. Damp. Slimy. *Where was he?* He paused a moment.

Oh yea, burial cave.

BOOM—everything was shaking again.

Aftershock, Moses nodded. He could see rubble falling all around. Strangely, he wasn't the least bit concerned. 'It was appointed *only once* for a man to die,' Yeshua's words echoed reassuringly in his mind. *He wasn't going anywhere.*

The tremor began to subside.

Moses paused, letting it fade, remembering Yeshua's final instructions: "Ladies and Gentleman," he'd announced. "You're heading to the surface to pick up your bodies. Upon reanimation, please rendezvous at Mount Nebo. Westside summit. Overlooking Jerusalem. I have a few stops to make. Wait for me there."

Moses stretched, getting his bearings and his legs. The rendezvous point was just up the hill from his current location. Most would be arriving from Jerusalem—a solid four hour walk. That meant, he had plenty of time to kill.

His stomach growled. *Wasn't there a spectacular grove of wild figs along Nebo's southern slope?* His mouth began to water. *Fresh figs—it had been centuries.* He hopped up from his seat. Most of the others would do a little sightseeing, revisit their old stomping grounds, maybe even pop in and surprise a few distant relatives. *But wilderness was wilderness.* Moses' stomach gurgled again. And it wasn't like he hadn't already seen it, the first forty times. He smiled. *Four hours,* that would give him plenty of time to hit the grove, fill his belly, and climb to the summit before anyone had even arrived.

He glanced around, moving towards a shaft of moonlight streaming through a tiny hole in the rubble. *There—that was his ticket out.* He stepped forward, stretching one last time before he grabbed a large boulder and began the arduous task of clearing his exit.

—| 0000:00:00:17:05:54 AD |—

"You lose—*again!*" John hollered back to a heaving, sweat-drenched Peter still pressing his way up the quarter mile hill.

John paused, debating, hand resting near the mouth of the wide open tomb. "Sorry. Can't wait," he called to the disciple with half a hill still to go. "I'm going in!" He flashed a victorious grin and darted inside.

Peter raised a weary hand in protest, but John was already gone.

The tomb was dark and musty, narrowing quickly down a short corridor and dead-ending at a small, perpendicular burial slab. John stifled a shudder. Even in the playful light of the early morning sun, it was a little bit creepy. The hair on the back of his neck stood tall, his whole body tingling. It hadn't been but twenty minutes since Mary had crashed their 'disciples only,' all-night pity party, spouting tales of a risen Messiah. A confused groundskeeper? And an empty, abandoned tomb.

In her own words, Yeshua was very much alive.

John reached the end of the corridor. If what Mary had said was right, he was going to find the tomb quite empty. A chill shot down his spine. He wasn't sure which was creepier—finding a dead body … or a missing one.

"Is he there?" Peter bellowed, finally reaching the tomb's gaping entrance. He paused, his broad frame filling the doorway, blocking its minimal light.

"C-Can't tell.." John faltered, squinting and peering again.

"Wrong answer," Peter barreled into the cave, ripping a torch from the wall and wheeling up beside John.

"Is he—?" He held out the torch.

"..n-no—," breathed John. "He's gone."

Both heads were instantly spinning.

Missing body.. Opened tomb.. *What had happened? Had the body been moved? Stolen? Where were the guards? Was Mary actually telling the truth?* The two men stared in awe, wanting to believe, but trying to compute.

"A-rose!" John exclaimed.

"It ... certainly seems that way," hesitated Peter. "But he could have been secretly taken.."

"No. *A* rose—," John pointed to the neatly folded face cloth, carefully placed beside the discarded grave wrappings. It was folded and purposefully set aside, exactly like the napkin at Thursday evening's Passover Seder.

Peter's jaw dropped. No one but Yeshua could have known to do that. *Had the Master been telling them this all along?* "Y-Yes," he trembled, slowly connecting the dots. "A rose. Why he ... arose!"

Suddenly Peter was sweating again. This time for entirely different reasons. He grinned, joy detonating like fire in his soul. He couldn't help it, he *had* to nudge his wide-eyed friend. "I-It's origami.." the words came tumbling out.

"Yes," whispered John, eyes wild and alive. "It's origami!"

—| 0000:00:00:20:15:27 AD |—

When Moses finally broke through the rubble, the morning sun was high in the sky. His chosen path had taken him at a ninety degree angle, right out the side of the cave. *No matter,* he shrugged, wiping the sweat from his brow. *There was still plenty of time to—*

He turned towards the front entrance, and froze. There, standing outside the mouth of his wide-open tomb was his entire group of resurrected counterparts—*including Yeshua.*

Moses' jaw dropped. He scratched his head, confused. *How had they—?*

The group burst out laughing.

"We had bets on how long it was going to take you to dig your way out of that rubble," someone howled. "What were you thinking? You completely missed the exit!"

"Wait! Don't tell us—," a second ribbed. "You never noticed because you were too busy turning an eleven day task into a forty-year chore!"

The crowd was rolling again.

Moses shot his friends the look. "All that time to take bets and write jokes—yet, not a single one of you thought to help me out?!"

"You never asked!" they roared.

Moses turned to Yeshua—eyebrows, palms and shoulders raised.

Yeshua just grinned and shrugged. What could he say? *Moses never asked.*

"Fine—," Moses feigned his disapproval, although he was a little disappointed there would be no figs. "Shall we rendezvous?" He gestured towards the summit, turning and heading up the side of the steep, dry mountain.

"*Wait—,*" someone grabbed his arm. "No need to walk ... unless you want to."

It was Joshua.

Moses shook his head and stopped. "Wait—what? Oh, yeah right—," he conceded, squeezing his former apprentice's shoulder. "I suppose we can move at the speed of thought now."

Joshua nodded, a slow grin spreading ear to ear.

"So ... I ... probably could have just moved *through* that collapsed tomb wall?" Moses quipped, gesturing to the cave.

The crowd exploded.

Finally, the lights were flipping on.

"Don't know what I was thinking," Moses chuckled. "I could have easily stopped by the old fig orchard and—"

"Way ahead of you—," Joshua tossed something into the air.

Moses caught it.

Fig.

"Wild. Ripe. And all yours," Joshua grinned, handing over half-a-dozen more.

Moses took a grateful bite. *Mmm—better than he remembered!* "Have I ever told you how much I love you," he teased, wrapping an appreciative arm around his protege's neck. "You always did have a knack for actually *taking* the fruits of the land."

Joshua chuckled. "Not much has changed," he fired back.

"You still do the backbreaking labor, while I get the results!"

Moses smiled, mouth full of fig. "You and me. We always were a great team."

"We always were!"

Then they were gone. Disappeared like the others. Headed up to the summit, on their way back to Heaven.

CH55: THE FALL
0000:00:01:02:00:22 AD

Applause and ticker tape filled the air. Spectators lined the streets. Yeshua glanced back at the joy-filled procession stretching endlessly behind. *What a sight!* On one hand, it was a homecoming—a celebration of brothers, sisters, families, and friends—*of Heaven reunited!* On the other.. Yeshua looked down at Haylel, dragging along in tow. Well let's just say, no victory would be complete without showcasing the 'spoils of war.' He tightened his grip around the chains that bound his adversary's feet and grinned. One thing was certain—the spoils had never been bigger.

"*King.. of.. kings! King.. of.. kings!*"

Yeshua turned back to the affections of the crowd. Their approval was deafening. He threw back his head and laughed. *Had he really just pulled this off?* A sting operation, millennia in the making, hidden in plain sight for everyone to see. Heavens' biggest coup exposed. His smile stretched a mile wide as he peered at the holes in his hands. It had cost him everything, *but today it was over.* Oh, he felt like dancing. *Justice had arrived.*

The procession turned—rounding the final corner, heading down the final stretch. Yeshua's heart leapt. There it stood, towering in the distance. Spotless. White. Shimmering like polished pearl against the golden glass streets. *Home!* He sighed deeply, waves of nostalgia bombarding his soul. *Heaven's throne room.* On most days it looked more like a castle, but today it was a courthouse, decked to the hilt in full, courthouse regalia. Yeshua gazed fondly. Domes, columns, accents and arches—it had 'em all. *And of course, his favorite part*—the fully interactive colonnade; rows of hand-carved pillars, forty stories tall, crafted in the image of time-honored saints, watching and waving as the procession passed by.

Yeshua ran down his mental checklist:

Court date? *Set.*

Perpetrator? *Under arrest.*

Leading witness? *Ready to attest.*

He smiled as he tugged on Haylel's chains. The evidence was collected. The legwork was done. All that remained was showing up and winning his case.

Smack. *SMACK.* Smack. *SMACK.*

Haylel jolted awake, his helmet bouncing hard against the courthouse steps.

Smack. *SMACK.*

He tried to sit up—but someone was dragging him by his ... feet?

Smack. *SMACK.*

His hands and legs were tied. There were crowds on all sides. *And an endless procession behind?* Smack. *SMACK. What was happening?* He felt so weak.

Slowly, the memories returned.

SMACK.

Then they were inside.

A courtroom. Haylel glanced around, trying to—*WOOSH*—he shot up on his feet, two massive angels lifting him from either side.

Cherubim, he nodded, recognizing their markings.

Feet together.

Hands behind his back.

Clink, click, buzz—clumsy chains fell as bands of light snapped securely in their place. *Ahh,* he was free to move, but.. *Ouch,* not too quickly. He tested the strength of his bonds—*cutting.*

One cherubim stepped back. *Click. Hiss.* Haylel's helmet decompressed and lifted off, revealing his true identity.

Blinding light.

Sudden chatter.

Whoa—Haylel clamped his eyes shut tight, ignoring the speculative prattle. *Let them talk.* Right now, the room just seemed so much *brighter* than he remembered.

Bang. Bang. Bang. A gavel sounded, calling the court to order.

"All arise, the honorable judge, Elohim, presiding."

There was a flurry of movement as the procession, *The Assembly*, a cloud of witnesses, Spirit, and pretty much all of Heaven rose to their feet.

Haylel didn't move, he was already standing. Instead, he rolled his neck side to side, breathing deep, mentally preparing. The atmosphere was invigorating. He was beginning to feel strong again. Clear. Sharp. Dangerous. He glanced around, excitement rising. Courtrooms were his forté, he was more than ready to clear up this little ... misunderstanding.

"Who calls this case before the court?" Elohim's voice boomed like thunder. He reached for his gavel, opening the books before him and taking his seat.

"I do, your Honor." It was Yeshua. The proceedings were underway.

"State your name for the record."

"The Word. Yeshua. Your son."

There was murmuring.

"Occupation?"

"—King of the Jews.."

More murmuring.

Elohim leafed through a tall stack of papers, searching his opened books. "I see no formal charge against you. Nor is it your predestined time." He frowned, glancing up from the bench. "State your case. Why are you here?"

"The Defendant," Yeshua pointed to Haylel. "I'm here to press charges." He cleared his throat. "One count: Gross Neglect. One count: Failure to Protect. One count: *First Degree Murder.*"

The air went out of the room.

Elohim turned to Haylel. "How does the Defendant plea?"

"Not guilty, your honor."

"You're certain?"

"Very."

Elohim raised an eyebrow and a gavel. "Then, by the laws of the Universe, and the bylaws of *The Assembly*," his gavel fell. "Let the proceedings begin."

More movement.

More books being opened.

Yeshua stepped forward, addressing the room. "Your Honor, Spirit, Ladies and Gentlemen of the Court, Witnesses, Fellow Citizens of Heaven and Earth," he nodded to each in turn. "I stand before you today to attest, beyond any shadow of a doubt, that the Defendant, Ha-satan, and the infamous 'garden snake of old' are, in fact, one and the same. And to prove that the Defendant, this 'garden snake of old,' has finally gone too far—undeniably transgressing Heaven's perfect law."

The room buzzed.

The gavel banged.

Yeshua turned to the crowd, motioning for them to settle. "Long ago, before the inception of time," he began. "In a little, back room within these very halls—the Defendant made a binding oath, swearing to uphold the sanctity of Heaven and Earth by governing the channels between." Yeshua shifted his stance, countenance growing solemn. "His job? To facilitate the budding relationship. His mission? To protect all parties involved." Brief pause. "As it has played out ... *he's done neither.*"

The room erupted.

"Certainly, he's played his part well," Yeshua waited for the room to die down. "Making calculated move after calculated move, furthering his own agenda. Pulling the strings by living above the law, while maintaining appearances of living within it." There was a long breath, a moment for the words to sink in. "But this time, he went too far. I stand before you as proof: Fully man. Fully God. Perfect in law *and* spirit. Blameless *and* incorruptible." Yeshua shifted gears. "Under his care, I should have been revered. Protected. Upheld. At the very least, unkillable." He held out his dripping hands for all to see. "Yet, I was offered up. Abandoned. Abused. Tortured. Maimed and martyred. All while under the "watchful eye" of this ... adulterous adolescent."

Yeshua surveyed the horrified crowd.

"Ladies and Gentlemen—I Am. *I am* the living proof—

the evidence beyond any shadow of the slightest doubt—that
the defendant is no longer competent, compliant, or capable of
upholding the office to which he was originally placed. For when
he was given a perfect man to protect, even the fully submitted and
blameless son of God, he still found a way to destroy him. And so, for
the atrocities committed against Heaven and Earth—and the blatant
misuse & abuse of his own laws—I move that the court charge him
with the highest offense." He pivoted to face the bench. "I move the
court charge him with *treason.*"

Treason? The room was in an uproar.

Bang. Bang. Elohim swung his gavel, "Order—," he thundered,
turning quickly to Haylel. "What say you?"

"Not guilty, your honor."

"You're … certain?"

"Very."

"May I—," Yeshua cut in, gesturing towards the defense.

"All yours," Elohim conceded.

"Haylel—," Yeshua challenged the defense directly. "Did you
not accept the position offered to you on the day of your creation,
to rule over Heaven as CEO—second-in-command—answering to no
one, save Elohim himself?"

"—I did."

"And did you not accept the position offered to you on
inaugural day of *The Assembly,* to rule over Second Heaven as Earth's
'Covering Cherub?' Watching over Earth's inhabitants, guiding and
governing their budding, intergalactic relationship with Heaven?"

"—I did."

"And in the midst of the garden, did Adam not choose to eat
from your tree, and your tree alone?"

"—He did."

"And on the sixth day of Sivan, 1446 BC. Did you not sit atop
the holy mountain, Sinai, and agree to uphold the laws of Moses,
which—by your own chisel—were carved into two tablets of stone?"

"—your point?" Haylel growled, suddenly very much
annoyed.

"Well—," Yeshua wrapped it all up. "If, by your own

admission, you were fully in charge of Earth … chosen by Adam, set in place by Elohim. Then, why—when a man existed who perfectly upheld your law—did you not perfectly uphold him?"

Haylel stiffened. *How dare the Prosecution insinuate … in front of everyone.* "First things first," he glared. "How is it even possible that you exist? I own every man on Earth, and every generation that comes from him." He opened his cloak, producing a well-worn deed. "Even if you did somehow manage to come directly from the one you so foolishly claim your Father to be—based on the precedent set by Heaven's own judgment of the 200 Ambassadors—Heaven can no longer use humans to create any type of offspring … hybrid or otherwise. It is *illegal*," he slapped the deed down, leaning in towards Yeshua. "*You fool … do you not see?* By the very admission of your own existence, you have subsequently disqualified *yourself*." A dark chuckle escaped his lips. He stepped back, pleased to no end. "It's over. You cannot exist. Close the books. Court adjourned. Case dismissed."

The crowd froze. Stunned. Silent. *Was it really ending this quickly?*

"That is true—," Yeshua held up a commanding hand. "You have spoken accurately to say my seed came directly from Elohim, my Heavenly Father. *It certainly did*. And just as Adam's seed bypassed you, so mine did too." He flashed a broad grin. "As for my earthly mother. Should we summon her? She will gladly testify that she was not taken, not used, not abducted, nor abused. In fact, it was quite the opposite, she *offered* to carry me of her own free will—*as a virgin*." He leaned in, matching the intensity of the defense. "As for Joseph—the earthly man to which she was betrothed—he is here now," Yeshua gestured towards the gawking audience. "Speak to him and see. Does he object? Find out for yourself. Ask him if my earthly mother was not as pure and chaste as the driven snow on the eve that they finally consummated their marriage."

Haylel scowled.

The crowd relaxed.

"As far as precedent," Yeshua hammered on, correcting the lopsided narrative. "It was actually the *illegal actions* of your

Ambassadors, which gave me the *legal right* to engage a willing and cooperative human participant in my conception—so long as it was engaged in such a way as to satisfy the guidelines and stipulations set within your judgment. Thanks to you, a 'free willed, virgin birth' was both, lawful and completely justified." He hesitated a moment, thoroughly enjoying the cloud of confusion now resting on the defendant's dumbstruck face. "So if I may," he enunciated slowly, "redirect you to my original question: *Why*—when a man existed who so perfectly upheld your law, did you not perfectly uphold him?"

"*Fine,*" Haylel fumed, temper flaring. "Let's play your silly games." He set his jaw, regrouping and shifting tactics. "You claim perfection," he waved his hands sarcastically. "Yet there were numerous occasions when you were caught, outright, breaking the law. Take Shabbat, for example. Did you not perform an obscene amount of healings on that day? Not to mention the time you and your leather-necked minions picked and ate grain from someone else's field. Were those not works?" He raised an eyebrow. "Even thievery?" His hands came down hard on the table in front of him, wrist-bonds sparking. "Had I actually committed the murder you so glibly accuse me of, *would I not be well within my rights?*" He looked to the crowd. "Is there not substantial evidence, across a multitude of grounds, that this charlatan has, in fact—a multitude of times— broken the law? Is not even *one* of those many afore-mentioned infractions, more than enough to completely absolve me from keeping my end of the deal?"

Yeshua quieted, casually scanning the walls, searching their familiar surfaces until the half-baked rant had come to its full and unfounded end. "The Ten Commandments for Dummies," he slowly read aloud, pointing to a plaque he was particularly fond of. "Number Four: Honor the Shabbat and *keep it special.*" He turned to Haylel. "Which is more *special*?" he probed. "To *feast* on Shabbat, or to starve? ..to be *whole*, or to be afflicted?" He grabbed a quick breath, hammering his point home. "If the law calls for Shabbat to be the most holy and thus, '*special,*' day of the week, than shouldn't Shabbat be the day—above all other days—*to thrive*?"

He waited for a response.

Any response.

Nothing.

"As for eating from another man's field," he turned to the crowd. "Cannot the King who owns everything, eat freely from the tenant's field of his choosing?"

Suddenly Haylel was furious. "Was it not your *own* people who took you into custody?" he hissed. "Who handed you over to Pilate? And cried out for your execution?"

Yeshua nodded and gave a slight shrug.

"Was it not your very *own* lips that released your spirit? Admitted Elohim's betrayal? And sent you plummeting into the afterlife?"

Yeshua stifled a grin.

"And was it not *Elohim* who placed you on my doorstep? Leaving you to rot in Hades? Not so much as a Chihuahua, much less a rescue dog in sight?"

Yeshua couldn't hold back, he gulped a deep breath, loosing a loud, hardy laugh. "Guilty as charged!"

"Then, I rest my case. Clearly, I had no hand IN THIS MATTER, WHATSOEVER!" For a moment Haylel swayed like a drunken sailor, the tiniest dribble of drool cascading from the corner of his mouth.

Yeshua almost rolled his eyes. "Did you not just hear yourself admit to taking the oath at *The Assembly,* and to upholding the laws of Moses on Mount Sinai? In whose possession lay the keys to *Death, Hell* and *The Grave*? On whose lapel were they bound? Are you inferring, under oath, that it was not your *sole* responsibility to step up and correct the situation?" He threw his hands up in the air, eyes beginning to blaze. "Shrewd as you are. You expect the court to believe that an innocent man—potentially the son of God—shows up on your doorstep unannounced, and you didn't feel the least bit obligated to get to the bottom of it? If for no other reason than to cover your own pointed tail?"

"Of, course not—," Haylel lowered his voice, quickly regaining control.

Silently, he chided himself. He'd gotten so flustered, he'd

almost forgotten the ace up his sleeve. He paused, straightening his cloak, taking a moment to enjoy the limelight.

"Did you not say?" he slowly recalibrated. "And I quote: 'Pater, eis cheiras sou paratithemai to pneuma mou?' or 'Father.. into *your* hands, I entrust my spirit?'" He cleared this throat, voice settling once again to a purr, palms innocently raised. "Were those not your own words? A petition *to Elohim*, made by *you?* Who was I to stand in the way of *your* appeal?"

BOOM.

Ace dropped.

He was off the hook.

Haylel stepped back, cocked his head innocently to one side, and flashed a wicked, wicked grin. "But you're here now," his arm swept generously toward the bench. "Appeal."

That, was about all Yeshua could take. He squared his shoulders, narrowed his gaze, and lowered both barrels. "More accurately translated," he informed the defense. "'Pater—,' means Protector, Upholder, *Founding* Father, and Patriarch." His eyes burned white-hot, locking with Haylel's, dredging the depths of the deceiver's wretched soul. "As Earth's 'Covering Cherub' and deed-toting owner, were *you* not my protector, upholder, *founding* father, and patriarch?" He paused, letting the tension fester. "That statement was *NOT* an appeal to my benevolent, heavenly Father," his voice dropped to a hard-core whisper as he slowly pulled the trigger. "That statement was my direct appeal … *to YOU.*"

BOOM. *Silence*—beautiful, awkward silence.

Somewhere a mic dropped.

Haylel blanched, slowly going white as ash. He reached for the table to steady himself, beads of sweat dotting his suddenly furrowed brow. "*I—, H-How—,*" he stammered, trying to form the words. His face grew tense. Frustrated. Confused. That answer wasn't even in his ballpark of 'anticipated responses.' His legs began to tremble. He went weak in the knees. He could feel the victory slipping from his grasp. There was so much to say, but no way to *spit … it … out.* The room began to spin around him, then squash and stretch as rage stampeded his soul. His stomach churned. He felt hot.

Sick. Unstable.

He had walked right into that.

RIGHT INTO..

Checkmate. Yeshua smiled, quietly turning to the bench, "Your Honor, the defense is right. I would be a fool not to take this opportunity to submit my appeal." He lowered his head, dropping to one knee. "Abba, I have done all that you asked: Become a servant to all. Obedient unto death. Even submitting to my most bitter of enemies. Now I turn the entirety of my future over to you." He glanced at his floundering counterpart. "Judge rightly between us, Father. Do as you see fit."

The courtroom fell silent.

Slowly, Elohim cleared this throat. He looked at his two sons. Both conceived in flawless perfection. Both perfectly and equally loved. Yet one bowed low before him, humbled and broken; while the other clung desperately to his laurels, too proud to admit unmistakable defeat. He shook his head, pushing aside his books. There was only one way to handle a conundrum of this proportion. He lowered his gavel, lifted his eyes—and after a long, deep, thought-filled breath—launched wholeheartedly into his reproof.

"Haylel," he began. "My Covering Cherub. My strong, unyielding hand. You know the rules. *If any man keeps my commands, he will live.* That promise is as old as Eden's two trees, themselves." He paused, peering sternly over the bench. "Certainly, you were granted permission to test Yeshua, to discover his motives. But when the line was crossed, and he arrived in Hades without a single spot or blemish, was it not your duty to uphold the law you had sworn to protect?" He leaned back, arms crossed, a hint of remorse lining his words. "You were given ample time—six hours on the cross, seventy two hours in Hades. Yet you squandered it all. On what? Show and spectacle? Fog and lights?" His tone tightened. "You knew what would happen on day four—you had three days to correct the situation before the situation became permanent." He raised a questioning eyebrow. "So why didn't you? Why were you left dragging your feet? Certainly you weren't scared of me. You said so yourself: Am I not so "naive" as to choose to believe you, even when you lie directly to my face?" Elohim's expression didn't hide the pain of betrayal, even as he flashed a terse, all-knowing grin. "Haylel, I gave you years. Centuries. Millennia. Sent you prophets, priests, and kings. I drew up blueprints, laws, and books. Confronted you passively. Confronted you face to face. I gave you every opportunity to change. Every opportunity to step back into your appropriate lane, to resume your appropriate position. Yet you chose to ignore them all," his eyes welled with heartfelt sorrow. "And so—after much frustration," he straightened a stack of already straight papers, letting a silent tear fall. "I did the unthinkable … *I sent you my son.*"

The crowd sat riveted.

"It was nothing new," Elohim explained. "Just as Eve partook of your fruit, Mary partook of mine. Just as you sent your ambassadors to Earth, so I too, sent mine. Just as you wrapped yourself in flesh to tempt Adam, so I wrapped my son in flesh to tempt you." He glanced up, choosing his next words carefully. "I made no move of my own accord, I followed *only* your lead. Tit for tat. Eye for an eye. Strictly adhering to every stipulation and guideline set, in complete compliance to the precedents determined *by you.*" He leaned forward, his voice growing grim. "Haylel—you have no one to blame but yourself. I gave you my son, placing him completely under your rule. Like Daniel under Darius, it could have remained that way forever," Elohim was firing on all cylinders. "But you weren't OK with that. You had to have it *your* way. So you took what you wanted when you thought no one was looking. Except this time *all of Heaven was*—and you were caught, red-handed, elbow-deep in the cookie jar, chocolate plastered to the very corners of your face." He stopped, almost daring the defense to interject. "Haylel, I gave you everything you ever wanted: Power. Position. Prominence. Perfection. The opportunity to be God—*just like me.* But you squandered it all. Destroying everything you touched. And now," he nodded towards the prosecuting bench. "Even the very cookie you stole—stands here testifying *of your guilt!*"

Haylel's face looked drained. "That … i-is all well and good," he quickly diverted. "We could stand here splitting hairs all day. But when it comes right down to it, it's simply my word against his.

Prove it," he bowed with a smirked. "Place his blood on the altar. Pass him through the fire. Offer blood and body, *right now*, as a living sacrifice. Let's see exactly what impurities they do or do not contain." He folded his arms smugly across his chest. "Let's remove all speculation—beyond any shadow of doubt."

The crowd went silent, almost dreading the reply.

"I will do you one better," Elohim surprisingly upped the ante. "What say you? Should we stoke the fire seven times hotter? Let's see if my son is not only who he says he is, but if he, in fact, *is* a brand new creation."

The room stifled a gasp. *Seven times hotter?* No being, save Elohim himself, could survive.

Haylel nodded his agreement.

Immediately, Spirit swirled into action. To the right of the bench, at the front of the room, she manifested the altar and fire. Surrounding it with a whirlwind of color and lights, she stoked it seven times hotter, even as she shielded the room from its damaging effects.

A pathway opened.

Elohim motioned.

Yeshua stepped forward, passing through the walkway and up to the altar. He looked at it fondly—remembering the day he had fashioned it. A grooved, circular basin surrounding an ornate golden box—armrests, headrest and a well-padded back completing the ensemble. It was a golden seat. A powerful seat. Haylel's seat. Full of manna, miraculous life, and the law. Two Cherubim hovered far above it, covering it with their wings, stoking it with flames of their own. On Earth, this seat was known as the, 'Ark of the Covenant.' In Heaven, it was Elohim's right-hand throne.

Yeshua knelt beside it. Raising a hand over the fiery box, he opened his fist, letting precious blood flow. It sizzled as it hit the red-hot seat, spilling down over its edges and filling the basin below.

Woosh—a blinding flash of light erupted, bursting into flames.

Yeshua stepped back, watching his offering burn ... except, it didn't burn. He stifled a grin. It wasn't that it wasn't accepted—no, the flames were proof of that—it was just that this offering was so pure, so undefiled, so holy, *it couldn't be consumed.*

The crowd gasped, they had never seen anything like it.

Yeshua turned. *One last test to pass.* He looked at the raging flames. White hot. Blazing. Burning all around. For any creature less than full-blooded, Elohim, this was certain death.

Without hesitation, Yeshua stepped through. No countdown. No long deep breath. No suspenseful climatic pause. He couldn't help it, he was much too excited to wait.

The crowd roared.

Haylel looked stricken.

Yeshua flashed the room a dazzling grin, while he danced a little jig in the flames. It was settled. No dispute. *He was a brand new creation!*

With a nod and a smile he offered Spirit his arm, taking the slender hand of his Mom. Then, mother and son—choking back tears—stepped fearlessly out of the flames and into the heart of the Father.

Yeshua was home.

Elohim turned to his trembling, former Cherub. "YOU HAVE BEEN MEASURED AND WEIGHED—," he boomed, raising his gavel. "AND YOU HAVE BEEN FOUND WANTING!"

The gavel came crashing down.

"Haylel, no longer will you be called by your given name. From this day forward, you shall be called, Lucifer. For you will appear as a light before men, but your illumination will lead only to death—and every life who follows its guidance will ultimately come to a bitter and unexpected end."

The gavel came crashing down again.

"I hereby decree," Elohim turned back to the court. "That— effective immediately—Lucifer be stripped of his office, dismissed from his throne, and removed from his seat at, *The Assembly.* In his place," he beamed. "I am pleased to appoint, Yeshua, *my son*—the very one he tried to destroy."

BOOM—waves of solar flares exploded across the heavens as Elohim's gavel came crashing down a third and final time. Lightning raced across the skies. Galaxies trembled. Stars realigned.

The courtroom shook, unsettled, everyone falling to their knees as the edict made its way swiftly across the multiverse.

In the distant Milky Way Galaxy, Earth rocked and reeled, its moon fracturing to the core. Mars—Earth's twin planet—tilted and shifted, skidding wildly out of control. Its orbit expanded, flung wide across the solar system, all positional influence over Earth, permanently and physically removed.

"*NO—,*" Lucifer roared, lunging for his now worthless deed. "*YOU* did this to me!" He pointed a trembling finger at Elohim, the deed crumbling in his hand. "Earth is *MINE!* Man chose *ME!*" His entire frame shook with uncontrollable fury as the remaining deed turned to dust. "*You thief. You back-stabbing CROOK.* You set me up! How can you punish me for a world *YOU* gave me? You hypocritical piece of.."

"*ENOUGH—,*" Elohim thundered, his reprimand crackling with conclusion. "Mankind has suffered long enough." He slammed the books shut, rising from his seat, eyes and aura on fire. "Son of Perdition," he blazed. "No one did this to you. *You did this to yourself. No one set you up, the truth has simply been revealed.*" He leered over his bench, his final words piercing like double-edged swords. "You hard-hearted, self-absorbed devil. In the midst of destroying mankind, and senselessly murdering my son on a tree, did you ever stop to think that maybe—just maybe—what you were doing to them, *you were also doing to yourself, and to me?*"

"Ahhgggggggg—," Lucifer rushed the bench—*HE WOULD NOT BE DENIED!*

Elohim shook his head, dropping silently to his seat. *Unbelievable,* a quizzical little smile washed over his all-knowing face. *Was he really being forced to confront the imminent assault of a tantrum-throwing toddler?* He paused for a moment, observing Lucifer with what appeared to be deep, deep pity.

Then he lifted a finger ... *and swiped left.*

THUD. Lucifer went limp, skidding sideways across the floor.

It was over.

Elohim turned to his bailiffs. "Gentlemen," he gestured

towards the unconscious body, emotion overwhelming his voice. "Kindly remove this corruption from our court. For behold," he paused, beaming at the presence of his newly appointed son. "I have just made *all things*, brand new."

CH56: BEGINNING OF THE END

They sat alone. Three figures, deep within the recesses of space—walled in by nothing more than the absolute darkness around them. The only light present was the soft ethereal glow emanating from within the figures themselves. They spoke earnestly, in hushed tones, occasionally pausing to crack a smile or share a private joke, but never lingering for longer then the briefest of moments before they were wholeheartedly back on track. There was no telling how much time had actually passed. The circular table, around which they huddled, overflowed with books, blueprints, edicts, programs, songs, scrolls and more—each painstakingly handcrafted down to the smallest of details.

"We can't just send him off, *minimum security*."

Elohim looked up from his work. "Why not?" he inquired, penning the final touches on his now completed manuscript and permanently closing the book.

"Because." Spirit gave him '*the look.*' "We all know … if I don't personally escort Lucifer into captivity," she flipped open the lid to her perpetual gum dispenser and shook out two twinkling cubes. "He *WILL* escape!" She snapped the lid shut—*hard,* squinting her disdain for the story's current ending. No way was she going to let this gaping oversight slide by unaddressed.

Elohim chuckled, eyes dancing with delight. "That will only happen," he reassured, "if everything goes … according to plan!" He laughed out loud, delighted by the look on Spirit's face. He offered up a powerful hand, requesting some gum of his own.

Spirit handed over both radiant cubes, glancing down at the two remaining in her palm. *The Law of Sacrificial Giving!* She popped one into her mouth. "According to plan?"

"You know—two trees? Growing in the garden of every heart?" Yeshua gently cut in. "The Truth or The Lie. Battling it out for ultimate control?" He grinned, no longer able to restrain his own growing excitement. "A future where every life on Earth is nothing less than a free-willed, high-stakes, individually-tailored, epic-sized, *CHOOSE-YOUR-OWN ADVENTURE!*"

"He'll go rogue," Spirit countered flatly, clearly unimpressed. "And with no more accountability, what's holding him back from doing *absolutely anything?*" She swallowed hard, nearly choking on the diabolical thought and then on her bubblegum.

"How 'bout this?" Yeshua smiled, dangling a familiar set of keys high in the air. "*Death*, *Hell*, and *The Grave* will no longer be at his disposal ... and thus, anyone who resists, *he* will be powerless to stop."

"A good start. But what about deception?" Spirit fired back. "He will still have deception ... and anyone *deceived* will be powerless to stop *him.*"

"Agreed," Elohim rejoined the fray. "Which is why we will need a family on Earth. Sons and daughters who can see through the lies, sort through the muck and the mire, stand up against his vigilante evil, and shut it down at every turn." He nodded his 'thanks' for the gum, pocketing the pieces for later. "A family whose pure intentions and selfless love will compel Heaven—nay, *force* Heaven—down to Earth."

"And how, pray tell, do we acquire such a family?" Spirit devoured her remaining piece, chewing fiercely.

"My blood," Yeshua smiled. "They will enter the bloodline through me."

"Still—they will need help," Spirit closed her eyes, imagining the countless complications of the coming scenario.

"Which is precisely why we'll be sending them someone else," Elohim agreed. "Someone unbeatable. Free of Earthly law. Able to be everywhere, at all times. Capable of holding the darkest deceptions at bay!"

"Someone with killer highlights? Unending whit? And ninja-like reflexes?" Spirit blew an aggressively large bubble, watching as her masterpiece lifted off and floated away blinking into the surrounding darkness.

"Definitely someone with an endless supply of bubblegum," Elohim teased.

"Who can teach man how to be unstoppable?"

"Only when unoffendable.."

"To follow rules and regulations?"

"How about, personal instruction.."

"To be cousins and in-laws, followers and fans?"

"Let's go with, kings and queens, sons and daughters.."

"You're on!" Spirit grinned, karate chopping the air. "But—," she froze mid swing. "You know the devil is gonna take serious advantage of me being restricted to the spirit realm. He'll blind man's eyes. Claim I don't exist. Make those who do follow me seem weird and crazy," she turned to Elohim. "Then he'll project his own nefarious actions onto you. He'll swear you're a, 'distant, hard-hearted, old fashioned, angry, prude.'" She leapt up from her seat, pacing, hands flailing in every direction. "He'll claim your son never existed: That he never really died. Never really rose. Was never really your son at all. He'll invent denominations, departments, systems and agencies, red-tape and bureaucracy to mask his endless conspiracies. Non-profits to fund his agendas. He'll push fake news, fake religions, fake disease, and fake end-time scenarios. Propagate pyramids, pyramid schemes, genetic restructuring, and social justice for Artificial Intelligence. He'll hypersexualize pop culture, demonize the truth, place taxes on thin air, restrict transportation, use children as currency, and castrate the church. Not to mention trans-humanism, the alien deception, meteor cover ups, singing purple dinosaurs, and a whole host of other impossibilities." Spirit paused, swallowing hard. "Then, after he kicks you out of everything—dragging your name blasphemously through the mud—he'll stand up claiming to be the actual returning, reincarnate 'Son of God,' and attempt to steal all your credit."

Ahhh—the mother of Heaven and Earth deflated, collapsing to her seat and burying her face in her hands. "Perhaps Yeshua *should* go back. He can talk to everyone out-loud, face-to-face—no confusion, no distance, no misunderstandings."

Yeshua reached out and took Spirit's troubled hand. "It all sounds well and good, but at some point don't the training wheels just need to come off? Besides—," he chuckled. "When the devil's pushed too far, and our family is forced to choose between living in hell-on-earth or simply becoming unoffendable—isn't that when the game truly begins?!" A huge grin lit his radiant face. "*And isn't that when Heaven finally starts to become unstoppable!*"

Spirit looked up, her countenance already transforming. *Of course,* she beamed, *how had she forgotten—they were the ones with the current win, win! If the devil backed off—Heaven's Kingdom would grow up. If the devil doubled-down—Heaven's Kingdom would wake up.* Yeshua was right. *They couldn't lose!*

She leaned forward, smiling mischievously. "How silly of me to fret over something as trivial as *minimum security,*" a rejuvenated giggle erupted. "I know just the guards to send!"

And with that, it was settled.

Yeshua stood to his feet. "Ladies and gentlemen," he bowed long and low. "May the games finally begin!" He flashed a dazzling smile, blew both his parents a kiss—and with his belt blazing bright—headed for the nearest exit.

…

Pitter, patter, pitt—Yeshua's sandaled footsteps struck up a sort of muffled cadence as he moved briskly across the infinite darkness and into the well lit throne room. Up ahead he could already see his exit—two very white, very polished, seamless, sliding, double doors with a barbershop-style chair sitting catty-corner, just to their right.

Vintage leather. Extra padding. Facing the back wall. Yeshua smiled—those were clearly Spirit's touches. He glanced to his right, immediately captivated by the endless army of Heavenly Hosts, frozen in suspended animation. There were literally trillions upon trillions. Every size, shape, color and creed. Hanging, midair, waiting for one word to awaken.

"Welcome!" Elohim's voice thundered in the distance.

Yeshua grinned, picking up speed. *That was the word—* the masses were already stirring. A few more steps and he pulled alongside the lone reclining chair. His heart leapt, moved by the striking beauty of the creature within.

A Cherub: Perfect. Pure. And beautiful.

Yeshua wheeled to a stop, *he had to ...* Haylel looked so innocent basking in the effervescent glow of Elohim's eternal greeting. It just didn't seem possible that he would ever be capable of doing the things he would eventually do. Yeshua stared for a moment, weighing the consequences of what suddenly felt like a cataclysmic decision. *Oh, that there were some other way,* he reached up, quietly removing the set of keys hanging from his own shoulder. *He knew what he had to do.* With all manner of stealth and precision he leaned over, silently clipping the keys of *Death, Hell,* and *The Grave* onto Haylel's left lapel.

The mighty cherub began to stir, peaceful eyes fluttering.

That was his cue! Yeshua spun, stepping quickly through the automated exit doors. Turning one last time, he basked in the latest swell of heaven-sent energy. His belt flared, bright as the noonday sun. Power surged from his being. At the last moment, he caught Haylel's eye, two immaculate white doors sliding silently shut between them.

Then he was gone, back on the move.

There was no time to waste, he quickened his pace. There were planets to make. Gardens to grow. Mankind to create.

He stepped outside, stopping on the strangely vacant doorstep of the soon to be forever-bustling, throne room. *This was it,* he grinned. His next step would take him to the most forgettable corner of the most forgotten galaxy, on the back side, of the wrong side, of the far side, of the multiverse; propelled forever into the pages of the greatest story of all time. He bowed his head—stance wide, knees bent—every muscle begging to blast epicly out of the atmosphere in a blinding flash of fire and light. *BUT*—he slowly stood—why do all that when one could simply move at the speed of one's own thoughts? He grinned, the scene casually changing around him, leaving him hovering over a formless, churning, watery chaos.

He turned to greet Spirit and his Father, hovering along beside him, the three taking a moment to link up—arm in arm.

Deep breath.

Gun depress.

There was no going back now.

It was rags to riches. Beauty from ashes. Tragic loss to epic overtime win. *Ready or Not,* The Word lifted his voice. *His-story—was about to begin.*

EPILOGUE I: THE RISE

Whirrr. BANG. Eeeeeeeek. The patty wagon came to an excruciating stop. Shuddering, it backfired loudly, a cloud of rainbow-colored smoke exploding from its quivering exhaust.

The wiry driver shot his bulky partner a sideways glance. "Checkpoint," he grumbled, pulling the hood of his cloak forward, concealing his long, brooding face. An impatient flick of the wrist signaled his partner to do the same. "What seems to be the trouble, officer?" He cracked his window ever so slightly.

A towering angel bent down and peered inside. Ignoring the question, he cupped both hands above his eyes, pressing hard against the tinted glass. For a moment he paused, noting: *One prisoner. Two guards. Prisoner sound asleep.* He moved a finger to his ear, listening intently to an updated dispatch feed. Pulling out a flashlight, he looked again: *One prisoner. Two guards. Prisoner sound asleep.* Seemingly satisfied, he stood up and patted the hood, motioning for them to go.

The engine roared to life, launching the wagon slowly into motion. The prisoner shifted and moved, jostling awake. Groggy, he lifted his head, instinctively tugging against the fiber optic chains binding his wrists.

"Where we headed?" he prodded the driver.

"Auschwitz.. Alcatraz.. Azkaban.. What's it to you?" the snide remark wafted back through the laser-barred partition.

The prisoner grunted his dissatisfaction, but quickly fell silent, all attention returning to ridding himself of his chains.

For quite some time the cart rumbled on. Out of the city. Out of the suburbs. Out, through the boonies, and into the wide open country.

What luck—, a smirk began to weave its way across the prisoner's pursed lips. *The further they traveled away from the city, the weaker his chains seemed to become!* He glanced around, keeping his excitement in check. *The bars on the windows looked to be waning as well!*

Down a dirt road—then another, and another—each more narrow than the last. *Where were they going?* The prisoner racked his brain. Lush, golden prairie grass stretched as far as he could see. This was the middle of nowhere. The far side of Heaven. He knew this place well. There wasn't so much as a shed with a barbed-wire fence, much less any sort of state-run correctional facility.

The cart came to a stop.

Now was his chance. The prisoner lunged forward, thrusting his hands through the weakened window bars and around the driver's neck. Choking—*hard.*

"Mas— Err—," struggling words erupted. "Mast— Er—."

Prophet?!

He squeezed harder.

The other guard shook with laughter.

BEAST?!

More laughter.

"—*Master!*" Prophet managed to tear himself away.

Lucifer fell back hard against his seat, ripping off his chains. "Get me out of here!" he roared.

Prophet was already out of the cab. "Fifteen seconds," he scowled, rubbing his neck with one hand and holding up a small, metallic orb with the other.

Transient Portal!

BEAST moved quickly to the rear of the wagon, tearing its industrial armored doors effortlessly from their hinges.

With a twist and a toss, Prophet's orb went flying.

The trio watched as it rolled to a stop, humming softly.

For a moment, *nothing..*

Nothing..

NOTHING..

BOOM—it exploded into a twenty-foot fireball.

"Our exit, boys.." Prophet grinned, disappearing inside.

BEAST immediately followed suit.

Lucifer wasn't quite so quick to oblige. With a grunt and a growl, he wheeled to a stop, eyes wildly roaming the vast deserted plain. *What do you do to the world who has forever rejected you?* The question burned like dry ice in his veins. *He had given Heaven everything.. EVERYTHING.. For what?!* He raised a defiant fist.

Tick. Tock. Tick..

Lucifer glanced toward the ever-vexing, ever-perplexing, ever-distant clock tower. *What a joke*, he scoffed. *Like some sort of pestiferous yo-yo it was, what—beginning to wind up?*

The Dark Lord scowled at the mysteriously rising numbers, his forked tongue clamped between fiercely resolute lips. *Yes—he would MAKE them pay,* he vowed, a drop of cold-blood escaping pursed lips and tumbling down to the prairie grass below. *After all—,* he tossed aside his shredded chains. *Revenge was a dish best served..*

Pffewww—the portal flickered, quickly beginning to fade.

That was his cue.

Lucifer turned and sidestepped through. *All bets are OFF,* he silently raged, falling like lightning towards an undisclosed Second-Heaven location. *As far as he was concerned, the game had only just BEGUN. But this time*—a ravenous roar exploded from blood-thirsty lungs—*they were playing … FOR KEEPS.*

EPILOGUE II: WANT MORE?

The crazy thing is, this story doesn't have to end here. Potentially, this is just the beginning. Sure, the details of this book are largely fictional—historically reimagined narratives, wrapped around cosmic real-life events. But the reality is, if you truly want in on the action—to take on your God-given role in history, to get in on the fight, and have a real, open, honest, two-way, interactive, personal relationship with the living God of the Universe—*you can*.

It only takes two things:

1. Honesty

2. Yeshua

Flagrant, blatant *honesty* ensures that God *will* answer back. And *Yeshua* ensures that *THE living God* (not some other, fallen, lesser, dead god) will be the one *who* answers back.

Since I have absolutely no idea where your current "Earth-experience" has landed you on the aforementioned, "spiritual spectrum;" here are a number of awkwardly honest prayers that you can pray (in Yeshua's name) to move you deeper (towards God).

Feel free to pray the appropriate one(s) in your own words, but ONLY if you *really mean it* to the BEST of your ability, with *ALL* the heart you can muster.

Otherwise, no worries ... but don't waste your time :)

For the curious "Tester:" *God. I don't know if you exist. But this book kinda made me think.. and if you are real, talk to me. Show yourself to me. Let me feel your energy. Your presence. Your life. Communicate with me in some real, tangible, obvious way. A way that I will know—beyond any shadow of doubt—that You, God, the one true living God, are the one talking back to me. And that you do exist. In Yeshua's name. So be it.*

For the calloused "Hater:" *God. You're pathetic. I hate you. You're a crutch and a let down. All your people are hypocrites and liars. You've been absent my entire life—and honestly, I haven't missed you. But this book made me think.. maybe some other, lesser god has been the one causing all the trouble in my life and then blaming it all on you. Maybe there is some far-fetched, 'Hail Mary' of a chance that you actually are real. That you actually do care. And that you actually are good. If so, please show yourself to me. Talk to me. Let me feel your energy. Communicate with me in some real, tangible, obvious way. A way that can't be denied. A way that I'll know—beyond any shadow of doubt— that you are real and you really do know me. In Yeshua's Name.. Do it.*

For the future "Son or Daughter:" (Anyone ready to open up their line of communication with Papa God permanently): *Papa God, I know you're real. I have no doubt, and I want to be your kid. Adopt me. Change me. Teach me your ways. Make me a part of your Kingdom. A member of your family. I ask your son, Yeshua, and your Holy Spirit to fill me, right now. To inhabit my mind, my heart, my body, my soul, my personality, my sexuality, my psyche, my being, my essence. Every part of me! You have free reign, and total permission, to do anything you need to do. Change everything you need to change. Heal everything you need to heal. Live in me. Fix me. Restore me. Set me free. Right now! Change my heart to WANT to do everything you want me to do. Permanently open and restore my lines of communication with you—the one, true and living God. And help me protect those lines of communication above all else. Because true life comes from true relationship. And I want true life. In Yeshua's name. You rock. Amen.*

And we could go on:

For the Addict.. For the Prostitute.. For the Pharisee.. For the Deep State..

But the point is not for me to put words in your mouth, or to lead you in some trumped up, spiritual "incantation." The point is relationship—real, normal, interactive, relationship. The point is for you—in your own words—to be completely *honest* about where you're at, and where you want to go … talking to God like a friend, a dad, or even (if this is where you're at) as an enemy.. (in Yeshua's name).

Remember, God is a person. He's not some set of rules, some cosmic ethereal force, a Bible-toting social club, or even some sort of supernatural secret society. *He's simply a father.* A good father, with your best interests at heart, who actually wants to help. *But ONLY if you want it. ONLY if you ask for it. And ONLY if you DON'T play games.* He has no interest in a billion more Lucifers running around—paying him homage, being kind to his face, virtue signaling their own "goodness" to everyone else, and then doing whatever the "hell" they want to do behind his back. We've all read the story. We've all lived on Earth. One Lucifer has been more than enough.

Now, certainly, we don't have to be perfect. God isn't looking for perfection. We just have to be *honest* about where we are at, and open to God changing us and taking us where He wants us to go.

For example. If we love our addiction and are completely bound to it, but want out of its perpetual destructive life-style … *say that.* If we hate that we have to turn tricks for a living, but it's the only thing paying the bills … *say that.* If we don't really love God, mostly just ourselves … *say that.* If we only want to escape Hell without the hassle of a relationship … *say that.* If we truly want to sleep with every <fill in the blank here> on the planet … *say that.* It's not so much about *what* we say, but *how* we say it. Honesty first. Humility second. He already knows the truth.

There is so much more we could talk about. Like how it's God's job to *change* our heart (and our job to simply be open and honest about what's going on in it). Or, how every god requires a sacrifice – and the choice we each must ultimately make is: *Do we sacrifice somebody else, or sacrifice ourself?* But this is an Epilogue. If you want a book, download the free PDF version of, *Desktop Revelations Vol 1, Spiritual Warfare,* from the 'Spiritual' section of the 'Help/Tutorials' page at elciProductions.com [www.elciProductions. com/help.htm]. Or better yet, check out the books of Matthew, Mark, Luke and John in the Bible.

Another great resource is, YouTube. Search: Sid Roth, Elijah Streams, The Deep End with Taylor Welch, Tony Merkel and The Confessionals, Right On Radio, Jamie Winship, Todd White, Troy Brewer, Robby Dawkins, Keven Zadai, Lance Wallnau, Robin Bullock, Jenna Winston, Jennifer Bagnaschi, John Ramirez, Nathan Reynolds, Jessie Czebotar, Bread Beckers, Ryan Ries, Marcus Rogers, Rachel Hamm, Anna Khait, Joseph Prince, Cindy McGill, Kat Kerr, Katie Souza, Nancy Coen, BRIDE Ministries, Delafé Testimonies, Ian Claton, Pete Cabrera Jr, Darren Wilson, WP Films, Victor Marx, Graham Cooke, Priscilla Shirer and/or Andrew Wommack, and go from there.

All that being said. If you're honest. And relentless. And willing to let Yeshua change you from the inside out. Then, *welcome to life as you've never known it!*

EPILOGUE III: THE STORY BEHIND THE STORY

Now I know what you're thinking. How in the holy name of God's green Earth, was this gregarious goober (yours truly) chosen to pen such a world-changing, hard-hitting, mind-blowing manuscript?! *Funny..* I remember stumbling out of *The Matrix*—opening day, matinee—*and thinking the EXACT SAME THING.* I was completely blown away. Not only by the mind-bending, reality-altering, world-shattering constructs unpacked in that cinematic masterpiece, but also by what it must have taken for one, single, creative genius (Tom Althouse) to actually mastermind it. *How in the..?* It was staggering. Among all the wild scenarios my pea-brain could conjure up, only one thing remained certain—*it wasn't anyone like me.*

Fast-forward, twenty-some odd years: So, how is it that I'm the one hugging the very first copy of *Desktop Revelations, Vol 2, The Fall*, my pen-name somehow boldly embossed across the bottom of its Marvel-esque style cover?

Actually, as weird as it sounds, I had very little to do with it. All I can say is, "I never chose to write this book—this book sorta chose me.."

Let me attempt to explain.

Do you remember Pepe Le Pew? Yea—that Looney Tunes skunk who skipped his way through life, blissfully unaware of his own stink? Well.. uh.. um.. yea, that was me. Bad breath—for upwards of thirty-nine of the first forty-six years of my life, and counting..

At least, I think.

Herein lies the conundrum.

Looking back, I have hundreds, if not thousands, of stories. Bizarre, random, red-flag moments—that I was completely unaware of at the time—but for whatever reason hung around in the recesses of my permanent memory-banks. Things that just didn't add up, didn't make sense.

For example: The time my 5th grade teacher, Mrs. Fox, pulled me aside and gave me (irony of ironies) a red pill. It was the same type of pill I was given back in 1st grade to practice brushing my teeth. (I had thrown that pill—a blue pill—in the trash). She kindly explained its purpose, and asked me to try it. I did. Admittedly, I brushed and brushed. And after five full minutes of spitting bright red dye, no end in sight, I finally quit. I was like, *dang—that was tough—never doing that again.*

Lesson learned ... NOT.

About that same year, my Dad came home one day with an odd request. He handed me a large, colorful brochure and suggested—"*Ventriloquist School!*" Random, as I had never expressed any sort of remote interest in ventriloquism, *EVER*. But writing jokes and doing stand-up seemed kinda fun, so I was like, "This could be cool."

A day or two later he came home toting a large Popsicle stick—the kind you get at the doctor's office. Reminding me of said, "Ventriloquist School," he proceeded to suggest that I hold the Popsicle stick in my mouth—horizontal across my back teeth—and try to talk. Obliged, I attempted this feat with a grin and a lisp that sounded somewhat like Donald Duck meets Elmer Fudd.

And—that was that.

Perhaps the experiment did not change anything significant about my stink, because "Ventriloquist School" was never brought up again.

Flash-forward to late September, ninth grade. Marching band was well under way. It's Friday night dinner and Mom says, "Your friends are coming over in the morning, be sure to brush your teeth tonight." Weird. Because, one—what are you talking about, "my friends are coming over?" And, two—when do I ever *not* brush my teeth?

But ... September *is* my birthday month, and I prefer surprises, so I didn't pry.

Now unbeknownst to me, my mom had received a phone call earlier that week from some super-cute, super-peppy Senior squad-leader-chick letting her know, "the DHS trumpet section would be swinging by the house between four and five AM to pick me up and cart me off for some traditional freshman hazing. Would that be OK? And if so, could she (my mom) please let them in?"

Apparently, my mom is totally cool with hazing because she readily agreed :)

In all honesty, the "hazing" was super fun—I got to wear a clown suit (along with fifteen other oddly dressed freshman), sing "You Are My Sunshine" to our band director (Mr. Shine), do marching drills (in said clown suit) around the school's parking lot, get kicked off of said parking lot by the cops (not in clown suits), grab some IHOP for breakfast, and return safely home—all before 9 AM. Which brings us full-circle back to Mom's 'tooth brushing' suggestion. *Was that a helpful, yet subtle, hint?* Cuz—uhh—lesson not learned.

Wow. There are so many things.

How about the time my younger sister got up the nerve to mention specifically that something "stunk." (We were the only two in the room). I laughed and said the only comeback that popped into my head. "It's probably just your breath blowing back in your face."

Now at the time, I was being completely facetious. I couldn't smell anything and thought she was just giving me a hard time. But knowing what I know now—her crushed look and lack-luster reply makes so much more sense.

Sorry sis. Hope you weren't traumatized. You never stank a day in your life.

And what about my older sister? She used to chew Wriggly's Big Red bubble-gum all the time, like an addict. Seriously. It was one piece out, the next piece in. Complete 'chain chewing.' I called her on it once, and the girl who always has an answer for everything was like, "*I dunno—(chew, chew, chew ... <new piece> ... chew).*"

My apologies sis, if that over-compensation had anything to do with you being so closely related to the town "stinker." :)

Lesson not even noticed.

And who can forget the time 'Aussie Andrew' shook my hand,

looked me square in the eye, and in front of everybody said, "You stink." I should have gotten some sort of clue then, *right?* I mean, the incident punched me in the gut and brought tears to my eyes.

But alas, no such luck. I was clueless.

In my defense, this *was* the same guy who frequently pushed me in midair, sending me flying dangerously off-balance whenever I drove past him in basketball. And the same guy who repeatedly borrowed my clothes for so long, that I was often left wondering if I'd ever see them again.

It just so happened, that on this particular day, he'd managed to land the "coveted seat next to the cool kids," and I thought he was just trying to play the part. The insult hit me like elitist-rejection, not truth.

Point-blank lesson, totally missed.

And then there was: Mom buying me dental sealants in college (no reason).. My in-laws buying me a Nettie Pot after college (no reason).. Oral care products regularly appearing in my Christmas stockings (no reason?).. Personal water requests at group meals magically—and repeatedly—upgrading themselves to sweeter, more "breath freshening" beverages like coke or sweet tea (oops—again. no reason).. Gigi (Great Grandma) persistently refusing my arm (but then, willingly taking my brother-in-law's arm) for aid in crossing streets and climbing steps, etc. (no reason?).. Dan, Mark, and Justin— three very cool dudes who often got grumpy (and very uncool) whilst talking to me at school (no reason).. Danny (a different Dan), nearly passing out when trapped next to me on an overcrowded and temporarily stuck Kyle Field elevator; and then avoiding me like the plague afterward (no reason?)..

Then there was: James, my college party buddy, outright ignoring me at random and inopportune times, usually when I was seated too close.. That increasingly—all to common—warm, welcoming *silence* when I'd walk into a room.. Inside dinner parties moving outside, when I RSVPed.. Outside dinner parties moving inside, when I un-RSVPed.. Friends seemingly unable to get comfortable around me.. Copious amounts of shoulder-to-shoulder ("facing the sunset") conversations.. Living perpetually stuck in the 'hug and move on' greeting-zone.. Regularly feeling "emotionally stiff-armed," "overlooked," "avoided," and so much more..

Now don't get me wrong, I wasn't totally ignorant. I did notice something was "off." The relational distance, the subtle rejection, the social inconsistencies—I could sense all that. However, the blame was often misplaced. *I was ugly or uncool.. They were shy or insecure.. I wasn't good with people.. They were having a bad day..* These perpetual half-truths kept me at bay; leaving me circling the truth, whilst scratching my head, confused. *Why did people repeatedly treat my friends (and later, my wife) different than they treated me? And why did they treat me so inconsistently? It didn't make sense.*

Still—I was beginning to wake up.

One last story.

Grad school had finished … (but only just) … and all my college friends were back together for a day at the lake—some typical "fun in the sun." Evening falls. Its been a long day of making waves and rock'n the beach. We're all lazed out, sprawling in armchairs, marshmallows roasting. A song comes on the radio. It's Britney Spears. I grunt a giggle and speak up. "Wouldn't it be funny if you lived your whole life and totally missed out on something everyone else knew?"

Now I was just thinking radio, pop-tune, pop-culture. You know: Justin Timberlake.. Britney Spears.. The Beebs.. Like, wouldn't it be funny if every time you walked into a room, some certain song (or artist) had just finished playing; and every time you walked out, they just so happened to broadcast again and … *you totally missed it? You totally missed them!* How funny would that be? How would you ever know? How would anyone ever know?

Come on, that's a funny premise. And at the very least, a great conversation starter.

"Shut up. You're being stupid," my friend grouched, immediately changing the subject.

..Or..not? … I scratched my head, trying to figure out what had just crawled up his s'mores. *Maybe he thought I was hinting at something taboo, like gossip or Jesus..* Still, the instant tapped nerve at the mention of what felt like such a light-hearted and potentially

funny premise struck me as strange. *What could have caused it?* I was
beginning to seriously speculate..

OK—*quick time-out:*

To be clear, what I'm *NOT* saying is that all of the above
"evidence" has to be concrete proof of me being stinky or having bad
breath. I get it. Oral care products really do make great stocking-
stuffers. Shoulder-to-shoulder conversations really do work for
sunsets. Insecurities really do come into play. In fact, many of the
social-distance discrepancies above could very well be innocent
misjudgments. An "off" day. Textbook "projection issues." Symptoms
of third-party gossip. Or a million other things.

Case and point:

In my lifetime, over the years, I've been hit on by way more
than my "fair share" of ... *DUDES.*

That's right—*dudes.*

And—not to throw a complete curve ball here—but clearly
my sexuality (which has never been questionable to me) is at least
perceived as being somewhat questionable to others.

That being said: a repeated misdiagnosis of this caliber could
certainly lead to many of the relational issues/nuances/distances
noted above. However, this argument loses it legs the moment one
attempts to explain the many times my sexually "liberal" and/or
"more diverse" friends have treated me in *exactly the same manner.*

All I'm saying is, that from my perspective, over my past
30+ years of personal experiences, the *ONE* thing that seems to
make *EVERY SINGLE* other thing fall magically into line, (aside from
assuming that *EVERYONE in the world* is a complete, "misdiagnosing
homophobe,") would simply be: me having a classic case of, *Pepe Le
Pew Syndrome*—living blissfully unaware of my own stink.

But I digress.

Let's move on to the "great awakening.."

Skip to 2007, my 30th birthday. We're at *IT's* (a big pizza
place, full of fun, friends, and family games). For about nine months
now, my "enlightenment" has steadily progressed. Like a massive
sewage dump, the comments and distance, the actions and reactions,
the offers of gum, water, snacks—and all manner of passive-

aggressive innuendos—have been raining down on me, daily. I'm beginning to think <don, don, dahhh: cue suspenseful music> *I might actually have a bit of a stink issue.*

Nahh.. its been years. Someone would have told me something point-blank by now ... right? I lean over a fence, high-fiving a go-cart driver as he passes.

"Sir, please stop interacting dangerously with the carts," my reprimand booms out over the loudspeaker.

Oops, I turn to dodge the heat, striking up a conversation with a friend who's just arrived.

She gets quiet.

I figure she's shy.

"Riders, hand the attendant your token and select your cart," the voice booms again.

Our turn!

We hop to the floor and make our picks. Engines are revving. Excitement is building: *Three.. Two.. One.. —Go!* The race is underway. I take the lead. And the win. It's the start of a super fun night, *so.. uh.. um..*

Why can't I find anyone?

I walk around, sorta bouncing from group to group, each one oddly indifferent to me. *Strange,* it's *my* birthday, and even my wife has gone off with my brother and the "shy" girl. And that's when it hit. Really hit. I mean, these were my friends, the people closest to me for the last decade—roommates, groomsmen, workout buddies, teammates—and they were acting eerily similar to the people at work, church, (and pretty much everywhere else right now, in my life).

Passively indifferent. And so ... distant.

Maybe I do. I mean, really do.. stink!

And with that, the proverbial dominoes began to fall.

I'd like to say that I went weak in the knees, dropped to the floor and/or threw-up a little in my mouth. But my initial reaction was more like a 'slow sinking feeling,' as memories, moments, comments, and/or former life-experiences sluggishly resurfaced; each epiphany replaying through the sudden clarity of my brand new "stinky breath" lens, and falling—*right ... into ... place.*

Dang.

At first I felt super embarrassed. 'Betrayed' might be a better word. I felt like the rug had just been pulled out from under me. Like I had been living a lie. Like I could no longer trust anyone. It wasn't so much about the issue itself (although that was certainly awkward), but about *how long* the issue had been going on, unchecked. I felt like that cop who ate donuts for breakfast only to find a big blob of crusty, bubbly glaze plastered to his mustache at dinner. *Really? All day long, and no one said a word?!*

But wait. It gets better.

So you'd think—now that I'm painfully aware—I could just run home, adjust a few oral hygiene habits, and everyone could finally move on with my new, fresher, better smelling life. (It certainly seemed like that was the scenario everyone else had been silently banking on). There was just one, slight problem—I already had rock-solid oral hygiene. Sure, I added a tongue scraper. Took my gargling a little more seriously. And cut the excess ranch, jalapenos, and salsa from my diet. But you're talking to the kid who's never had a cavity in his life. *There really wasn't much more I could do.*

And that was the hardest blow.

The morning I realized no extra amount of brushing, flossing, gargling, and/or bubblegum chewing would significantly alter my stink—I hit an all-time low.

I'd be lying if I told you there were no suicidal thoughts. There were. And for three long days they quietly hung around, loitering in the back of my mind. But on day four, I was like, "No. Not even an option." *And that was that,* my heart was settled. By the Grace of God, I never had those thoughts again. Not that it made walking out the next awkward decade(s) of life any easier. It didn't. But I, at least, was no longer struggling against myself.

Long story, super short.

So, after about three years of serious floundering; I finally started confronting. Hardest thing I've ever done. But I really saw no way around it. To my frustrated amazement, I never got any straight answers ... *FROM ANYONE.* Instead, I got brilliant side-steps, like:

"Hmm, never noticed.." or "Don't even mention it, I'm used to being around smelly jocks.." or "That's alright, smells don't bother me.." I even got some genuine, heartfelt tears. And while those tears did temporarily soothe my soul, no one gave me anything I could use constructively, or even explained what the situation looked like from their perspective. *Nothing*.

I will say, in their defense, it wasn't like I really pressed the issue. I was battling my own fear of confrontation, and fear of man. Not to mention the insecurities of feeling betrayed, and the embarrassment of feeling perpetually, uncontrollably stinky. Just the fact that I was occasionally forcing the can of worms out into the open felt like huge victories to me.

Still, aside from some very temporary positive relational changes, nothing really shifted. This was almost worse than before. Now I wasn't just in a hole, I was *stuck* in a hole. *Stuck in me.* I was reaching up, reaching out, and nobody—I mean, nobody—wanted to help. *Why?* It blew my mind. Could they not see my struggle? Was it not affecting them? Did they really care more about 'saving face' than saving me?

I began to speculate: Maybe it had been going on for so long, it was too embarrassing for *them*. Or, maybe they actually *liked* it this way. Maybe the issue was more about something else. Or maybe there was something much more sinister at play? I couldn't figure it out. How was I caught in this 'Twilight Zone' of a world where I was the only one telling the truth and everyone else was lying? *Absurd.*

Yet somehow, that was my reality.

Over time, my subconscious became obsessed. All day, every day, two questions bombarded me: *Was it breath? Was it not breath?* It wasn't like I could just look in a mirror and find out. I needed real-time, third-party feedback if I was ever going to have a shot at correcting the issue. I was at a loss. I didn't want to be the guy who really did stink, but acts like he doesn't. (Weird.) Nor did I want to be the guy who doesn't stink, with a complex like he does. (Double weird.)

So for years, that's where I lived: Feeling like the lone truther, caged in a world of liars. Not big, bad liars. Just little, white liars. Smiling faces, whose casual indifference and "noble intentions" to "not hurt my feelings" were completely ruining my life.

BUT GOD.

Now, thank God for God, because just as my source of life from man was drying up, my source of life from God was beginning to explode. I began to hang out with him daily. Then twice a day. Then all day, every day. He became my "one thing." My stability. My safe-space. My peace and happiness. My inner strength. My *mighty* inner strength. My joy.

In short, God became my addiction.

Funny thing tho—even as I felt His presence and power increasing, and heard his insights into many, many subjects—He never once mentioned the breath thing ... *not ever.*

That was somewhat troublesome.

Still, as one might expect, this strange scenario did drive me to ponder one simple question, very deeply: *How do you catch a liar?*

Or more precisely.

How do you catch a liar, that wont stop lying ... EVER? You know, when every excuse has another excuse, every justification another justification. When stories shift, and blur, and change, endlessly ... I mean, even when everyone flat-out knows the truth, that sort of liar can never be caught. *Why?* Because there's nothing to pin them to..

—Unless..

A new idea hit.

Unless, you somehow *CATCH THEM*: in the act, red-handed, in a way that can never be denied!

Bingo—my answer had finally arrived!

Like a breath of fresh air <ba-dum, ching>, 'renewed hope' rose, sparking dreams of hidden cameras, staged cocktail parties, and reporters from *Dateline NBC* capturing all the background chatter surrounding my life. If anyone could, Chris Hansen would get to the bottom of this!

..BUT, then again—going on national television to 'out' all the people closest to me probably wasn't the best way to resolve my personal issues. Not if I wanted to preserve the relationships, anyway. *There had to be a better way..*

Then one day, I had a novel idea (literally): "If God were in my shoes, what would *He* do?"

I chuckled. *Yea right, like God would ever have to deal with bad breath and perpetual liars.*

Then it hit.

Wait a minute—wasn't satan a 'perpetual liar?' I mean, he *was* the 'Father of Lies' [John 8:44]. Wasn't that the kind of liar who would never, *NO NOT EVER*, tell the truth?

Yea.. so.. how did God catch him?

I thought for a moment, my religious upbringing kicking in.

Well, of course—yada, yada—*God sent his son, Jesus, to the cross, to defeat the devil and save us from our sins..* I was quoting verbatim.

Wait a minute! Something shifted. I could almost hear the tires screeching to a halt. *What if CATCH and DEFEAT were actually synonymous terms?*

Yea—*so Jesus went to the cross to CATCH the devil.* I began to see the crucifixion in a whole new light. *Jesus literally BECOMING the cookie in the cookie jar, so that he could testify, first hand, to exactly WHO it was who ate him!*

Wow. If that was legit—than Jesus coming to Earth *was a total heaven-sent, covert, Psy-Op!*

BUT—wait a minute, my world came suddenly unglued. *IF Jesus went to the cross to CATCH the devil … Than, uh—um.. wouldn't that mean the devil had NOT been caught yet?!*

Suddenly my religious upbringing was tearing at the seams. Tires falling off the cart.

And if the devil had NOT been caught yet. Wouldn't that mean the devil was STILL God's right hand man, second in command?

Gears jammed, smoke billowed, clutches popped: Worldviews were shifting.

Yea, cuz … according to Matthew 10:24, didn't Jesus take BACK the keys to Death, Hell, and The Grave?

My jaw dropped.

TAKE BACK?! So that meant—for like, FOUR THOUSAND

YEARS—the devil LEGALLY owned them?

I was blown away.

And if the devil LEGALLY owned them, (the keys, that is)*—than why didn't he just LEGALLY kill everyone and be done with it? Why was he so willing to play along with this wildly inconvenient, "Promised Messiah" charade for literally millennia? I mean—why jump through hoop after hoop, invent scheme after scheme, take chance after chance, when one could simply "pull the trigger" and LEGALLY be done with it all, in one fell swoop?*

The answer hit me upside the head, like a block of rogue ice in an arctic Eskimo shower. My jaw dropped. My blood ran cold.

BECAUSE—it was an INSIDE JOB!

The palm of my hand smashed hard against my forehead.

Of course! I rolled my eyes. *It only made total sense. The devil wasn't raging AGAINST the system, because he WAS the system! He WAS the woke CEO, the corrupt CIA, the compromised global government. He WAS the crooked blackjack dealer; counting all the cards, controlling everyone's hand, and calling all the shots. He wasn't scared to lose, because he thought he COULDN'T lose! The Fall—HIS fall—it hadn't happened yet!*

HE WAS PLAYING BOTH SIDES!

My mind was blown, there were so many implications.

No wonder the God of the Old Testament seemed so "schizophrenic." He sorta WAS—he had the devil as his CEO!

Passages of scripture bombarded my brain.

This must be why we see Moses being commissioned by God in Exodus 3, and one chapter later, that "same God" is coming to kill him.

That's Owner vs CEO!

And why we still find the devil showing up in Heaven and answering directly to God in the book of Job.

The fool's still on the payroll!

It also explained why God would allow a reportedly "rogue" devil to afflict Job in the first place: 1. He's trying to teach/show/change the devil (in hopes of avoiding the fall). 2. It's a promotion for Job (from religion to relationship). 3. This is a concerted effort to provoke Job to pray a very specific prayer [see Job 9:33], opening lawful access for

Heaven to initiate a conversation with Abraham (ultimately sending God's Living Word to Earth). AND 4. *It reveals the age-old conundrum of why a "good" God would ever allow an "outlaw" devil to waltz right into His throne room, demand his favorite kid (Job's) destruction, and not only agree … but never lock the worthless fool up!*

On and on it went.

There was: Daniel's delayed prayer [in Daniel 10]. The argument over Moses' body [see Jude 1:9]. Jesus' strange concern with secrecy [circa Luke 4:35, Matt 9:30, Mark 8:26 & 30]. Why God seemed so distant & angry in the Torah/Old Testament. And why Jesus even had to go to the cross in the first place.

It was all making so much sense!

Suddenly, I froze, the true weight of this revelation starting to press in. *This wasn't just huge, this was EPIC! It was so much greater than my personal pea-brain, social-distance, hygiene issues. The world needed to know! And it needed to know … NOW!*

Tears welled. *How was it that I had been chosen to attempt such a monumental, impossible feat?* In that moment, I was overwhelmed. Awestruck. Horrified. Emboldened. Undone. I had no idea how this would ultimately play out; I only knew one thing:

I was ALL IN.

Admittedly, this new insight initially solved nothing pertaining to my personal life. It was still four more years until I could completely accept the fact that I might be perpetually stinky the rest of my life. And nearly twelve more years until I could openly talk about all aspects of 'said issue' without stumbling across some sort of hidden internal emotional landmine.

However, that very same decision to "forsake my personal issues for the sake of the greater collective good," was ironically the very same decision which ultimately enabled me to transcend my limiting circumstances, and step onto the ladder up and out of my "impossible" situation. *How?* It did two things: One: It gave me a purpose. And Two: It gave me a reason for my pain.

That was huge.

Suddenly, my curse had become my blessing. My pain, my answer. No longer were insurmountable obstacles keeping me *FROM* my destiny, they were actually the very vehicles taking me *TO* it!

Sure, I still had a lot of hurt and frustration ahead. (Some of, my toughest—most excruciating years were still in front of me.) But everything, at the core, had flipped. I had flipped. AND best of all, I now had the perfect platform with which to publicly discuss the "Twilight Zone" of a conundrum that had become my life!

The water was parting.

The path was drying.

Finally, there was a way out!!

...

Now, please note—I'm no one special. What God did for me, *he will more than do for you!* God is no respecter of persons [Rom 2:11]. If at some point you find yourself in my shoes—trapped in a prison, trapped in YOU—remember *there is hope! There is a way out!* My way was a book. Yours might be a song. A business. An invention. A revelation. A joke. A narrative. Or a million other prearranged, preordained things. Just know, these troubles are not because you are 'less than' or somehow 'irreparably broken.' But rather, it's because there is something so GREAT, so INCONCEIVABLE, so HEAVEN-SENT that God wants to do in and through you, that the enemy of your soul is doing everything he can to get you to take yourself out before your light can manifest.

The Catch 22? If you will turn to God. Run to God. Let him heal you and direct you. Then the very prison you were put in to kill and destroy you, will become the very elevator, lifting you effortlessly to the top [see Genesis 41]. *Don't miss out on your ride!*

...

But I digress. So, what about my friends and family? How did everything wrap up in real life?

Well, I'm pretty sure everyone (me included) was glad I didn't actually go ahead with the Dateline NBC solution :) And truth be told, I'm still walking (and working) a lot of this stuff out: Yes—some of the third-party gossip has finally come to light. And some of the gossipers have plainly been exposed. And yes—some of the "skeletons" unduly projected onto me, have finally returned to their proper, original owner's closets.

However, here I sit, (2024) five years after writing the previous portions, no closer to any finite resolution then ever before—other than to say, it seems to be undoubtedly obvious that there is some sort of 'stink' clearly involved. Now, whether that is some sort of physical breath issue, or simply the natural repercussion of the hard to hear, soul slapping, truth filled, "offensive" words often coming out of my mouth. I don't know. Maybe it's witchcraft (supernatural stink is actually a thing). Or some sort of perpetual 'thorn in the flesh.' Maybe it's gossip at the hand of some accusing spirit, "close friend" or dare I say, government agency. Maybe, like Jacob's son Joseph [see Genesis 37], it's simply the 'culminating embodiment' of the perpetual unspoken offense of being overly open and overly confident (and a wee bit too obnoxious) in 'who I was created to be.' Heck, maybe it's not even me. Maybe it has more to do with the hidden secrets that God's light in me exposes in the people around me. Or simply the fact that I was dropped, smack dab in the middle of the mindbendingly supernatural war over writing this book. Maybe, like Elohim himself, it's simply the fruit of those closest and most jealous of me, spinning self-serving narratives behind my back, putting me and others at perpetual relational odds. I don't know. I may never know.

Any suggestions?

Still—all spirit, soul or physical stink aside—I do know two things:

One. I humbly apologize *to you*. Past, present, future. For all undue offense—spoken/unspoken, intended/unintended. (Save any time I speak or obey Papa God's direction, Word, or Truth). And of course, for any physical stinkiness I have/did/will potentially emit. I'm sorry. Truly sorry.

And Two. Rest assured, no matter how this all eventually plays out—like Joseph and his brothers [see Genesis 42]—*ALL IS*

FORGIVEN!

100%.

Sure, that doesn't make mistreating me OK. It certainly doesn't make the lies told about me true. Or allow the liars to get off of God's hook, Scott free. But, they *are* off of mine. Because, by the incredible Grace of God, I accept the loss. I receive the pain and the shame. The rejection, distance, and undue frustration. The life, time, reputation and energy that I will never—no, not ever—get back.

But I willingly take the hit. I really do.

Why?

Well—again, like Joseph—God will (and in some ways already has) more than made up for it. Besides, I'm sure—had I been in their shoes—I would have done the *EXACT SAME THING.* I mean, if I'm completely honest, this whole conundrum sorta—*um, more like, TOTALLY*—forced me into becoming the man I am today. I mean, it certainly pried my stubborn, white-knuckling fingers off the world's lame, dying, death-cult, forbidden-fruit, fake, "game of life." And let's face it, it's not like I'm some, "amazing Christ-like figure," who boldly, willingly, fearlessly, selflessly ran to his cross to save the people he loved most.

Quite the opposite!

I was simply ostracized, ignored, quarantined, social-distanced, shamed, blamed and perpetually kicked out of every game (every man-made system), until one day I finally accepted my fate and discovered (that after Jesus took away all the pain) I was left strangely unbound, unshackled, and wildly free! ..It's a bit like the story of, *Brier Rabbit.* Or those four lepers in 2 Kings 7.

So thank you friends. Thank you family. And strangely, most of all, thank you devil. You literally forced me out of your twisted, shallow, mind-controlled, death-cult systems—and into the pure, unconditional freedom found in the loving arms of my amazingly unstoppable, beyond good, most gracious Heavenly Papa!

Honestly, looking back, my only redeeming quality was purely the fact that I simply kept running to God. He's done the rest. And while the journey has, at times, stunk terribly <ba-dum Crash>, I am uber grateful to have traversed (and somehow survived) it. After all, look at the book, the man, the family, and the relationships that have resulted from it! Not to mention the culture, the future, and impacted world to come! It has become my real-life, right-now, living-proof testimony to the undeniable, supernatural, transformative power of Papa God; and to what he can do when he takes a man, an irreparably broken man, made to look like a fool and a liar, and reveals to the world—he actually (in divine wisdom) *is telling the truth!*

Histories will shift.

Societies will change.

Personal futures will alter.

And when the dust finally settles, and all the smoke clears: *Nothing less than ALL of eternity will have been changed ... FOREVER!*

Ask me then, "Was it worth it?"

Much love. As ONE. Your humbled stinker.

- L.A. Carnevale

- THE END -

ABOUT THE AUTHOR

Fledgling author L.A. Carnevale is a nobody. He gets that. When God put the call of author, producer and culture-shaper upon his life, he was the first person to bring that glaring fact directly to God's attention. Oddly undaunted, God's call remained. So L.A. answered. *Desktop Revelations, Volume 2, The Fall* was book number four of that call.

Now, with a novel, self-help, and multiple children's books under his belt, (not to mention the copyrighted music placed on over half-a-dozen cable and prime-time network stations), it has become strikingly apparent—*L.A. is still a nobody!* Which means he is undeservingly blessed to live a life that forever points to *The Somebody*—and that is a life he wouldn't trade for anything. He looks forward to the books, music, and more which is sure to follow … and to all that God has for him and his family in the future.

Of course, when L.A. isn't busy being a nobody, he enjoys hanging out with his family, laughing—*a lot*, spinning new narratives, dropping blazing beats, crushing Mario Cart Wii, war boarding, war walking, war calling, and generally doing just about anything that will get the devil's bloomers in a wad. His deepest passion is to bring wholesome, funny, unashamedly truth-infused entertainment to an overly-propagated (and somewhat socially confused) culture … *whatever that means!* But mostly, he just loves to hang out with his Heavenly Papa.

He currently lives with his family in DFW Texas. *God bless Texas!*

www.elciProductions.com
www.desktopRevelations.com

PAY IT FORWARD

Like what you read? Pay it forward. Purchase a copy for someone else today, at: **DesktopRevelations.com** (click on 'The Fall' > click on 'Fuel The Movement')

Desktop Revelations, Volume 2, The Fall was initially published using a divine think-tank, 'Pay It Forward' concept. The idea was for ALL first-generation customers to pay exactly $0.00 for their first copy. In other words – each copy was 100% prepaid. Allowing us to give every copy away, 100% FREE, (including shipping & handling).

We then place the life of the book in *your* hands. Assuming you love the product, we give you the opportunity to invest (or not) in a future-generation customer's copy. So forth, and so on.

In this way, we can both maintain a business and give our book away, 100% free, forever, to EVERYONE who wants it.

Of course, if additional copies are desired – additional copies may be purchased at: **DesktopRevelations.com** (eventually expanding to: Amazon.com, BarnsAndNoble.com, and more).

However, to ensure our *Pay It Forward* concept initially takes hold— for the first number of year(s)—it will *only* be available through our personal, in-house website at: **DesktopRevelations.com**

May our world never be the same! *Much love. All God's best!*

"AND IN THOSE DAYS, the devil—who is Haylel, Lucifer, the Father of Lies, the Son of Perdition, the Deceiver of Many—will become so unveiled, so unpopular, so clearly exposed; that the only way he will EVER be able to re-emerge and rise on the public scene again, will be if he PRETENDS TO BE JESUS CHRIST, HIMSELF.."

www.ingramcontent.com/pod-product-compliance
Lightning Source LLC
Chambersburg PA
CBHW020230110726
47898CB00004B/1213